Introduction

The characters in Bloodlines-Traces and their stories could be anyone's story; anyone who can trace ancestry; anyone whose great-great-grandmother answered to the call for women's liberation; anyone whose predecessors fought for freedom, justice and equal rights for all, in a quest to improve the plight of the poor and weak in Victorian and Edwardian times.

In fact, these stories *are* what create our lives today. Had it not been for the courageous acts of war correspondents witnessing the atrocities in Gallipoli during the First World War and taking action, many more would have died in the hills of the Dardanelles and less people would now have the opportunity to read what happened to the journalists who saved their future.

We owe our ancestors gratitude for the path they paved for us, even if we feel we would have done it differently. Not only do we grow when we learn during one lifetime, we do the same while developing ourselves through generations of one family and owe it to our children to do the same for them. While the fight for justice has changed in the sense that the fine line between poverty and wealth, fame and obscurity, have different dimensions, compared to the standards of the 19th and 20th century, the battle is still the same in how we all strive to be recognized for who we are and what we are capable of. Many of those answers lie in what our predecessors did before us.

On an evolutionary level, hopefully now more than ever, humanity is gaining understanding of the need for collaboration rather than division, all themes that found words in *Bloodlines - Traces*.

Following the advice of proofreaders, a **Macpherson family tree**, was inserted, adapted from 'Cathy's notes' as used while researching her Macpherson genealogy. The adjoining '**Who's Who**' gives a short description of main characters. **Reader's Notes** can be found at the back of the book, referring to the historical sources parts of the narrative is derived from.

To conclude; we invite you to www.touchnotthecat.com which features reviews and pictures, as well as blogs on how certain chapters and characters came to life during the process of writing Bloodlines - Touch Not the Cat and Bloodlines -Traces.

D1390611

Synopsis Bloodlines-Touch Not the Cat

After fleeing Ballindalloch in 1895, to escape the wrath of Laird Gordon Macpherson, gamekeeper's son Alexander Stewart finds his way in Boston, Massachusetts, thanks to the help of Irish immigrant Michael Devane and his son Sean.

The wilful laird's daughter, Katherine, stays behind in Scotland to find she is pregnant with Alexander's child, and even though her father Gordon has mysteriously vanished, and can no longer prevent the lovers from reuniting, Katherine chooses a different path for reasons of her own.

116-years later, Raleigh policewoman Cathy Macpherson succumbs to the request of her husband David Stewart, to give their marriage a second chance and joins him on his genealogy quest.

Next to uncovering the secret of the laird's disappearance, Cathy also finds clues to the true relationship between Alexander and Katherine, the lives they led, and how the consequences of their actions live on in the next generations of Macphersons and Stewarts.

Thomas McKerley & Ingrid Schippers

Bloodlines - Traces

Macpherson family tree

Lachlan
B:1810

Gordon (married Elisabeth; 1841 - 1895)
1835 - 1895

William (Chicago?)
1841 - 1920

Gordon
1861†

John
1862 - 1915
M: Victoria

James
1864 - 1940
(Raleigh)

Thomas
1866

Alexandra
1896

two earlier kids
+
Charles Edward (Eddie)
1917

Donald
1869

Lachlan
1872

Katherine
1877 - 1954

Donald
1907 - 1944

Alistair
1910 - 1980 (new laird '44)

Thomas
1930

Angus (Sr.)
1931 - 2000

Margaret
1933

Euphemia
1933

Spencer (gramps)
1933

Jim (pop)
1951

Me

Diane Coxl

Angus (present laird)
1954

John - George - Angus Jr.

Who's Who: The Main Characters in Bloodlines -Traces

U.S.A. present day

Diane Cox (1949), granddaughter of **Edward Macpherson.**
Jim Macpherson (1951), grandson of Edward Macpherson, cousin of **Diane Cox**, father of **Cathy Stewart**, father in law of **David Stewart.**
Cathy Stewart (1976), born **Macpherson**, Homicide Detective from Raleigh, North Carolina. Married to:
David Stewart (1969), Travel Writer

Scotland present day

Angus MacPherson (1954), Laird of Ballindalloch.
Thomas Macpherson (1930) nicknamed Uncle T. by Cathy Stewart, retired Black Watch officer, uncle of **Angus Macpherson.**
John Macpherson (1977), Account Manager for Eastern Europe with the Royal Bank of Scotland, eldest son of **Angus Macpherson.**
Maggie and Euphemia Macpherson (1933), younger twin sisters of **Thomas Macpherson, aunts to Angus.**

Victorian/Edwardian Times

Gordon Macpherson (1835- 1895), Laird of Ballindalloch from 1867-1895, married to **Elisabeth** (1841-1896)
John Macpherson (1862), eldest son of **Gordon & Elisabeth**, married to **Victoria Galbraith** (1865)
Alexandra Macpherson, only child and daughter of **John & Victoria**
James Macpherson (1864) younger brother of **John**
Katherine Macpherson (1877), youngest and 7th child, sister to **John and James**
William Macpherson (1841), younger brother of **Gordon Macpherson**
Edward (Eddie) Macpherson (1917) registered in the 1920 census as member of the household of **James Macpherson** (1864) in Raleigh North Carolina.
Alexander Stewart (1875), son of **Jane Black** and:
Robert Stewart (1855), gamekeeper of Ballindalloch from 1874 – 1896
Donald Simpson (1832), butler at Ballindalloch Castle from 1868 – 1903
Mary Montgomery, (1844), personal aid to **Elisabeth Macpherson** and caretaker of **Katherine and Alexandra**

PROLOGUE
Wednesday 22 July 1896, Ballindalloch Castle, Banffshire, Scotland

The pain shot through her lower back.

Around her, servants were busying themselves bringing fresh warm towels and bowls of steaming water. The family doctor fumbled underneath the linen sheet covering her body.

"For Christ's sake help me," Katherine cried out, her face reflecting the agonising pain jolting her body.

Even though she was totally absorbed by the process of giving birth, her mind slipped to a dormant layer of anger. Katherine wished she could toss off her constricting nightgown with its long sleeves and high collar. She felt it was suffocating her and it didn't hide a thing! With the Swiss cotton clinging to her sweat soaked body she might as well have been naked.

Carried on the wave of the next contraction a feeling of frustration rippled through her body. For a moment she wished she could disappear into nothingness, free from all she could not escape, unless she would pass away.

Had it not been for the knowledge, university was waiting for her, Katherine would gladly have given in to a call of the Grim Reaper. She was not ready to be a mother and felt guilty. Even though her life had been turned upside down, she already loved the baby, but had promised herself not to tread on her mother's path. Trading her maternal rights for John's consent and funding to go to Edinburgh had been a heart breaking decision, but at least her child would be raised within the family.

Katherine's eldest brother had his own reasons for condoning his sister's actions. To satisfy and distract his wife in their childless marriage they were to raise the child as their own, also providing a suitable heir while his sister's outrageous decision to study medicine would certainly quell all other rumours.

It was time peace was restored and normal life resumed.

Part I

Some people are your relatives but others are your ancestors, and you choose the ones you want to have as ancestors. You create yourself out of those values.

Ralph Ellison, 1914 - 1994

It is easy to say how we love new friends, and what we think of them, but words can never trace out all the fibers that knit us to the old.

George Eliot, 1819 – 1880

CHAPTER 1
Friday 7 June 1895, Chicago, Illinois, USA

The coach bringing fifty-four year old William Macpherson to Mort Pullman's house, hobbled its way over the dusty road, causing the whisky bottle Macpherson was holding to shake its content. He had brought a twelve-year-old to share with his friend. They both needed cheering up. Ever since the strike, Mort's fame had turned into dangerous exposure. He couldn't even show himself in the streets anymore without fear of assault.

Ahead, despite the noise of the galloping horses, unruly chanting could be heard. The loudness of the din told William it had to be a large crowd. The strike had changed a lot, turning the natural division of classes into a mere shadow of its former self. George Mortimer Pullman had been successful with his Palace Car Company. With the depression of 1893 and declining business, he had seen himself forced during May 1894, to release more than one third of his factory workers, two thousand people. To further protect his precarious financial situation, he had also refused to reduce the rents of the company housing of Pullman Town. It had made the people revolt. With the backing of the American Railway Union, the workers in Illinois went on strike, the boycott rapidly spreading nationwide with Pullman refusing to go to arbitration.

Across the country, Pullman cars were not being worked. It was dire as almost 250,000 were on strike throughout the USA. Hostilities increased. Thirty strikers had been killed in a Chicago riot. Marshals and thousands of army troops tried to keep the trains running. The situation was deteriorating.

A heavy object crashed on the carriage roof, causing Macpherson's fiery temperament to utter a stream of muttered curses. He sensed they were now slowing and could hear the tumult closing in. The carriage was only moving at snail pace and the noise of the crowd was becoming louder. William drew the curtains and latched both doors. They were now under siege, the crowd slapping and kicking the carriage. The noise of the throng was scaring the horses, their nervous high-pitched neighing alarmed William. They came to an abrupt stop.

Crack! A pistol fired, followed by the loud hail of Paul, the elder of the two coachmen. "I will shoot dead the next man, woman or child who touches this carriage. Be on your way."

A few seconds of eerie silence followed. William nudged the curtain just enough to observe the crowd retreat reluctantly. A drone emerged from the crowd, softly at first but soon swelling to angry shouts. 'Pullman out, Pullman out.' The carriage started moving, gathering pace. William leaned back, stretched his legs with a sense of relief, yet cursed under his breath. Didn't they know what was good for them? Hadn't Pullman contributed to the lives of working class families? The ingenious method to raise Chicago was all Mort's invention. He saved the whole town from certain flooding by Lake Michigan, protecting the livelihood and homes of thousands and thousands of people. Mort Pullman had also changed the face of travel, designing the sleeper railway car, making train journeys more comfortable and less time consuming. A man who had improved the world, deserved better than to end up a prisoner of his own being.

Maybe it was the recognition of injustice, which fortified the kinship between Macpherson and Pullman over the years. William Macpherson had tried to create a rewarding life, based on the belief his well-being was down to sheer endeavour, rather than the wealth of his family. As God was his witness, it had not been easy leaving Scotland, but he *had* been successful establishing the whisky import and distribution business.

Unrewarded love had cast a shadow over all he had achieved. William's thoughts shifted to his older brother, even though it was a place he did not gladly go. Gordon had it all; the title, the land, the wife, all derived by birth right, and took it all for granted.

It would have been only natural for Elizabeth and William to wed. From childhood they shared an unspoken bond of two souls destined to be one. Yet their parents had thought differently. Elizabeth was to be the future laird's wife. Now it was William's fate to recognise she was lonely, married to a man who only knew how to live his life through cultural inheritance.

Had it been God's test to challenge William's resilience, or punish him for his sins, he would have understood. Why Elizabeth should suffer eluded him completely. She had always conducted herself like the perfect wife. Yet after ten years of marriage, Gordon had retreated into his own living quarters, suggesting it was best for Elizabeth, so his irregular working hours would not intrude on her wellbeing.

William knew, that if it had not been his brother's duty to produce heirs to Ballindalloch, the marriage would have been one of rational convenience only. He wondered if Gordon ever sought pleasure in anything. His brother habitually seemed to face life in earnest, without a glimpse of humour or zest, making William and Gordon complete opposites.

The carriage shuddered. A wheel had crunched over a deep rut in the track. William found himself struggling, when the carriage careened at an alarming pace.

"Are you okay Mister Macpherson? I am sorry," bawled Paul from above.

"Get on with it man," William shouted.

After what seemed an eternity, the familiar creaking of the iron gates being opened to Pullman's house, somewhat calmed his tested nerves. Sanctuary for a few hours!

Perhaps he should leave Godforsaken Chicago, defy his brothers warning and return to Ballindalloch. Elizabeth's letter burning in his pocket certainly gave him good reason.

CHAPTER 2
Sunday 7 August 2011, Brooklyn, New York, USA

Diane Cox made herself comfortable in the lazy chair facing the flat screen television, waiting for the next rerun of Grey's Anatomy. She'd already seen the series, but allowed herself her secret fancies and felt it was a perfect legitimate way to pass a Sunday afternoon. Deciding on a scoop of ice cream to enhance the experience, Diane eased herself from the chair when the voice of an anchor man came on air. She glanced out of the window looking onto Willow Street.

All was quiet as usual. Brooklyn Heights was a luxury for Diane. Bobby, her late husband, had a successful career in pharmaceuticals with Pfizer and even ran for Borough President for the Republicans. He had passed away in 2006 after a short illness, leaving her with financial security including her fully paid up home. Her kids were scattered over North America getting on with their own lives. She had considered moving to smaller low maintenance accommodation. Dawn, her dearest friend, had recommended the new East River State Park complex.

The words coming from the television now drew her attention;

'A policewoman from Raleigh, North Carolina, literally stirred up some dust in the Scottish Highlands yesterday at an estate by the name of Ballindalloch. The Castle is situated …'

Slowly Diane sat back down, eyes glued to the screen. A helicopter view zoomed in on a yellow digger, half way buried in the remains of a wall and the image of a young woman appeared in the left upper corner of the screen. The commentary highlighted how American tourist and prime suspect Cathy Stewart had been arrested. The broadcast finished with a light-hearted quip on building relationships with Scotland.

When the programme turned to the weather chart, Diane got up and walked to her laptop on the lounge table. Opening the browser, the screen flared up immediately. On Sundays she often left her computer on with Skype open. She was a keen Facebook user, primarily to keep up to date on what her kids and grandchildren were up to.

She Googled 'Ballindalloch' and almost immediately hits appeared, giving similar information to what she had just seen on television. Diane sat deep in thought for a while, gathered herself, went to her bedroom, and opened the closet holding her winter coats, the top shelf packed with boxes. In too much of a hurry to get a stepladder, she pulled over her dressing table chair, ignoring the thought of Dawn who recently suffered a nasty fall standing on a stool. Diane hauled herself to reach the top shelf. Impatiently she removed some items and tossed them on the bed behind her, until she found what she was looking for. Carefully, she removed a leather bound photo album, holding it reverently in both hands.

Grey's Anatomy would have to wait.

CHAPTER 3
Thursday 11 August 2011, Ballindalloch Castle, Banffshire, Scotland

"I've had an interesting discussion with Mr Brocklebank." Detective Inspector Peter Duckett confronted Thomas Macpherson.

Born and raised in Govan, Glasgow, in a working class housing scheme, Duckett was a street fighter. In the 1980s Govan was a place where life was a question of survival. His father worked in the shipyards, and his mother stayed at home to raise their five children. Peter was the oldest. By the time the last of the children left the house, his mother was an alcoholic. Peter's two brothers followed the shipyard path, and his sisters worked in the city; one at a bakers shop, the other at an accountants practice. His parents separated in 2002 and divorced two years later.

Duckett was staring across the library table into the senior man's eyes. Subconsciously rubbing his chin, the tall broad shouldered policeman waited for a reaction. Three walls with glass door-enclosed shelves, packed with books from floor to ceiling, made the room seem tranquil and private. A bay window offered a splendid view of a flower garden.

Uncle Thomas, as he was known within the inner circle of the Macpherson family, sipped his tea and smiled slightly at the inspector.

"Drink your tea Inspector before it gets cold." The handsome and agile looking veteran seemed totally relaxed.

"Mr Brocklebank told me you actually directed Mrs Stewart to the exact spot of the castle wall, she should...shall we say... remove? Isn't it so Mr Macpherson?"

"I have no idea what you are referring to," Thomas replied, taking his time to cross his legs.

The detective pursed his lips. "I know your background Mr Macpherson, a distinguished career in the military. Black Watch, right? A Colonel no less, served your country all over the world!"

"*Our* country," Thomas corrected.

"You know well enough what I refer to sir. What you did five days ago was out of character. The media reports must have tarnished your reputation. What puzzles me is how you knew the specific spot in the castle wall."

Curtly, Thomas Macpherson interrupted. "Why are you concerned with the reputation of an eighty-one year old man, who just wants to live his twilight years in peace? Look inspector, all I did was to try and help Mrs Stewart get out of the digger, as I feared for her safety."

"What is your relationship with Mrs Stewart? It seems you get along well. You were seen late on the Saturday morning going upstairs together. Was this in preparation for what was to come?"

"No it was not, we were both heading back to our rooms."

"So you didn't go to Mrs Stewart's bedroom?"

"At my age inspector, I don't think so."

Frustrated, Duckett ran his fingers through his wiry brown hair and stood up. "Let's get back to what happened later. Billy, Mr Brocklebank, phoned Mr Christie and told him you were striding in front of the JCB, shouting 'over here lass'; directing her in other words."

"Billy can get excited. I take it you also spoke to Kenny?"

"What is your relationship with Kenny Christie?"

"Stop playing games Mr Duckett. You know fine well we served together in the Black Watch. He was my right hand."

"Exactly! And it seems to me, he is still your confidante, so he would tell *me* whatever *you* asked him to say. How did you know the body was there Mr Macpherson?"

Thomas remained silent and simply shrugged his shoulders.

Duckett tried again. "The whole thing was planned. We know Mrs Stewart barged in on John Durie's home early in the morning, asking the curator questions on the disappearance of Gordon Macpherson. He showed her some old newspaper clippings from 1895. In the afternoon, by sheer coincidence, she hijacks a JCB and with your help slams into the castle dungeon. And guess what? There are the bones of what will be surely identified as Gordon Macpherson. The poor bugger finally unearthed, after a hundred and eleven years. It was all planned wasn't it? We know you met Mrs Stewart after she returned from Grantown Museum. Mr Macpherson, can you deny any of this?"

"You're from Glasgow are you not?" Thomas inquired casually. "What are you doing here son? Shouldn't you be chasing drug runners, murderers and other nasty people? Why are you interested in a damaged wall and some old bones?"

Feeling insulted, Duckett glared at Thomas. "You must know Mr Macpherson there is still a high media interest. All I'm trying to do is tidy up some loose ends. Off the record, I think this family could do a better job at being so called sophisticated. You must have known all along Gordon Macpherson was under your feet. Christ maybe you've known for bloody years! You convinced Mrs Stewart to do your dirty work."

Thomas Macpherson looked Duckett straight in the eye. "You have a vivid imagination. This meeting is over." Thomas left a dismayed policeman without even a simple goodbye.

CHAPTER 4
Friday 7 June 1895, Ballindalloch Castle, Banffshire, Scotland

Elizabeth Macpherson lay in her four-poster bed, almost disappearing in the huge quantity of bedding covering her thin body. In spite of all the layers she was shivering. Her feet and hands felt as cold as ice. It was early afternoon judging by the daylight streaming in through the French windows. A blackbird sat on the ledge and seemed to be eyeing her, adjusting the angle of its head with abrupt swift movements.

A wave of tiredness flooded Elizabeth, making her feel much older than her fifty-four years. She knew her time was due and felt at peace with it. If there had been chances to change her circumstances, she'd let them slip. She had become too good at hiding her real condition. She knew she should try and fight, but felt too exhausted from being taken for granted, even if everybody always praised the way she supported her husband, her children, had taken care of the young Alexander, and was there to help the sick and poor in the local community. *But they never asked what I wanted.*

Perhaps the only person who had known what really moved Elizabeth was Mary Montgomery. At sixteen, Mary had joined the Macpherson household when Elizabeth and Gordon were just married. Mary had quickly moved from chamber maid to personal aid of Lady Macpherson. She witnessed all children being born and intuitively knew exactly what was going on, quietly supporting Elizabeth to meet her obligations. 'You are my working half,' Elizabeth had remarked once, embarrassing Mary who in her down to earth way felt it was only her duty.

Yet truth be told, Mary *was* taking care of Elizabeth, to such an extent Gordon and the children were oblivious to the severity of her condition. Elizabeth felt in some respect it was better. Why upset her children unduly? All were busy with their own lives.

The only thing she wanted to settle before leaving the earthly plane was the matter of Katherine. Her youngest and only girl had shown to be independent and of bright-witted character. Elizabeth felt it was exactly these characteristics that could endanger the family balance, and felt guilty. She had seen her daughter's struggle with Gordon, had understood her reasons and never said a word. It was too embarrassing. As mother, she needed to set an example. How could she reprimand Katherine on behaviour she could well understand? Elizabeth cringed at the thought. She pulled up her knees to her chin and wrapped her arms around herself, wishing she could remove the shame from her consciousness. A new coughing fit sent red hot flames through her chest.

Had she possessed her daughter's wilfulness, Elizabeth would have eloped with William and settle down somewhere far away. Yet it had not been part of her character to oppose the hand that supplied her. She had always been a compliant wife, except for one time. In a way she felt it was a sign from God that the union had been immediately blessed with a child. For Gordon, it had been a devastating acknowledgement of what he had always denied. In his own protective way, he cared for his Elizabeth, yet knew she preferred the attentions of his brother. As a result, Gordon had retreated into complete emotional silence.

Now, with the friendship between Alexander and Katherine, Elizabeth felt it was time to allow the couple their space and freedom.

CHAPTER 5
Friday 7 June 1895, Chicago, Illinois, USA

"I certainly would never go to Britain. Hattie would have a stroke," Pullman said, admiring the colour of the 'water of life' in his glass. "I'd advise you to stay put my friend; you are an American now. This is where you've built your fortune for the past two decades. You and I are not men to retreat with our tail between our legs when matters change."

William Macpherson stared into his whisky glass before taking a large gulp. "It's different for you Mort. You were born in this country. I'm a Scot and will be so as long as I live. Christ, when the crowd stopped my coach, I thought, what the hell am I doing here? This strike is getting out of hand. I feared for my life."

"You arrived safe and sound. The riots only serve me well my friend. They will discredit the Unions. I hired the Pinkerton Detective Agency to arrange such events. The press will publish how an unruly crowd threatened a poor defenceless man. The agency will make sure the details and more, are printed."

William sat back and smirked at the deviousness. "You scoundrel, it's a good thing I have you as a friend rather than a foe. Did you know Pinkerton was Scottish? I believe he was from Glasgow, not my favourite city I must admit."

"I don't care if he was a nigger from the South. I only need them to earn their exuberant fees." Pullman leaned back and stretched his arms. "So why are you contemplating going back to Scotland?"

For a moment William hesitated, unsure if he should reveal more. "You should know I didn't leave Scotland because I wanted to. It was my scheming brother who put me in a position where I had no choice but to leave."

"No choice? Man, we always have choices!"

"My brother would agree with you when they are *his* to make," William grunted, "and in this case I have to admit the choice *was* his. Gordon knew North America had a thirst for whisky. To get me out of the way, he easily convinced his partners I was the right man to grow the trade here. 'The Grants have a mutual admiration of your talents,' he said, the scheming bastard!"

"Whether you agree or not, your brother spoke true. What you pulled off with the President was brilliant."

William looked away. "It wasn't me. It was Carnegie who ordered the whisky to be delivered to the white house.

"But, I know Andrew well enough William. He only does business with the best. If it hadn't been you in charge of DCL, he

14

would never have ordered the cask of Scotch. He knows you have what it takes to discreetly handle such a situation. Anyone else would have been brow beaten by the patriots who want to sell their own spirits."

"I understand why bourbon sells, it's cheap, it's American and there is a lot out there," William remarked, "but I will continue to push the quality of our drink and trust the Scots here prize their inheritance and spread the gospel." Holding up his glass, he continued, "Mort, our whisky even *looks* better."

"To each their own William, but fact remains it takes diplomacy and courage to take on the Americans at their own game. You have done the perfect job."

William did not comment on his friends praise but was grateful for the recognition.

"So how did your brother manage to force his hand on you?"

William threw his friend a quick glance.

"It's a tedious story. He also meddled with Cooper & Waddell, you know, my so called partners in Inverness, who I am sure were happy to see the back of me. The truth be told Mort, I was not pulling my weight in the practice and more concerned on other matters, rather than traipsing to and fro with clients to the courts, pleading with inexorable half drunken judges. Furtive person that he is, he manipulated these facts, the ever righteous laird, my brother Gordon Macpherson."

Mort leaned back in his chair. In spite of his pride of having a strong American lineage, he had to admit Europe was appealing. He appreciated the resonance of the word 'laird' for instance. *Perhaps if a feudal system had been in place in America, the strike would never have happened.*

"Sorry William, but maybe your brother was correct. It seems to me that life in Scotland wasn't giving you the gratification you sought."

William leaned back and reflected. He had arrived in Toronto in April 1877, representing the newly formed Distillers Company Limited. Known as DCL, the conglomerate was made up of six distillers and merchants from Scotland. William's legal experience was recognised to be of great value, to understand and comply with complex law regarding alcohol standards and controls in Canada and America. He spent the first three years establishing distributors and retailers. It had proved to be a difficult task with local competition of Club Whiskey. In 1880, the whisky industry had experienced a major break. The phylloxera bug destroyed French vineyards. Wine and brandy production plummeted. In particular, the English craved for blended whisky, being deprived of their trusted cognac and claret. The

15

result had been a huge shift to consumption of whisky around the globe.

Despite the American competition and growing concern around prohibition, with the rise of the Temperance movement, William had convinced DCL to trade from headquarters in Chicago. He and his most loyal employees had moved in 1886. William purchased a detached house in downtown Maxwell Street. Chicago was a huge commercial and industrial city. DCL secured a lease of a modest office in the Home Insurance Building, a ten-story skyscraper on the corner of Adams and LaSalles. In Chicago, he had blossomed into a maverick, a traveller and an all-round raconteur.

Cautiously, William eyed his friend. On one hand, he wanted to confide in Mort what had made him leave Scotland. On the other, he was worried the response would be unwelcome. If he were to tell Pullman his true reasons for wanting to go back, Mort would probably advise him to let matters be and avoid causing more damage; be grateful for what he had achieved in America.

"There was also the matter of my brother's wife," Macpherson probed, to see how his friend would react.

Pullman raised his eyebrows but said nothing. He picked up the bottle of Scotch and poured two generous refills.

"She was forced into an arranged marriage, sought refuge elsewhere and gave birth to a girl, eighteen years ago now," William paused, "years after she and my brother had separate living quarters."

The fire crackling in the hearth was the only sound in the room. Amidst his own current situation, Pullman could not find it within him to consider William's problems to be something of great concern.

"Women," Pullman said crassly, "nothing but trouble what?"

William looked up at his bearded friend. "This is different."

Pullman contained a sigh. To him, women were most of all a necessity to secure the continuation of a family line. Hattie had gifted him with four fine children. "Is your brother still there?"

"Yes he is for sure."

"Why bother? What makes you think he will want you there now?"

William expressed a grim smile. "I'm sure he won't, but Elizabeth is unwell and she worries for her daughter's future, she..." Searching for words he blurted, "It's just that history is repeating itself."

Beginning to find the discussion tiresome, Mort absentmindedly asked, "Is the girl being forced into an arranged marriage?"

"Oh no, on the contrary!" William sniggered. He knew for a fact Katherine would never be forced into marrying anyone. "It's even worse in a way. She is doing what Elizabeth never dared! She is ignoring my brother's command by her involvement with the gamekeeper's son." Looking at Mort sternly, he concluded, "I'm going back to put things right for Elizabeth, myself and more importantly, for our daughter."

The foreboding Elizabeth was soon to die eluded him completely.

CHAPTER 6
Thursday 11 August 2011, Ballindalloch Castle, Banffshire, Scotland

"Come in," bellowed Angus Macpherson seated behind his desk. He had not been looking forward to the meeting. Nervously, he drummed his fingertips on a closed laptop.

Duckett stepped into the study with confident movements and closed the door. Angus felt uncomfortable. He wished Duckett would show some emotion rather than contained demeanour.

Peter glared at the smallish rotund man. Angus looked uneasy when the inspector pulled up a chair uninvited and sat down opposite. In a soft, but firm voice Duckett opened, "I was surprised you dropped the charges."

"Do you want a tea or a coffee inspector?"

"No thanks. Why did you, Mr Macpherson?"

Angus stood up, removed his dark brown jacket, draped it over the back of his chair and sat back down again.

"Mr Macpherson?"

"Well, I didn't see the point of charging Mrs Stewart. For one; she did unravel a family mystery, God rest Gordon's soul, and two, she is a Macpherson. Blood is thicker than water inspector."

"You sound as if Mrs Stewart is your long lost sister. What is her connection to your family? Cousin, at least ten times removed?"

Angus forced a thin smile. "I take it there is no such thing as a Clan Duckett. If there was, you would know all clan members are 'cousins' no matter how far removed from their roots."

The remark annoyed Peter. Unlike Thomas Macpherson, Angus didn't seem to target his observations deliberately to get him off balance, but his aloof manner had the same effect.

"Don't you think it is remarkable Mrs Stewart knew exactly where to direct the JCB?"

Angus jumped. "I do indeed inspector, she is an amazing lady and she must have some psychic powers way beyond my imagination. I never believed in such ..."

Duckett raised his voice and interrupted, "It must have cost you a lot of money to repair the damage."

Angus paused to consider his answer. "All things being equal Mr Duckett," he finally produced, "whilst I do not condone Mrs Stewart's actions, our tourist numbers have gone through the roof over the past few days. This will fund the repairs. In addition we still have our insurance claim."

"Insurance! Surely they will never pay out on an act of deliberate destruction?"

Angus leaned back in his chair, feeling more comfortable with the way the conversation was now going. "Oh yes they will. I was a corporate lawyer for many years. I know how to tread the law."

The policeman stood up and leaned over to Angus, forcing him to look up. "Even the courts can't deny Mrs Stewart knew exactly where to guide the JCB. Somebody helped her. I do recall you were in a state of shock when you arrived at the scene, but you must have realised what was going on."

Angus dropped his head and returned to tapping on the computer.

Sitting back down, the detective continued, "Do you remember when I told you we found a body? We were in the tearoom."

"No," muttered Angus, "I was in shock as you have just stated."

Duckett paused and produced a small notepad from his jacket, flicked through the pages and read out, "Mr Angus Macpherson; quote: 'Oh my God, he's been found'. Do you recall those words Mr Macpherson? It was as if you knew he was *there* to be found."

Angus looked up wishing he was somewhere else.

"If I did say something similar I am not surprised inspector."

"So you *knew* they were Gordon Macpherson's bones?"

It was now Angus who stood up and leaned across the desk to glare at Duckett. "Who else could it be? We don't have a habit of running around Ballindalloch murdering people and tossing them into a dungeon! The mystery of Gordon Macpherson's disappearance is a well-known story in these parts and it was just an educated guess. He was the first person to spring to mind when you told me human remains had been discovered."

"The police report at the time concluded Mr Gordon drowned in the Spey, did it not?"

"I never believed in a drowning, ask the family. I have always found it highly unlikely. Gordon's body was never recovered you know... um ...until now."

Duckett gave a wry smile. "Maybe you disputed the drowning because you and Thomas Macpherson knew the whereabouts of the body?"

"Think what you want! I have to say I am appalled by your implication. If my uncle and I had known of Gordon, we would have informed the authorities. What kind of people do you think we are?"

The inspector shook his head. "I have witnesses who saw Thomas Macpherson help Mrs Stewart guide the digger to the exact part of the castle wall."

"That is preposterous inspector, why would he! Now if you'll excuse me, the Royal Scotsman coach party is due to arrive any moment. It is customary I welcome them. Their trip includes a stopover at Ballindalloch for afternoon tea. I need to go. Enough has been said as it is. I suggest you close the case."

Angus left the room without giving Duckett a final glance, leaving an ill-tempered inspector behind.

CHAPTER 7
Thursday 11 August 2011, Ballindalloch, Banffshire, Scotland

Duckett arrived promptly in the small office adjacent to the castle tearoom, for his one o'clock appointment with Cathy Stewart. When he announced his arrival, he was told she hadn't been seen all morning.

He wasn't offered a seat. All attention was directed towards The Royal Scotsman passengers, who were at the beginning of a guided tour. Irritated, Duckett walked outside.

Everyone in this bloody castle is treating me as if I was a tourist who hasn't bought a ticket, especially Thomas, the arrogant old bastard calling me 'son'. With the corners of his mouth pulled down, he silently mimicked Macpherson's words, *Are you from Glasgow son? As for the laird, he is some piece of work.*

The sound of someone running on the gravel made him turn his head towards the ivy arcade connecting the tearoom courtyard and the gardens. Cathy appeared from under the foliage. Her face was flushed with the combination of exercise and highland air, her hair tied up in a high ponytail, wet from perspiration. A damp towel hung around her neck. Even with no makeup or fancy clothes, Duckett had to admit Cathy Stewart had a natural, appealing presence.

"Hey there Duckett," she greeted him casually. Her cycles of breath were still fast, her mouth slightly open.

"Nice day for a jog," he said, hiding his annoyance over the fact she had failed to be on time.

"Yeah, should do this more often."

Cathy seemed distracted. She had forgotten the appointment. "So, what do you want?" she asked, hiding her embarrassment by vigorously drying her hair with the towel.

Duckett felt another flush of frustration. "I would prefer to sit while we talk," he said, clipped.

"We could park here." Cathy pointed at a wooden bench conveniently located between the flowerbeds.

"I prefer we go inside."

Cathy knew well she irritated the life out of Duckett. "Let's just do that inspector."

Duckett followed her through a corridor with small, low bay windows. An abundance of pictures and paintings adorned each side of the hall. The passage was narrow. Billy Brocklebank approached from the opposite direction. They all had to sidestep a little. Cathy took the opportunity to ask for beverages.

"Billy, could I please have a bottle of water, a large bottle if you don't mind. You inspector, what is your tipple?"

Before Duckett could answer, Billy muttered, "You'll have to get your own drinks I'm too busy, sorry."

Duckett observed the friction between the Scot and the American.

Ignoring the tension, Cathy led Duckett into a modest sitting-room where she promptly sat down on the windowsill and crossed her legs. Duckett sensed she was trying to be distant, an old police trick he knew all too well.

"Okay fire away, it is your show after all."

"Call me Peter," he counteracted. "We *are* fellow detectives after all."

Cathy feigned innocence. She knew well enough they were going to cross arms and lock horns.

"Thanks Peter, please call me Cathy."

"So tell me *Cathy,* do we in Scotland conduct ourselves differently compared to the Raleigh PD?"

A sudden feeling of not being in control overwhelmed Cathy. "I wouldn't know, I'm not the one at work here."

Duckett gave a sardonic smile, "What brought you to Scotland, to Ballindalloch?"

"My husband I guess. He traced his ancestors, the Stewarts of Ballindalloch. Shall I bore you with details of Alexander Stewart?"

"Please don't. It's the Macphersons I want to discuss and what you did on sixth August and why."

"Okay."

"Why did your husband not join you on this trip?"

"He did, he just happened to arrive a few days after me. He had prior business in London."

"He arrived too late to stop you."

Cathy smiled and took a deliberate pause. "Sorry, but it amuses me you think David could stop me doing anything."

"I believe you arrived on the Thursday before the incident," Peter went on, ignoring what he considered a feminist remark.

Cathy just nodded.

"And you had never met any of the Macphersons of Ballindalloch before?"

"Not in this life for sure. It was my first visit to your wonderful country Peter," she said, managing to make Duckett uneasy.

"And why may I ask are you still here? Your husband went back to the US."

"David is none of your business," Cathy snapped.

Grasping the opportunity, Duckett smiled. "Fair enough, I do hope you have the necessary visa. So you arrived on Thursday, the fourth of

August. What did you do from the Thursday to the Saturday afternoon?"

"Look Peter, let's cut to the chase. Since coming here all I heard or imagined I heard, was the mystery of a laird missing since 1895. I don't know what came over me on the Saturday, but I just knew it was the reason why I was here."

Cathy's features became serious. The redness on her cheeks had gone and she seemed to be staring beyond Duckett.

Duckett laughed out loud, but Cathy didn't flinch.

"Yeah right! Images in your mind directed you to Gordon Macpherson's bones. Maybe Gordon was shouting at you," he mocked.

Cathy had the urge to sock him on the mouth, but remained calm.

"I'm just wondering why you are protecting Mr Thomas Macpherson? It is obvious he was the one who had the knowledge. You simply followed his instructions."

Cathy stood up and stepped closer to the detective. "You know Peter I don't understand why you are still investigating this. There was no homicide. What happened to Gordon Macpherson and why, we'll never know, will we? What is your motive to keep on stirring up the past? You are upsetting these good people. What interest is it to the police? It will be established the bones were Gordon Macpherson's and he died in the tunnel. If you enjoy family history so much, why don't you research your own? It should be easy with your surname."

They both stared at one another for a few seconds. Duckett's facial colour had visibly changed from bland to dark red. He coughed and shuffled his feet, the scraping of his shoes the only sound filling the room.

"Let me leave you and the family at peace for now. I'm sure you will contact me if you recall anything of importance."

Cathy summoned a benevolent smile. "If you'll excuse me I have to call my husband and my buddies at the PD," she lied and shimmied out of the room.

CHAPTER 8
Saturday 2 November 1895, Ballindalloch Castle, Banffshire, Scotland

The dishevelled figure of Gordon Macpherson nervously scurried around the study, his beard still damp from the heavy rain that caught him on his way back from Grantown. Twice he had been there today. In the early morning to report the theft, and in the afternoon, to watch with his own eyes, Alexander board the train to Perth. The lad would have been foolish to do differently.

Back behind the desk from which he had initiated the Stewart boy's departure, Gordon found it hard to concentrate on the task ahead. He knew more dissembling was required to avoid any trace of the scheme he had designed to rid Ballindalloch of the gamekeeper's son. Nobody else was allowed to work in his study, but still needs must. His notes to Anderson seemed the most significant to dispense with, although the man had yet to confirm the last steps of his mission.

His hands still cold and stiff from the afternoon excursion, Gordon clumsily crushed the most revealing papers and walked over to the fireplace. Simpson had made sure the maids had kept it alight. Just as he tossed the proof of his foul play into the flames, the chimney-clock chimed the hour of six, making Gordon jump. A cold shudder ran down his spine and he could feel his heart pound in his chest. The clock was the last present his wife had gifted him for Christmas, six months before her death.

Gordon tried to shift his mind to more profound tasks to be performed, but first he anxiously opened the cabinet storing his whisky, grabbed a bottle and poured a generous glass. Gratefully, he felt the liquid burn his throat.

A movement caught his attention outside the window. A man stooping over a lantern helping him through the evening darkness was making his way towards the main entrance. Gordon wasn't expecting any visitors, even more so, he was not ready to see anyone and hoped Simpson would deal adequately with whoever was coming his way. Voices in the hallway told him otherwise. It was the gamekeeper, Robert Stewart, who sounded extremely upset.

"I insist on seeing him now," Stewart boomed.

"Robert," Simpson hushed, "you cannot. The laird must not be disturbed at this time."

"He *is* disturbed and I'll disturb him even more," Robert continued to bawl.

Gordon could hear Stewart's boots marching towards the study. Frantically he looked around as if trying to find a place to hide. The heavy door to the study flew open. Robert Stewart walked straight up to Macpherson.

"What have you done to my son?" he bellowed. "Where is he? Who gave you the right to send him away? Has he done you any wrong? If so, it should be reported to the police. What in God's name is going on here?"

Trying to overthrow Stewart's confidence, Gordon pushed out his chest in anger, his face colouring bright red. He shouted, "I now know from whom your son inherited his impertinent behaviour Mr Stewart! Calm yourself before you judge my actions!"

Taken off guard, Robert stopped in full stride, his breath still rasping and with obvious difficulty. He'd always given Gordon Macpherson the respect he deemed necessary, but what had happened today, erased all previous understanding of the way the world was divided. Alexander *was* his world. He had gratefully accepted the Lady Elizabeth's proposition to raise his son within the Ballindalloch walls. Ever since her untimely death, Gordon's behaviour had dramatically changed.

"Robert, sit down and listen. I had my reasons. You have to understand."

Like a hawk eying its prey, Robert Stewart watched the laird. Reluctantly he sat down on the chair closest to Gordon.

"Do you want a dram?"

"No! I want answers," Stewart growled fractiously. It occurred to him, even though Gordon Macpherson and he had spent much of their childhood together, be it divided between the castle and the gamekeeper's lodge, he had never enjoyed his company.

Lady Elizabeth? She was totally different, an understanding woman. When she had taken on the reins of Ballindalloch by marrying its laird it had been easy to converse with her regarding the happenings on the estate and its families. Gordon could be aloof, like an actor playing a role in a stage play.

"Lady Elizabeth would never have condoned this."

Stung by the gamekeeper's words and in no mood to be reminded of his departed wife, Gordon stood up and walked over to the decanter, pouring himself another whisky with his back to Stewart, using the absence of eye contact to deliver his message.

"As you say Robert, your son should have been arrested and in fact I did report the theft to the police only this morning, but I wanted to give the boy a chance."

"Theft! What theft?" Robert asked with malice, getting up from his chair. "Alexander would never steal. You know that just as well as I do."

Gordon turned and faced the gamekeeper. "Well I'm not so sure," taking advantage of the puzzlement creeping over Robert's face.

"What in heaven's name are you implying man!"

"Look Robert, I don't want to go into details but jewellery has disappeared and the police have reason to believe your son was the culprit. Pending the investigation, I thought I'd give Alexander a chance and give him means to become invisible for a while until the tide has turned; calmer water so to speak. It was the only way I could think of to save all of us from shame."

Gordon had thought long and hard how he was going to explain Alexander's absence to Robert and the other inhabitants of Ballindalloch. He would deal with the real hazards when needed.

Robert's silence unnerved Gordon more than he cared to admit. Never before had he seen his gamekeeper in this state. A trickle of sweat dripping on his brow, made him wonder if he had perhaps used the wrong arguments.

"Look, let's be fair here Stewart. The friendship between my daughter and your son was unbecoming. It was high time he left Ballindalloch. You must see this. Now, if you'll excuse me it has been a distressing day for me too, believe it or not. I have not even had my supper yet, which I believe is being served now. I'll be quite happy to discuss more in the morning. Goodnight Robert."

"Aye, well, maybe you are right. Miss Katherine and Alex did spend too much time together. I tried to tell him and I wish he had left this damn place, but not in this way. It should have been his choice to do so, or mine, but not yours! You have made my position here untenable." At that, Robert marched out of the study feeling very unsatisfied. For now, he could do nothing but accept the situation.

***

After a sleepless night and a struggle to stay awake during the morning church service, a tired Robert went looking for his friend Simpson, the head butler of the house, to seek his opinion and advice. Robert felt mentally exhausted.

Donald Simpson lent a sympathetic ear to Robert's ranting and raving. Reading Alexander's note, indicating he had to leave within the hour, bound for America, Simpson agreed with Robert, Alex was no thief. He also shared how distraught Miss Katherine had been by her father's deceit. She had in fact confided in him with her intent to visit her best friend Heather in Edinburgh and had asked Simpson to arrange transport to Grantown train station.

Robert, at a loose end, then went looking for coachman MacLean. Maybe if he could get all the house staff on his side, they could convince Gordon to have a change of mind.

"Be sure, there will be more water to flow under the bridge," MacLean predicted, waving his finger in the air.

On his way back to the lodge, Robert saw Gordon heading towards the river, dressed in fishing attire and carrying a rod. He considered approaching him, but thought better of it. Only on entering the lodge, did it strike Robert; *fishing in November, how odd?*

***

An hour later, John Macpherson, Gordon's eldest son, made himself comfortable in the leather club chair beside the drawing-room fire. Dressed in a dark-green velvet housecoat, his feet resting on a footstool, he buried himself in a newspaper. An article on bicycles being responsible for declining book sales in the United States had drawn his attention. John sniggered. *Bicycles indeed! They were a pathetic invention for the middle class, trying to keep up with progress.*

A strange rumble and a soft shaking of the windows drew him away from his readings. Astonished he looked around. The room seemed tranquil. Dust particles were dancing in the afternoon sunlight that fell through the window. He heard a shout from downstairs. This was unusual for the Ballindalloch household, especially on a Sunday, when quietness was held in high regard.

Tossing his newspaper to the floor, John stood up and walked towards the window. He saw nothing unusual outside, just Robert Stewart walking towards the field where the Aberdeen Angus was grazing.

John shrugged his shoulders. He wished for some peace. Breakfast had been unnerving enough. Little had been said after discovering Katherine had left at the break of dawn without having asked permission. Father's mood had been unbearable.

Just when John turned away from the window to go and look for Simpson, hurried footsteps in the hall announced someone approaching.

"Sir!" It was the stable boy Callum. Normally, he would never dare enter the private quarters. "I beg your pardon sir, but I think you should go downstairs. Something has collapsed in the old scullery." The boy looked peculiar. There were streaks of dust all over his clothes and face.

"Go look for my father," John ordered. Quickly, he made his way towards the kitchen quarters. A strange mingled scent of dust and fungus came floating towards him. He found MacLean in the scullery, coughing and waving his arms at a cloud of dust still spreading through the darkened space. The panel, used to close off the old whisky tunnel, lay on the floor.

"I'd say part of the tunnel has collapsed Mr John," MacLean remarked on the obvious.

Over the years many stories were told of the ancient dungeon beneath the existing structure, especially the story of a severe flood in 1829. This topic occasionally kept the late night conversations in the servant's quarters going. Some claimed they could still hear the screams of the whisky smugglers who were trapped and drowned in the dungeon.

"Where is Simpson, why isn't he here?" John asked, not knowing what to do with the situation.

"I believe he's with Robert sir."

"Impossible, I just saw Stewart walking towards the river."

An uneasy silence hung between MacLean and John Macpherson. The estate hummed with gossip on what had happened the day before, especially Robert Stewart's threat to follow his son's footsteps and leave Ballindalloch. Simpson and the gamekeeper were close friends. Everybody was now waiting to see how the butler would react. Simpson had paid a huge contribution to the upbringing of all the Macpherson children, including the fostered Alexander.

John ordered MacLean to leave.

"Go find Simpson. Tell him I need him here now."

Stunned, MacLean hurried himself out of the scullery.

John noticed the old brass lantern, usually hanging beside the coal cellar door, was missing. As children, he and his brothers would often explore the tunnel. He wasn't remotely tempted to go in now, the dust irritating his throat. He was just about to leave, when Simpson arrived.

"Where were you man? We've been looking all over for you!"

"I'm sorry sir, I was engaged," Donald Simpson answered, not bothering to remind John, he was not on duty on Sunday, unless there was an official function to perform.

"Get someone to close this off," John commanded, "and don't even think of going in, it's too dangerous."

"Yes sir," Simpson answered. "I'll see to it immediately. Have you seen your father? I think he might want to be informed."

"Callum is searching for him," John answered. "You just take care of everything here."

CHAPTER 9
Wednesday 7 September 2011, Grantown-on-Spey, Morayshire, Scotland

Cathy strolled into the Grantown-on-Spey Museum, clutching a gift-wrapped bottle. It had been a humid day, forcing her to take advice on using an insect repellent to combat the ferocious highland midges. Dressed in casual attire of blue denims, a sleeveless dark blue top and trainers, she approached an elderly lady behind the reception desk who was busy opening a parcel of books.

"Good afternoon, is Mr Durie available?" Cathy asked the petite, but resilient-looking woman.

"Has been a fine day has it not?" the lady volunteered, as she tidied her red woollen cardigan. "Let me check." She picked up the telephone. "Who can I say is calling and the nature of business?"

Cathy guessed the woman well knew who she was. The dramatic happenings of the fourth of August and her subsequent arrest, had been widely discussed within the local community. The national and local networks swamped the town with journalists, attempting to unravel more details of her and the Macpherson family. An agent for CNN had even made an attempt to interview Durie, who had rebuffed all journalists by merely informing them Mrs Stewart had simply wanted some information on the well-known local mystery of 1895; the disappearance of Gordon Macpherson. Cathy had been quite surprised to hear of his placid reaction after the way she had forced herself into his home.

"Mr Durie knows me, Cathy, Cathy Stewart and it is pleasure, not business."

"Let me find him for you. I'm quite sure he is upstairs."

Cathy sauntered into the main hall of the brightly lit museum. It was empty of visitors. Cardboard partitions sectioned off the exhibits into various categories. Cathy peered at a historical display, consisting of old pictures and posters from the town. The surname 'Grant' dominated the descriptions of the exhibits. She overheard the receptionist on the phone informing the curator of her presence.

"Mrs Stewart, John, um, Mr Durie will be here directly."

Before Cathy could respond, John Durie appeared from a doorway. A tall gawky man, dressed in fluttering slacks, clumsily walked into the hall.

"M-Mrs Stewart, what brings you back here?" he stammered. "I thought you would have r-returned to the USA."

They shook hands and Cathy gave her best smile. "Still here I'm afraid, but I promise I will not give you any more hassle. I just wanted to apologise for my unannounced visit to the museum last month. It must have been quite an ordeal for you, you know, imposing myself on you in the manner of an interrogation. I just wanted to show you I am not altogether incorrigible. I would have come earlier, but needed some time to shape up. I hope this will help compensate for our first acquaintance." She handed Durie the bottle. "Let's say it's a peace offering."

Without hesitation he took the bottle. "There is no n-need Mrs Stewart but th-thank you anyway."

"I hope you enjoy whisky, Cragganmore to be precise. When I reflect on how I barged into your home it makes me cringe. I can only tell you how sorry I am."

The curator pushed his wiry grey hair back. Embarrassed by her prolonged apology, Durie gestured they should wander further into the hall. "W-would you want to take a more p-proper look around this time?" he asked.

Durie went on to explain the history of the building and its contents. There were various sections showing the town's past, its industries, people and local arts and crafts. Cathy was trying to show interest, but most of Durie's words passed over her.

"How long have you been the curator?"

"I p-prefer to think of myself as a historian. I have b-been here for many years, too many. I'm a bit of a d-dinosaur I'm afraid."

Cathy stopped in her tracks and stared at a framed black and white photograph on the wall. She stepped closer to study the image. Two women were smiling back, their arms looping around one another.

"I'm afraid this p-picture is rather indulgent of me. It has no historical value to the museum. It's a p-picture of a family ancestor."

"She," Durie pointed to one of the women, "is part of the Durie family tree."

"Where and when was the picture taken? Do you know?"

"I wouldn't be a historian if I didn't know, would I?" She is my great-great-grandmother on my father's side, depicted here on the grounds of Edinburgh University. The y-year is 1897. Why do you ask?"

Cathy turned to the photo and pointed. "Because the girl next to her is Katherine Macpherson."

CHAPTER 10
Sunday 3 November 1895, Edinburgh, Scotland

"Katherine! What brings you back so soon?" exclaimed a surprised Heather Durie, having said her goodbyes only yesterday. "Ignore the mess," she added apologetically, "the children have been playing and Nanny has Sunday off. Is everything all right?"

A glum Katherine Macpherson stepped over a wooden rocking horse and threw her oldest friend a relieved look. "I'm so happy you're home; sincere apologies for my impulsive behaviour. It was only early this morning I made up my mind to come back."

"It's perfectly alright, you are always welcome here," Heather responded, meaning every word.

The small hallway of the second-floor abode, just off Princes Street, offered little room. Heather took Katherine's coat, hat and umbrella and ushered her into the sitting room.

"Auntie Katie, Auntie Katie!" The voices of six-year old twins Claire and Oliver filled the air with happy shrieks, "you've come to take us to the park and feed the ducks," Claire chimed.

Spontaneously Katherine went down on her knees to give the twins an affectionate hug, wrapping a slender arm around each of them.

"Not exactly you mischievous pair," she said, smiling broadly at their enthusiastic welcome, "but I promise we'll go some time soon."

Malcolm Durie appeared in the doorway of the study, adjacent to the sitting-room. "Katherine! What an unexpected pleasure. What brings you back so quickly and on a Sunday? I'm surprised your father allowed you to travel."

"He doesn't know I'm here to be honest." Getting back on her feet, Katherine smoothed the folds of her skirt. "We had a rather nasty argument I'm afraid."

Malcolm was not surprised. A close friend of the Macpherson brothers, he'd often witnessed Gordon's strict regime. He had also observed over the years a young Katherine growing up into an independent young lady, somewhat a contrast to his wife Heather, a long-time friend of the laird's youngest child. The women's friendship had continued after Durie married Heather, with Katherine visiting them frequently, especially after the twins were born. The bond between Katherine and Heather was predestined. Although of different characters, they shared a passion for science, culture, novels and art. These same interests had drawn Heather to fall for the professor, who was now a Dean of Edinburgh University.

Katherine loved spending time with the couple; sometimes staying a few days, taking weight off Heather's shoulders by entertaining the twins.

"Children, your room now please," Malcolm instructed. "You can come back later. I will call you."

The twins groaned in harmony. They gave Katherine a wave before leaving.

"How was your journey?" asked Heather.

"Terrible! Changing from one train to another is such an annoyance, so time consuming. The railway companies don't care as long as they are lining their pockets. It could be so much more efficient. I feel as though I have been living on trains the past few days."

"Well, sit down and relax while I get us some refreshments," Heather suggested.

Katherine chose a spot on the far end of the couch next to the window offering a view over Southbridge. People strolled in the autumn sunshine, some women with parasols. Horses and carriages found their way on both sides of the road, either going in the direction of the train station or further south. Katherine sat silently, watching Malcolm concentrate on preparing his pipe.

"Here we are." Heather came in carrying a tray with a pot of tea, a porcelain jar filled to the rim with milk, a matching sugar bowl and a plate of shortbread. "This should cheer you up."

She sat next to Katherine and served the tea. "Now, to what do we owe the honour?"

"It is father," Katherine opened, clearly agitated. "He's sent Alex away under the most horrible pretence, accusing him of stealing mother's jewellery. Now I understand why father suggested I visit you for a few days, just so I'd be out of the way! I'm convinced he forced Alex. I cannot stay at Ballindalloch. I'm so angry."

After uttering a deep sigh Durie asked, "Do you know where Alexander is?"

"Heading for America I've heard." Katherine took a few moments to collect her thoughts to address what she had really come to discuss. After glancing at Heather, she turned to Malcolm. "I didn't plan to burden you with this till next year," she opened, "but considering the circumstances it can't wait any longer. I'm going to be rather forward." She cleared her throat and looked at Durie. "Malcolm, I know you are in favour of further education for women. I've been exploring the possibility of applying at Edinburgh University. In fact," looking somewhat guilty Katherine added, "Heather and I visited the campus last Friday, while I was here, didn't we?" Katherine was now looking at Heather.

Malcolm raised his eyebrows towards his wife. "You didn't tell me dear. Had I known we could have arranged tea ."

Heather's face blushed. "Katherine wanted me to keep it quiet. She has a rather revolutionary idea."

"I have an *enormous* request," Katherine took over the exchange. "I wanted to discuss it with Heather first. I was wondering, hoping … you could help me."

Malcolm Durie remained silent, causing Katherine to feel insecure. She stood up and walked towards the window. When she turned, her face displayed a pained expression. "I *need* to leave Ballindalloch and studying at university would be a dream come true," she pleaded. "It must be possible. Can you vouch for me, support my application?"

"Sit down Katherine, drink your tea," Malcolm Durie suggested firmly.
"Is this university notion an escape route from your father or are you serious?" Glaring at Katherine, he probed. "What do you want to study?"

Becoming emotional Katherine raised her voice, "Medicine, and to answer your question, yes! It *would* get me away from father's grip, but I know one thing. I would make a good doctor!"

Heather interrupted, "Katie, lower your voice please! You will frighten the children."

Katherine muttered an apology.

"You're aware, even with a degree, you won't be allowed to practice professionally?" the Dean remarked.

"I know, but times are changing! Maybe, when I finish my studies, things will be different and if not here, I can always go and work as a missionary. Mary Slessor did it, why not me! Or I could go to America, live with Uncle William. I believe women there have more opportunity to work."

Malcolm frowned. He thought she was being a tad naive. "Missionary! Leave Scotland! Katherine, now that would be rather drastic."

For a moment Heather and Malcolm caught each other's eyes.

"What is your heart following my dear?" Heather inquired. "Alexander, or your ambition to be a doctor?"

"Both perhaps," Katherine answered honestly. She sat back down on the couch and looked out of the window to avert Heather's gaze. "I'm enraged however with Alex for leaving so tamely; without putting up a fight. He could have at least left me a letter. All I know, he no longer wished to be with me. Nothing is left. My mother gone, now

Alex, friends are moving on or getting married and father insists time and time again I marry a Grant. It's why I came to you," Katherine said, now addressing Heather. "Of all people you understand me best."

"But will your father allow it? Will he fund your education?"

"Oh he will oppose it, but over the years I have learned how to combat him. He has given me plenty of practice," Katherine added in a grim tone. "But he can't force me to marry! I'd sooner escape to America than yield to his wishes."

"Katherine," interrupted Malcolm Durie, "have you considered the Edinburgh School of Medicines for Women? They are strongly connected to Bruntsfield Hospital and could be a more attainable solution."

"I know of the school, but it is a university I want and there is none finer than Edinburgh. I have my School Leaving Certificate. Together with references and your influence it should be ample to gain entry."

"I do not doubt your credentials Katherine and you are right, I *am* in favour of higher education for all, but not so sure if the general consensus among my colleagues is similar," Malcolm said, with a touch of irony. "Let me sleep on it and consider what can be done."

Katherine nodded her head in agreement.

"I will need time to convince the learned gentlemen. Also, your father's consent in writing and guaranteed funding will be required. The university, or I for that matter, must not be a stage for family disputes Katherine, so you need to swallow your pride and offer an olive branch to your father."

"I fully understand," Katherine replied firmly, "you'll get everything you need." There was no way her father was going to prevent her from doing what she wanted.

"Your family background will help considerably," Heather remarked. "Many students only attend evening schools of medicine to study part time because they have to work to pay for the college fees."

Tension visibly left her body. For the first time Katherine dared to believe she might have a chance and flashed a radiant smile.

"Hold your horses," Malcolm said, putting both hands in the air, "I can't promise you anything yet. The medical faculty has its excellent reputation to maintain. It will take me time to convince the Board to accept this wild suggestion as it could be perceived you are taking a shortcut. And even though your family background may give you advantages, it also comes with responsibilities. I hope you understand."

"I do Malcolm, I give you my word."

"Now," Heather said, patting Katherine's hand reassuringly, "finish your tea and let's go and fetch the children. First thing tomorrow morning Malcolm will have a telegram sent to Ballindalloch, confirming you will be with us for a few days. I am sure they will be concerned as to your whereabouts."

"I will arrange it dear," Malcolm Durie said, as he sparked a match and lit his pipe.

CHAPTER 11
Monday 4 November 1895, Ballindalloch Castle, Banffshire, Scotland

James Macpherson sighed as he rubbed a hand through his hair. His father's study was meticulous. It felt as if Gordon could step inside any minute. James was worried. His father had never been absent without notice. He glanced at his pocket watch. *Where could he be?* So much had happened over the past few days, Alexander's dramatic departure, Katherine leaving early Sunday morning. Simpson had assured them she had gone to the Durie's, but James knew his sister's determination all too well. It could well be, she was trying to trace Alexander. And then, there was the tunnel incident.

Silently, one of the characteristics of an experienced butler, Simpson had entered the study. "We have received two telegram messages Mr James. They are addressed to your father. Maybe it will explain as to his whereabouts," he offered hopefully.

John would normally be in charge of such matters when the laird was absent, but he was in Grantown to report their father's disappearance. Without further thought and with the aid of a letter opener, James retrieved the first message. He read anxiously. "Well, at least this confirms Katherine *is* in Edinburgh. Malcolm Durie sent it." The second message, revealed something totally different. It was from the Grant's agent Anderson;

To: Laird Macpherson.

Stewart aboard SS State of Nebraska

Stayed till boat sailed as agreed STOP

Anderson

James frowned.

"Sir?" Simpson's concern was genuine.

"That'll be all Simpson thank you. I'll call you when I know more."

Hesitantly, Donald Simpson took a few backward steps before turning to leave the room. He sensed James' confusion and dearly wanted to know what was going on.

Pensive, James stared at the message. *Why would Anderson be confirming Alexander boarded a ship?*

From the beginning James had found the whole story difficult to comprehend. He genuinely liked Alexander Stewart. Being raised in the same household, James always kept his distance so not to get too familiar. His sister had been breaking enough conventional rules with the gamekeeper's son. He did not begrudge Katie and Alexander their friendship, but agreed with his father, certain boundaries were being overstepped. They spent too many hours together, riding, in the library, game hunting and God knows what else, and without a chaperone. It encouraged gossip.

During Saturday's dinner, Katherine had been highly upset when their father broke the news of Alexander's departure. In front of everyone she had cursed her father.

A noise in the hallway made James look up.

"Simpson told me we have a telegraph message?" his brother John barked, still wearing his wet winter coat.

"It's from Anderson," James answered, "regarding Alexander Stewart."

Without a word, John snatched the telegram from his brother's hand and quickly read it.

"Why would Anderson send such a message?" James asked, as his brother's eyes darted over the paper.

John remained silent re-reading the few words as if they would disclose more.

"I'm sure father had his reasons." He looked at James. "Maybe he suspected Alexander would do elsewhere, and hired Anderson to follow him."

"And what would be his reasons?" James asked.

"I don't know," John snapped, throwing his hands in the air.

James wasn't convinced. As the oldest son and heir to Ballindalloch John was being groomed by their father. It often involved discretion. James knew, as a youngster, John had grown jealous of Alexander. The affection their mother showed Alexander and the way she had condoned the friendship of her only daughter and foster son had always bothered John. The jealousy had festered into resentment.

"But, if Anderson watched Alexander board a ship," James said, trying to choose his words carefully, "why not retrieve mother's jewellery?"

"Are you implying father was not being truthful brother?"

James retreated into silence.

With angry gestures John stripped off his coat and passed it to the butler who had followed him into the study.

"Simpson, you may leave now."

37

The butler hesitated. His loyalty to the family had always been impeccable, but what he had just witnessed aroused his anger. He marched out of the room.

Upset, Simpson set out to search for Robert Stewart and share what he had overheard. If the Macpherson sons were not going to confide in him then he would share his concerns with the gamekeeper.

***

"It is what I heard Robert." Simpson had found Stewart at home in the west lodge.

"Christ almighty. He's had this Anderson follow my boy. What is going on here Donald? We both know his friendship with Miss Katherine angered Gordon. I warned Alex often enough. But Macpherson should have talked it over with me! And I know one thing for sure Donald, Alexander is *not* a thief."

"Well it seems we can't ask the laird at this point in time. He's not been seen since yesterday afternoon."

Robert frowned. "Maybe he's in hiding, shamed by what he has done to my lad."

"Perhaps you are right, a kind of mental remorse. John went to Grantown Police this morning," Simpson said, in a sombre tone. "I am sure they will arrive directly to investigate."

Concerned, the gamekeeper looked at his friend. In spite of everything, he understood the butler's bond to the Macphersons. "I last saw him strolling towards the river soon after we arrived back from church. It looked like he was going angling. He was carrying a rod." Robert gave Donald a bewildered look. "What do you *really* think Donald?"

"Fishing you say, at this time of year? I don't know where he is Robert, but I have a bad feeling."

CHAPTER 12
Thursday 15 September 2011, 11.00 a.m. Ballindalloch Castle, Banffshire, Scotland

Cathy sat moping on one of the seats lining the bay window of the library, arms folded over her stomach, cushions propped up her back and her feet resting on the opposite seat. She had tried to make herself comfortable but the attempt to relax was in vain. Her mind wanted to launch into action, her muscles felt stiff with restraint. Cathy had always been overly active, ever since her first steps as a toddler, sometimes driving her mother to the brink of despair. Amongst her childhood friends, she'd been the first to climb trees, build campfires and initiate excursions, a natural leader of the pack.

The copies of the 'Alexander letters' provided by Wayne Stewart were lying on the table next to her, together with her notes. They didn't reveal their full story as yet. She had met Wayne and his wife Eleanor, at the annual clan gathering a month earlier in August. They had travelled from Boston to visit the home of Wayne's ancestor. 'Reading his words in the land he came from gives me a kind of belonging,' Wayne had explained to Cathy. 'It's almost as if I'm fulfilling his wish to see Ballindalloch again.' At the time, the remark hadn't caught Cathy's interest. Now she had read Alexander's writings several times, she understood Wayne's comments much better.

When Cathy had asked Wayne how he had come into possession of the letters his answer had been that none of them were ever mailed. Cathy thought Alexander must have been writing out of a sheer need for normalcy. His abrupt separation from Katherine when her father pressganged him to America, must have caused a deep rift in Alexander's emotional stability. Cathy had no doubts Katherine and Alexander had been lovers. The tone of the letters contained disguised intimacy or at least a very close friendship. After arriving in Boston, Alexander had tried to create the illusion of sharing experiences and thoughts with Katherine. The final letter was dated April 1898 where he asked Katherine to forgive his intention to ask for the hand of a Sarah Gibson.

There was one letter in the bundle that stood out; dated November 1915, almost seventeen years after Alexander's last letter to Katherine. A James Macpherson wrote this letter to Alexander. Cathy impatiently searched her mind for reasons why this man would request a meeting with Alexander at the Boston Globe, to discuss something of a 'personal nature.' Her gut feeling told her there was more to it than met the eye. Who *was* James Macpherson anyway? What stunned Cathy was the letterhead. This James was from Raleigh!

Too many things had happened since she'd arrived. Cathy had never been interested in genealogy, satisfied with the existence of parents and grandparents only. It was David, who was immersed in the Stewart research. Hell, it was what brought them to Ballindalloch in the first place. She had faint memories as a six or seven-year old, visiting Granny Macpherson, who lived in a retirement home, but the question of who came before her had never crossed Cathy's mind. Was James perhaps the missing link between her American family and the Ballindalloch Macphersons? Was he indeed her great-great-grandfather? Did this explain her striking resemblance to Katherine and why Uncle T was the spitting image of her father?

Cathy picked up the letter and read it again. Even as a copy, it showed signs of ageing.

MACPHERSON & SON BRICK MANUFACTURING
121 Fayetteville St. Raleigh, North Carolina.

November 12th 1915

Dear Mr. Stewart,
My name is James Macpherson, originally from Ballindalloch Castle, Banffshire Scotland. I have reason to believe you are the Alexander Stewart who left the same place around 1895. I take the liberty of writing to you as I wish to inform you on matters of a personal nature.
I plan to be in Boston for a few days on business and would propose we meet at your place of work on December 5th.
I would appreciate receiving a reply from you as soon as possible.
Thanking you in anticipation,

Yours in kindness,

James Macpherson.

Cathy pulled the collar of her sweater around her neck as if to protect herself against a draught, even though the sun shone abundantly through the window, keeping the crisp highland air at bay.

Did James actually meet Alexander? The address of Macpherson & Son Brick Manufacturer Co, Cathy had identified as one in the older areas of Raleigh. An internet search had revealed no such company.

Cathy stood up abruptly, gathered the letters and stuffed them in a plastic folder. She stared at the grounds. Not a soul to be seen. An uneasy feeling crept up her hairline. She felt as if the world had moved on without her. She needed to get on with things, get help on finding out who brought their family line to the United States. Not David; too much unresolved grief and blame. It was time to enrol her father.

***

"Pop can you hear me?" Angus had invited Cathy to use his study to telephone home whenever the Skype connection failed which it did often. Sitting at the huge Victorian-style notary desk, Cathy held the old fashioned receiver to her ear with one hand, while the other played with a pencil.

"I sure can. Are you getting fed up with your medieval surroundings Cat? Maybe it's time to come home." Jim still hadn't come to terms with the fact his daughter had chosen to stay in the Scottish Highlands. He could understand why she would shy away from facing her hometown after her actions had been exposed on national television, but she couldn't hide forever.

The local community in Wake Forest had known the public figures of Jim Macpherson and his daughter for years. They were still in shock and so was he. Up until now the records of both father and daughter as police officers had been impeccable and Jim had always been proud to show off Cathy's smartness, when she helped solve yet another case. Many town folk would also seek her or Jim out, even if it was to report a petty crime. For Cathy, to tear down an ancient wall of a Scottish castle had been incomprehensible. Jim found himself facing glares from people who had before always shown undivided respect.

"Not yet Pop, I'm not ready. How are you? Is Mom okay?"

"We are fine Cat. Your Mom is at a charity event for the Wake Hospice. We just wish you would come home."

"I still have too much to do here. Listen, I'm calling you coz I'm on to something and I need your help on research."

Jim Macpherson tried to suppress a sigh. He didn't want his daughter to think he wouldn't support her, but the truth was he was getting pretty weary with her behaviour.

"I can hear you sigh in Scotland," Cathy teased, three thousand miles away. "I know you think I'm mad, but I'm on to something. Do you want to hear?"

In spite of his reluctance, Jim smiled. His daughter's charm to get what she wanted was familiar ground for him. "Okay, shoot!" he retaliated, actually curious now. He had to admit his daughter's stay in Scotland had triggered some genealogy interest within him as well, especially after the phone call he'd received.

"Well listen to this. In 1915, a James Macpherson, originally from Ballindalloch, owned a brick manufacturing company in Raleigh, in Fayetteville Street."

James took a sharp intake of breath.

"You know of him?" Cathy had heard her father's wordless response.

"I do now."

"Very funny," Cathy snapped. "I know you Dad, what are you hiding?"

"Well, as it happens, I got this call from a Diane Cox."

"Diane Cox? Who is she?"

"She is a long lost cousin from New York who found my number after contacting the Raleigh PD." After a short pause Jim added, "She was actually looking for you."

Cathy remained silent not wanting to stop the flow of information.

"Mrs Cox saw the report on TV you know, the happenings at Ballindalloch and recognised the castle name. She's got pictures of the grounds given to her by her mother."

"So who was her mom?"

"Hang on, I'll get my notes. I went to the State library to check. Her mother ..." Jim continued while leafing through his papers, "was a Maureen Douglas Macpherson, born in 1933 in North Carolina. She was the younger sister of your grandfather, my aunt. She died in New York, 2006."

Cathy, taking notes said, "It makes Diane Cox your cousin Pop. How come I never heard of her?"

"Oh you know how it goes Cat. They moved in the fifties. We lost contact except for the occasional Christmas card. I was just a kid. I never even knew her married name."

Cathy gathered her thoughts. "When I was debating if I should go to Scotland or not, you mentioned pictures your grandfather Eddie had seen. Pics from Scotland, and he used to tell you stories right? But you never saw any photos."

"Correct."

"So what were these pictures, do you know?"

"I'm not done yet Cat. Diane told me her mother mentioned *her* grandfather, James Macpherson, had been quite a wealthy man until the great depression of the thirties. Guess how he made his money Cat?"

"Let me take a wild guess. He made bricks?"

"Yep."

"James Macpherson, your great-grandfather?"

"Hold your horses Cat. I went to the library and found this James and family on the 1920 Census records. This lists all people living in the household on the 1st January. Let me read out the details for you." Jim cleared his throat. "James, head of household, age fifty-six, occupation is listed as 'owner of factory', origin, SCO for Scotland. Josephine his wife, age fifty-seven, nothing listed under occupation, origin SCO. This is where it gets interesting Cat. A Raymond is listed. Son, age thirty, origin, SCO, occupation, Sales Executive and Edward, indeed my grandfather Eddie, son, age three, origin, USA. There is also a housekeeper, a Matilda Ward.

"So, my hunch was right?" Cathy said, without feeling convinced.

"Don't you think it is strange though?"

"What is?"

"One son aged thirty the other aged three. Twenty-seven years apart!"

"So? They didn't use birth control?"

Jim sighed. "A baby in their fifties Cat, I don't think so! Curious thing is, I searched for Eddie's birth certificate but drew a blank. I will go back to the library and this time pay for research assistance."

Something was bugging Cathy, but she couldn't grasp what it was. "Go back to the library as soon as possible. You know what Pop?" she continued, "I am discovering our Celtic heritage is not only celebrating Robert Burns, Tartan Day *or* wearing the right tartan. It's being able to truly embrace the culture; to respect and appreciate what we have been given, without us becoming a kind of new world Celts. I've been told by more than one person I was sent here for a reason and they are right. It's not done yet. Somewhere along the line things are not what they seem to be. Finding Gordon's bones, is the catalyst for something else, something maybe even more important, I feel it. No! I know it."

"Who is this I am listening to? The daughter who wasn't sure she wanted to accompany her husband to Scotland on his genealogy quest?"

"I don't mean to sound weird Dad, I'm just trying my best to express how I feel. I now know the reason for my constant sleepwalking and the dreams I had while growing up. You and Mom never discussed it with me. *Just bad dreams* you would say. Well they weren't."

"Are you now telling me you are clairvoyant?"

"No," Cathy responded, trying to keep impatience out of her voice. "I just seem to see things from the past, feel and smell them. And what happened in Wake Forest only made it worse."

Jim remained silent. His daughter being shot, her life only saved by a thread, thanks to the quick action of Steve Hicks, had been life changing for him too, but he never had been able to express it, not to Cat, not to anyone.

"Pop, it's a curse, not a gift, and my sightings are less frequent than when I was a child. In one way it is a relief, in another it pressures me into wanting to reunite these visions with the present. I seem to have no choice. It's why I am here. It's my destiny."

Back in Wake Forest Jim sighed, "Cat, I love you and will do all I can to help, in spite of my doubts about all you've just said. So what's next?"

"Email me a copy of the census and find the birth certificate of your grandfather Eddie."

CHAPTER 13
Sunday 2 February 1896, Ballindalloch Castle, Banffshire, Scotland

A narrow beam of moonlight streaked through an opening in the drawing- room curtains. As if to hide even more what was being discussed, John Macpherson drew them entirely shut. The fire crackling in the hearth created a false atmosphere of security. What they were debating was never to go beyond the walls of the castle. It wasn't even supposed to be disclosed to their brothers. Fortunately, they were scattered around the globe, in Donald's case serving in the Royal Engineers and Lachlan in Australia. They should know as little as possible about what was going on.

James broke the silence. "Katherine, the only way I see fit to solve this matter is to find Alexander, bring him back and the two of you get wed. I cannot concur with this ridiculous plan. It's wrong! I won't change my mind."

Katherine looked at her tall handsome brother affectionately. With his straightforward way of addressing matters, James, once again demonstrated why he was her favourite brother. She had quite opposite feelings for John who could be very self-centred.

"But James, this is not only dependent on what is morally right or wrong," she said. "It's the rest of my life at stake here. What sort of future would Alexander and I have at Ballindalloch? No one would accept us. And think of the future of our child. What would people say? Who would accept the child? Where would it belong? It would always be at a disadvantage."

James tugged at his cigar nervously, turned away from Katherine and stared into the fire, leaning one elbow on the mantelpiece. He didn't want Katherine to sense his panic on the decision he was asked to make. "I do not understand how you could have let it come this far! Do you really think Alexander does not know you are pregnant? The man is no fool!"

"It only happened once James." The thought of her brothers assuming they had a fully blown affair made her blush. "I know it shouldn't have, but it did. I cannot turn the clock back. Strange as it may sound, maybe part of me doesn't want Alexander to return. He has chosen to leave for his own reasons rather than face the ridiculous charges father made against him and even though I believe he is innocent of stealing, I do find him guilty of deserting me. I've always stood up against father, why couldn't he?"

"Because he knows his place," John's high-pitched tone added. "I don't understand James, why you will not cooperate, when even our sister agrees this is the best solution. The child will be brought up as the respectable heir of Ballindalloch. You will have to agree it beats going through life as the child of a gamekeeper. Besides, even though I might not agree with her ambitions, our sister has different plans for her life and so it seems does Alexander Stewart. Isn't it so Katherine?"

James had to admit Alexander's behaviour had been perplexing. Nothing had been heard from him. James had gone to Glasgow to speak to Anderson. He had told James that other than making sure Stewart would board the ship, he had been given no further instructions by the laird. The whole situation was unsavoury. Now, Robert Stewart understandably was planning to leave as well. James found it hard to believe that Alexander had departed without as much as a letter to Katherine. The two had been so close. His sister was right. Alexander had chosen to desert her rather than to stand up to Father.

Yet to agree that John and Victoria adopt the child was too easy. James felt Alexander should pay for his faults, pick up his responsibilities. With the laird's disappearance unresolved, the charges filed with the police in Grantown had not been pursued. They could be dropped and Alexander reinstated. They should not have indulged in such shocking behaviour. James still struggled to accept his sister's conduct.

"May I remind you once more brother," John interrupted James's thoughts, "there is more than one aspect to be considered. Victoria and I have waited eight years as you well know and still our marriage has not been blessed with a child. Ballindalloch needs an heir and this could well be our only chance."

"But it is not right John. You know our mother would never have agreed." James glared at his sister. "Have *you* considered how she would have felt Katherine?"

John was beginning to lose his patience. There were many matters to be taken into account and they could all work out for the better if only his younger brother would be willing to cooperate. Scandal would be avoided, their sister could get on with her life and Ballindalloch would have its heir from the oldest son, as it should be. It was time for a different approach.

"Are you sure you are refusing to cooperate for the right reasons my dear brother? We're all well aware the control of the estate would pass on to your family if I did not produce an heir."

As if stung by a nest of hornets, James swirled away from the fire and took a few steps towards his brother who involuntarily backed away.

Katherine looked on in horror, racked in guilt. She had never seen her brothers behave in such a way. "Stop it! Please stop!"

46

"Katie, I do not understand how you can choose such a challenging path over taking care of your own child," James uttered, trying to restore his composure. "There is no need for you to go to university. Why can you not just be content raising your child? You have all the help needed here. Eventually people would come to accept the situation, they will come around. I never thought I'd hear myself say this, but as you always say, times are changing."

"Only if people force those who oppose change," Katherine responded. "I have no future here. I have no choice. John and Victoria will adopt. And I know you find this difficult to understand James but I *want* to study medicine. Even before I discovered I was pregnant, I had it all arranged with Malcolm Durie. He is going to help me to secure my place." She drew in her breath, "I know you all think I'm not in my right mind, but to be honest, I don't care. I cannot spend my life here otherwise you might as well bury me now. And anyway, I will see my child when I return between semesters."

"But the child will not know you as her mother Katherine." James pleaded. "It's not as things should be. Think of how difficult it will be to keep this under the carpet. Perhaps you fail to understand now, after all you are only eighteen, but you will someday regret this, believe me."

John interrupted,"I think we understand your heartfelt point of view James, but it's time to take the bull by the horns."

A combination of despair over how his sister was going to ruin her life and the attitude of his oldest brother made his anger return. "What has become of you John? You are making a serious mistake. I cannot and will not condone this."

"What will you do? Call the constabulary? Tell them you won't allow your pregnant unmarried sister to have her child raised by her own brother and his wife?"

James felt a lump in his throat. Ignoring John, he turned to Katherine and said gently, "For some time I've been contemplating opportunities in America and it now seems time to pick up the glove. I choose not to be part of a household entangled in this sort of deceit. I plan to correspond with Uncle William and seek his advice on an investment in North Carolina."

Katherine was shocked and yelled, "Oh James, not you as well. You must think of Josephine and the children. They can't leave Scotland, they belong here!" If there was one family within the Macpherson clan who set a wholesome example, it was James's. They'd married young, clearly much in love. Together with their two children born in succession soon after, they had brought nothing but joy to the family.

James, torn between anger and pity, looked at his sister. "Josephine is in full agreement and it may prove to be the making of the boys. I will not interfere with *your* plans Katherine, but I cannot support them either. Should you need my advice, my door is always open, but any help will not include you giving away your baby."

***

The next day, James was busy in the study, when John stepped in unannounced and handed him a telegraph message.

"It seems your prayers have been already been answered, sent from New York." It was dated 31st January, announcing William Macpherson was expected to arrive at Ballindalloch within a fortnight. Time for John to have a discussion with the future grandfather Robert Stewart, and get him out of the way before Katherine started to show.

CHAPTER 14
Wednesday 28 September 2011, 11:30 am Ballindalloch Castle, Banffshire, Scotland

DI Duckett walked into the library carrying a briefcase in his left hand and a large envelope clutched under his right arm. He sat down at the centrepiece table. The Macpherson delegation, consisting of Angus, his eldest son John, the Black Watch veteran Thomas and Cathy Stewart were already seated opposite, a blank expression on all their faces. Duckett was sure none of them were as innocent as they would have him believe.

"This meeting is not to judge you or any of the lairds before you Mr Macpherson," he started, addressing Angus in particular. "I just find it remarkable nobody ever knew a body was underneath the castle, and a laird no less."

"It seems to me you are suspicious about a lack of knowledge on events of a hundred years ago Mr Duckett." It was Thomas Macpherson who spoke. "Do you have intimate knowledge of *your* ancestors?"

Duckett combed his hand through his unruly hair. "I think the comparison to my family background Mr Macpherson is not relevant."

"Thomas is correct," Angus cut in, "why do you think we should be aware of what happened here so long ago? Your persistent innuendo is becoming tiresome."

The policeman cleared his throat. John glanced at his watch, "I don't mean to be rude," he said, "but I'm expected at the bank by four, so could we please stop bickering. I believe this meeting was to review the forensic report?"

"Autopsy report," Duckett corrected.

"We are also in the midst of the funeral arrangements inspector," Angus added. "The Press is on my back and I do have a lot to prepare."

"I appreciate you all have other pressing engagements and I'm sure we can discuss more at a later date," Duckett replied, with a hint of sarcasm.

With all Macphersons watching him, Duckett reached for his leather briefcase, methodically placed it on the table next to the envelope, clicked open the latch and produced a rather bulky document.

"I hope you do not think we are going to review the complete file now inspector," Thomas remarked. "We would prefer to read the contents in private. I'm sure you have already digested the detail. Providing us with a brief summary will suffice."

49

Cathy smiled innocently at Duckett. She knew arranging this formal gathering was Duckett's effort to apply continued pressure on the family in the hope new information would surface. Instead, it generated the opposite effect.

Duckett glanced around the table. "I will leave the file with you. I can also send you a soft copy if you so desire."

"That would be appreciated," Angus mumbled. He was perspiring quite heavily and was preoccupied, frequently dabbing his head with a handkerchief.

Duckett nodded and continued, "The file contains the police reports from Grantown and Inverness, as well as the autopsy results from Raigmore. If you have any questions please call me. As expected they confirmed it was Gordon Macpherson, and the year of death is close enough to the date when his disappearance was reported, 1895." Duckett paused, expecting some reaction, but it didn't transpire. He went on, "cause of death was a broken neck, induced by a fallen rock. Death would have been almost instantaneous. The formal verdict was; 'death by misadventure.'"

Silence filled the room. Duckett pushed the envelope towards Angus. "These are the laird's belongings he had on his person. They are now legally yours."

Angus's complexion had paled and he seemed to be losing his concentration. He just sat staring at the envelope.

"Are you okay?" Thomas gave him a concerned glance.

Patting his chest, Angus replied in short breaths, "I think it must be a little heartburn."

Cathy stood up and extended her hand to the inspector. "I am sure the contents will be viewed in good time. Pass on our thanks to the staff at Raigmore."

"What a splendid initiative Catherine," Thomas mumbled. "I was beginning to get itchy feet." In a louder voice he added, "Goodbye inspector, we'll get back to you if we have any questions."

"All right I'll leave you to it, but I have to ask you to read the file as soon as possible. I am also a busy man and want this case closed," he lied.

"Are you okay to continue Dad, because we can do this later," John asked, after Duckett had left.

"No, let's get this over with, I am fine."

John looked concerned. "Well at least the authorities are satisfied with our statements," he said, flicking through the report.

Cathy frowned. "You think so John? Duckett seems to be rather annoyed the charges were dropped, and the official line makes me some kind of crazy woman. Destroying an ancient castle wall on the basis of a bogus dream wouldn't sound too convincing if I were on the case."

"I can only thank you Catherine," Angus said, "for not exposing the Macpherson family. We are forever in your debt and um... so is Gordon. Our reputation would be ruined if the full facts were known."

Cathy looked at Angus with a weary smile, "Don't forget I am also a Macpherson."

"So, what are your plans Cathy now this is all over?" John asked.

"If you have no objection I want to stay for a while. There are a few things I still want to do."

"Stay as long as you want my dear," Angus said convincingly.

John measured her up, "What about your job and husband?"

Cathy twitched her nose. "I need to be here a while longer. I have more exploring to do and knowing David, he will probably return. He still has his travel guide to finish."

"As long as you don't knock down any more walls my dear," Angus joked with a nervous laugh.

"Promise," she said. "I must admit I'm quite intrigued by the Katherine and Alexander story." A tinge of regret crossed her face. John had hit a nerve without realising it. She had never taken the time to inform David what she had uncovered regarding the Stewarts, even though it had been *him* who had sown the seeds. Cathy wondered if he'd been in touch with Wayne and Eleanor Stewart.

"Katherine ended up in the US," Angus volunteered. Looking at Thomas he continued, "Thomas met her you know, when she was quite an old lady. What brought her here do you know?"
Thomas smiled. "I have no idea. What I remember most was her accent. It was so unusual. Mind you, I was just a young lad at the time."

"Maybe she came for a clan gathering?" Cathy queried. "Angus you showed me pictures of past gatherings. Do any date back to... how old were you Uncle T?"

"It was before the war, but let's do this first." Displaying a commanding manner Thomas picked up the envelope. "As far as I'm concerned this will be the last message from beyond." He ripped open the envelope and scattered the contents over the table. Simultaneously, the four of them leaned forward.

Lying on the table was an open blackened silver vesta-case with three matchsticks inside, a gold pocket watch and chain, a dulled silver propelling pencil and an enamel miniature portrait of a woman, set in a gold rim. Cathy picked up the tiny portrait.

"Gordon's wife I presume," Angus remarked.

"Whoever she was, she was a beauty," Cathy murmured, inspecting the little picture closely. On the back were the initials 'WCR'. Next she picked up the pencil, gave the barrel a twist and a lead popped out, still intact. "Well I'll be damned," she said, wiping the barrel on the sleeve of her sweater. She looked at it again, breathed heavily on the pencil and rubbed the silver between her thumb and forefinger.

John who was busy holding the watch guessing the weight asked, "What are you doing?"

"There is an inscription on the pencil, hold on." After a few seconds Cathy looked up at the men. "Why would Gordon have a pencil inscribed DCL Chicago?" she asked, handing the pencil over to Angus.

Angus lengthened his arms as far as he could but had to take Cathy's word for it. He couldn't read the tiny characters.

Fiddling with the pencil he pondered, "I would guess it could have been a gift from Gordon's younger brother. I believe he was a whisky trader in the States."

"Was he the one who got murdered?" John asked.

"No, that was a cousin, Malcolm. He was smuggling booze from Canada during Prohibition and got shot." Angus glanced at Cathy with a humorous look on his face and added, "Maggie would tell you Al Capone shot him but it would be more likely Mr Capone ordered his killing."

Cathy smiled slightly at Angus while her mind switched back to police mode. *Maggie ... the family encyclopaedia! During the days surrounding the clan gathering last August and the quest to find Gordon, Maggie had ultimately been the one supplying all relevant information. Maybe it is time to have a talk with her again.*

"Where is Maggie these days? I haven't seen her here since the gathering" Cathy probed.

"Home of course," Thomas answered. "My sisters live in Laggan close to Cluny Castle. It's just south of Newtonmore."

Cathy made a mental note to get their address and phone number. "I have been checking out my North Carolina roots," she volunteered. "Maybe Maggie and Euphemia can fill me in on some gaps."

John raised his head intrigued with the idea.

Cathy caught his look, "I have made a connection to a James Macpherson," she said, before returning her attention to the pen. "Angus, do you know if this brother of Gordon, William, was married?"

"He was a younger brother, is all I know. We don't know for definite if the pencil was his. But I will give you the family tree details.

52

This will give you some information on all of Gordon's siblings and his extended family." Angus was now interested to find out for himself.

John cleared his throat. "Cathy, just think, you married a descendant of Alexander Stewart, while at the same time you could be from the family who owned the estate where Alexander was raised. It's bizarre. Going by the picture I showed you of Katherine Macpherson, you must admit you are her double."

Cathy nodded, "I remember the picture, Katherine and her niece standing by the river." She wondered if she should share with John, her find in the museum. "If you were in my position wouldn't you want to research a little deeper?"

"I sure would. I do not believe in coincidence. So anything I can do to help you Cathy, all you have to do is ask."

Filing that offer for future reference, Cathy turned to her attention to Angus. "You better make some changes to your website Angus. There is no ghost anymore."

"I don't think so Catherine. After all the publicity, the tourists have been flocking here. We will leave the ghost story for at least another year."

Cathy walked towards the door. Gripping the handle, she turned back to the men. "Thank you for allowing me to stay on."

The men watched their American 'cousin' walk out of the library.

"She must be apprehensive," Angus said, turning to his son. "By just looking at her you can tell."

"I knew it the day she arrived here," Thomas chipped in.

"I can't get my head around she married a descendant of this Alexander Stewart," John said. "I meant what I said Dad, I want to help her in any way I can. We all should. We owe her."

Somewhat concerned, Angus looked at his oldest boy. "I agree John, but make sure your intentions are for the right reasons."

So much for our history son; you are our future.

CHAPTER 15
Sunday 9 February 1896, Ballindalloch, Banffshire, Scotland

Returning from the Sunday morning service at Inveravon, using the Church Walk leading back to the castle through rolling forest land, John spotted the lonely figure of Robert Stewart some twenty yards ahead.

The conversation with James and Katherine last Sunday had not left his thoughts. He knew his wife's expectations were set high by now. John worried Katherine would change her mind. He recalled the suicide of a business associate's daughter some years ago, after her newly born child had been taken away because of her unmarried status. John shrugged his shoulders. Emotions were not his forte. *Why do people create such upheaval when practical solutions can be found?* It was time to talk to Robert Stewart. If there was one man he didn't need around it was the future grandfather. John needed to act quickly. Stewart would be smart enough to realise the child was fathered by his son and he could influence Katherine's decision. Quickening his step, John tried to catch up with the gamekeeper's long strides. Just before reaching Stewart's lodge he called out, "Robert, can I have a word please?"

Reluctantly Robert stopped and turned. "I don't have anything to discuss with you."

John's resolve faltered, taken aback by the tone, "It won't take long it's regarding your position." He took a few more steps forward. The men now faced each other, John panting slightly.

"Look," Stewart growled. "Don't try convincing me to stay. I leave next month, my passage is arranged and nobody is going to stop me."

"Really!" In an effort to hide his relief John tried to sound stern. "I take it you were going to inform me of this?"

"Yes, the same way your father informed me of *his* decisions. Now if you don't mind, I have other things to do."

"May I inquire how you secured other employment without having a reference from me?"

"I didn't. I am going to join my son in America. We'll do fine without help from the Macphersons." The gamekeeper continued his way along the garden path, disappeared into the lodge, slamming the door behind him.

John was pleased how Fate had dealt the cards, but at the same time felt as if he was the only person remaining on the estate.

CHAPTER 16
Wednesday 28 September 2011, Ballindalloch Castle, Banffshire, Scotland

Cathy was in her bedroom busy on her laptop, checking her emails while logged in to Skype, waiting for her father. He had sent an email stating he had new information regarding Eddie Macpherson.

It was almost midnight. Cathy was seated at her desk, dressed in pyjamas, her feet bare. She was feeling a bit depressed. Looking at the chipped pink nail polish on her toes, she noticed they needed some attention. She wondered how much longer she could stay in Scotland. Her savings were rapidly running out and she did not want to ask David for money.

Wearily, Cathy opened an email from Steve Hicks, her partner at the Raleigh PD. Her job was still open and he pleaded she should come home.

Steve had saved her life. Last year, Cathy had been shot at point blank range, when she and Steve were tracking down a suspected killer through the woods of Wake Forest. Steve had driven as if possessed and managed to get her to the Raleigh Hospital in the nick of time. While Cathy recovered over the weeks that followed, unbeknown to her, he had taken the brunt of the blame. Their boss had been infuriated they hadn't waited on backup arriving.

Hicks' email also disclosed he was going to be a father again. Sissy was due in June next year. Cathy knew him as a wonderful father and could easily picture his excitement. For a fleeting moment she felt a tinge of jealousy. If David and she had been parents, how different things could have turned out.

Next, Cathy read an email from Sherry and Jacki. It was sent from Sherry's Yahoo account quite late the day before. They probably sank two bottles of wine at Backfins Crabhouse, their regular meeting place in Wake Forest, before sending the mail.

Sherry Jones and Jacki Merrill were two of her dearest friends. They had gone to the same schools, played in the same softball teams. Sherry was going through a nasty divorce, but going by what they wrote, things seemed to be progressing. Jacki, as usual, had a new girlfriend and proclaimed this one was going to last. It made Cathy smile. The longest relationship Jacki had was with Tina. It had lasted six months. Their message ended with, 'Please come home Cathy, we all miss you and that includes David.'

Cathy wondered what they discussed with David. She was sure they felt sorry for him and had told David she was being a bitch running out on him and all of her friends, but they didn't know half of it!

The familiar sound of the Skype incoming call snapped Cathy out of her thoughts. Jim's face appeared on the screen, instantly lifting her spirits.

"Hi sweetie, how are you? It must be late for you."

"I'm good Pop. Yeah it's around midnight here, you and Mom okay?"

"We're doing just fine. Your Mom is out at her yoga class. She joined up last week."

"Finally! I kept telling her she should give yoga a try. Anyway, what's new?"

"You look tired Cat. Are you sure everything's okay?"

"Honestly, I'm good. It's late and I just need some shuteye. So tell me."

"Okay, finding Eddie's birth certificate was not easy. Eddie was born in North Carolina, on June twentieth, 1916, at 141 Newlane. He was registered Charles Edward Macpherson. It threw me initially. For whatever reason the name Charles dropped over time."

"And the parents were?"

"Father unknown, but the mother was one Alexandra Macpherson. She was twenty years old, her normal residence was 266 Central, Los Angeles, California, Country of Origin; Scotland. And get this. She was an actress. Let me hold up the paper to the camera."

Cathy went silent. The name rang a bell. While crunching some dates in her head, she stared at the image of the North Carolina State Board of Health.

BUREAU OF VITAL STATISTICS

CERTIFICATE OF BIRTH

County: Davidson
Township: Ascadia

Full Name of Child: Charles Edward Macpherson

Boy/ Girl: Boy Number in order of birth: Married: Y/N; N
Date of Birth: June 20th 1916

FULL NAME AND AGE: *Unknown   Alexandra*
Macpherson (20)

RESIDENCE: *266 Central, Los Angeles, CA*
COLOR: *White*
BIRTHPLACE: *Scotland*
OCCUPATION: *Actress*
CERTIFICATE OF ATTENDING PHYSICIAN OR MIDWIFE:

I hereby certify I attended the birth of this child who was: *Alive*
Dr David Stansfield
At: *141 Newlane Ave, NC*
Witness: *B. Connelly*

REGISTRAR: *DW Tweedie*
DATE: *26ᵗʰ June, 1916*

"Cathy, are you still there?"

"An actress wow," Cathy paused. "Are you sure this is the same Edward?"

"It's the only Macpherson boy born in North Carolina matching the census birth period using the name Edward."

"Have you ever heard of an Alexandra in the family?"

"Nope, the name means nothing to me. What are you thinking Cat?"

"Grandpa Spencer or Grandma... Did they ever discuss Eddie's background or an Alexandra?"

"Cat, my parents never discussed any family history with me and to be honest I was never interested."

"Fantastic job Pop. I think I will grab some sleep now. Please email a copy of the certificate."

"Let us know when you are ready to come home. We miss you and so does David."

If David misses me so much, why does he never get in touch?

"I'll think about it, but only after Gordon Macpherson's funeral which is scheduled for October seventh. Say hi to Mom, I really need to go, bye."

Cathy picked up her family tree notes. Up until now she had been convinced her research would connect her family line to James Macpherson, the brick manufacturer in Raleigh. Finding Eddie's birth certificate however had given that lead a strange twist. From her papers Cathy also retrieved the copy of the Macpherson family tree Angus had given her. She ran her finger over the document. Above the name Alexandra (born 1896) were listed as parents; John Macpherson (born 1863) and Victoria Galbraith (born 1867). She tapped on the two names above John: Gordon, (born 1840), and Elizabeth Douglas, (born 1842). Cathy found no previous female with the name Alexandra. She focused on John's line and in particular the names of those before him. No Alexandra.

Maybe she was named after Victoria's mother or grandmother.

The information on Victoria only showed her full name and age, but no details of her parents.

Cathy closed the file and pondered who could help find out more on Victoria Galbraith's family. A gut feeling told her there was more to Alexandra than met the eye.

CHAPTER 17
Monday 17 February 1896, Grantown-on-Spey, Morayshire, Scotland

William Macpherson leaned forward to look out the window, as the train slowly rolled past the woodlands into Station West of Grantown-on- Spey. His joints felt stiff. The last stretch from Perth had been uncomfortable. If it hadn't been for the cable regarding his brother's disappearance and Robert's boy leaving, he would never have attempted a journey this time of year. He wished he had taken some rest and stayed the night in Glasgow, before the train journey to Ballindalloch.

He still thought of home as the place where Elizabeth resided, unable to imagine Ballindalloch without her. This was different. He would soon walk into the castle knowing she was gone. His mind's eye produced the image of the family mausoleum. He hoped Elizabeth had found peace. William felt guilty. Perhaps if he had not meddled in his brother's marriage she might have suffered less. On reflection, the interference on Elizabeth's life started with the imposing auld Lachlan, their father. He insisted Elizabeth be the wife of the future laird. To Gordon's delight, he won in the end. Who was to blame? *We all played a part in Elizabeth's unhappiness.*

A porter opened the door of his train compartment. William stood and inhaled the cold highland afternoon air, which smelled of smoke and oil. Attendants were already busying themselves retrieving luggage.

"Mr Macpherson," a familiar voice cried out. Standing on the steps of his compartment William could easily oversee the crowd. He detected MacLean near the entrance to the platform, his long coat and scarf flapping in the breeze. With his walking stick William pointed towards the luggage car, indicating where he was to collect his baggage. MacLean disappeared into the crowd of bobbing hats and plumes.

William sighed. He wished he didn't have to do this. Telling Katherine was perhaps the least of his problems. She might actually be pleased. What bothered him was confronting his nephew John. He couldn't have his daughter be the only one to know, isolating her in the same way it had estranged Elizabeth. Truth needed to be told. Perhaps he could suggest Katie should move to Chicago. She was a bold girl who would easily find her way.

An out of breath MacLean appeared. "I have your luggage sir."

"How is life holding out for you man?"

"I'm well sir thank you."

"Good, let's get on with it." Reluctantly William stepped onto the platform, keeping one hand on his beret.

The road to Ballindalloch looked muddy and difficult to manoeuvre. Patches of snow covered the land on either side of the road. William had joined the coachman up top.

"Would you prefer to sit inside sir? It is going to be a cold ride up here."

Anticipating he could extract some information out of the coachman on what's happened at the castle these past months, William said, "I'm well aware, but I think you could do with an extra hand."

"Aye, that is so true. Last Friday, this ride would have been impossible. We had the heaviest snow fall in years."

The thirteen miles from the station to Ballindalloch would normally take over an hour. It took them three. By the time they arrived daylight had faded. A damp dark winter cloak covered their surroundings. Leaving MacLean to settle the horses, an exhausted, chilled to the bone, William, stumbled into the hall. Filled with concern, Simpson greeted him and immediately took William's coat and beret and ordered hot drinks and blankets to be brought to the kitchen. The cooker range would supply the heat.

"Uncle William," John Macpherson appeared, attracted by the commotion in the hall. "Would you like to come and sit in the library?"

"Not unless you use the books to stir up the fire," William shivered through chattering teeth. "Sorry son, the kitchen will do for now."

Hiding his irritation over his uncle's immediate display of stubbornness, John led the way to the back of the house. William and John never cared for one another. Growing up, John had observed his uncle spent a lot of time in the company of his mother. He had felt jealous the way she always seemed delighted when William was around. William in turn never took to John. He was his least favoured nephew. The boy was too much of an introvert in William's opinion and this trait on occasions made John socially handicapped.

As the men huddled around the stove, Katherine barged into their sanctuary dressed in an oversized worn Aran sweater and woollen trousers. "Good grief Katherine what happened to you?" William grinned at her appearance, actually liking what he beheld.

"Good evening to you too Uncle William, and what fool may I ask would wear flimsy clothing on a night like this?"

William already felt himself warm up and gave her a broad smile as she walked over to hug him. Coming home wasn't so bad after all

John, Victoria, Katherine, William and James Macpherson sat around the dining room table. James was giving an account of his treacherous journey from his home in Inverurie to Ballindalloch. Simpson made sure the fire had been well stacked and had prepared a hot toddy for everyone, using an old recipe from his mother, except that he had to resort to using sugar instead of honey and boiling water with the whisky. The coals blazed and sparked fighting the bitter cold, tickling the backs of those sitting closest to the windows.

William shivered. "We should have stayed in the kitchen, the house staff are more comfortable than we are I tell you," he muttered.

"We wouldn't want them to eavesdrop on our discussion uncle," John said. "We have a matter of the utmost importance to relay."

And so do I boy, William thought.

James threw his brother an annoyed glance. "I thought we were going to speak of this in the morning," he counteracted. He had hoped to have a private word with William before the full family was involved.

"I thought it would be better for all to get this out into the open immediately James. I do not want uncle to be misinformed," he said, giving his brother a meaningful glare.

Curious, William turned his attention from James to John. "Let's have it," he said lifting his toddy.

"Perhaps I'm the most appropriate person to provide the news. I'm after all the one with child." Katherine's voice sounded crisp and clear.

In an uncontrolled gesture, William slammed his glass on the table causing a splash of his drink to spill.

"For God's sake Katherine, have you no pride!" John shouted. He had wanted to convey this in an entirely different manner, informing William they were going to adopt and why Victoria and he had agreed on their noble act.

William had been confronted with many unexpected challenges in his lifetime, yet all he could do now was to stammer incoherently.

"D-Don't you shout at her," William said, glaring angrily at John. He turned and stared at Katherine. "Are you...but how... you mean, I'm..." Fortunately, he found himself finishing the sentence in thought; *I'm going to be a grandfather...*

Next to exploring the circumstances under which Gordon had disappeared, the goal of his visit to Ballindalloch had been to reveal his true relationship to Katherine. Now, William's mind was quick enough to wait.

After the first dust of Katherine's announcement had settled, John took it upon himself to explain his plan. The child was to be registered as John and Victoria's.

"And what makes you think you can be a mother to another woman's child?" William asked Victoria.

John glanced at his wife and responded on her behalf, "She will look after the child as if it was her own, and I will be a dedicated father."

William was troubled by a sudden thought. Nobody had said a word regarding the father. Much to everyone's annoyance William stood up and commanded, "I've heard enough. This makes The Charge of the Light Brigade a well thought through plan." He put his hand out to Katherine. "We need some time alone. Let's go to the drawing-room Katie."

Both Macpherson brothers regretted seeing them leave. They would have preferred the opportunity, each for their own reasons, to steer any conversation between their uncle and sister.

The small drawing room was warm compared to the rest of the house. It was especially used in winter with a fire ready to be rekindled at all times. William tossed on some extra logs and used the bellows to get the fire going. Katherine made herself comfortable on the Chesterfield. Remaining standing at the mantelpiece with his back turned towards her, William opened softly, "I take it the father is one Alexander Stewart."

"A quick assumption," Katherine remarked.

"Your mother informed me she was not entirely happy about your friendship with Alexander."

Confused, Katherine looked at her uncle. Unlike Gordon, her mother had never objected to her bond with Alexander, yet they had never really discussed the matter. Katherine felt a stab of remorse. She should have known her mother was unhappy with her liaison with Alex. More and more she recognised how much her behaviour must have troubled her family.

"I'm sorry," she mumbled. At the same time, she was annoyed her mother's concern had been shared with Uncle William.

William now faced Katherine. "This arrangement with John and Victoria cannot go ahead. I hate to be the fly in the ointment, but what is Robert's view on all of this? Does he know he is going to be a grandfather?"

Katherine's blank stare unnerved William.

"Jesus Christ, he doesn't know!" William struggled to keep his temper at bay. "And how may I ask are you going to avoid Robert when you are showing? I'm not having any of this."

"Uncle William, Robert Stewart is leaving next month."

"Leaving, where?" William was now irate. "Did John dismiss him? If he did, I'll have his guts for garters."

"Please calm down, you are upsetting me. Robert is going to join Alexander in America. Mr Stewart will be long gone when the baby shows. And anyway, I do not want Alexander to know he has a child. He left me here in the lurch."

Back in control of his emotions, William said softly, "Katie, we need to talk this through some more, when we are all less tired." He stared at Katherine and thought how vulnerable she looked. "There *is* something I need to tell you Katherine. My intention was to inform you first and eventually the whole family. Given your situation, I think it would be wise to keep this between us for now. As you might have guessed, I didn't come here in midwinter just to pay a courtesy call."

Intrigued, Katherine observed her uncle's profile in front of the dancing flames of the fire. His face partly disappearing in the shadows, made it hard to read his expression. In an effort to create an atmosphere of more familiarity, William walked over to the couch and sat beside her.

"I think I may well match the shock you gave me," he said, after a deliberate pause. "There is something you need to know and I sincerely hope it will not influence your condition."

Katherine pulled up her eyebrows in wonder.

"Why would it?"

"Because I don't think you could possibly anticipate what I'm going to tell you."

Katherine probed her mind.

"You see, your mother and me …before you were born…we… Damn it Katherine there's no simple way of saying this," William blurted out. He stood up and without looking at her continued, "I don't know any other way to say this. I love you. *I* am your father *not Gordon.*"

Katherine was surprised at how easily she digested his words. Even though her conditioned mind flatly rejected any possibility of William being her father, her heart responded differently. Uncle William and she had a natural relationship. All the years he would come over to celebrate Hogmanay or spend the summer season at Ballindalloch, had been a feast. He would take her horse riding in midwinter or shopping in Elgin or even Aberdeen or Inverness. On reflection, the way they had bonded was far removed from the relationship she had with her father.

"Did father… your brother know this?" she asked, stunned by her own self-control.

It didn't surprise William her pragmatic attitude would produce this as her first question. In spite of her femininity, Katherine's mind often functioned as any male. William cherished this feature, no matter how unbecoming it might be to others. "We never discussed it," he said, sitting back down, "but he must have known. It was why I moved to the United States. It was the proper thing to do."

"Did you miss mother....and me, when you moved away?" Katherine asked, hearing her voice falter at the last word. She couldn't help think how different her life would have been if her Uncle William and mother had married. While she could adapt to this revelation, it was hard to fathom her mother as being anyone else than a faithful wife of Gordon Macpherson. Katherine simply could not imagine her mother sharing William's bed. A look of vulnerability descended on Katherine's face making William cringe inwardly.

"It was guilt I felt," he mumbled. "It is hard to explain."

A feeling of doom crept into Katherine's awareness. What about her child? Would it have to fight John the way *she* had fought Gordon? Would the child grow up in a miserable household? John and Victoria replicated Gordon and Elizabeth in many ways. Would they set the example she would want?

"Is that why you are against John and Victoria adopting?"

William grunted, while visibly shrugging his shoulders. He hadn't even said anything yet. Katherine had an uncanny way of getting straight to the point, which, on the one hand he had to admire, yet on the other, could be confrontational.

"Who am I to judge what you do Katie," he formulated carefully. "Growing up without a father would prove to be arduous for any child, but I understand why you don't want Alexander here. Follow your heart is my advice. I can only offer my support to ensure you and the child's wellbeing. Perhaps you and the wee one can spend summer seasons in Chicago, instead of me coming here. I could talk to John."

Katherine sighed. She couldn't shake off the foreboding feeling she was overlooking something. She felt overwhelmed and incredibly tired. William observed her changing mood.

"It must have been a rough few months for you Katherine. Your mother passing away, Gordon disappearing and Alexander leaving, a lot to come to terms with. And you with child and now this."

Lost for words Katherine searched her mind. The reality of the situation now hit her with full force. Nervously she got up from the couch and paced up and down the room. "We must never inform John or anyone else for that matter in the family about this. John could well change his mind about the adoption, feeling it could be one scandal too many. We must never tell anyone Uncle William. It would change everything including mother's reputation. She doesn't deserve that."

William looked Katherine in the eye. "Your mother's legacy would be my main concern, but what's done is done. It could actually give you good argument to join me in America. You could have the child there without embarrassment. Once in Chicago we could say you're a young widow. Nobody would know different."

Feeling unsteady, Katherine sat back down. "What if it is not what *I* want? What if I desire the child should grow up here, at Ballindalloch?"

William felt himself becoming impatient. "But Katherine, for as long as I can remember you've wanted to get away from here," William exclaimed, gesturing at the room with his hands.

"Exactly," Katherine said. "To go to Edinburgh, is what I want. Uncle William…father…." Katherine was pleading, tasting the strangeness of the word, "I want to be a doctor of medicine. And I would still be close enough to see the child …"

William felt utterly exhausted. "I've had enough for one day," he said, "I need a bath and some rest and you should get some sleep as well. We'll continue this conversation in the morning." William walked towards the drawing-room door, briefly placing a hand on Katherine's shoulder. He sincerely hoped she'd come to her senses and move to America.

***

The next morning, William found John in the kitchen sitting near the cooker range reading the newspaper.

"Is there anything of interest in the paper John?" William queried.

Flinching at the sudden question, John quickly looked for something worth reciting, " Only an article about the memorial service in London in honour of Beatrice's husband Prince Henry, two weeks ago. He died of malaria in Ashanti. Our Donald is out there you know."

"Have you heard anything from him?"

"No, the last letter was many weeks ago. I made him aware of father but nothing else."

"Good," William replied, "there is no point adding to his concerns, I'm sure he has enough on his plate. Where are Thomas and Lachlan hiding out these days? Word of their father's disappearance would have been upsetting. Are they aware of their sister's position?"

"Why upset them unnecessarily? Thomas has many interests uncle. He spends most of his time in London and Paris. He is still in the civil service in what capacity I have no idea. He's hardly ever home." Thomas and John differed in age by almost four years. "In fact, the last time he was here was at mother's funeral," John recalled.

William flinched when John referred to Elizabeth. "And Lachlan, what's he doing? Is he married yet?"

Lachlan, the baby of the Macpherson boys, was the nephew William favoured most.

"He left Ballindalloch last September. He is in Australia to the best of my knowledge, designing bridges. An adventure he called it. Father paid his passage; character building he told us all."

"Australia, I'll be damned," William exclaimed. "I wouldn't walk over any bridge designed by Lachlan."

John cleared his throat. "He writes often. He asked if I could provide as much notice as possible when we arrange father's memorial service."

William, raising his voice a tad said, "There will be no such service until we find Gordon, do you hear? We will arrange a proper burial."

John was taken aback by William's tone. "Which brings me to the topic of the tunnel, I want to know what happened," William said, peering out of the window at the gentle snowflakes falling on the deserted landscape.

"Tunnel? What do you mean?"

"MacLean told me the old whisky storage tunnel collapsed on the same day our Gordon disappeared. Why didn't you inform me?"

"We have more important matters to discuss. I need to settle affairs between Katherine and Victoria and would appreciate your approval." Even with John being acting laird of Ballindalloch, important decisions had to be made with the full agreement of the most senior family members. It was an unwritten rule.

William shook his head. "This is simply a formal contract between your sister and your wife isn't it?" He lifted the lid of a pan on the cooker and eyed bacon and eggs. Travelling always left him ravenous.

"You have to admit," John said, "it is not an everyday situation. I would have preferred to father a child of my own, but it seems God thought otherwise."

Carrying a generous plate of rashers and egg, William sat down next to John and greedily attacked the offering. Still chewing William muttered, "It seems to me it has more to do with Alexander Stewart rather than the good Lord."

"We prefer not to be reminded," John replied, his face displaying a thin smile. "It is a good thing he has gone."

"Wouldn't it have been better to get him back and bear the consequences?"

John sniggered. "It's well seen you have not been here for a while. Your niece has turned into a wilful young lady. She doesn't *want* the child, we are doing her a favour believe me. She *does not want* Alexander to know anything."

"Knowing the Stewarts, I feel for Robert. I think the matter is," William spoke in between chewing, "she doesn't want to stay here! I suggested last night she should come with me to America."

"It is out of the question!" John reacted. "Why would she? In any case she plans to go to Edinburgh. Our Katherine has it all arranged. Malcolm Durie has secured a place for her at university. She will move sometime in August."

In spite of himself William had to smile at his daughter displaying the same reluctance to conformity as he always had. "Then we'll have to respect her decision," he commented wryly. "It only leaves the tunnel to discuss." William had stopped eating and was observing his nephew. He wondered why John was so reluctant to discuss the incident.

"If you insist let's go and have a look, but there is nothing much to see."

Together John and William made their way to the disused scullery. William coughed, "The look and smell in here reminds me of a pigsty," he said, looking around the place he recalled so well from childhood. "Has anyone looked inside at all?" he asked, as they dragged the wooden panel away from the tunnel entrance. A pungent stench caught them by surprise. A scurrying of rats could be heard further inside.

"I want to know the cause of this stench," William demanded.

"And arrange an inspection for structural damage on the storage room above."

"The storage room is fine, we checked. Maybe the rats built themselves a nest and created a weakness. I have forbidden the staff to enter; it would be far too dangerous." John hoped Simpson or Stewart would not converse with William. They had been insistent the tunnel should be searched.

"I agree John, but I'm talking of hiring experts. Have you not once considered there could be a connection between your father's disappearance and the collapse of the tunnel? The police must have investigated; what did they say?"

John remained silent.

"You didn't inform them did you?" William said, looking at his nephew, eyes narrowed.

67

"No, I didn't. What would father be doing in there?"

"In our childhood, your father and I spent many hours in there, albeit without our parent's knowledge. I plan to meet up with the Grantown Constabulary next week. I am not impressed how their investigation has been conducted. I know the story of disappearing jewellery; the Alexander Stewart theft. It's all nonsense! You know it and I know it. From what I have learned of Katherine and Alexander, one can speculate on Gordon's motive."

"What an insult," John cried out. "How dare you even suggest he had an ulterior motive; Father never even knew Katherine was with child. None of us knew, until Doctor Kennedy confirmed the cause of her complaints last month."

"Which is when you concluded it would be better for Katherine to give her child to you and Victoria?"

John looked annoyed. "It's settled. I've already explained. What else do you want to hear?"

"I know well enough my brother would never have agreed," William replied, hoping his remark would not reveal too much of his inner emotion. He stared at his nephew. "You and Victoria had better look after Katherine's bairn as if it was your own, otherwise you will have me to answer to. Are you listening to me John?"

"Yes, you need have no worries."

"One other thing, you provide all the support Katie needs. The girl has had a torrid time this past while and she will be under a lot of pressure in the coming year, having the baby and going to university. Anything she asks for; you give her, do you hear?"

John was cringing under his uncle's scrutinised gaze. "Yes, yes. Uncle... will you mention the collapsed tunnel to the police?"

John's reasoning suddenly became apparent to William. What good would come from excavating the tunnel? If nothing was found it would attract needless suspicion. If Gordon was indeed there what else would they find?

"My God! It's a wonder Robert Stewart hasn't informed the police!"

"We must consider Katherine's condition" John remarked.

William didn't directly respond, instead gestured they should move the wooden panel back. He then asked, "Has Katherine or James mentioned the tunnel?"

As both men shifted the panel back in place, John answered, "No, James is his usual withdrawn self and Katie just wants the mess cleared up."

"Get the castle checked for structural damage but first brick this tunnel," William ordered.

John didn't answer.

"On second thoughts, brick the whole fucking scullery!" William walked briskly towards the kitchen feeling engulfed in guilt.

CHAPTER 18
Friday 7 October 2011, Ballindalloch Castle, Banffshire, Scotland

"You did the auld laird proud Angus," said a portly James Grant sitting in his chair puffing a large cigar, holding a glass of whisky in his other hand. Grant, a close associate of Angus for many years was now in semi-retirement.

The group of men had gathered in the sitting room, making their way from Inveravon Church after attending the funeral of the Laird Gordon Macpherson. Angus had poured all the men a generous glass of malt.

James Macpherson piped up, "I bet you never trust Billy to pour whisky."

Everyone laughed as James added, "Did you see Billy in church? You would think he knew Gordon personally the way he was greetin'."

Angus sitting beside his son George nodded. "It was the most surreal experience for everyone I am sure. I am glad it is all behind us now. It's been a difficult few months for the family I can tell you." George put an arm around his father's shoulder. "John mentioned the tourist numbers are up on last year. Each cloud has a silver lining does it not?"

"No doubt," Angus's eldest son John sounded from the far corner of the room, standing beside James Grant's son Peter, and Doug Stein, owner of Glen Fraoch, a small privately owned distillery known for producing superb malts.

"Oh yes," Angus said, "An amazing increase. Many just stand and gawk at the repair work being done. It is quite amusing. I am going to extend the season till the end of this month. I wish the salmon in the Spey were thriving as much. The return of fish born in the river is well down. The Fishery Board's position is that the decline is due to climate change. I don't dispute it, but sooner believe it's the water you guys pump back into the river that's causing the problem."

"That's not fair Angus," Peter Grant commented. "You know we meet the legal standards set by the water authorities."

"Aye, well maybe they've got their sums wrong,"

"Where *is* Mrs Stewart?" asked James Grant, diverting the conversation. "Is she still here?"

It was John who replied. "Cathy has gone to her room. I think today was too much. The crowd outside the church overwhelmed her, not to mention the media." John caught himself thinking Cathy probably couldn't wait to get on the web and update her father. Before the funeral service started, he had overheard her talking with Maggie and Euphemia regarding a James Macpherson of Raleigh, North

Carolina. Though Maggie had provided little knowledge of this James, she had only been too happy to find someone willing to listen to her other family anecdotes and had shared some stories on a William Macpherson, the 'Chicago brother' of Gordon. According to Maggie, William had lived in sin with an American vaudeville actress. John had never heard of such tales and put it down to drivel. It had made him wonder though, if he would want to know more on his family line, if he would be third or fourth generation American - Scottish.

James Grant guffawed. "Well, Catherine Stewart is one lady and a half. Pretty one as well, you should move in there John."

"You behave James," Angus said flippantly. "Catherine is a married woman. Fine fellow he is too, her husband, David Stewart. Just you keep your nose in your own glass."

Changing the subject, Angus asked, "How are you enjoying playing the hospitality role?" Turning to Peter Grant, he added, "I bet your old man still tries to help you with his way of thinking?"

Peter laughed. He was now CEO of the Grant dynasty succeeding his father. "Not quite Angus. Playing golf keeps him busy."

James Grant added with some doubt, "The market is so buoyant." He looked at Doug Stein. "I'm sure you have similar numbers Doug. The North America's, India and Eastern Europe are particularly strong, is that not so Peter? The domestic market is a different story though. If the export market keeps growing and I'm sure it will, even more distillers including us will need to import more barley from ..." James paused, "... from England."

The whole room burst into laughter.

Doug commented on Grant's remark. "Glen Fraoch has seen the same trend. Our growth in the last few years has been almost too much to manage. The past twelve months however have been difficult. As you guys know, I am busy working on securing investment to expand over the next ten years. Being a comparatively modest player, we are constantly facing takeover bids. I keep refusing of course."

James commented, "Peter told me of the Ukrainians. I hear Suntory plan to expand. Mind you I am sure the Japanese will be after the big boys. I can understand your position Doug. We will help if push comes to shove, won't we Peter?"

"We have already discussed this with Doug at Board level, so don't feel you are alone."

"Actually, on hospitality," James jumped in, "we have a group from the Marriott Hotel chain planned for next spring. A delegation is coming over from the States with half a dozen prize winners of some competition. Can we include Ballindalloch in the itinerary?" He turned to Doug Stein who was standing by the window. "Also Doug, we could include an hour or so at Glen Fraoch. What do you think?"

"Thank you James, just contact Linda and confirm the date and times," replied a sombre Doug.

"I expect discounted tickets for the party, Angus." James said.

Everyone laughed, "I'll check if our margins can cope with five percent James."

"You drive a hard bargain Angus. If Mrs Stewart is still around perhaps she could do a tour of her August capers," James said.

There were a few smiles but nobody said anything.

Sensing his comment was not received well, James turned more serious. "What a way for the auld laird to die. The Macphersons have been traipsing over Gordon's bones for years and nobody knew a thing until Mrs Stewart showed up. She has become a bit of a celebrity."

In the far corner of the room, Doug Stein was oblivious to the banter. Lately he found it hard to enjoy the usual business windups. The current developments at his own distillery weighed heavily upon him. He felt tired and older than his fifty-five years. The thought of going home to an empty house disturbed him as well. Normally he would not give it a second thought as he enjoyed a bachelor's life. Tonight was different. He found his mind kept drifting to the way Gordon Macpherson must have died, the horror of the laird's last thoughts, all alone in a dark tunnel facing death. Quietly he left the room and made his way outside to call a taxi to take him to Elgin. As the taxi driver slowly steered his car through the Ballindalloch private exit fifteen minutes later, he was still trying to push away the black cloud hovering in his brain.

CHAPTER 19
Tuesday 11 October 2011, Wake Forest, North Carolina, USA

David Stewart sat staring into the blue glow of the computer screen. Only a desk lamp lit his study, casting a shadow of his tall frame on the wall behind him. His right hand was cupped over the mouse only one click away from booking a ticket to Aberdeen. He was hesitating. David was still angry. Once again, the Macphersons were bullying him. *The story of my life!*

His father-in-law had been quite demanding. Their conversation had left David unsettled and again made him question his marriage.

"What sort of husband are you?" Jim had shouted, ferociously shaking his finger. "Either *you* go get her back or I will, and don't think you'll be welcome here if I have to be the one to straighten her out!"

Reflecting on the conversation made David slip his hand from the mouse and reach out for the last drops of the Glenlivet sitting next to his laptop. *I'm such a klutz, always letting the Macphersons rule my life. Do I want her back? Maybe it should be about what I want for a change?*

With a sigh David stood to get a refill. Except for his conscious choice to change his career from an account manager with a hardware company to becoming a travel writer, little in his life seemed to be in his control. When he'd met Cathy so many years ago, she had been the one to make a pass at him. A year later, it had again been her, proposing they should get married and settle down. He had wanted to of course, but in retrospect it felt the initiative was always taken from him. At the time of their marriage he had been head over heels in love with Cat. Then, he was oblivious to how she and her father took charge from fucking Christmas dinner to almost everything else in his life.

For a long time David had not resisted, but by gate crashing his genealogy research, Cat had taken one step too far. His ancestor Alexander had tickled his imagination. From rural Scotland in the late Victorian era to a career at the Boston Globe was quite an achievement. Sometimes David wished he could step into a time machine to witness how his ancestor had coped with what must have been a time of enormous change. Shortly after he'd found out Alexander's place of birth, Cathy had taken command, uncovering a key piece of the Stewart family history. On the one hand he should be grateful, on the other the way she did it was unforgiveable for him.

Her actions had even jeopardised his professional assignment to write a travel guide on the Speyside Whisky Trail, as well as his wish to visit Alexander's place of birth. He would have to return and round up his research, yet with his father-in-law prompting him to go and convince Cathy to come back to North Carolina, the writing of the guide had again been put in second place.

David glanced at Alexander's death certificate. Wayne Stewart had emailed the copy. The single sheet of paper listed over twenty deaths. A line, halfway down the list depicted the details of Alexander's death;

RETURN of WARRANT OFFICERS, NON-COMMISSIONED OFFICERS AND MEN OF THE *"War Correspondent"* **KILLED IN ACTION**

Or who have DIED whilst in Service Abroad in the War of 1914 to 1918

RANK	NAME	COUNTRY	AGE
War C	*Alexander Stewart*	*Scotland*	41

DATE and PLACE OF DEATH	CAUSE OF DEATH
5 Jan 1916, Gallipoli	*KIA*

Certified to be a true Extract from the Return of Deaths in the War 1914 -1920 of people born or attested in Scotland.

RJ Donaldson, Assistant Registrar General.

Killed in Action, Gallipoli.

The book he discovered a few days later had put a totally different light on his priorities. At first, David had been astonished. He had researched the web for weeks on this World War I battle in the feeble attempt to find anything on Alexander Stewart's exploits as a War Correspondent. He discovered many disturbing articles written by Alexander in the Boston Globe and the Times of London. The more he read, the more interested he became in the bloody conflict. Glancing at the pile of books he had purchased on the Gallipoli campaign, his eyes went to the book lying open on the small sofa; a hardback, published in 1930.

At first, when he had read page 303, he almost missed it. *Just wait until I share this information with Cat and all the other Macphersons; not by email, not by telephone, not by Skype.*

Click, ticket booked.

CHAPTER 20
Saturday 22 February 1896, Ballindalloch, Banffshire, Scotland

The soft clinking of knives and forks finding their way around the breakfast plates was the only sound to fill the room. Holding a tea and a coffee pot, Simpson surveyed the family. At the head of the table John was hiding behind a newspaper avoiding contact with his uncle who was sitting to his left. William had been far too secretive to his taste. He didn't disclose any details of his talk with the police in Grantown, and his abrupt approach to the employees on the events over the past few months only ensured an unhappy and silent bunch of workers. All these discussions without John's involvement disturbed Simpson.

"Looks a great day to go out riding," Katherine said, breaking the silence. The snow was gradually disappearing with daylight turning the grounds into a softer shade of white.

"You'll do no such thing," William retorted curtly, "not in your condition."

"Oh stop fussing. I'm young and strong."

"Don't tempt me young lady, you've caused enough trouble as it is," William muttered.

Katherine smiled. She knew William's words didn't match his real thoughts. He cherished the thought of becoming a grandfather and wished he could share it.

"Perhaps you could join your uncle and James this morning?" Victoria suggested. "I understand they are going shooting."

John looked up from his newspaper. "Don't be absurd Victoria. In Katherine's condition it is better she just stays at home."

"You can't Katie," William said, "James and I need time to discuss his move to America and I have asked Robert Stewart to join us."

"All right," Katherine agreed, tossing her napkin on the table. She didn't want to be anywhere near Robert. "If you'll excuse me, I'm going to the library." Katherine had acquired some new medical books on pregnancy and childbirth, typically written by male physicians. Conditions for women in childbirth could improve dramatically in her opinion. It was ridiculous that men in this day and age dictated to women what they had been doing all by themselves for centuries.

On leaving, Katherine stopped at the door and asked, "John have you and Uncle William had time to discuss what's to be done with the tunnel? It's been three months." The strangeness of calling him 'uncle' now was ringing in Katherine's ears.

"William and I have discussed the situation and it will be taken care of Katherine," John said. "We will close off the old scullery completely."

"I'll see you here at lunchtime Katie," William interrupted. "I might go to Grantown. You may want to join me while you can still walk in town, you know..."

It wouldn't be long till Katherine would have to confine herself to the house with her pregnancy starting to show. William understood all too well how difficult it would be for her.

"I would appreciate that very much." She blew William a kiss and went on her way.

William stood up from the table, excused himself to Victoria and John.

"Uncle William, are you ready?" James's head popped around the door. He had chosen to eat his breakfast early to avoid the family. The tension was not palatable for James when all family members were together.

"Give me a few minutes James and I will meet you outside."

***

"Pull!"

Callum the young stable boy, with a shilling in his pocket, crouched in the sodden wild grassland some one hundred yards ahead and released the trap. The machine gave a metallic screech as the spring freed and the disc arched into the air. *Bang!* Instantly fragments of limestone burst in the skyline and disappeared without trace.

"Good shot Robert!"

Robert Stewart un-cocked the Winchester 1893; the cartridge dropped close to his feet. The smell of smoke lingered in the cold winter air. All the men were dressed in heavy hunting jackets, breeches, hats and boots. Snow dominated the landscape, and the clarity of the highland winter morning, provided the illusion you could reach out and touch the hills in the distance.

James Macpherson looked at his uncle and said, "It's a wonderful way to keep your eye in for the grouse shooting is it not?" his breath vaporising.

"Aye, it is." William glanced at Robert who was busy reloading his shotgun. "For sure none of us will be here for this year's shoot." He produced a silver hipflask, took a slug and handed it to James. "Here it will warm your belly." He turned to Robert, "Come over here man, have a drink."

Robert joined the other two shooters and was happy to taste the whisky. William had invited him to the shoot. After some persuasion, Robert had reluctantly agreed.

In the distance Callum, who was standing but only visible from the waist up, was flapping his arms around his body in the effort to keep warm. The small boy looked vulnerable as if he could be the next target.

"Isn't it rather peculiar we will *all* be in America shortly? What are *your* plans Robert?" James asked, turning to the gamekeeper.

Robert hesitated and gave a thin smile. "I don't have anything planned other than to be with Alexander for a time and wait and see what transpires."

William with a serious look on his rugged features said, "Aye, James I would never have believed we have arrived at where we are now." Turning to Robert, his voice earnest, "Our Katherine and Alexander have caused all this trouble. What is done is done and we should remember only yesterday they were children. Robert, tell your boy to stay away. I know he was wronged, but he made up his mind to go, so he'd better stay where he is. You tell him I do not want Katherine …"

James interrupted, "Robert, we are saying this in everyone's interest."

"Gentlemen," said the gamekeeper putting his hands in the air, "I do not need your idle threats. I cannot vouch for my son, but I for one will never return to Ballindalloch as much as it saddens me. The Stewarts have served here for a long time." Contemplating on what to say next, Stewart peered over the land his family had tended for generations. "I can accept the wrong doings of Alexander and his friendship with Miss Katherine, yet cannot condone how the laird and then his son have dealt with the situation. Thank you for asking me along, but I should go now. I wish you good fortune."

Robert slung the un-cocked gun over his left shoulder, turned and made his way back to the lodge.

Both men watched him trudge through the snow.

"Can you live with this uncle?" James asked softly. "Do we have the right to deny Robert and Alexander?"

With his own delight on becoming a grandfather burning his conscience, William was unable to answer. Instead he offered, "I went to Grantown and had a meeting with Campbell Ramsay, Superintendent of the Banffshire Police."

"Regarding father I presume."

"Yes. Ramsay was aloof. He asked the local sergeant to join us, a Robbie Grant. Mr Ramsay only looked at the case notes for a couple of minutes. 'Death by misadventure'," he said. "I told him I was extremely dissatisfied with how the police handled the case."

"What was his response?"

"Bloody told me I could complain to the High Court in Edinburgh, but given everything, I would be wasting my time. Arrogant man he was, I wanted to punch him in the mouth. I'll tell you James, I might have well talked to a slab of granite from your quarry. Speaking of which, have you had anybody interested regarding the sale?"

"I have a potential arrangement for a long term lease. My connections here, in Glasgow and in London have helped me greatly to move to North Carolina. I do not want my family here a moment longer than necessary."

"Isn't brick making a wee bit different from digging granite James?"

"It's the same principles uncle, and what better country to build?" James paused, "I wish we could rebuild our family."

"Can I ask you a question James?"

"Sure."

"If things were different, you know, regarding Gordon, Katherine, the Stewart boy, would you still be going to America?"

James took a few moments, "No."

William frowned, stepped forward a few paces and cocked his shotgun.

"Pull!"

Robert Stewart stood leaning over the ship's railing on the starboard side of the SS Furnessia. He was pondering over his reasons for leaving Scotland. He was certain his son who had sailed only five months before, had done the same.

The steamer, part of the Anchor Line fleet, was one of the modern type of vessels whose size, speed and comfort, made the passage across the Atlantic a much more easy and agreeable endeavour than was the case in times gone by. With her 445 feet in length, 6500 tons of gross tonnage and two funnels, she made an impressive sight.

The promenade deck stretched from a point nearly amidship to the stern of the steamer, and was surmounted by a deckhouse of which one half was utilised as a comfortable smoking room.

The sailing was unusual, as the Furnessia had been chartered to ship the Yardley & Lapsley museum pieces, circus equipment, menagerie and performers back to America after their tour of Europe.

Robert had been fortunate to secure a second-class saloon ticket on the passage at a cost of nineteen pounds, as the number of passengers and crew were reduced to 120, due to the massive cargo of the touring entertainers. At the Anchor Line Union Street office in Glasgow, a small crowd had gathered outside the building, hoping some passengers would happily sell their ticket for a profitable gain.

They had been at sea for seven days. The first four days had been pleasant enough, but this morning the ship's captain had issued a storm warning. He had predicted it would delay their arrival in New York as they would have to port in Halifax, Nova Scotia, to replenish coal for the boilers. The swell of the ocean was now severe and rolled the ship from side to side in a consistent motion.

Robert felt it was safer to return to his cabin on the forward Main Deck. His room accommodated five other passengers; three men and two women of similar age to Robert. Berths were allotted in rotation of purchase and numbers marked on the tickets. Passengers were provided with all necessaries for the voyage, including a liberal supply of well-cooked provisions. Robert had little appetite. Seasickness was rampant throughout the ship. It was difficult to ignore the retching of his fellow passengers.

In his cabin, Robert's thoughts returned to Ballindalloch. His childhood had been a happy one. He had spent most of his early years at Inveravon School, playing and exploring the grounds of the estate;

the woodlands being his most treasured part. Church at Inveravon Parish on Sunday was mandatory. The Sabbath was sacred on the estate and nothing else seemed to happen or be allowed on a Sunday. His father was a staunch Presbyterian, as *his* father was before him. Robert never met his grandfather or grandmother Stewart. He was to learn much later, that his grandfather was a God fearing man from Aberdeen. He had been the gamekeeper of Ballindalloch, but died in a mental institution when he was only forty-five years old. When he was committed to the asylum his wife went to live with her family, leaving Robert's father, to fend for himself as a young man.

John Stewart had been a tall man with handsome rugged features. He grew a bushy beard in winter and shaved it off in spring. As a gamekeeper, he was responsible for maintaining the game, bird and fish population of the estate, a skill Robert learned from him.

During school holidays he often accompanied his father. He once watched him shoot a fox. He taught Robert the need to eradicate as many predators as possible. Foxes, magpies, stoats and birds of prey were a danger to the wildlife, precious to the laird.

Robert loved it when his father borrowed the estate coach and took his family to Elgin for the day. His mother, everyone called her Bettie, always looked so elegant. She would dress in her best clothes knowing she would be viewed riding in such a fine carriage. Bettie was a soft-spoken woman, slender build, with jet-black hair and hazel eyes. Robert adored her. She would often ask him to brush her hair in the evening, while she would hum her favourite tunes. On their days out in Elgin they would dine in a fine tearoom and sometimes he would be treated to a proper barbershop haircut or new boots and clothes.

The ship plunged, startling everyone in the cabin. Robert's stomach seemed to meet his throat and for the first time he began to feel unwell. He swallowed his excess saliva. The women were crying, with the husbands trying to console them, hiding their own fear.

The Furnessia made her way through the storm, proceeding at twelve knots, heading for the entrance of Halifax harbour. The crew experienced intermittent visibility and heavy seas. Unbeknown to everyone on board, the ship was twelve miles off course to the west of the harbour.

In an effort to distract himself, Robert returned his thoughts to his family. He recalled visits of aunts and uncles, usually in spring or summertime. His mother's sisters, Jenny and Maisie from Crovie, would stay for a few days and they would sometimes bring Granny Campbell. None of his cousins ever visited and he did not recall anybody else from the Stewarts appearing at Ballindalloch. Robert had a faint recollection of visiting Crovie with his mother. He remembered it as a tiny fishing village with one street. His uncle had taken him on a fishing boat. They had spotted dolphins.

As for the Macphersons, he could remember the auld laird and his wife. He didn't see them much though. His mother told him to stay away from the 'big house' as she would refer to the castle. He would often come across Gordon and his wee brother William. They were a good bit older than Robert and occasionally would give him a few pennies to do some errands; cleaning boots, fetching coal or wood for the fire.

On the bridge of the Furnessia, officers failed to take soundings. Nor did they post a masthead lookout, reduce speed or wake the captain as they approached the unfamiliar coast. They somehow did not spot the Sambro, the large landfall lighthouse there to warn mariners of the rocky shoals to the west of the harbour entrance.

Robert thought of his aspirations of studying engineering, but all changed in 1874 when his father died. The story went he had confronted a poacher close to the Monks Cottage in the woodlands. During a fistfight with the culprit he had collapsed and died. At the time Robert had been accepted by Dundee University, when Laird Gordon offered him the apprentice gamekeeper job and promised help from Henry Ingles, the gamekeeper of the Grant Estate in Elgin. Robert, even at nineteen-years old, was already skilled in many of the gamekeeper duties. The salary on offer of thirty pounds had been a major factor in his decision.

A year later, he married Jane Black, whom he had befriended through attending church services and social events. Jane soon discovered she was with child. Their son, Alexander, was born on 17th April 1875. Robert's salary, a modest rent for the lodge and all the fresh food from the estate made life comfortable for the young family. Jane secured work at the castle, switching from House Maid to general-purpose worker or being a Between Maid, working in either the house or the kitchen as needed. She earned sixteen pounds a year and was allowed to bring the baby. The other house and kitchen staff helped her with Alexander. Tragically she died in 1884 of consumption, at the age of only twenty-seven. It had forced Robert to learn quickly how best to look after his eight-year old son. Eventually, Lady Elizabeth Macpherson had taken Alexander into the 'big house', to be raised and educated together with her own children.

Robert smiled at the memory of teaching a young Alexander and Miss Katherine how to gut rabbits, hares and fish in a similar way he had been taught by his father. *Those days have gone. Now here I am running to Alexander. Will I burden him? What will I do? Surely country estates in America will need keepers?* Robert thought of

Gordon, John, William and Miss Katherine. She had been in tears when he gave her a hug before leaving the estate. *The poor girl had a difficult time and didn't seem to be looking after herself.* He had noticed Katherine had not been her usual lively active self and had gained weight. The person he would miss the most would be his friend Donald Simpson.

***

At two fifteen am local time, on sixth April 1896, the Furnessia struck an under water rock off Marr's Head, Meagher's Island, Nova Scotia. The crew lowered lifeboats, but they were all washed away or smashed. Due to heavy seas, ripped open hull, fire, explosions and bursting of steam pipes, the ship quickly filled with water and flipped on its side. Some tried to swim, or climb ropes to a wave swept rock or the barren shore. Residents of the tiny fishing village of Lower Prospect and Terence Bay, soon arrived to try and rescue and shelter any survivors. There were none to save.

CHAPTER 22
Thursday 23 April 1896, Ballindalloch Castle, Banffshire, Scotland

Uttering a desperate sigh Donald Simpson sank on the reading chair facing his bedroom window. His dark brown eyes sought out the familiarity of the fields hosting the rear entry to the castle, the view partly blocked by a wing added by the Macphersons in 1783, when they recognised more space was needed. Many generations of Macphersons had lived here, all leaving their own influence on the structure.

Simpson wondered how Gordon Ramsey Macpherson would be remembered. He had been laird from July 1863 to the third November1895, the date of his disappearance. Frantically, Donald's brain searched for reasons that could justify the terrible losses and sufferings of the families residing on the Ballindalloch grounds.

Why did Robert's boy have to go? Alexander was a trustworthy lad, always willing to help others. And smart too, a talent for writing uncovered by Mrs Roxburgh, the children's English tutor. Simpson had always felt comfortable with Alexander, unlike the Macpherson boys.

"Think Donald, think," he muttered, resting his head against the chair. Never before had Simpson felt this division between duty and what he believed was justified. Of course, there had been unpleasant moments when he was requested to execute commands he actually opposed. Donald reflected on the time some years ago when the laird caught Miss Katherine in the library reading 'inappropriate' books. As a punishment she was banished to her bedroom, her door locked. He had been assigned the task of serving the young lady her meals. The girl had refused to eat. Genuinely caring for her wellbeing, he expressed his concern to Katherine's mother. Fortunately, Lady Elizabeth quickly persuaded her husband to end his futile punishment. This episode had made Donald question his loyalty towards the laird.

After the tragic death of Lady Macpherson, Donald Simpson often stood up for the laird's only daughter. It had been him who helped her escape to Edinburgh without her father's knowledge. That same day the laird disappeared. Donald questioned his own actions. Had he stepped out of place? Had he altered Fate? Would Gordon still be here had Miss Katherine not gone to Edinburgh?

Simpson was utterly frustrated with himself and his obligations. Until now it had never been a problem to follow instructions, 'with the occasional bit of improvising' as he would call it, to serve his own convictions. This time it was different.

Before leaving, Robert Stewart had confided in him he would be living with Alexander in Boston and provided a forwarding address. Donald Simpson was now facing a major dilemma. Should he or should he not inform Miss Katherine of Alexander's whereabouts? Would he be helping or doing a disservice? In one of his son's letters that Robert shared, Alexander had described in detail the episode of being summoned to the study by Gordon Macpherson, the envelope containing a prepaid ship's passage to America and two hundred dollars. Alexander could have said no! Instead he chose to leave. Donald was sure the boy had no idea of Miss Katherine's condition. *What would have happened if he had known? Would he have made the same choice?* It was not his place to inform Alexander, but should he give Miss Katherine the opportunity? With his friend now missing at sea, he was the only person who had Alexander's address.

His mind was in turmoil. Was he, Donald Simpson, the one to inform the son of his late friend of Miss Katherine's condition or give *her* the opportunity?

Abruptly, Simpson stood up. He had made his decision.

CHAPTER 23
Tuesday 11 October 2011, Boat of Garten, Scotland

The passengers of the Royal Scotsman were soon to wake up. The yellowish glow of the first beams of autumn sunlight peeking over the horizon, gave the countryside a romantic air. The Victorian-styled train stood silent alongside the platform, blending with the rural surroundings. One would almost not notice the locomotive was missing. Early birds voiced their morning calls and a few rabbits played in a nearby field. Animals were still the dominant proprietors of the landscape and gave the impression nothing had changed in hundreds of years.

The only foreign sounds stirring were the soft thuds and bumps made by Train Manager Ross McKenna, who was helping to prepare continental breakfast for those passengers who wished to dine in their cabins. A Steward, Richard, on his maiden trip with the Royal Scotsman, had just gone to deliver coffee and toast to a Mr Stein.

Doug Stein was sitting by his writing desk, dressed in his usual business attire; suit, white shirt, smart tie. He was an early riser. He had already been reviewing the distillery Operations Plan for the coming six months. He enjoyed the train journey much more than he had anticipated. If it hadn't been for the Grabowski Group arranging everything, it would never have occurred to him to travel on the Royal Scotsman.

Doug was quite delighted with the deal he had struck securing a supply of sherry casks. The Ukrainians had surprised him. He was sure the casks would only be made available if he accepted their offer of buying a percentage of his distillery. During the past two years, they had consistently applied pressure to the board members to sell their holdings. This time, their offer had been staggering. 'But I will never sell,' he told them, 'over my dead body.' *Buying him a ticket for the Royal Scotsman wouldn't change anything!*

Surprisingly, they accepted his position and reached an amicable deal on the casks. Doug had thought of calling the office with the good news, but then thought it could wait. The major issue facing the Board was cash flow. The bank supported their business plan and offered a long term loan. The interest rate was such, the Board decided to explore the private sector. Doug frowned. So far, their efforts had not come to fruition. A knock interrupted his thoughts.

"Good morning Mr Stein," a voice sounded behind the door, "your morning coffee." Doug recognised Richard's voice, one of the attendants, a gentleman in his own right who had provided excellent service.

Doug opened the door. Ignoring all decorum the attendant rudely walked in, bumping into Stein in the process. As he stumbled, Doug registered the absence of a serving tray. A strange feeling of foreboding overcame him. Confused, he hardly noticed the arm curling around his back, while the steward pressed his body against him and pushed his other hand against his chest. Doug's heart was racing and he gasped for breath.

"Hush Mr Stein everything is okay," were the last words he heard as he slumped to the floor, eyes staring with a perplexed gaze.

***

In the neighbouring cabin, Diane Cox opened her eyes and looked over at her friend Dawn, who was still in bed. Their twin cabin though small, oozed luxury and comfort. Wood panelled walls holding candle shaped lights, a beautiful wooden writing desk with drawers, standing next to Diane's bed, and a small square shaped cabinet underneath the window of which the top could serve as a table.

The fact Dawn's bed was situated at a forty-five degree angle with Diane's, gave the women some privacy. Diane had to lift her head to actually see her friend. Dawn still seemed sound asleep.

A sound, a feeling, had alarmed Diane, but she wasn't quite sure what it was. Absentmindedly she looked at the leather bound photo album lying next to her on the desk. Perhaps one of her vivid dreams had left her apprehensive. She often had those lately, disturbing images of unknown places, yet always with familiar faces staring at her as if she should know exactly where she was and why.

A soft thud in the cabin next door caught her attention. A disturbance must have awoken her. A door opened and closed. Diane was quite sure it was Mr Stein's, the quiet director of some whisky factory. Travelling alone he was. She then heard crockery rattling and someone curse; unusual for the Royal Scotsman. It sounded like an accident with the morning breakfast service.

Diane had coffee brought to her cabin each morning. She badly needed it to wake up, especially with jetlag still keeping her drowsy. They'd boarded the train only a day after arriving in Edinburgh from JFK. Dawn had needed some persuasion to join Diane on the trip to Scotland, but was thoroughly enjoying the experience.

Expecting the steward to knock on her door next, Diane threw her legs over the side of the bed, stretched her arms high and yawned. Nothing happened. Intrigued she got up, unlocked the door and peeked into the corridor. A tray, covered in spilled coffee and drenched toast, stood abandoned on her right, opposite Mr Stein's door. She felt a draught. It made her shudder. Someone had opened a door to the platform. Conscious of being in her pyjamas, Diane quickly retrieved a dressing gown she had purchased, especially to wear on the Royal Scotsman, a bright red robe, the back decorated with oriental birds. She stepped into the corridor. The passage was empty. The row of windows lined up one after the other depicted an empty platform, except for a man briskly walking away from the station. Peering, Diane noticed he was wearing a familiar uniform. He stepped into the front passenger seat of a black car parked next to the station house. It took her a moment to recognise it was a Royal Scotsman attendant's outfit. On impulse, she walked into the next carriage to follow the car as it drove away. Puzzled, Diane stared at the distancing rear of the car. The sound of a swing door from the far end of the carriage made her turn and scurry back to her compartment.

The flash of a red gown disappearing behind the door was all Ross McKenna saw.

***

The engine of the Royal Scotsman came to a complete stop. Silence returned to Boat of Garten. The wildlife of the surrounding Cairngorm National Park seemed undisturbed. The locomotive had returned to pick up its tail. Only the carriages stayed overnight at the Boat train station, while the locomotive remained in the much busier station of Aviemore.

Ross McKenna had discovered a dead body. The train drivers had been instructed by the head office to keep everyone on board. Inside, the train attendants busied themselves to clear the dining room car known as Raven. The police required a makeshift room for Detective Inspector Peter Duckett and his team to conduct a round of questioning.

The dead man had been found under suspicious circumstances; fully dressed and lying on the floor of his cabin with no obvious trace of illness, struggle or robbery. A death on the train could be a problem, be it natural or otherwise. The famous journey attracted tourists from all over the world for 'the experience of a lifetime'. Travel writer Vivien Devlin, had described the Royal Scotsman as a 'Palace on Wheels'. Negative publicity could dent the reputation.

The slamming of doors announced the arrival of two cars from the Grantown-on-Spey Police Department. They had parked behind a coach, of which the driver was making a frantic call on his mobile. He was supposed to drive his thirty-six passengers to Ballindalloch Castle as part of the tourist's itinerary. In the turmoil, no one had thought of informing him differently.

From the leading car DI Duckett and Sergeants Tom Baxter and Shona Boyd stepped out. The second vehicle held a doctor, a forensics expert and a photographer, who had all been quickly assembled, after the Orient Express Company had sounded the alarm.

"Not your average luxury holiday eh," Duckett mumbled over his shoulder to Baxter, who habitually walked one step behind. Peering from the windows of the luxurious observation car, thirty-five pairs of eyes jostled for position to watch the group of officials move towards the train.

"Look at them," Duckett said, "They remind me of prisoners."

Baxter observed the assembly of people, apprehension visible on their faces."It's a lot of money to pay sir to be stuck inside. I feel for them actually." Baxter and his wife had just been on a bus tour through Greece, staying over in different hotels. He wondered how he or his wife would have felt if one of the co-passengers on the trip had been found dead and the vacation would have been stalled.

"Good morning ladies and gentlemen," Duckett opened, as he stepped into the observation lounge. He'd done a quick survey of the cabin where the deceased had been found and left it to the experts.

"My name is DI Duckett and this is Sergeants Baxter and Boyd." Duckett waited on his colleagues to give the audience a short nod. "There's no need to panic," he continued. "We're just following official procedures. When someone is found dead under unexplained circumstances, we need to rule out foul play. The doctor is with the deceased, but we need to ask you all a few questions just in case you may have heard or seen anything to help us with our investigation. Your information will be treated confidentially. We will be questioning you individually in the dining car Raven. It might take a while. So I'm afraid your excursion for today will be delayed."

"But I have an appointment at Ballindalloch," a slightly overweight woman called out. She was wearing trainers and a bright light blue sweater and dark blue slacks.

'Sorry ma'am, but we can't make exceptions."

"It's an important meeting," the woman added cryptically.

Duckett observed her while trying to keep a neutral look on his face. *Ballindalloch will have to wait.* "I assure you we'll not take up any more of your time than is necessary."

He turned to Baxter and Boyd and whispered; "Get me the person who found the body and find out who is in charge. When I am done with them, get me the American woman who complained she would be late for her Ballindalloch appointment."

***

"Why did you go and check on Mr Stein?" Duckett asked Ross McKenna, ten minutes later in the dining car. At McKenna's instructions, one of the attendants had placed a decanter of water and a flask of black coffee and condiments on the table. McKenna poured them all a coffee. Baxter sat on Duckett's right, ready to take notes.

Stirring his coffee McKenna said, "I saw Richard step into a black BMW and drive off. I was confused. He should have been serving morning refreshments."

"Where were you?"

"The corridor, next to the pantry, I was helping prepare in-cabin breakfasts, when I spotted Richard. I wondered, where the hell is he going? I immediately walked to the front carriage and found an abandoned tray in front of Mr Stein's cabin. He ordered early morning coffee. So, I knocked on his door. When he didn't reply I used the master key, went in and found him," he said, his voice now faltering.

"This Richard, did he drive the car himself or did he get into the passenger seat?"

"There was another person in the car, the driver, but I didn't see him, or her."

Duckett pulled his mobile from his jacket and fast-dialled a number. "Do you have a description of this Richard and any photos of him? What is his family name?"

"Richard Stillwater, and yes we have a logbook of all staff members together with their picture."

"I want a copy of Stillwater's file."

"I'll get it for you now," McKenna said, and left the Raven.

The inspector now believed this was no accident. Duckett had to alert the Aberdeen HQ and Special Branch.

McKenna returned with the details and picture of Stillwater. Duckett quickly read the document and looked at the manager. "I notice he was a recent hire. Was this his first time on the train?"

"Yes it was; our new employees have on the job training. I don't understand what is going on. Why would Richard …? Oh my God, I simply can't believe..."

"You must not mention this conversation to anybody," Duckett said firmly. "This is strictly between you and the police. Do you understand what I'm saying?"

"Yes inspector," replied a shocked McKenna, who now slowly began to feel the impact of what he had witnessed.

"Good. Now did you observe anything else before you found Mr Stein?" Duckett asked. "Think carefully," he urged, knowing the mind tends to erase its memory shortly before traumatic events.

McKenna thought deep. "Well, there was one thing," he said, searching his mind's eye. "There was a passenger in the corridor, wearing a rather flamboyant morning coat, which is unusual."

"Why unusual?"

McKenna snapped back to being the manager. "Passengers don't walk around in their pyjamas inspector. This train is a hotel, a five star hotel. All the facilities our guests need are in their rooms. Would you walk around a hotel lobby in your pyjamas?"

Touché, Duckett thought, *and I don't even wear jimjams.* "You used the word flamboyant?"

"Yes, a loud colour. A housecoat, it was bright red, silk I think, decorated with birds of some sort."

"Was it a man or a woman?"

"I only got a brief glimpse, but I would guess a woman."

Duckett instructed Shona to go to the observation lounge and find the person who owned the red morning coat. The lady who had the appointment at Ballindalloch would have to wait. To Duckett's surprise, it was the American woman anyway who walked into the Raven.

"Did you bring ID ma'am?" officer Boyd asked.

"Yes, I have my passport right here." Nervously she rummaged around in a travel bag and handed Duckett her papers.

"Diane Cox?" he read out loud, raising his eyes to the woman.

"And your name is again?" the lady asked firmly. She didn't seem taken with the proceedings.

"I'm DI Peter Duckett and this is Sergeant Tom Baxter. I'm sorry to inconvenience you in any way. I am sure you understand we have a serious matter at hand and we have to ask you some questions."

Mrs Cox nodded.

"Was it you who was seen outside your cabin this morning wearing a red morning coat?"

Diane blushed. "Are you implying I had anything to do with the death of Mr Stein? If so, I want to speak to a lawyer, I'm sure I have the right to remain silent in Scotland as well!"

Duckett suppressed a sigh. *She had seen too many movies.* "Mrs Cox, you were seen. If you noticed or heard anything we'd be much obliged."

Diane took a few moments to gather what she would say.

"I heard someone curse and went to take a look. I saw a man wearing a steward's uniform get into a black car. I then went back to my cabin."

"Before, did you see or hear anything suspicious?"

"No Inspector I did not."

Duckett was disappointed. "Are you here on holiday?"

"What else would I be doing on the Royal Scotsman, Inspector Duckhead?" Diane snapped.

Duckett frowned, not sure if the woman was purposely mispronouncing his name. "My name is Duckett if you don't mind and only you can answer the question Mrs Cox."

Diane Cox hesitated for a moment and said, "I'm actually combining business with pleasure."

"Can you state the nature of your business?"

"Let's just say it's some real estate interests."

Duckett all too well remembered the location of her appointment, but wanted her to say it. "Any place in particular?"

"Yes Ballindalloch, I told you I have an appointment. Mr Macpherson is expecting me. I tried to call him but my cell phone has no signal."

"Are you interested in buying the castle?" Duckett inquired, unable to hide his surprise.

"No!" Diane answered impatiently. "Look, I don't see how this has anything to do with your investigation and I want to keep the appointment."

Curious, Duckett used some of his authority.

"Can you confirm for us, Mrs Cox that Mr Stein had nothing to do with your planned visit to Ballindalloch?"

"You are mighty impertinent inspector! I'm here on personal business!"

Duckett withdrew from the conversation allowing Baxter to wrap up. He wouldn't want to be sued for improper conduct, knowing Americans were quick to take people to court. Yet he was dying to know what sort of business this Mrs Cox might have with the Macphersons.

"The Orient Express Company will arrange a taxi to Ballindalloch, Mrs Cox, so you can still keep your appointment."

CHAPTER 24
Friday 24 April 1896, Ballindalloch Castle, Banffshire, Scotland

Katherine lay on her four-poster bed waiting for lunch. To avoid the company of her sister-in-law, she had instructed Mary to have her meal served in her room. Victoria was on her own, as her husband was in Inverness attending a meeting to review a newly passed law on land boundaries. John was worried the revision might negatively impact the estate.

She had tried to make herself more comfortable using extra pillows propped behind her back, her knees supported by a roll cushion. A copy of the Celtic Magazine lay idle next to her. Her brother had given it to her after she'd bitterly complained of her confinement, yet the periodical failed to interest her. But then nothing did. Not even her cherished library books could offer comfort now, her mind filled with recurrent self-lashing thoughts. She felt everyone had deserted her; Mother, Alexander, Gordon and now Robert Stewart, missing at sea. William had returned to Chicago, but she had not heard from him since.

As if to protect her unborn child from her thoughts, Katherine placed her hands on the bulge beneath her stomach. The child responded by moving towards the warmth. It made Katherine cringe with remorse. Was she going to condemn her baby to a life she was eager to run away from herself? Would she, as James had predicted, regret her actions? Should she instead pick up the responsibilities and resolve what she had caused to happen entirely by her own doing? Never before had she felt so lonely. She had pleaded with John to be allowed to go to Edinburgh and visit Heather Durie, yet her brother had been relentless. There was no way she was going to be permitted to reveal her condition to the public eye. Heather was trying to support her friend as much as possible through long letters and infrequent visits. The Duries had been quite abashed when hearing of Katherine's condition. Malcolm Durie had given Katherine a stern message. Although her place at university had been secured, he now wished he had never helped her. Should the University Board ever discover her unmarried predicament, they would most certainly never allow her to enter the first semester. As it was, the Board of the University of Edinburgh held firm to their decision that women were not yet allowed to fully participate. "The days where Sophia Jex Blake and her friend Edith Pechey had been accepted only to attend part lectures have not yet passed," Malcolm Durie had explained.

After William's departure, having to stay within the walls of Ballindalloch had brought Katherine on a constant verge of panic. Their private goodbye had been tearful. The veil of their true relationship now removed, the bond that had always been there, was even stronger. Having to keep it a secret made her feel even more isolated within the family.

John had threatened the slightest misbehaviour on her side would be cause to cancel their arrangement. It had brought Katherine to a point where reason at times eluded her. The movements of her unborn child were a constant reminder of what had passed between her and Alexander. She wished she could ignore it, but felt an overwhelming urge to get her horse saddled and ride to the derelict lodge deep in the woodlands she and Alexander had used as their sanctuary, just to feel a little closer to the father of her baby.

Victoria was just as much a prisoner of the house as Katherine. To enhance the illusion the baby was hers, Victoria had also been restricted to the castle and was forbidden to attend social functions or undertake visitations. In addition, John had ensured there would be no formal events at the estate until August.

Even though bound by the same circumstances, Katherine and Victoria had passed the equator of being able to share their pain. The age gap didn't help. Over the years, Victoria had grown used to treating her husband's younger sister as a minor. Katherine was after all only ten-years old when John and Victoria married.

Katherine continued to doubt whether her brother and his wife were suited to raise her child.

At the same time, Katherine had also put her hopes on Victoria. She had seen Victoria change during the marriage. She had become careful choosing her words when addressing her husband and at times would flare up and show unexpected resilience in defending her rights. Katherine strongly suspected the reason her brother and Victoria didn't have children was due to a lack of sexual relations. For the two women to share such intimate detail would be unheard of. In an unspoken agreement they avoided getting too familiar.

Taking her own childhood as an example, Katherine anticipated it would be Donald Simpson and Mary Montgomery, who had helped raise her and her brothers, who would do most of the care taking of her child. With Katherine spending university breaks at Ballindalloch, the child would not lack affection. A knock on the door announced the arrival of lunch. To Katherine's surprise it was Simpson who brought the meal.

"Where is Mary?" Katherine asked, pushing herself from the bed to move to the small table where Donald had placed the tray.

"Thought I'd bring it to you Miss Katherine," Donald replied, "to give Mary a hand."

Simpson's remark gave Katherine a twinge of guilt.

"As usual, I'm causing all sorts of trouble Simpson. I feel for poor Mary, her having to take care of me day and night."

"Miss Katherine," Simpson blurted, "to be honest I have a personal reason for helping out."

"What is it?" she queried.

Donald took a moment, "I know it is none of my business, but I've thought long and deep and realised I am probably the only one in possession of certain information on Alexander Stewart."

Katherine had taken a seat at the small table and was now staring at Simpson, not a feature moving on her face. She feared what he had just said. Of course it had crossed her mind Simpson would have heard through Robert Stewart of Alexander's whereabouts. Donald and Robert had been very close. Simpson had to be devastated.

"I understand your concern," she said carefully, "and, believe me, I am grateful." Katherine meant what she said. Simpson and Mary were the only people remaining at Ballindalloch she could rely on. "I am not interested in anything to do with Alexander, it would not make matters more bearable."

Annoyed for not succeeding to stand up for what he felt was important, Simpson heard himself stammer, "T-this is also to help Alexander Miss Katherine. You may find what I am going to say impertinent, but I think he would want to know and do feel he should have a say in matters." Summoning up courage he added, "Especially seeing the price we all have paid for this."

Katherine uttered a deep sigh, immediately supressing the enormity of the truth. "Yes well, even though you might be right, it will not change anything. Thank you for your effort, but it has to stop here. Please take the tray. I have no appetite and want to be left alone."

"But…"

"Please Mr Simpson, let it be."

CHAPTER 25
Tuesday 11 October 2011, Ballindalloch Castle, Banffshire, Scotland

Kenneth Christie, the Macpherson family driver and odd job man around the estate, broke the tranquil silence of the drawing room where Cathy sat studying a book on Celtic ancestry. "You're needed in the library urgently."

Somewhat reluctant, Cathy uncurled herself from a comfortable leather club chair.

"What's wrong, do you know?"

Christie knew everybody's business more than anyone else on the estate. "It's a woman from New York who came in with the Royal Scotsman."

Cathy gave a deep sigh. She routinely went into hiding when the *Orient Express* excursion arrived fortnightly. She'd discovered many visitors came to view the devastated wall and to look for *her*. "I thought the tour had been cancelled, something to do with a death on the train?"

"This lady came alone by taxi," Christie said. "I believe she had an appointment."

Cathy briefly raised her eyebrows. "Do I have to go?"

"I think Mister Angus may need a hand in this case."

When Cathy stepped into the library she immediately caught the uneasy atmosphere. A spirited looking lady in her sixties, sitting at the centre table eyed her with curiosity. Angus sat opposite, looking utterly uncomfortable.

"Sorry to bother you my dear," Angus said, "but this lady insisted on meeting you. She tells me she is a relative of yours."

Cathy studied the woman's face.

"I've been dying to meet you. I've seen the report on CNN you know," the lady said in an unmistakable Brooklyn accent.

Not another one, Cathy thought.

"You certainly don't waste your time beating around the bush do you," Cathy retorted. "A relative you say?"

"Sorry," the lady replied. She got up from her chair and proffered her hand, "I'm Diane Cox and very pleased to meet you Cathy Macpherson."

Unable to hide her surprise, Cathy cried out, "You are my father's cousin!"

A short but tangible pause filled the room. Angus' unease visibly increased. "You two *do* know each other?"

"No," Diane said, her gaze still locked on Cathy, "but I did have a chat with her father before coming over the Pond, just to make sure."

"Make sure of what?" Cathy asked.

"Oh, just to clarify some family related matters. It was then I heard you were still here"

Without looking at Angus, Cathy slowly sat down on a chair beside him while continuing to observe Diane Cox. She could strongly sense Angus's discomfort. The woman had clearly come with an agenda.

"So you travelled all the way from the States to see me for yourself?" she asked, curiosity grabbing a hold of her. She was careful not to push it to far though, with Angus obviously in distress about something.

"Well to cut to the chase," Diane responded, "I have reason to believe I directly descend from this family, the Macphersons of Ballindalloch."

"Mrs Cox, I already explained," Angus cut in, "there are many Macphersons in America. Their ancestors or they themselves all came from Scotland at some time. We have Macphersons from all over the *world* visiting us," he added, making a wide gesture with his hands. "At the end of the day we are all one family."

Undeterred Diane continued, "You don't understand Mr Macpherson, I have done my homework. I have proof, *solid* proof I am a descendant of an heir to Ballindalloch, born here in 1896."

"Whom exactly are you referring to?" Cathy asked.

Before answering, Diane turned to Angus first. "Her father," she said, pointing her thumb at Cathy, "also has the same family line. That puts *her* in the same position as me."

"Answer Catherine's question please!" Angus said impatiently.

"Alexandra Macpherson, the daughter of a John and Victoria Macpherson. I believe John was the boss of Ballindalloch at one time?"

Angus rolled his eyes. "The word you are looking for is *laird.*"

Diane now turned to Cathy.

"Until we did our research, I could only recall vague stories from my parents of how our family originally came from Scotland. But I watched the images on television of *you,* Cathy, and what you had done here. It was the Ballindalloch name I recognised."

Angus and Cathy sat quiet, both for their own reasons.

"We started with known descendants in the States. You know it saddens me how over the years I never realised I wasn't taking the time to discuss family history with parents, grandparents, aunts, uncles and so on. Now I do not even have a brother or sister to go to."

Cathy gave a wry smile. She could relate to the woman's regret. Angus glanced at his watch. "Mrs Cox, please would you get to the point."

"Where was I? Oh yes, we found the birth certificate of my grandfather Edward, or as he was known Eddie Macpherson. That led us to where our American roots began. Edward's mother, Alexandra Macpherson, was born in 1896, in this place, maybe even in this very room."

Angus exuded a tired sigh, disgusted at the thought. "Who is 'we'?" he asked.

It took a moment for Diane to fathom Angus's question. "Oh, my son and I did the research. He can be quite the amateur sleuth. We managed to find Alexandra's birth certificate without too much difficulty. Scotland has wonderful genealogy databases, all online as well. My friend Dawn and I are going to the National Archives building in Edinburgh as part of our holiday."

Cathy remained silent, recalling the recent phone call with her father. So far she hadn't heard anything new.

"When Alexandra's father, a certain John Macpherson died, the estate should have been passed on to his eldest child, right?" Diane paused and stared at Angus, who just shrugged his shoulders. "What I want to know," Diane continued, "is why a young woman in 1917, who was heir to a Scottish estate, would trade in that life to become a single mother in Hollywood."

Angus frowned, "Are you sure it's one and the same person?"

"You're darn right I am, why do you think I came all this way?" Diane produced a letter size paper from the small backpack beside her chair and handed it to Cathy. "This is a copy of the birth certificate of Alexandra's son Edward, my grandfather and *your* great-grandfather."

Cathy stared at the birth certificate. It was identical to the copy her father had emailed.

"It was tricky to find. As you can see, he was registered as *Charles* Edward," Diane said.

"Let me see," Angus said, waving his hand impatiently.

As Angus ogled the document, Diane casually added, "From what I've learned, Alexandra was quite a well-known actress. Even did a movie with Lillian Gish, a famous silent movie actress in those days. Her profession might explain why an uncle who lived in your hometown, Raleigh, North Carolina, raised her son. This uncle was also born at Ballindalloch. I have a copy of *his* birth certificate as well, a James Macpherson. In fact I even have James Macpherson and his family, listed on the 1920 Census. It shows Edward, listed as *son*, age three and *that* matches the year of his birth. Eddie had been adopted."

Diane Cox handed Cathy a small bundle of documents. "You will find Alexandra's death certificate among this lot detailing her parentage. Poor girl, gave her baby away, never married and died comparatively young." Diane smirked, "It's quite conclusive!"

"Proving what?" Cathy clipped.

"You are here for a reason."

"Excuse me?" Cathy said, raising her voice starting to feel annoyed with the insolence of the woman.

"After I called your father, I figured you may well have made the same discovery as we did, which is what brought you to Scotland. As I said earlier, we both descend from Alexandra *and* I have pictures."

"What pictures?" Cathy and Angus asked in chorus.

Carefully Diane picked her leather bound photo book out of her bag. "These photographs, they belonged to my mother. When she died they were among the few things I made sure I inherited. As a child, I would spend hours looking at them, fascinated by the idea my ancestors lived in a castle. It made me feel as if I were a princess." Diane smiled melancholically for a brief moment before adding in a smug tone, "And then, years later I see the castle on television."

Cathy parked the array of questions overwhelming her and forced herself to listen.

"My grandfather Edward must have given them to my mother. I suspect *he* in turn inherited them from *his* mother, who we now know was Alexandra. I simply never queried who my grandfather's mother was. Until now that is."

Again, Cathy could relate to Diane's train of thought.

"There are quite a few snapshots of the Ballindalloch Castle and grounds," Diane said, opening the picture book. "Here is my great-grandmother when she was a child standing by a river with a young lady. I'd say you resemble her," Diane remarked looking at Cathy. "Have a look."

It was all too familiar for Cathy. John had given her the exact same picture in August. He had told her the child was the niece of Katherine Macpherson, posing with her on the banks of the River Spey. Deciding not to give anything away, Cathy diverted the subject. "I have heard of the actress Lillian Gish, but never one called Alexandra Macpherson."

"Oh you wouldn't have," Diane replied. "She worked under a stage name, Alexis Stewart."

CHAPTER 26
Thursday 23 July 1896, Ballindalloch Castle, Banffshire, Scotland

"It's a what?" shouted Laird John Macpherson.

His wife Victoria had found John in the study writing a letter to his bank in Inverness. He had tossed the pen on the desk, splattering ink over the paper.

"Yes dear, Katherine has had a girl. Both the child and Katherine are well."

John stood up and walked slowly towards his wife. "This changes everything. My God! A girl! Victoria, do you not understand? Please tell me you are not as thick as the walls of this house."

Victoria's eyes filled with tears. "Don't you dare talk to me in that manner! I am your wife, no matter what." She lifted the skirt of her gown slightly and made for the door. On an afterthought she turned. "Didn't you ever consider it might be a girl? If not, you are the one who lacks any intelligence. It is after all a one in two chance, my dear husband."

Victoria slammed the door leaving John to simmer.

***

"How are you Katie?" asked John. Katherine was propped up in bed by an abundance of pillows. The drapes were open, allowing the sunlight to spill into the room. It was a bright morning, the temperature being cooled by the highland breeze.

"I feel a little weak, but I hope to be riding by Saturday again. Can't wait to get out of here," Katherine said, trying to hide the conflicting emotions her brother's presence summoned. Holding her baby girl for the first time had thrown her into turmoil.

John didn't know what to say next. "Can I get you anything, tea or lemonade anything at all?"

Katherine braved her anxiety. "John I think we should talk. I know you wanted a male heir."

"I admit I am disappointed."

Tears rolled down Katherine's cheeks. "John she is a beautiful baby. Promise me you will love her the way I do and will never deny her rights. She *will* make a fine laird one day."

"Katherine please, you must consider my position in all of this." John tried to take Katherine's hand but found her pulling away.

"Brother we cannot change anything! It's too late. What is done is done. Alexandra will be a wonderful lady, a daughter who will bring

100

pride to our family. God! If ever a family needs pride it's ours. You and Victoria had better be the most upright parents ever to walk on Ballindalloch land." Katherine wiped away her tears. "*You* have tasks to do now John; a formal announcement, register the birth and you'd better inform the family and your acquaintances. Oh and don't forget to send a telegram to Uncle William and James, they will be anxious to hear the news."

John avoided the fiery expression on his sister's face. "I hear you named her Alexandra," he said. "Isn't that a bit obvious? It could well stimulate gossip."

"It was agreed I could name my baby and it will be Alexandra. From this point onward, I want to know I can entrust her in your care." John stared into space for a few moments and said, "Alexandra will be looked after well and I despair you would ever think otherwise. I hope you find what you are looking for Katherine." He walked away. As he stood outside the bedroom door, he could hear Katherine sob. He wondered if they had made the biggest mistake of their lives.

CHAPTER 27
Tuesday 11 October 2011, Ballindalloch Castle, Banffshire, Scotland

"I'm done with this," Angus cried out impatiently. The atmosphere in the library with Angus, Cathy and their American visitor from the Royal Scotsman had turned tense. "Mrs Cox, I appreciate your concern for the integrity of your ancestry, but I'm sure our family handled whatever it was that happened with the utmost diligence. I will inform our lawyer and contact my son, John Macpherson. The Waddell firm has been looking after us for generations, I'm sure they will be able to shed light on this matter."

Cathy's mind flashed back to when she first arrived at the castle. Angus had provided all genealogy information willingly in this room.

"This concludes our meeting for now," Angus said, pushing away from the table. "I cannot help you further at this stage."

"It's not money or the estate I'm after if that's what you're thinking," Diane offered. "Put yourself in my shoes! What would you do?"

The phone rang and drew everyone's attention. Thankful for the distraction, Angus immediately picked it up. It was the Administration Office switching an urgent call from Glen Fraoch Distillery. Angus visibly blanched. Alarmed, Cathy watched Angus reach in his pocket, and produce a little plastic pill container. Squeezing the phone between his cheek and shoulder he used both hands to retrieve a pill and tossed it in his mouth.

"I think you'd better go Mrs Cox," Cathy said.

Confused Diane stood up. Her initial confidence diminished. "But when will I hear from you again? I'm only here for three weeks. In truth it was the main reason for booking this vacation."

"I understand and I'm sure Mr Macpherson will handle this to the best of his knowledge. Believe me, he has done the same for me, but right now you need to leave."

Before Cathy could usher Diane out of the library, Angus hung up the phone.

"It's Doug Stein," he said, staring wide-eyed at Cathy. "Found dead on the Royal Scotsman."

"He was my neighbour on the train," Diane cried out. "He was the reason I was late for my appointment. The police questioned me."

Pale and shivering, Angus slowly sat on the sofa. "Get that woman a taxi," was all he could produce.

CHAPTER 28
Wednesday 12 October 2011, Ballindalloch Castle, Banffshire, Scotland

"I knew him well Catherine," Angus said with sad eyes. It was the morning after Diane Cox's visit. Cathy and Angus were seated on a sofa in the drawing-room overlooking the grounds. From the window, cattle could be seen grazing in the distance. "We often met up, mainly at whisky events. Our family has major investments in the industry. He was as much a friend as he was a business colleague. In fact, I am his executor, not a task I am looking forward to. Didn't I introduce you to Doug at Gordon's funeral? He was with the Grants. We all came back here for drinks after the service in this room. My sons were here as well.

"I didn't join you guys, remember? When I got back I went straight to my room."

"Oh right, I forgot," Angus replied, annoyed by his confusion.

It concerned Cathy to see how upset he was.

Angus sighed. "Perhaps it was a heart attack. Doug was under a lot of stress. Glen Fraoch is a private company and facing some challenges. Doug mentioned some Ukrainian conglomerate had been offering staggering money to him and his shareholders in an attempt to buy them out. He kept refusing, but was concerned other stockholders would indeed sell. He was proud of Glen Fraoch's history and wanted to make sure it remained Scottish. I wonder what will happen now."

"Have you talked to the family?"

"Doug didn't have any. He was an only child and his parents died a long time ago. From what I know, over the years he has been in a few relationships but never married. There are no siblings I'm aware of. The lawyers will have to sort it out."

Cathy felt tired. She yawned, closed her eyes and leaned her head back on the sofa they shared. Angus gave her a sympathetic look.

"All this must be tedious for you Catherine."

Not opening her eyes Cathy just smiled. The discovery of her family's connection to Gordon had shaken her more than she cared to admit. It was surreal. The coincidence of how her family roots and her husband David's, seemed to be connected, was also mind blowing. Yesterday's meeting with Diane Cox had sparked the unanswered questions even more. Last night she had shared her findings in a phone call with her father, but nobody else, yet. "It's a lot to take in over a short period of time Angus."

Cathy had laboured into the small hours of the morning, the Macpherson family tree documents scattered on her bed. She searched the web for 'Alexis Stewart' and using Wikipedia, she uncovered; details of her movie career, her birth shown as 1896, Scotland, her parents John and Victoria Macpherson, Scotland, her death in 1934, age thirty-eight. No spouse was listed. Following Diane's trail of thoughts, Cathy wondered when Alexandra had left Scotland and more importantly why?

Cathy also checked ship's passenger lists to try and find out when Alexandra moved to the States and who she might have been travelling with. Not having a precise year or exact location, hundreds of Macphersons and Stewarts were displayed. Would she have sailed during the war years 1914 to 1918? Too fucking difficult! She searched census records in California and the Carolinas but had found nothing. The family tree of the Ballindalloch Macphersons hadn't given away anything on Alexandra's life either. It mentioned no spouse or children. Diane indeed had done her homework, and more. Cathy wondered how John was going to deal with the woman's questions.

Snapping herself out of her doze Cathy sat up. "I'm sorry Angus I don't know what came over me. Can I ask you something?"

"Ask away my dear. What is it?"

"Your father, according to the family tree, was also called Angus right?"

"Yes, why do you ask?"

"Well, you told me once about the 'president to president' concept, you know passing on family confidentialities from one laird to the other, but did you actually enjoy a good father and son relationship? I mean did he confide in any personal matters? You know maybe involving *his* father or his wife's parents?"

Angus thought carefully before answering. "No, but what I will say is my father adored my wife. She was the organiser of the household. You have probably noticed I am not the most methodical person and I miss my wife's support and love. I loved my parents, but my father was the one who was quite distant, not just with me, but the whole family." Angus dropped his voice. "You are being diplomatic for a change aren't you? What you want to know is if I was aware of Gordon's tragedy and if my father knew and all the previous lairds."

Cathy gave a wry smile. "Go on, don't let me stop you." She was in fact unsure what she wanted to hear. The phenomenon of naming children after their parents kept ringing in her head.

"I know Thomas told you his story, so you must know his father, Donald Macpherson, who was the laird at the time, knew what Thomas uncovered," Angus said, feeling comfortable, pleased even, to be talking to Cathy. "Donald died just before the end of the war. *His* younger brother, Alistair Macpherson became laird as Thomas was only fourteen. When *Alistair* died, the title was passed on to my father Angus, even though Thomas, or Uncle T as you call him, was old enough by then to take on the lairdship. He was after all the oldest son of the former laird, but Thomas declined, preferring his life in the military over staying at home farming cows and fishing salmon."

"So your father was never officially told?"

Angus smiled at her terminology. "Not *officially*, but he certainly knew for he told me, on a dreich day while he and I were out hunting and took a rest at Lagmore stone circle."

"That's what you tried to tell me on the day of the clan gathering," Cathy said, remembering how nervous Angus had been.

"Yes my dear, a delicate subject. I could hardly believe it at the time. It certainly changed my aspirations of being laird. My father never revealed his source though. It wasn't Thomas, I know *that* much. Thomas and I discussed it years later when I was laird."

Cathy smiled benevolently. "So how do you think your father knew?"

"Catherine I can only guess. Maybe through his uncle, *Donald,* Angus emphasised in the effort to help Cathy keep track of the names. Anyway my dear, until you came along, this was all hidden in the past. I thought differently for a while, but let me say again, you did the right thing uncovering Gordon's remains, so you need never worry your pretty head."

"I am just amazed Angus, the police authorities at the time did not discover what happened. According to the tree, Gordon had six children. Wouldn't they or the staff at the time have checked the tunnel?"

"I wouldn't know, I wasn't there was I?" Angus said jovially. "Maybe the family and the police were in some kind of conspiracy."

Cathy looked at Angus knowingly. "Mm … maybe, who knows? It could well be that the jewellery Uncle T found beside Gordon's body in 1940, were the jewels Alexander Stewart was accused of stealing. Do you think it is likely they all knew?"

"Maybe they did Catherine, but my dear it's something we will never know. The jewels were never seen again anyway, which is a shame. They'd be worth a small fortune today."

Cathy chuckled. "Thank you for your trust Angus, and the reassurance. To this day I still don't know *what* I was thinking. By the way, does John or any of your sons know?"

"At some point we need to let go Catherine. So the answer is no, and I trust this conversation will stay strictly between us."

"You betcha! No need for concern there," Cathy said, glancing at her watch. "I have an appointment this morning in Elgin with Iain Macbeth, the curator you recommended."

"I don't think you will discover anything new on your Macpherson ancestry in Elgin Catherine. You know what? Maybe another talk with Maggie would throw some light. After all, she did put you on Alexander's trail."

Cathy smiled at the memory of Maggie and her twin sister Euphemia whom she first met the night she arrived at Ballindalloch. "Do you have Maggie's contact details so I can give her a call?"

"I'll get you the details."

"Okay thanks, now I need to get out of here to clear my head."

Angus said, "I'd better call James Grant and Peter." He sighed, "Poor Doug!"

While checking to see if her bag held all the information she needed, Cathy casually asked, "Where is Uncle T, do you know?"

"He is in Perth for a few days, for what I do not know. He can be such a secretive man."

Touché, thought Cathy.

***

Cathy was humming to the music on the radio, as she drove out of the parking lot of the Elgin Family History Centre. She was now more confident driving on the wrong side of the road. Using John's Ford Focus, she made her way home via the scenic route. She enjoyed exploring the region. It also allowed her thinking time. As predicted, the meeting with Mr Macbeth had proved fruitless. The picture of Katherine Macpherson in the Grantown Museum and the silver 'DCL Chicago' pencil nagged at her. She made up her mind to call John and arrange a visit to Edinburgh.

Eight miles from Elgin, a road sign caught her attention; 'Glen Fraoch Distillery' and in smaller letters underneath; 'Luxury quality single malt.'

The name rang a bell. *Doug Stein's!* On a hunch Cathy took the turn. The buildings of the distillery were simply styled from earlier times. The grey stone walls although dank, sparkled in the morning light. Two tall chimneys towered from the main building. The courtyard held five parked cars. Cathy pulled into a visitor's slot. A plaque outside the main entrance was displayed;

Glen Fraoch Whisky

We have the slowest distillation process in Scotland preparing the perfect casks, before they receive their first drop of spirit. Our whisky matures for at least 15 to 20 years before it reaches our customers. Glen Fraoch gives you pause to reflect when investing valuable time and infinite care, you can create something of real worth.

"Afternoon," a voice greeted, when Cathy stepped into a small reception area. A desk and a wide cupboard against the back wall were packed with bottles of whisky, many in presentation cartons. A young man in his twenties wearing jeans and a black fleece sweater took his time studying Cathy. He seemed to enjoy the experience.

"Can I help you?" he asked.

"I'm just having a browse. I saw the road sign for the distillery and thought I'd have a look. I might just buy a bottle," she said, thinking of a gift for John. "I recognised the name of the distillery. I'm staying close to Boat of Garten and know someone who was a good friend of your boss."

"Mr Stein," the lad answered, "It was such a shock for everyone here."

Cathy continued inspecting the whisky offering. "Have you worked here long?"

"Seven years come January. Most of my family have worked here over the years."

She gave him a friendly glance. "You don't look old enough. Sorry what was your name again?"

The lad was taken by Cathy's presence. "I'm Craig, pleased to meet you."

"I'm Cathy. Seven years is a long time Craig. They must pay well here."

"Aye, we do all right."

Inspecting a bottle closely, Cathy asked, "Where did Mr Stein live?"

"Elgin, I've been at his house a few times. I still cannot take it all in. It's been a disastrous few months all in all."

"How's that?"

"First of all we had an unexpected production shutdown a couple of months ago. In my time, it's never happened before!"

"What caused it?"

"A maintenance issue," he said, with a hint of sarcasm, "was the management statement. Oh and we had a fire in the loading bay just around the same time. Electrical fault we were told."

Cathy handed him a bottle. "I'll take this one please. Who is the chief engineer, the person responsible for maintenance?" She handed Craig forty pounds. "Keep the change."

"Thanks. He is quite new. Only joined the company …"

"Who wants to know?" asked an attractive woman, who stood in the doorway. She was tall, slim and dressed in a dark blue trouser suit, silk blouse and wore heels. Are you with the police or a reporter?"

Cathy looked at Craig who was clearly embarrassed and responded, "Yes, I'm a police officer, but I'll come back at a more convenient time." She brushed past the woman on the way out.

"You do that," the woman snapped. She turned to Craig, "Can we have a wee chat?"

Craig looked outside to watch Cathy climb into her car. *I know her face.*

From where, he couldn't remember.

CHAPTER 29
Wednesday 12 October 2011, Morayshire, Scotland

Peter Duckett and Shona Boyd were enroute to Glen Fraoch Distillery. Since the early hours, they had been in Bishopmill, a northern suburb of Elgin. Boyd was driving a Mercedes C-Class Saloon. The sergeant felt uncomfortable with her boss being unusually quiet.

"If there is one distillery in this area Guv, there must be twenty," she said, trying to break the silence.

Duckett remained staring out the window, "Aye, I suppose."

They took a turn at the Glen Fraoch road sign. Boyd slowed the car over the speedbumps towards the carpark. As she switched off the engine and released her seat belt Duckett said, "Let me take the lead Shona, but don't be shy if you think I miss something." Duckett was fond of Shona Boyd. She was going to be an outstanding officer, unless she married the arsehole she had been dating for the past eighteen months.

Their morning at Bishopmill had been close to a waste of time. Duckett had a warrant to enter and search the home of Doug Stein. The modest detached house on Kennedy Place displayed nothing of interest. Each room in the house was immaculate and everything appeared to be in its proper place. Framed pictures decorated the walls of the lounge, bedroom and study, including a black and white picture of a couple Duckett assumed were Stein's parents. The other pictures were of large groups attending gala events. Shona had checked the back garden, garage and Stein's parked Jaguar XF. Nothing of interest was found. Both officers had searched the study; a tidy desk top, each drawer organised; stationery, envelopes, some Glen Fraoch branded glasses. Shona had opened a three-drawer filing cabinet, using the keys found on Mr Stein's person. The bottom drawer contained documents and marketing brochures relating to the distillery. The other held domestic bills, maintenance agreements, bank and credit card statements and other personal papers. Among them Duckett had found a folder containing Stein's last will and testament. He had noticed it was dated May 2009 and confiscated it to read later.

The police officers also talked to neighbours. They tried the houses on either side of the Stein property and two directly across the street. Only two of the four houses had been occupied; an elderly couple and a housewife whose young daughter constantly interrupted the interview. All were consistent in their answers though. Mr Stein had been a private gentleman with few visitors who rarely accepted invitations to street events such as the annual summer barbeque. Their relationship was an occasional chat, when meeting in the street.

"Not exactly a socialite," Boyd had commented to her chief.

"Probably due to his work," Duckett speculated. "He would be with people day and night in the office, travelling and attending all sorts of commercial events. He probably needed some kind of escape."

Duckett scampered with Boyd from the distillery car park to the reception lobby. "I swear there is snow in the air," he muttered looking at the sky.

The receptionist greeted them, Gloria as it said on her name tag, a smartly dressed young woman. She had been expecting the officers. "You two should have coats on. You'll catch your death out there."

Boyd thought Gloria's skirt was too short and noticed her top stopped short, exposing her navel.

Before either could respond the door opened and Angus Macpherson walked in. "My goodness," the laird uttered, "we meet again."

Duckett was surprised to see the laird. "Indeed Mr Macpherson. What brings you to Glen Fraoch?"

Angus sighed, "My inspector, you always have so many questions. I haven't even taken my coat off yet. You must be here to do with Doug's death I take it?"

"We are. This is my colleague Sergeant Shona Boyd."

Angus simply nodded as he gave Shona a quick glance.

"Can you spare a few minutes Mr Macpherson?" Duckett ventured.

"I do have an appointment, but if you insist."

Gloria, eavesdropping, mentioned the small meeting room near the reception was vacant. They all entered and Boyd closed the door.

They all sat around a small circular table. "I have a meeting in…," Duckett glanced at his watch, "in ten minutes, so I won't take up much of your time." Arching his eyebrows, he went on, "May I inquire as to the purpose of your visit Mr Macpherson?"

Angus gripping his coat over his lap reluctantly answered, "I am the executor of Doug Stein's estate and I have an appointment with the company lawyer as I need to establish a meeting schedule with the Board over the coming weeks. It will be my responsibility to make sure Doug's wishes are not compromised in any way."

Duckett thought of the unread will in his possession. "If you are the executor you must have known Mr Stein for some time."

"I did indeed inspector."

Duckett turned to his sergeant, "Shona, can you fix up a meeting with Mr Macpherson when we have more time?" Turning back to Angus he asked, "Are you on the Board?"

"Good grief inspector, no I am not. I told you I am …"

"Do you have personal interest in what will now happen to the company?" asked Duckett.

Boyd squirmed in her seat, feeling uncomfortable at her chief's tone.

"Are you trying to wind me up inspector? My family have absolutely no involvement in Glen Fraoch or stand to have any personal gain from Doug's death." Once again, Angus realised how he disliked Duckett. "You might have ten minutes," he blurted, "but I am already running late. Good day to you both."

***

The boardroom on the second floor was comfortable and spacious. It held a conference table surrounded by ten seats, each place equipped with a water glass on a company coaster, together with a notepad and pen. Full-length windows overlooked the courtyard providing a pleasant view of the countryside. The police officers waited in silence, Duckett doodling on a notepad.

"Good afternoon." A middle-aged gentleman dressed in a smart suit walked into the room. Duckett and Boyd stood up. "I am Anthony Edwards, Company Secretary." The man was clearly English. Shaking hands, Peter made the rest of the introductions.

As they sat, Edwards opened, "Shocking business, I still cannot believe Doug has gone."

"I am sure all the employees feel the same Mr Edwards," Boyd said. "We just want to ask a few questions about Mr Stein and the company."

"Of course, I am only too happy to help. Our company lawyer will join us. She is busy in another meeting right now, but will be here as soon as she can."

"No problem, but can we start now?" Duckett asked. Edwards nodded. "Mr Stein owned fifty-one percent of the company stock. Can you provide us with the details of all the board members and their shareholding?"

Surprised by the question, Edwards cleared his throat. "Well there is Mr Peter Grant. He is CEO of Grant's ..."

"I know the Grants," said Duckett. *The Macphersons of Ballindalloch and the Grants are as 'thick as thieves'.* "So what investment has Grant made?"

"The board members with the exception of Mr Stein and one, other have a five percent holding."

"Who else has a similar stake?" asked Duckett.

"Stuart McBride of Glenfarclas and Iain Cuthbert. Iain is the Chairman of the Scottish Whisky Society."

The names were not familiar to Duckett or Boyd.

"And we have Margaret Burns," Edwards added.

"The novelist?" asked Shona. "She made a fortune Guv from her crime books. She lives in Elgin."

"Margaret is also an entrepreneur and a fine ambassador for our industry," Edwards supplemented.

Duckett, who only read newspapers, stared at the Englishman and asked, "Who else is on the board?"

"Sean McCarley, our Vice Chairman. He is an Irishman from County Antrim. He is an expert on environmental studies."

"What of the Macphersons at Ballindalloch? Do they have any involvement in Glen Fraoch?"

Edwards cast a puzzled look. "In the business none whatsoever, however, Mr Angus Macpherson is Doug's executor."

Boyd looked at her boss and frowned.

"Never mind leave it for now," Duckett murmured.

"When you own five percent stock or more, one is entitled to sit on the board," Edwards continued. "We do have a twenty percent stakeholder in Glen Fraoch. The Broadside Holding Company, represented by Mr Walter Brodie."

"Can I have the contact details of all the board members please?" asked Duckett.

Before Edwards could answer, a woman entered the room. Being tall, her smart black trouser suit enhanced a slim athletic build. Her glasses were perched on top of her forehead "I am Ann White, White with an 'I'. I'm the company legal advisor. I am sorry about the delay," she offered in a scholarly manner. "Prior appointment I'm afraid." She placed her briefcase on the table and shook hands with the officers.

Using his notes, Duckett outlined what they had already covered with Edwards and asked, "How well did you two know Doug Stein? Not as the boss but as a person, his private life."

Ann was first to answer. "He was almost a recluse outside of work. I have been with the company for almost four years and to be honest, Doug just lived and breathed work. Didn't he Tony?"

Edwards agreed and added, "His grandfather founded Glen Fraoch you know. Doug was paranoid on building the business and preserving the heritage."

"Was there anyone in the company he was particularly close to?" Sergeant Boyd asked.

"Why all the personal questions?" queried White. "Are there suspicious circumstances at play?"

"We believe it may well be the case Mrs White," Duckett said firmly.

White paled and looked at Edwards before addressing Duckett. "My God! What happened inspector?"

"I am not at liberty to divulge anything at this stage, as it could prejudice the investigation. Can you please answer the sergeant's question?"

"No inspector, not to my knowledge," responded Edwards. "I'm not aware of anyone special. He treated everyone pretty much the same."

Duckett sighed. "From what we've learned so far, offers have been submitted over the past year or so, to buy-out Glen Fraoch. It seems Mr Stein was unhappy with one particular company."

"Yes," agreed the lawyer, "Grabowski, a Ukraine based outfit. They represent many clients in Eastern Europe."

"Who was the client they were representing in this case?" asked Duckett.

"We have no idea. Without any hesitation Doug and the other board members rejected the offer. Walter Brodie was the exception. He suggested we should at least have some dialogue as they could well be a good contact for other aspects of the business. You see inspector; major investment is required here. Maybe you can comment Tony?"

Edwards took time to explain the company's need to grow. A significant cash injection was required to fund new stills and expanded raw material inventory storage.

"I should add inspector, the company constitution clearly outlines Glen Fraoch must remain British. Even to the point if we were bought by a British company the clause would carry over."

"The new owner could not sell out to a foreign company?" asked Boyd.

"Correct," White confirmed.

"So Grabowski were wasting their time?" asked Boyd.

"To acquire full ownership, yes. Doug owns, or should I say owned fifty-one percent. There would be no barriers to Grabowski trying to buy as much as they could of the remaining stock." White continued, "I will get you a copy of the constitution before you leave."

Boyd leaned forward. "You would think Grabowski would have been aware of the clause?"

Ann answered, "I have no idea sergeant. All I know is that I drew up the papers, responding to both offers made in the past year. There was no legal requirement to mention the clause, so I didn't."

"You said Walter," Duckett looked at his notes, "Brodie was keen to find out more on the Grabowski offer?"

"Oh yes," Edwards replied. "Broadside would make a fortune."

"Why not just sell their twenty percent to Grabowski?" Duckett asked.

"It was not the basis of the offer. They wanted a minimum of fifty-one percent," replied White.

"Well, if I was Brodie and wanted to make a bundle of cash I would have contacted Grabowski and offer them the Broadside stock. At least they would get a seat on the board. Don't you think?"

"You'll have to ask Walter," Edwards cut in.

Duckett remained silent as he continued jotting notes.

"What will happen to Mr Stein's stock?" Boyd queried.

Ann White cleared her throat. "I am working flat out to establish a Board of Trustees who will manage the business. Doug had no family."

"I need you to provide the details of trustees when appointed Mrs White," requested Duckett.

"Of course inspector but it's going to take some considerable time. By the way, it is Miss."

"Anything out of the ordinary occurred in the past, say twelve months?" a stone-faced Duckett asked.

"Out of the ordinary?" asked Edwards.

"Yes, at the distillery or from a commercial perspective."

The lawyer smiled. "Don't you talk to your colleague inspector?"

"Excuse me? What do you mean?" asked a perplexed Duckett.

"Your colleague was here earlier, an attractive woman with an undoubted American accent. She was snooping around the shop charming young Craig with all sorts of questions."

Duckett was speechless, his surprise obvious.

"She left rather abruptly when I interrupted their chat."

Boyd turned to her boss, "I think it's time to have a natural break Guv."

***

Duckett's mood changed for the worse after hearing Cathy Stewart had been sniffing around the distillery. Back in the boardroom with Edwards and White, he was extremely irritable.

"Before we start, here is a copy of the constitution I promised." White handed Peter a document dated 1998. The clause regarding British ownership was on the first page. Duckett read the details and noticed a small print addendum.

"Thanks." He pushed the document to Boyd. "I asked you earlier if there had been any unusual events in the past year or so."

Anthony Edwards leaned back in his chair. "Two things come to mind. In the past four months we have lost a few major customers in Europe and India. Our agents could not come up with any solid reasons why they dropped us, they just did. I can provide you with the details."

"How many accounts is a 'few'?"

"Seven to be precise; two of them are Indian."

"You said two things?"

Edwards clearly was concentrating on how best to structure his response. "We had to shut down production during late August, water contamination. We've never had any incident of this type before. Doug was horrified, all of us were. Water is a vital resource of our product as I'm sure you are aware."

"Where do you get your water from?" asked Boyd.

"We draw from tributaries of the River Lossie for malting, mashing and reducing the alcoholic strength. We also draw a lot of water from the river for coolant purposes. You know, condensers, in the still house. But Officer Boyd it had nothing to do with our problem."

"I don't understand Mr Edwards. What do you mean?"

Edwards looked at Ann for support. She leaned forward and said, "The contamination was from *inside* the distillery. Our scientist calls it 'turbidity' caused by fine insoluble materials. The presence of iron was found in our plumbing inspector, similar to problems of many years ago, when we used cast iron mains. It was baffling."

"Sabotage?" Duckett asked.

Both Edwards and White flinched. "I'm sure it was inspector," Edwards responded, "The problem has not recurred. Doug insisted we told the employees it was a maintenance issue and to say no more."

"Was there any sign of a forced entry prior to you discovering the contamination?" asked Duckett.

"Not to my knowledge. Ann, did you hear of any break in?"

The lawyer just shook her head.

"Well thank you for your time. By the way we will return Mr Stein's computer and mobile as soon as possible." Duckett glanced at his colleague, "Any further questions Shona?"

"Only one more request. Please provide us with a complete list of all employees; date they joined the company, references, their job descriptions and so on. Also please supply a similar list of employees who have left the company in the past six months and the reason for leaving. The same applies for contractors and the name of their employer."

"Especially any people who left the company shortly after the water incident," Duckett said. "One last question, was Mr Stein a religious man?"

Edwards without hesitation replied, "Oh yes, he worshipped at Saint Sylvester's in Elgin. It's on Institution Road. Doug was a devout Catholic."

"Thanks, we will be in touch."

CHAPTER 30
Wednesday 12 October 2011, Glen Fraoch Distillery, Morayshire

Duckett clicked on his seatbelt and started the car. "Shona, we're going back to Elgin to speak to the priest. You never know what Stein might have told him in confidence." As Duckett manoeuvred his way out of the car park he commented, "Quite a productive discussion with Edwards and White.""Definitely boss. The water issue was deliberate for sure, an inside job. It could have been an employee who was royally pissed off for some reason.""Have a look at the constitution. Read the addendum below the statement on staying British." As they made their way, Shona read the opening page.

"Now *that* is interesting. The clause can only be revoked if Glen Fraoch *is* threatened by administration or liquidation."

Duckett seemed pleased. "I do believe we are close to finding a motive Shona. Lost customers in Europe and India, water contamination, the leader dead; Christ the company is going to be run by trustees, who will never have the passion, drive and commitment of Stein. Shona, this smells of some Ukrainian Mafia hit. Make life hell for Glen Fraoch and over time, bring them down." The DI paused and added, "Paid cash for his train ticket as well. Who the fuck buys a ticket costing thousands of pounds using notes Shona? Not Doug Stein."

Boyd leaned back and stretched her legs. "Circumstantial as it may be Guv, I bet you a pound to a penny an employee or contractor hasn't been seen since the water incident."

"I agree. Let's go through the motions and contact the other board members and get their take on events. The shit will hit the fan tomorrow morning when the media report Doug Stein was murdered. This is way over my head. Let's try and find the priest. When we get back to the station you prepare the report and we let the chiefs and Interpol get on with it."

Shona looked out the passenger side window. "Can I ask you a personal question sir?"

Duckett laughed out loud. "*Sir* she says, this must be a good one. Go on, spit it out."

Boyd faced her boss with a stern look. "Why do you have a hang up with the Macphersons? The way you pulled the laird into the meeting room and asking Edwards and White if the Macphersons are on the board of Glen Fraoch. I could see the confused look on their faces."

"Shona, it's just a hunch the Macpherson family are not what they seem. But you are right. Your reprimand is justified."

There was an awkward silence in the car. Shona broke the atmosphere. "You ought to find yourself a woman Peter and get laid. I bet *Miss* Ann White would oblige. Or even better Mrs Stewart she's a stunner you must admit."

Peter grinned at Shona. He knew she had once again hit the nail on the head. "Aye well maybe you are right, but Mrs Stewart is not my type Shona," he lied.

"By the way, maybe one of us should interview Craig, you know the lad in the distillery shop."

"No, I am not going to encourage Mrs Stewart's interference."

"Then what *are* you going to do?"

Duckett smiled. "You leave Cathy Stewart to me."

***

Saint Sylvester's Church was set back on a quiet residential street, a short distance south of Elgin town centre, a grand sandstone building with a slated roof. The wooden double doors were open.

As both officers approached the church, a middle aged man appeared in the doorway dressed in jeans, a woollen jumper and wellingtons.

"Good afternoon," he said, inspecting the visitors thoroughly. "I take it this is not a courtesy call?"

"Correct, we're police officers. Do you know if the chaplain is around?"

"You are looking at him. I'm Father Thomas Reagan. And you are?"

Duckett made the introductions and the priest asked, "May I see your ID's please? I believe it's what one should ask?"

The officers smiled and duly obliged. "We are conducting an investigation into the death of Mr Doug Stein," Duckett opened. "We believe he was a member of your church."

"Come inside," the priest offered solemnly. Father Reagan closed the doors and gestured for them to sit on the vestibule chairs. "What a sad loss. He was a good living person, but troubled these past few months. Mr Stein was also a generous man. He was a major contributor in the building of the sacristy and meeting rooms in 2000."

"So you have known him for a long time?" asked Boyd.

"Oh yes, I would guess around fifteen years."

"You said he was troubled, in what way?" Duckett queried, as he made his notes.

The priest took some time before answering. "When I heard Mr Stein had passed away, I couldn't help reflecting on our conversation some weeks ago. He looked extremely stressed. Did he contact you?"

"We are from the Grantown Constabulary," commented Boyd.

Father Reagan looked pensive. "Maybe he called the Elgin Police."

"Why would he want the Police?"

The clergyman leaned forward. "I don't really know. He told me he had some serious problems at work. I asked him what kind of problems. He muttered a bit on not knowing what to do and was considering going to the police. I asked if he wanted to tell me more but he seemed anxious to leave."

"Did he have any friends at the church, maybe someone he sat beside?" Boyd asked.

"No, and to be honest he wasn't a regular. He travelled a lot you see. Why are you conducting an investigation?"

"It is routine for all sudden deaths Father. Thank you for your time." Peter handed him a card. "Call us if you think of anything else. Shona, call Elgin and check if Stein contacted them."

The priest opened the doors and they all stepped outside.

"I apologise for my appearance. We have a gardener, but I help when I can. I like to think I'm green fingered."

Watching Shona pace up and down making her call, Duckett pulled the collar of his jacket around his neck. *Maybe we will be done with this case soon.* Climbing into his car, his mobile rang.

***

Duckett's hunch had been right. It was Edwards who called, with details of a security contractor who had left the company the day before the water contamination was discovered. Duckett requested they email the information, including a scanned copy of the man's picture. It seemed an identical situation to Stillwater of the Royal Scotsman. A call from Shona to the Elgin police confirmed they had no record of Doug Stein lodging any form of complaint.

Back at Grantown, Duckett made a few phone calls. The first was to the Grampian Police Headquarters. He discussed at length what had been discovered so far with the Chief Constable Gardner, who was co-ordinating with Interpol. The conversation took over an hour. Duckett's second call was to Ballindalloch Castle.

Through the open door of his office, Duckett could hear Shona tapping on the keyboard. He yawned and wondered for the umpteenth time in his life how he ended up a policeman. Like his father, as a young lad from Govan he had mixed with many shady characters. Always on the take, spending what little money he had on fags and beer. He went with his pals to Ibrox Stadium to cheer on their beloved Rangers Football Club, singing their sectarian songs, cursing, getting into scrapes with opposition fans over nothing. His father didn't provide him any guidance. It had been his mother's older brother, Uncle Teddy, who handed him an application form to join the police force.

Snapping out of his thoughts Duckett made his way out of the station informing Boyd he would be back in an hour to review the report. He was going home for a quick shower and a change. The call to the largest stakeholder in Glen Fraoch, Broadside Holdings, could wait until the morning.

CHAPTER 31
Wednesday 12 October 2011, Ballindalloch Castle, Banffshire

The Skype jingle on her laptop beckoned her attention, just as she came out of the shower. *Shit!* Cathy glanced at the time on her computer, quickly wrapped a towel around her and clicked the answer key.

"You are early David," she said, sitting down by her desk.

"And a hello to you too Cat."

"We did agree on seven my time. I'm not even dressed yet."

"Aren't I the lucky guy? Giving me a peek at what I'm missing?"

"You said in your email you have some information for me?" Cathy ignored his remark.

"So much for the age of romance Cat," he said flippantly. "Listen, I'm coming over. I plan to arrive in Grantown on Tuesday twenty-fifth October."

"Why?"

"Jesus Christ Cathy, is that all you can say?" He paused, waiting for a response, but none came. "Okay then, because I have your father on my back. Your mother never talks to me as it is. She just gives me the 'it's your fault' type of look."

Cathy leaned forward. "If you are coming all this way to try and make me come back with you, forget it. I'm not done here yet." As she spoke, it slipped into Cathy's mind she still needed to follow up on Angus's advice and contact Maggie, to check if she had any family gossip on Alexandra."

"Don't be so self-important Cat, at least I'm trying. Anyways thanks to you, I never finished the travel guide. So I plan to get it done. I need the commission. I also hope to have a grown up conversation with my wife on what she plans to do with the rest of her life and if I am included." David was unable to hide the anger in his tone. Correcting himself to a more mellow approach he continued, "Cat, can we please have serious time together? We do need to talk this through."

"David, I agree we need things sorted one way or the other. But I do need some more time here. Some new stuff has come up."

"What stuff?"

Cathy articulated the discussion with Diane Cox and how she had traced her Macpherson roots back to Gordon, his son John and John's daughter, Alexandra. "So David, if she is right, then I am from the same line."

"Things might not be as simple as they first appear," he said.

121

"Maybe so, you are the expert, but if you were in my shoes wouldn't you want to investigate further? I'm going to Edinburgh. I came across a picture of Katherine Macpherson taken at university there. My gut feeling tells me to do some research on her. She was the aunt of Alexandra."

David remained silent.

Cathy was a little surprised he didn't pass any comment on Katherine, whose life after all, had intertwined with David's ancestor, Alexander. Disappointed at his apparent lack of interest she made up her mind to end the call. "I don't have much time David, I have another appointment due."

David managed to curtail his annoyance. "Enjoy Edinburgh," he said, trying to sound as though he meant it. "I'll email you my flight details."

Cathy took a moment to study David's image. *Did she still want him or was it time to call it a day?* "Let's talk when you get here. Say hi to Sherry and Jacki for me. I'm sure they are spoiling you with sympathy."

Cathy stood up and clicked the red button, giving David a brief shot of her semi-nakedness.

***

"Why did you drag me out here at nine o'clock in the evening?" Cathy asked, tossing her black leather jacket over the back of the nearest chair.

Peter Duckett sat in the dingy office of Grantown-on-Spey Police Station and stared at the American woman. Firmly he ordered, "Sit down."

Cathy scraped a chair over the floor, sat and crossed her legs. As she looked around the room her thoughts returned to the day she was arrested. "You know I hate this place Peter."

Duckett didn't waste any time on pleasantries. Leaning forward he asked, "Why the hell were you at Glen Fraoch Distillery this morning asking questions to young Craig under the pretence you were a police officer? I could have you arrested and kick your ass all the way back to the States."

Taken aback, Cathy glared at the inspector. "I needed to buy a bottle of whisky," she finally managed, "a gift, and it was certainly not for you."

The brawny policeman sighed and leaned back in his chair. "Cathy back off with the crap. I'm serious, for your own good. I don't believe in co-incidences. You obviously heard Doug Stein had died otherwise you wouldn't have been anywhere near Glen Fraoch."

"Okay Peter, I will come clean. I was driving back from Elgin and noticed the road sign for the distillery. In the morning Angus had been upset. Mr Stein was a close business associate and friend. I know you think I'm a crazy woman, but I just felt drawn to the place. My intuition took over."

Duckett hesitated as his anger subsided. "You should know it was not natural causes. Doug Stein was murdered."

"What!" Cathy exclaimed her thoughts returning to Angus. "So my hunch to visit Glen Fraoch ..."

"Listen," Duckett cut her off, "don't get involved. This will be a high profile investigation. It's in your own interest, stay away."

"Peter what happened?"

The Scot sighed and after a few moments he said, "Watch the news tomorrow, it will be nationwide. I'm telling you this as a cop. I've never experienced anything like it in my life. It reminds me of a fucking James Bond movie. Raigmore Hospital called me with the results. There is no doubt Mr Stein was murdered."

"Nine out of ten homicides, the perp is usually known to the victim."

She can't help herself. "I know, but we already have a prime suspect, a bogus employee on the train."

Duckett rubbed his face with both hands. He was tired. "He vanished without trace. We contacted the airports and train stations, but it's probably too late. We had a detective go to Leith today to interview the HR folks who hired him. Apparently this guy was as English as strawberries and cream, well his accent was. We also have witnesses at the Garten, who mentioned they had seen him running from the station and jump into a black BMW."

"A train attendant! Jeez if he is the perp and didn't mind being known to everyone, it makes it an unusual case." Cathy frowned and stared at the policeman. "Looks like a professional hit to me."

"Yep! What we all suspect. My chief in Aberdeen is already in discussions with the Police Commissioner in London."

Cathy's mind was dancing. "I told you I was chatting with Angus this morning. He mentioned some Ukrainian Group have been trying to buy Stein's business."

"I know of them," replied Duckett. "I have been at the distillery today and met up with the company secretary and their lawyer. Diageo also tried some years ago, but this one is different. The big wigs are checking them out."

"Any other leads?" asked Cathy.

Duckett hesitated, unsure if he should continue.

Aware of his predicament she said with a benevolent tone, "Only tell me if you want to."

"Well there are a few pointers. For example, the company lost some large customers without any good reason and they recently had an unplanned production shutdown."

"And they had a fire in the loading bay," said Cathy.

"What!" Duckett exclaimed. "How do you know that?"

"Calm down Peter. The young guy in the shop, Craig, told me."

Duckett sighed and scribbled a note to ask Edwards and White why they never mentioned the fire. "I have been a busy lad today. To tell you the truth I'm knackered."

"You do look tired Peter, go home and get some sleep."

"I wish," responded the policeman. "One more thing, we had all the passengers and crew of the Royal Scotsman interviewed. One of them is a business associate of the Macphersons, a Mrs Diane Cox. What's the story there Cathy?"

"You are something else Peter Duckett." Cathy stood up, but Duckett gestured she should stay.

"Cathy, give me a break will you? I only asked a simple question. Is there anything on Mrs Cox I should know?"

"I can assure you do not need to concern yourself with Mrs Cox. She has absolutely nothing to do with your homicide case."

"Okay, fair enough."

"Listen, I could get into trouble if my bosses found out I have shared all this with you, so do me a favour and back off. Let me get on with my job. Do you hear?"

"Are we done?"

Why do I never believe her? "Yes for now."

She forced a smile. "Don't work too late."

As Cathy put on her jacket, Duckett ogled her body. *I really must get laid.*

CHAPTER 32
Thursday 13 October 2011, Grantown-on-Spey, Morayshire, Scotland

Peter Duckett's bungalow was situated close to the dormant Grantown-on Spey train station. Presently, there was no Mrs Duckett. There used to be. Fiona Jackson, an attractive brunette, with an amazing smile, with legs as Duckett would say, 'going all the way to her armpits'. They met at his local barber shop in the summer of ninety-three. It was Fiona's first day at work and Peter was her first customer. They married in December 1994 in Springburn, Glasgow. It didn't last long. Just over two years into their marriage, Peter had been offered a CID position in Inverness. It meant promotion, more money and a comfortable 'police home' on the outskirts of the city. Despite his pleas, Fiona had no intention of leaving Glasgow. She was from a large integrated family. Fiona was one of four children. She had an abundance of aunts, uncles and cousins scattered all over Glasgow. She would constantly refer to a relation using the word 'our', *our* Sandy, *our* Kevin... When they first met, Peter assumed these were siblings, but as he would learn later, they were in fact cousins or relatives even further removed. After they married, he was welcomed into Fiona's wider family circle, but he quickly became tired of his house being invaded by her relatives.

Meanwhile he was fast becoming a competent officer, but not without cost. He was spending less time at home as the demands of the job increased. His mental health also took a battering. He had to endure the most horrific scenes. Murders, suicides, drug related dens, car crash victims, abuse of women and children and poverty on a scale he had never imagined, and he encountered some of the worst 'low life' people in Glasgow. This put a strain on their marriage. A major rift in the relationship with the Jackson family occurred when *our* Archie was arrested for pushing drugs to kids at Springburn High School. Alistair, Archie's father, tried to convince Peter to help get Archie released. Peter refused. This caused considerable tension at home, spilling over to Fiona's full family circle. Archie was sent down for five years and Fiona's family turned their backs on Peter. When the Inverness offer arrived, Peter was ecstatic, convinced it was an opportunity for him and Fiona to start over. Fiona didn't share his opinion. The couple went their separate ways. With no kids involved the divorce had been quick. Fiona never married again, although Peter did hear through the grapevine she had a live-in boyfriend.

Dressed in a housecoat and slippers, Peter sipped a mug of tea staring blankly at the television, waiting patiently for the BBC morning news. At seven am, the Stein murder as expected, was top of the show. It was Chief Constable Gardner who faced the media. The report drew parallels with the infamous Georgi Markov murder in 1978. A Bulgarian dissident, he had a pellet of ricin fired into his leg by an umbrella while walking over Waterloo Bridge in London. Although the KGB was thought to be responsible, nothing was ever proved. Markov died three days later. Raigmore Hospital had found the same poison in Stein's body, probably injected. The official post-mortem announcement confirmed heart failure killed Stein, resulting from shock. The TV journalist explained ricin was found naturally in castor beans and would have been lethal anyway, as it prevents body cells making the proteins they need. Images of the Glen Fraoch Distillery, and the Royal Scotsman train docked in Boat of Garten, appeared on the screen.

Duckett pondered. He had been disappointed the lab didn't find any clues on Stein's hardware and mobile phone to assist the investigation. The outcome on the office and home telephone records was similar. Duckett switched off the TV. He was happy not to be named in the BBC report. Peter had provided his bosses with a complete status on the investigation so far and probable motive. He wondered how the big wigs in Scotland Yard and the Foreign Office would follow up the Grabowski Group connection, the cash payment of the train ticket, Stillwater, the missing Glen Fraoch contractor and the customers who cancelled their contracts. He was relieved it was not his remit. His next step was to contact the board members.

Glancing at the mantelpiece clock he wondered if it was too early to call Broadside Holdings. *Shit!* The business card given by Edwards with the contact details was at the station. Among some items he had brought home to browse, he picked up Doug Stein's Filofax and flicked on the 'B' tab. A telephone number for Broadside Holdings was there. From the first four digits, '0131' Duckett knew it was an Edinburgh number. He picked up his mobile and stared out the window into an empty street. He tapped in the number on his mobile.

'You've reached the voicemail of John Macpherson. I'm sorry I can't take your call right now, but if you leave your name and number I will get back to you as soon as I can.'

It took Duckett a few seconds to compose himself before leaving his message.

Part II

The Second Sex, a book on the history of feminism by Simone de Beauvoir, published in 1949, was put on the Vatican's *Index Librorum Prohibitorum,* the list of forbidden books and formally abolished in 1966, as it was considered 'immoral'.

Katherine Macpherson's story starts seventy years earlier...

CHAPTER 33
Friday 9 October 1896, University of Edinburgh, Edinburgh, Scotland

The stench from the body was hardly bearable. Even sitting on the sixth row of steeply racked benches in the modern theatre, Katherine was tempted to cover her nose with a handkerchief. Professor Weatherbee's constant scrutinising gaze kept her from doing so.

"Miss Macpherson, would you do the honours please," he called out.

Many of the twenty-three students sniggered expectantly, on what was to come next. Wriggling past her fellow freshers seated around the dark wooden circular arena Katherine found her way to the nearest staircase leading down to the dissection table at the centre. Professor Weatherbee stood waiting and handed her a scalpel without further comment.

To emphasise the fact it was her problem to solve and not to expect any help, he took a few steps back, retrieved his vinaigrette from his right pocket and held the silver perforated scent box under his nose.

Katherine turned towards the corpse on the dissection table illuminated by daylight from the glassed dome roof, only a white cloth draped over the male genitals. Katherine wondered if they had chosen the gender on purpose, especially since her assignment was to open up the inner thigh to examine and describe how the tendons served as a connection to the skeleton. A woman studying medicine was seen as an absurdity which made her audience blind to the fact their disdain only fuelled Katherine's persistence to succeed.

Her fellow students didn't know whether to be besotted with the attractive Katherine MacPherson or attempt to crush her arrogance. She *was* undeniably beautiful. Her height did not distinguish her in any way from most male students. On the contrary, some of the freshers were shorter than her, which added to their discomfort.

Katherine seemed oblivious to all this.

"We have been studying how skeletal muscles are connected to the bone. Most of these muscles are attached to two bones through tendons." The professor glanced at Katherine. "Isn't it so Miss Macpherson?"

Katherine nodded in agreement.

"And what do we call the place on the stationery bone which is connected to the muscle Miss?"

"Origin," replied Katherine.

"And the moving bone?"

129

Looking firmly at the audience she replied, "The insertion."

Ignoring Katherine, Weatherbee addressed the students. "We are now going to look at the adductor longus muscle and its tendons. It is a long, triangular muscle running from the pubic bone to the femur. It functions to adduct or move the thigh inward and assist in flexing and rotating it to the side. Now, if you please Miss Macpherson, in your own time."

Katherine picked up medical gloves from the trolley next to the dissection table. The rubber gloves were an invention made a few years earlier by William Stewart Halsted, to prevent medical staff from developing dermatitis. She placed her gloved hands in a tray of carbolic acid. The smell was a mix of vinegar and rancid butter. She turned and faced the cadaver. Katherine confidently removed the white sheet exposing the left thigh and carefully placed the scalpel just underneath the pubic bone to make a long and deep incision. Using both hands she pulled the flesh back exposing the muscle.

Katherine gave a thin smile when she heard a student vomit and being ushered out of the theatre. The smell was repugnant. Katherine inwardly thanked Robert Stewart for teaching her and Alexander how to gut game.

"Everybody, gather round the table," the professor ordered.

The students shuffled forward, some more reluctant than others.

"Now observe the belly of the muscle between the tendons. The actual contraction is done by this part of the muscle." Weatherbee looked at Katherine. "Miss Macpherson will explain."

Katherine finished her assignment without embarrassment. Accurately, Katherine described the steps of the procedures to Weatherbee as if talking to a peer rather than a teacher at one of the most prestigious medical schools in the English speaking world.

"Look here," Weatherbee interrupted Katherine in mid-sentence. "Tendons are under extreme stress when muscles pull on them. So they have to be strong." He looked at the students and smirked. "I am sure Miss Macpherson's tendons are strong when both her adductor longus muscles are being pulled."

Nervous laughter echoed around the arena.

"Never trust a woman with a scalpel," one of the students joked, loud enough for all to hear. A rush of suppressed sniggering rippled through the group.

"Good thing he didn't have a choice," Katherine said crisply, nodding at the corpse. She walked smartly to a basin, removed her gloves and began vigorously washing her hands. Katherine was enraged by the professor's chauvinism.

Weatherbee eyed her critically. "You'll refrain from such impertinent behaviour in future Miss Macpherson. You are dismissed, please leave the theatre immediately."

Used to these kinds of blatant acts of hostility, Katherine didn't blink twice. She tossed her used hand-towel in the basin, curtsied and with purposeful strides made her way, the eyes of her fellow students observing the feline quality of her movement.

CHAPTER 34
Tuesday 1 November 1898, Edinburgh, Scotland

By the time she was in her second year of medical school, life at the university had become easier for Katherine. Her fellow students had grown tired of inventing insults that found no aim and secretly some of them had to admire her resilience, although few would ever admit that.

Being an independent woman in the public eye still caused her problems. She was sitting uncomfortably by the window on the first level of the horse-drawn tram, crammed with early morning passengers, destined for the city centre. Two sweating Clydesdale horses pulled the double decker vehicle. Katherine was wearing a high-necked dress with a white fluffy collar, covered by a fur cape. A flat brimmed yellow straw hat, banded in black ribbon and plume, completed her outfit. A short rotund gentleman next to her was struggling with the narrow seating. His overweight derriere was pushing her closer and closer to the window.

For the past two years she had travelled the journey six days a week. The four-mile excursion from Joppa, an eastern suburb of Edinburgh, to university could easily take thirty minutes. Although highly inconvenient and laborious she had little choice. The Joppa property had been in the Macpherson family for years. They used the large villa when in Edinburgh for business or to escape the harsh highland winters. Staying in city student quarters, had not been recommended by The Duries. She would have adapted to the basic facilities, but the requirement to share made this impractical, if not impossible. To break the monotony of returning to Joppa, Katherine would occasionally lodge with the Duries and enjoy the benefit of seeing Heather and the twins.

Katherine loved Joppa. The air was clean and she was close to the sea; to the north, the Firth of Forth coast, to the west Portobello. The villa was in the residential area of Brunstane Road. The 165-foot spire of St Philip's Church dominated the north side of the street. Last year, Katherine had befriended the minister, Martin Buchan. Her Saturday house cleaner Mrs Doyle had told Katherine the reverend was a freethinking preacher and on occasions his sermons could be controversial. The comment had triggered Katherine's inquisitive mind. In September she attended a Sunday evening service. The church had been packed with parishioners of all ages. She had been impressed by the minister's pragmatic approach. When delivering his talk on 'Thou Shalt Not Kill' relating to Britain's history of bloody hands, he walked up and down the aisles. Every few minutes he would ask questions to encourage the congregation's involvement. She had never seen any minister conduct in a way of conversing rather than a sermon.

A few weeks later Katherine had attended a Woman's Guild charity event where the same Reverend delivered a speech on the role of the church in combating poverty. At the end, when people were leaving, Katherine had approached the minister. She had asked his opinion on church influence on the financial institutions. Sharing a pot of tea, Katherine and Martin Buchan spent over an hour dissecting what could be done.

Martin in his late thirties was a bachelor. His marital status had surprised Katherine. He was good looking, well groomed and a wonderful conversationalist. He had proved to be of great assistance to Katherine, sharing his knowledge on Edinburgh and in particular the burgh of his birth, Leith. Martin and Katherine enjoyed occasional afternoon tea or supper.

Her studies were going well despite the obstacles related to her gender. Her exam grades were excellent. In the first year the curriculum had been varied and challenging; anatomy, comparative and human physiology and histology, chemistry, dissections and diseases of children. The second year was equally strenuous; more advanced anatomy, physiology, advanced chemistry, pathology, therapeutics and dissections. Even Professor Weatherbee's behaviour towards her had changed for the better. The year also included regular visits to the Royal Infirmary in Lauriston Place, situated on the edge of the city, to escape the smoky air of the centre. Katherine thoroughly enjoyed the practicality of the hands-on studies with patients who really needed help. Now, in her third year, the studies included, surgical anatomy, hygiene, bacteriology, principles and practices of medicine and surgery, gynaecology and obstetrics. She had already explored the fourth year subjects; nervous and mental disorders, otology, laryngology and dispensary clinics.

Positioned near the front of the tram, Katherine could easily see and hear the horses. She pitied the beasts, remembering the freedom *her* horses enjoyed at Ballindalloch. Thinking of the highlands, her thoughts turned to Alexander. It was exactly two years since he left Ballindalloch under a dark cloud.

Katherine tensed when she felt a hand pressing on her right thigh. Glaring at the revolting man pushing against her, she grabbed his wrist and thrust his hand away. Getting on his feet he whispered, "You are a fine sturdy girl my dear," and waddled towards the exit. Katherine was fuming. Her eyes darted around the packed carriage. None of the passengers standing close by seemed to have noticed anything.

Still furious she alighted from the tram at the new Royal Infirmary carrying a heavy satchel of books. It was a short walk to the medical building in Teviot Place but Katherine was pleased she was wearing a cape to break the biting cold breeze.

The Medical Faculty was housed between the hospital and medical building and boasted facilities for teaching, scientific research and practical laboratories; a complex known to everyone at the university as the 'New Quad'. Katherine walked across the grand quadrangle in front of the Italian Renaissance styled building. The courtyard was already busy with students, teachers and hospital staff. She observed a discreet delivery of a cadaver to a side entrance close to the dissection rooms. The three-story galleried Anatomy Museum displayed everything from whales to apes as well as human anatomy. She hoped one day she could bring Alexandra to see all this.

Fully prepared for a day of teachings on the latest changes in the practice of childbirth Katherine entered the building.

Katherine and the Reverend Martin Buchan sat opposite each other eating supper at the small dining table in the lounge of the church manse. Candles lit the room and a blazing coal fire cast intermittent shadows across the room. The atmosphere was one of privacy. Katherine was in an amiable mood and felt comfortable towards the handsome minister. She had made her way directly from university, but wished she had gone home to change. Martin was in a waistcoat, dark trousers, a short turnover shirt collar and a floppy bow tie, his hair short and his pointed beard well groomed. Katherine thought he looked dapper, his attire blending with his strapping build.

Most of their conversation had been of his four-year history as a minister and Katherine's time in Edinburgh. He had made her laugh a few times reminiscing peculiar experiences with members of the church, particularly at weddings and funerals. He told Katherine with amusement of the previous evening. Local children had been constantly knocking on his door, guising for Halloween, dressed as witches and devils, carrying their scooped out turnip lanterns.

Katherine complimented Martin on a newly acquired piece of furniture in the living room, a dark stained oak sideboard.

"How do *you* manage living in the villa? It's such a large house," Martin enquired.

"I only use a few rooms, the front public room, one bedroom, scullery and bathroom. A domestic cleans on a Saturday. She attends to the rest of the house."

"I have a similar situation. This house was built for a family of ten."

"Martin, what made you join the ministry, or am I being too inquisitive?"

"No I don't mind, it is a perfectly normal question to ask," he said courteously. "I always knew, even as a wee boy I wanted to serve God. I was one of seven children, the only boy. It was tough. There was no hand me down clothes for me, maybe the odd jumper and drawers." Martin laughed as the memory tickled him. "We would walk to South Leith Parish Church with my parents, grandparents, aunties, uncles, cousins and all. We must have looked a right bunch of toerags. The kirk session also controlled the school. It's now Leith Academy, but we all had to find work when we were twelve. It was an aunt who funded my training at the Church of Scotland College in Edinburgh."

"I am one of seven as well Martin, the only girl. Isn't it a strange coincidence?"

"It is indeed, but you wouldn't have had hand me downs would you?"

"Indeed," was all she could muster, somewhat embarrassed comparing her upbringing. "What occupation did your father hold?"

"He was a docker. My mother worked in a rope making factory. We all had to work hard. It was and still is a tough life for them."

Katherine wanted to ask more on his family, but sensed his discomfort. "Have you been busy with your football team?"

Somewhat relieved Martin's face lit up. "I try and get to see Hibernian as often as I can. As chaplain their demands are minimal I must say." His expression changed as he observed Katherine's obvious disinterest. "I know you don't follow football."

"It seems all rather silly to me, grown men chasing a ball. Last week I saw a large crowd in the street coming or going to a game. It is an intimidating sight."

After finishing their venison collops Katherine offered, "Let me clear the plates Martin."

"Leave them be Katherine, Mrs Ralston will see to them in the morning." Changing topic he said, "When you get your degree will you receive your diploma at the new McEwan Hall? They say it cost over one hundred thousand pounds to build."

Katherine, with elbows on the table and hands under her chin replied, "If I make it you mean. They don't want women Martin."

"Katherine, I have known you for quite some time. You are a spirited woman I am sure you will graduate and the medical world will change."

She frowned, "The sooner the better."

"How was today for the future Doctor Macpherson?"

Katherine sat back in her chair and grinned. "Something you know little of I think, childbirth. The latest practices and medicines available during pregnancy and delivery."

"Your assumption is quite accurate, I know little of having children, but do they consider in their lectures that many families may not have the basic education or money to obtain what is necessary? Have a walk through Leith for example. Most people still don't have two halfpennies to rub together. It's no wonder child mortality is so damning." The minister rubbed his beard and remarked, "Aye and how good has God been to me, working for Him in Joppa. Leith is a midden Katherine. It is an independent burgh you know. Many people assume Leith is part of Edinburgh Town Council, but it's not. Mind you, they do try to take control when it suits them. I sometimes think Leithers would be better off if it *was* part of Edinburgh."

"Martin, I was shocked when I discovered in many towns and villages, ash pits are still being used for human waste and the removal of refuse is only once in a while. It's disgraceful."

"In Leith, many homes have their water supply obstructed by ratepayers because of cost and they try to store water in the home. You know what happens then Katherine!"

"Contamination," Katherine confirmed. "I do want to try and help Martin. Many doctors all over the country are overworked, doing hundreds of house calls in their own time. More general practitioners are needed. I might not cure tuberculosis, but I am sure I can contribute. Maybe I am destined to follow my mother's footsteps. She did a lot to help the less fortunate."

"In good time I'm sure you will Katherine."

"Most Scots are receiving a standard of health care which at best is uneven in quality and at worse, non-existent. I sincerely hope by the time I graduate the law will have changed on women practicing."

"Time will tell," Martin answered. He seemed distracted. "Katherine, on your future … may I ask …How can I best say this? I've never done this before. These last few months Katherine I have grown very fond of you. You are the most attractive, charming and intelligent woman I have had the pleasure to spend time with."

A little flustered, Katherine retorted, "And I have equally enjoyed your friendship and I so appreciate your help in getting me settled in Joppa."

"Come to the fire and warm your bones," he said.

"Are you having problems keeping warm old man?" Katherine jested.

Martin smiled. "I'm only thirty-nine, but it is relevant to my question. I've gotten to know you as a bold woman Katherine, so I'm going to be forward as well. It is the only way to do this."

Katherine felt her mouth go dry. "Martin …"

"Please Katherine let me ask and you can have your say." For a moment they locked eyes. They each sensed the question and its answer, but it needed to be said out loud. "Will you marry me and have my children? There I've said it, will you Katherine? I would be the proudest man in the Kingdom if you were my wife."

Feeling light headed, Katherine walked back to the table and sat down. "I can't."

He walked over to her, clearly upset. "We get on well don't we? Is it the difference in age? Katherine I know many men who have younger spouses."

Katherine was visibly nervous. "You are a wonderful man and I'm flattered. I do love you Martin, as a friend. I just can't …"

"Because you are a daughter of a laird and well, you know my background."

"No Martin, it's nothing to do with *you*. How can you say such a thing?" snapped Katherine.

"I'm sorry," said Martin humbly. "Please accept my apology, but will you at least think on it? He placed a hand on her shoulder. "Take all the time you want, but please give it some serious consideration. I would be good for you and you …"

She looked up at Martin her face lined with concern. "Promise me what I'm going to tell you will stay between us."

"You have my word as God is my Maker."

"I'm a ruined woman Martin."

It took him a few seconds to realise what she meant. "So, you are not a virgin, it doesn't matter to me."

Tears were filling her eyes as she fought to control her emotions. "There's more Martin, I have a child, a daughter; she is being raised by my brother and his wife. I'm actually not allowed to raise this subject with anyone. How could I marry you and have your children when I already have a daughter? I would be deserting her."

A shocked Martin Buchan found himself unable to respond. He wished he could turn back the clock and had not created this irrevocable predicament. He sat down next to a sobbing Katherine and put his arms around her. She embraced the warmth of his body and felt the first signs of relief. Finally, she had told someone of Alexandra.

CHAPTER 36
Thursday 13 October 2011, Ballindalloch Castle, Banffshire, Scotland

Cathy was sitting in the hall, legs crossed, smartly dressed in a dark blue trouser suit and white blouse, her hair tied back in a ponytail. She was waiting for a taxi to Elgin Train Station. The overnight bag by her side was partly covered by a dark blue raincoat.

From the staircase a quizzical Thomas Macpherson asked, "Good morning Catherine. Are you leaving us at last?"

Looking at the old and wise gentleman, Cathy gave a wide smile. "Not quite, I'm off to Edinburgh. I'll be back tomorrow evening. John is helping me research Katherine Macpherson."

"Well I must say Catherine I admire your tenacity and hope you find whatever it is you are looking for." Thomas leaned over to her and in a conspiratorial tone whispered, "Angus keeps asking me what you are up to."

"I promise you'll be the first to know if anything new comes up," she charmed back.

"You have a fine day for travelling and I'm sure you will enjoy Edinburgh. Did you know in the 19th-century many people referred to the city as the Athens of the North? Much of the architecture was influenced by the neo-classical Greek style. You'll see it soon enough. Do let me know if I can be of any help."

Cathy stood up and quickly answered, "As a matter of fact Uncle T, there is something. Angus gave me your family archives and I was looking at the birth dates of Gordon and Elizabeth's children. I noticed Katherine was the only girl and the youngest, born after a seven-year gap. She must have been an unplanned baby."

Thomas smiled at her enthusiasm. "Most of the babies were unplanned in those days. You probably know more detail than I do. I can only guess though, Katherine must have been a bit molly coddled being the baby of the family and only daughter."

"Then maybe *this* one is more up your alley. What do you know of Gallipoli?"

"Where did Gallipoli come from young lady?"

"It's where Alexander Stewart died in 1916. He was a War Correspondent for the Boston Globe and The Times of London."

"Poor bugger," Thomas said, shaking his head. "Gallipoli was one great bloody battle in Turkey during World War I and was a huge embarrassment to the British Government. A lot of British and Allied troops died needlessly there lass."

"When I come back from Edinburgh, I plan to search the archives of the Boston Globe. I thought you might have some old contacts to help find out a bit more, you know military records and stuff."

The sound of a car horn from the driveway interrupted their conversation. "Your taxi I presume," Thomas said, as he opened the door.

She picked up her overnight case. "We can maybe catch up when I get back, if you are free."

Pecking her cheek he answered, "I'll be here. Have a safe journey."

***

The train arrived on schedule at Waverley Station. Cathy stepped onto the platform and glanced around looking for John. It was daunting to see so many people in one place after her long seclusion at Ballindalloch. People continually squeezed past her to get to wherever they needed to go, when luckily John appeared some twenty yards away. He waved and called out.

They quickly walked towards each other, hugged, with John kissing her cheek. "You look great Cathy. It's good to have you here."

"You look so ... so formal. Love the snazzy suit." *Jeez, he looks stressed.*

"I came straight from the office. I didn't have time to change into something more casual. While John picked up her overnight bag, Cathy's eyes darted around the station. They made their way onto an escalator to get to the next level.

"Busy place," Cathy commented. "It reminds me of city stations back home."

After only a few minutes and climbing a final set of steps, they entered Princes Street and turned left.

"As this is your first time in Edinburgh, tell me your first impressions," John probed.

Cathy glanced at the Princes Street Gardens and the buildings perched high, towering above in the distance. Directly in front of her was a huge intricate Gothic monument.

John could see she was intrigued. "It's the Scott Monument in honour of Sir Walter Scott, author of the Waverley novels." John looked back over the gardens. "Up there to your left is the Balmoral Hotel just above the station, and *there*," he said pointing to the right, "Edinburgh Castle."

Cathy stood for a few moments in awe, the early afternoon sunshine making her feel the warmest she had been in a long time. "John, it is beautiful. I wish I had planned to stay longer."

"Stay as long as you want. Are you hungry? Do you want a late lunch?"

"No I'm fine. I had a sandwich on the train. What's the plan to visit the university?"

"Anytime we want. The Faculty Head of the Medical Research Centre, a Robert Bell, is free up to five o'clock tonight. I gave him the details of Katherine in advance. The university campus is not far from here, within walking distance."

"Behind you is the shopping centre, if you are interested."
Instead, Cathy looked at the major road works going on all the way down Princes Street as far as the eye could see. "What's going on here?"

John grimaced. "They are building a new tram line, but let's not go there. He glanced to his right and quipped, "I see you have brought your own transport," he jested, pointing to a bright yellow JCB excavator, parked further down the street. Cathy laughed. They made their way towards the gardens.

Enroute to the university they stopped at a quaint coffee shop. Over their café lattes, John asked, "Cathy, tell me to mind my own business if you want, but why are you still here? Your husband and family must be missing you terribly. Is this family research your only reason for staying on?"

Cathy sighed and leaned back, bumping the chair of an older woman sitting behind, almost spilling her tea. "Sorry Ma'am, I do beg your pardon." The woman simply shook her head. Cathy forced a smile at John.

"You asked if it was the *only* reason, as if my family line was something trivial," Cathy responded in a gentle manner. "So yes it is my reason for staying. I want to know just a little bit more, although I must admit my Pop and Mom are pissed I am still here."

"Cathy, don't get me wrong. I am glad you are here, especially now, in Edinburgh. I was just wondering what your longer term plans are."

Cathy laughed naturally. "Long term for me at the moment is Monday week."

John's mobile rang. He retrieved the phone from his inside pocket and glanced at the display. "Give me a few minutes." He stepped out onto the pavement. Cathy observed John through the full length window of the coffee shop. *He's actually sexy, the suave gentleman.* She watched the breeze playing with his suit and the effort he made to pull the flapping jacket back in place, talking on the phone at the same time. She smiled at his antics. John had his back to her. *He must play sport.* The call didn't last long. He quickly returned and sat back at their table.

"Good news Cathy we have an appointment tomorrow morning at The Scotsman Newspaper. It's on the Royal Mile where we walked earlier, Holyrood Road. A friend of mine works there, Davie Deaking. He will help us search through their archives. Their records go back hundreds of years."

Cathy hoped they would uncover fresh information on Katherine Macpherson.

CHAPTER 37
Saturday 14 July 1899, Ballindalloch, Banffshire, Scotland

Eyes closed, knees slightly raised, wiggling her toes and supporting herself with the palms of her hands, Katherine lay back in the cast iron boat-bath enjoying the warm water submerging her body.

She had arrived mid-afternoon to an almost deserted house. The 170- mile journey from Edinburgh had seemed to take forever, due to the usual delays, especially in Dundee. To add insult to injury, when she arrived at Elgin East Station there was no sign of a waiting MacLean or any other coach to take her to Ballindalloch. This had infuriated Katherine. She had to hire transport at an extortionate cost. On arrival some forty minutes later, her mood was tested further when she discovered Alexandra was not at home. The warm and affectionate welcome from Donald Simpson and Mary Montgomery helped quell her temper. It had been warming to see them looking so well. Mary had been the one to suggest she take a bath in Victoria's bedroom. The main bathroom of the house was being renovated, with running hot tap water being installed. Katherine estimated it must be costing John a few shillings!

Mary had organised buckets of water be warmed on the kitchen range. Now relaxed in the tub, Katherine secretly smiled at her invading Victoria's sanctuary. She raised her lower body, submerging her head completely below the water. The noise of a door slamming gave her a jolt. She quickly sat up, causing water to spill and splash on the wooden floor.

"How dare you intrude my privacy," Victoria screamed. "This is my bedroom and you have no right to be here, none whatsoever."

Katherine's vision was impaired by soaked hair clinging to her face. Clumsily she wiped her face and managed to reply. "Victoria! It's good to see you."

Feeling mocked, Victoria marched over towards the bath and angrily threw a towel. "Cover yourself for God's sake. Have you no shame? John could walk in here."

She slowly stood up in the tub, taking time to wrap the long towel around her. As she stepped out of the bath she asked, "Where is Alexandra?"

"Downstairs. Now will you *please* get out of my bedroom?"

Silently, Katherine walked towards the door leaving a trail of watery footprints behind her.

Half an hour later, dressed in a comfortable blouse, cotton skirt and flat shoes she made her way towards the scullery. Katherine planned to stay for at least a week and spend some serious time with Alexandra. Approaching the kitchen quarters she could already hear the giggles of her daughter and the voices of Mary and Callum.

"Is this *the* Lady Alexandra I hear?" she jested peeking inside.

"Aunt Katie!" The four-year old rushed towards her. The young girl cuddled her aunt's legs. Katherine picked her up and hugged her.

"My goodness, how you have grown Alexandra! Let me look at you." Katherine gently placed her daughter back on the floor. The child was wearing a knee length dress with a lace trim at the hem, woollen stockings and button up boots. A large bonnet had fallen to her side. Her long hair hung in coils, a red ribbon serving as a hair band. Katherine gave her an admiring look. "You are as cute as a button but Alexandra, aren't those stockings far too warm for this time of year?"

"Yes Aunt Katie, I told Mother …"

"How was your bath Miss?" asked Mary.

"It was wonderful Mary thank you." Katherine then made an inquisitive face at Alexandra. "Why all the sniggering?"

The child gave Callum a shy glance. "Callum said you will probably fall off your horse when we go riding tomorrow," she stammered.

Callum smiled. "Just my way of trying to motivate her to practice Miss. Practice makes perfect, isn't that right?"

"I'll do my best," Katherine said jokingly.

"Does ten o'clock meet with your approval?" Callum asked. "Perhaps the three of us can go for a short ride in the woods. The little one is becoming quite a jockey."

"Good afternoon," John's sudden entrée silenced the banter. He kissed Katherine on the cheek before turning to the others. "Could we have a moment alone?"

Callum scampered and Mary took Alexandra's hand leaving only John and his sister. John leaned back and sat on the edge of the table. "You are looking well Katie. How long do you plan to grace us with your presence?"

Katherine pulled a chair close to the range and sat. "Perhaps a week or ten days, I'm not really sure."

"Stay as long as you want, providing you know your place."

Katherine ignored her brother's crass remark. *He's just insecure.* "How is Alexandra doing?"

"She is a most competent daughter Katherine. She could be at school now. Ahead of her years I would say."

"Good, her education is of paramount importance John."

"I know. You don't have to patronise me Katie."

"It is not you who concerns me."

John sighed, "Victoria is trying to be a good mother Katie. It's not easy for her. Alexandra can be so demanding …"

"John, stop making excuses. It is your responsibility to make sure Alexandra is loved and cared for. She is my most precious possession on earth."

"So it seems," John answered.

A distant clap of thunder distracted their conversation. What had been a sunny afternoon was to be exchanged for one of the highland's sudden rainstorms.

"How is Edinburgh?" John asked. "Better weather than here no doubt."

"Challenging. I need more money. Edinburgh is so expensive "

"Impossible, your grant is generous. You have the villa free and "

"You can afford it John. You must be spending a fortune. I've seen the work being done on the plumbing and who does the automobile belong to? I saw it in the courtyard when I arrived."

"The house requires new plumbing throughout. We're also having electric lighting installed. As for the automobile, Victoria and I are learning to drive the new contraption. We are sharing the vehicle with the Grants."

"And sharing the costs? How do you expect it to move around Speyside? What a complete and utter waste of money."

"You do not understand the modern automobile Katherine. It is an Alldays Traveller and it has a four horse power engine."

"I'll race it on Ranger any day of the week and win."

John shook his head. "Why don't you ask Uncle William for some funding Katie? He is doing rather well I believe, as is James. America is fortunate to have those two Scottish pioneers. In any case you are not getting one more penny from me."

"You are one sanctimonious man. Don't you dare try to undermine my … Uncle … William or James. They are good men." She was angry at her brother's attitude, but let it go, for now. "What news of Donald in Africa? Have you had any communication?"

"The last letter I received was months ago. It was heavily censored, so all I know he is still fighting the bloody Boers. Talking of men do you have one in your life yet? You are getting older Katherine and should be …"

Katherine stood up as if to leave. "Shut up! You sound like father." She still felt strangely guilty when referring to Gordon.

Undeterred John said, "Wait here a moment, I have something to show you." He left the kitchen and soon returned with a copy of the Times of London, folded open at page four.

"Have a look, blacks all over America, fasting in protest over unlawful lynching. It makes gruesome reading."

Katherine peered at the newspaper. "So what is your point?"

"It is a report by 'A. Stewart' of the Boston Globe ... do you think ..."

Katherine glared at him and threw the newspaper on the floor. "How would I know? Even if it is him so what? "

"Maybe Uncle William is right."

"Right, on what may I ask?"

"You should forget university and go to America."

Katherine turned to stamp out of the room when John added firmly, "Okay don't listen, enjoy your time with Alexandra but remember one thing."

"What?" Katherine asked, now standing at the door.

"You must seek permission from Victoria for everything concerning Alexandra's whereabouts. *She* is her mother."

Katherine turned and disappeared into the hall.

John frowned and stared at the scattered newspaper. His sister was uncontrollable. One day she could embarrass them all by making an unexpected move, he just *knew* it. He knew it was unbecoming to even think of such things, but he'd wish she would go away or some accident would befall her.

John's dark thoughts made the room seem cold and unwelcome. A familiar deep rooted anger overcame him. His thoughts drifted towards his mistress in Inverness. He pictured her long slender legs wrapped around his hips, causing a tingling sensation in his groin.

***

It was early on the third morning of her visit when Katherine still in bed pulled on the service chain. She hated requesting attention but this morning she couldn't face John and Victoria. A few minutes later there was a sharp knock and the door opened. Gratefully Katherine embraced the sight of Mary stepping into the room.

"Good morning Miss Katherine, I do hope you slept well. Is everything all right?" Mary sat on the edge of the bed.

"Oh Mary, I wonder what I'm doing here. John and Victoria would rather see me leave and in Edinburgh there is so much waiting for me to do."

Taking Katherine's hand Mary whispered, "You are here to see your wee one and if I may say you are putting on a brave face."

Katherine forced a smile. "Thank you Mary, but I am still torn in two pieces."

"Whatever do you mean Miss?" Mary wondered what was coming next.

"Here, I find myself living in luxury while the poverty in Edinburgh and Leith is appalling. I can't stop thinking of it. Mary, words cannot describe what I have seen. It's the children most of all. When I look at Alexandra so healthy clean and warm, food in her belly and being educated, I think ..." Tears of both anger and regret flowed down Katherine's face. "It is just not fair ..."

Mary moved an arm around her shoulders. "Aye, it's why I escaped to live and work here. But Miss, you are going to be a doctor, you can help ..."

Katherine jerked upright. "I'll never be a doctor, they won't let me Mary don't you see? And I'm going to need more money. John won't raise my allowance yet he is splashing pounds on a bloody automobile."

Mary giggled.

"What's so funny? I'm serious and ..."

"Listen to me," Mary whispered. "Ask Mr William or Mr James for some help. As for the auto thing, it's a ..." Mary bit her lip, "Maclean told me, a prototype, that's the word. It means ..."

Katherine had to smile. "I know what a prototype is Mary."

"Mister John and the Grants secured it for pennies Miss. They have to give feedback to the makers in Birmingham as part of a contract."

Katherine flopped back on the pillows. "Damn, I just feel so useless, while I could do so much if only I had the funds. Mother would have wanted me to follow my heart don't you think Mary?

Mary leaned closer. "Katherine, listen to me. You are a strong girl just like your mother, and you do whatever you see fit. God would never condemn anyone for doing what is right. So you get yourself educated and use your talent in Edinburgh or if you choose, this county."

"Mary I've seen things I never imagined possible. My guilt is beyond repair."

"Follow your instinct and don't you worry. The wee one will be fine. Me and Donald will make sure Alexandra is well looked after. Now what do you want for breakfast?"

***

147

As usual, Katherine's time at Ballindalloch was one of mixed emotions. She spent as much time as possible with Alexandra (subject to Victoria's permission). Picnics, horse riding, walks, visits to Elgin and Grantown and on one occasion swimming in a nearby loch. Katherine also made sure they spent study time together in the library. The feeling of nostalgia overcame her on one particular visit when Alexandra innocently asked, "How many times have you sat here reading Aunt Katie?"

Katherine received regular correspondence from William. He persistently invited her to Chicago. He had written that the liquor trade was going well in the USA. A lot of money was being generated into the pockets of the families in Scotland. He had warned the Temperance movement was growing stronger. William advised the threat should be taken seriously as well as the constant rumours on Prohibition. William expressed his annoyance with John. He never responded to William's letters. Katherine had smiled at William's request for a photograph of Alexandra. He always avoided using the word 'granddaughter' in case his letters would fall into the wrong hands.

James had also written. He and his family were quickly integrating in Raleigh, North Carolina. The construction business was booming all over the States. His company was thriving and he was struggling to keep up with the demand for bricks. His biggest challenge he admitted, was grasping the culture. Racism was rife and he had pangs of guilt at how cheap black labour could be employed.

On the morning of Katherine's departure the castle was as quiet as the day she arrived. At dinner the night before Alexandra had been instructed to say her goodbyes to her aunt as Katherine planned to leave early in the morning. Only Donald Simpson was there to bid her farewell with MacLean carrying her luggage to the carriage. Katherine took one more look at the foreboding surroundings.

How she hated Ballindalloch.

CHAPTER 38
Thursday 13 October 2011, Edinburgh, Scotland

After finishing their coffees, John and Cathy made their way directly to the university. They stood waiting in the small reception area where Robert Bell was to collect them personally.

Cathy looked at a plaque on the wall revealing the university was founded in 1583. "This place is older than the USA," she quipped.

A casually dressed man aided by a walking stick, limped towards them. His mop of light-brown hair touched his shoulders and his glasses were perched precariously at the edge of his nose. "Good afternoon I am Bobby Bell. You must be Mr Macpherson and …"

"Cathy Stewart," she said proffering her hand. "My maiden name is Macpherson."

They walked at Bobby's pace over a courtyard. "Skiing accident," he said pointing at his leg. "I have been strapped up for months. You would think working in the Medical Faculty, it would be fixed quickly."

They entered a small untidy office where three chairs and a desk made the room feel cluttered. Files of paper filled the room and the laptop on the desk hadn't seen a duster in months. A fortieth birthday card was displayed on top of a filing cabinet. Cathy was surprised as Bobby appeared to be much younger.

"I found some time to trace your Katherine Macpherson. She did study medicine here from 1896 to 1901, but didn't finish her medical doctorate." Bell handed John a document. "This will give you more detail of what she was studying, and the names of her fellow students for each year. Also you will find the address where she was living in Edinburgh."

"I wonder why she didn't complete the studies?" asked Cathy.

Bobby replied curtly, "She was expelled."

"Expelled?" Cathy echoed.

John said, "Kicked out of the university."

Cathy looked at Bobby, "What for? What did she do?"

Bobby Bell took off his glasses and looked at Cathy, "Sorry to tell you this, but the reason given was; illegal and inappropriate practice not tolerated by the university, fourteenth November, 1901 and it was signed by the Dean. It's all I have guys."

CHAPTER 39
Thursday 12 July 1900, Portobello, Edinburgh

The squealing of seagulls snapped Katherine Macpherson out of her daydream. She was sitting on the edge of a tartan shawl, wiggling her toes in the sand of Portobello beach. Her ivory white summer dress and petticoat were rolled up just past her knees revealing her bare legs. A drawing pad, pencils and remains of her picnic were resting on her lap.

Katherine often came to the beach to sketch. It was the only real leisure time she would allow herself. The ever-changing colour of the skyline always provided a fresh challenge. She also loved to draw the pier and the crowds of people coming and going, enjoying the human form and movement. Katherine squinted at the flock of gulls. The sunlight was strong and the sea breeze was cooling to the skin.

She had stopped sketching, distracted by her thoughts on the plight of the working classes. The poverty she had witnessed in Edinburgh and Leith was overpowering. The sharing of views with fellow students on what was going on in the world was a regular occurrence, but few did anything of note. The only exception had been a student protest against the futile death of thousands of young men fighting the Boers in Africa.

Her thoughts returned to the conversation she had with Martin Buchan, almost two years ago, regarding his home town of Leith. After many months of inner turmoil, Katherine was arriving at her decision on what she must do. She knew for certain her mother would have approved.

CHAPTER 40
Thursday 13 October, 2011, Edinburgh, Scotland

John and Cathy stepped out of the taxi on Morningside Road. Still carrying Cathy's case, John punched in a key code at the door of his apartment block. They walked inside a small lobby and entered an elevator. John hit the button for the second floor. Cathy had been unusually quiet on the short taxi ride back from the university. The doors shuddered to a halt and opened. Cathy followed John to apartment number 11C. John opened the door and placing his hand on her waist beckoned Cathy inside.

They entered a large contemporary style living area. "Quite a change from the castle," Cathy commented gazing around her.

The space was modern and sparse, only housing essentials. A black leather three-piece suite, a dining table with four chairs and a huge flat screen television dominated the lounge. Cathy smiled at the sterile decor. *No ornaments, no paintings or pictures, no flowers, no nothing. I wonder what happened to his girlfriend, what was her name? Ghislaine!*

She slumped onto the sofa while John disappeared into the kitchen to get some refreshments. "*That* was some turn up," Cathy called out. "Here I was expecting Katherine Macpherson to pass with honours, hoping I could trace her footsteps to becoming a Doctor Katherine Macpherson in the USA."

John was filling the kettle. "Yes, it was a bit of a bummer."

"I am learning John," Cathy said as he sat down beside her, "with genealogy you should be careful what you wish for." Cathy was feeling at ease. She tossed off her shoes, crossed her legs and folded her hands over her knee.

John studied her as she smiled. "Let's see what tomorrows visit to The Scotsman newspaper will bring. As a banker, I know a coin can spin differently from what you would expect. Let me first show you around. The guest room has an ensuite, if you want a shower. I was thinking of ordering a carry out rather than going to a restaurant. What do you say?"

"Carry out?"

"Yes, a meal *to go,* Thai okay for you?"

CHAPTER 41
Thursday 16 August 1900, Leith, Scotland

With the family villa in Joppa being too far from where she wanted to work, Katherine rented a flat in Greenside, a district of Leith. Her new home was directly above a tobacconist. At the shop entrance the proprietors displayed a wooden life sized figure of a Black Watch sergeant.

Edinburgh's port in the north was divided by the Water of Leith, with the northern section being mainly a fishing community and the south industrial. The population of 75,000 supported a variety of industries among which William Sanderson & Sons Limited produced VAT 69 and Mountain Dew blended whisky. A huge number of whisky warehouses could be found scattered around Leith to meet the growing export market. Rose's Lime Juice was another factory, which manufactured a completely different drink. A 'vitamin c' based cordial, targeted for seamen. Shipbuilding was buoyant, though mainly small crafts due to the shallow water.

Katherine's accommodation was a modest second floor flat. One public room, a bedroom and a gully-kitchen fitted with a Haden gas stove. The tiny scullery also had running clean water, which was of paramount importance to Katherine. The toilet was a shabby outbuilding shared by all the occupants of the building. The house was damp and poorly decorated. The main room had a bamboo table and two armchairs with a black-faced iron fireplace. The thin striped wall paper of the main room and bedroom was years old.

Katherine had scattered mothballs all over the house in the attempt to rid the damp odour. Over two weekends she scrubbed the house from top to bottom. She bought fresh linen for the single bed, new towels, cloths and medical supplies. Using different chemists in Edinburgh and Leith she purchased; bandages, antiseptic spray and dressings, ointments, oils, liver salt, hypodermic needles, medicine measures, thermometers, a stethoscope, disinfectant, soothing syrups and condoms. She had to order specialised medical instruments. Katherine moved most of her clothes, toiletries and study books from Joppa to Leith. It would be easier to commute to university from Greenside.

Her biggest problem was finding medical supplies which she couldn't buy or afford 'over the counter'. Many of these were readily available from the university. This is where Australian Alec Boswell Timms came into play. Son of Scottish emigrants born in Melbourne, Australia, he'd come to Edinburgh to study medicine, yet most of his time was taken up playing rugby. Intrigued by a woman with a strong determination like Katherine's, he'd struck up a friendship with her. Twenty-eight years of age, Alec was considered a mature student. He was now approaching his final term and paid little attention to what his fellow students thought of him or his relationship with Katherine Macpherson.

Katherine had shared with Alec her plan to help the people of Leith. While he did not completely condone her actions, Alec promised to help her obtain local anaesthetic products.

"I know Avril quite well," Alec had confided. "She manages the inventory of all the consumable products at the university medical store. I am sure they would not miss a few."

"One of your admirers I take it?" Katherine understood why many females would be happy to succumb to the handsome sportsman.

Alec just shrugged his shoulders.

"The point is can you trust her Alec?"

"Let's just say she is friendly towards me and yes, I am sure she is trustworthy."

"Try and get ethyl chloride, antifebrin, heroin and cocaine. Find the less toxic drugs if you can. Oh, and the new drug, aspirin. I know for a fact the universities all over Europe expect to receive a consignment of samples."

"Katie, if caught we could get expelled. Are you sure you want to do this?"

"I will take the blame, not you or Avril."

Boswell looked grave. "What you are doing is admirable, but nevertheless foolhardy. I implore you Katie, there is still time to change your mind."

Katherine looked at Alec and with a firm voice said, "My family is perfectly capable of riding out any storm. Alec, if we can save one child, only one, it will be worth it. Thank you for everything. You are a true friend and I will forever be in your debt."

"Hmm, I can think of a way how you could repay me," Alec flirted, lightly touching the tip of her nose with his index finger.

"Not in your wildest dreams!" Katherine responded playfully and pushed his hand away.

***

Katherine introduced herself to her neighbours at Greenside. She grasped the opportunity to ask them questions on local medical services. Mrs Duncan, an elderly lady who lived on her own in 'number 22', informed Katherine of a Dr Weir. According to the old woman, Dr Weir had lost his license to practice about a year ago. He had been accused of indecent behaviour when treating a ten-year old girl. He had been convinced to resign rather than face the scandal of a court case. Mrs Duncan added with venom, Peter Weir was a drunken scoundrel at the best of times, always reeking of whisky. Only a young Doctor Carmichael remained in the area, Mrs Duncan added, but he was 'aye chasing his tail' making it almost impossible to secure an appointment.

Katherine knew she had to track down this Peter Weir.

***

It was a Monday evening. Katherine had finished her day at university, had a quick meal at home and then set off for the Black Bull public house. It was only a stone's throw from her flat. Mrs Duncan had informed her she would probably find Dr Weir in the pub. Outside, above the entrance the eyes of a solid brass bull's head lit up the doorway. It was with trepidation she walked inside to the smoky and inhospitable bar. The gas lighting had been turned low. Glancing quickly around the spacious room, she observed a group of men of mixed age. As she walked towards the bartender a few cat whistles sounded.

"Excuse me," Katherine addressed the barman. He was busy wiping beer tumblers with a filthy looking towel.

"Squeeze me did you say? My pleasure lady," he replied, glancing for approval at the group seated in the corner. Everyone laughed.

"Ask her how much for a poke?" a voice rang out. Chuckles filled the room.

"I'm looking for a Dr Peter Weir. Is he present?" Katherine was trying to keep calm and ignore the sultry comments. She could smell the barman's rancid body odour and took a backward step.

"He doesn't do abortions Miss but I can inspect your credentials. I have comfortable quarters upstairs." More gaiety followed. One of the men walked towards her, he was no older than twenty. He smiled at Katherine, "Just ignore this lot my lady."

From their table somebody shouted, "Oh my lady."

"They don't know any better, you will find Peter on Old Sugarhouse Close, number ten methinks. Go left and first left and the second street on your right."

Katherine thanked him profusely appreciating his polite vocabulary and quickly made her way out of the alehouse. Outside she took some deep breaths and walked the dimly lit street making sure to avoid any unpleasant looking characters. Ten minutes later she found Weir's house.

The door was ajar. She knocked and slowly walked inside. Two candles on a sideboard lit the room. An elderly man was seated behind a small table cluttered with dirty plates, glasses, cups and empty bottles. It was obvious he had been sleeping. The room stank of rotten food and urine. His un-studded shirt was hanging out of stained trousers and his waistcoat was open. Katherine observed his toes peeking through his socks.

"Who the hell are you?" he asked.

"Mr Weir, Peter Weir?"

"Who is asking?"

"May I sit down Dr Weir?" She looked around the squalid room for an appropriate spot.

Weir gave a small chuckle. There was no obvious place for her to sit.

Katherine walked towards him and extended her hand. "I am Dr Macpherson. I'm new to the area and I understand you were a doctor here for many years. I was hoping you could spread the word to your former patients. I am now available for evening surgeries during week days."

The old man slowly stood up. His legs seemed hardly able to support him. He eyed Katherine from top to bottom. "A wee girl, a doctor; kiss my arse." He laughed out loud, "Just when I think I've seen it all you come along, a female practitioner." He ogled her and licked his lips. "Aye well, things must have changed. I'm not sure men will want you tampering with their privates unless they get inside your drawers."

Katherine remained collected. "Will you help me? I have been told only Dr Carmichael remains in these parts and I'm sure many children and women, if not the men, would welcome more medical assistance Mr Weir. As a doctor yourself you must surely agree."

"I don't believe you, a doctor, you? Get the hell out of here before I ..."

"Listen Mr Weir whether you believe me or not doesn't matter. I am here to help. You should know of all people how dire the situation is. Think of the wee ones."

The old man slumped back into his chair, his watery eyes still inspecting her. "Aye you are right there. My sister's granddaughter was a poor wee soul. She died last year, only five she was." He looked again at Katherine. "If I do happen to mention your name to a few *Doctor* Macpherson, word will spread fast. I hope you know what you are getting into."

Katherine just nodded her head. "Will you?"

"What's in it for me?" he asked with a lurid look.

Katherine pulled a half-bottle of whisky from her coat. "Would this bear any influence?" She gave the bottle a shake.

"Clever girl aren't you?" Without hesitation he snatched the bottle, opened it and took a long gulp.

"Thank you," was all Katherine said, placing a calling card in his hand, and escaped from the house.

***

In the evenings Katherine passed her time studying the medical intervention impact on the nervous system. She had borrowed books from the university library on methods to treat pain, using local or general anaesthetics and drugs such as morphine.

On the Thursday evening following her visit to Peter Weir, a young woman came to her door. She was holding the hand of a boy no older than four-years. The lad looked malnourished; skinny as a rake and as pale as the driven snow. The shabbily dressed woman was tearful and nervous.

"Doctor Macpherson, I am Annie Livie. Doctor Weir told me where you live. This is my boy David. Please help him, he is poorly."

And so it began. Katherine Macpherson had opened a 'can of worms' and there was no turning back.

CHAPTER 42
Thursday 13 October 2011, Edinburgh, Scotland

John and Cathy sat at the dining table eating directly from polystyrene boxes. Cathy had showered and was wearing John's 'RBS' terry towelling housecoat, John a T-shirt and jeans. They spent most of the evening reminiscing, sharing experiences of their childhood, school, friends and family. Eventually talk turned to their professional lives. So far Cathy hadn't revealed any real details on her experiences as a Raleigh cop.

She continued to steer the conversation towards John. "I thought you looked tired at the train station this afternoon. Is everything okay John?"

John forced an uncomfortable smile. "Not really, the whole financial market is still in turmoil. Not just here, it will be the same in the States. You know since 2008 we have had thirty-four thousand jobs lost. Between us, the latest rumour is the RBS Group will have their credit rating downgraded. My father keeps asking how secure my job is. RBS seems to be constantly in the news for all the wrong reasons."

"And *is* your job safe?"

John sighed, "I am thinking of resigning and starting afresh. I hate how the situation affects me. I'm working in the Foreign Investment space, primarily in Eastern Europe; Russia, Ukraine, Georgia and so on. These guys now have more capital to invest than the whole of the UK, so my days are numbered for sure. The big bonus times are over. Anyway I don't want to dump all my woes on you Cathy. Remember the day before the Newtonmore games, the week you arrived? It embarrasses me to think how you witnessed me drunk as a skunk. It was my way of escaping from all the shit going on. I am not going to wait on the Grim Reaper knocking on my door. Cathy, please do not mention a word to anyone, especially Dad. He needs everything to be in control."

"Promise, my lips are sealed. Do you know Angus had a visitor from New York?"

"Yes, a Mrs Cox claiming to be a descendant of our family line and related to you?"

"Yes, a distant one. I never met her until she showed up. Who knows maybe she is our missing link?"

John looked serious. "My father called me. He was quite upset. I am concerned. He takes everything so personal. I told him I would deal with Mrs Cox and not to worry."

"Mrs Cox is not deluded John, she seems to be the genuine article, but I'm not sure what her motives are."

John nodded. "Our lawyers, Waddell & Drummond, are on the case. Mrs Cox is in Edinburgh next week as part of her holiday. I plan to meet her and wrap this thing up."

Cathy admired John's confident attitude, "My hunch is this Diane Cox will not be a difficult lady to deal with. By the way, did you discuss Mr Stein with your Dad?"

"Yes, we were all distraught. I knew Doug well. He was a good man."

"Well it's certainly keeping Duckett busy."

John leaned over towards her. "There are evil bastards in the world Cathy. I hope they get the culprits, in fact you should offer your services to Mr Duckett."

Cathy went quiet for a few moments and drained the last of their Chardonnay. "John I do see things, in my mind that is. I could tell you of many experiences I have had over the years. Last year, September, I was ..." Cathy paused and stared at the ceiling ... "I'm not sure I can do this," she mumbled, her eyes now glistening.

John cupped her hand and whispered, "Cathy you don't have to...."

She turned, gazed at him and blurted, "I was shot John, fucking shot, in some godforsaken wood in the middle of nowhere. He stood there a few feet from me and ..." Cathy couldn't continue.

John sat quietly and waited a few moments before asking, "Did they get the guy?"

"Oh yes, Hicks shot the bastard dead. I found out later, but you knw what, I experienced going from severe pain to tranquillity within seconds. I could smell burning cotton and flesh, I could hear the pitter-patter of raindrops on the foliage above. The most beautiful butterfly landed on my knee. It had dark red wings with black edges and I knew I was heading for another place. Later, in the emergency room I saw myself from above, my own body lying on the table as if I was watching a movie." She stared into John's eyes. "John I was dead, I am sure something dragged me back. I know the doctors did their stuff, but it was more. You know the cliché of your life passing before you when you are in your final moments? Well it is true John, I've been there. It all makes sense, my childhood, my adult experiences. Since coming here I have had numerous people telling me I am here for a reason. I feel it too and it is why I'm staying on. Does it make sense or what?" Cathy recovered her composure and looked intensely at John. "What do you think? Am I a crazy woman?"

"Cathy you are a brave woman. To go through what you did takes guts. And you have changed Ballindalloch, for the better. You are one special lady."

"Well thank you kindly sir you are not so bad yourself," responded a bashful Cathy.

Intuitively she leaned over towards John's cheek and caught his typical masculine scent, a mixture of something primal and faded after-shave. She closed her eyes and found herself kissing his lips instead. Slightly hesitant, John pulled her towards him. A litany of emotions overwhelmed her; excitement, guilt, embarrassment, while at the same time she was startled at how natural it felt to do this. Most of all she felt longing, a long forgotten feeling, coming from deep within. Their kiss became more passionate. Cathy felt her heart racing. John shifted his body to move closer, but then the moment passed. Cathy opened her eyes and looked into his. Gently she nudged him back.

"I'm sorry John." Her voice sounded soft and shaky. "I cannot do this." You are one desirable man, but as much as I want to I just can't."

John sighed, kissed her forehead and stood up from the couch. "I understand and I'm sorry. It's just I'm ... never mind. I'll clear up, it's getting late and you should get some shut-eye. It's been a long day. Sleep well and I'll see you in the morning." He made his way to the kitchen.

***

In the unfamiliar bed Cathy tossed and turned. The mattress was comfortable enough, unlike her thoughts. She had without doubt wanted John and under different circumstances she would have willingly given herself. She hadn't felt the need for sex for such a long time, until now. She was aware John's bedroom was only a few steps away and for a fleeting moment thought of joining him. She sighed and turned on her side. *For all I know we might be related!* Subconsciously twiddling her wedding band, she felt guilty as her thoughts turned to her husband. She had said the exact same thing to him after he had convinced her to join him in Scotland.

CHAPTER 43
September - November 1900, Leith, Scotland

Over the next few months a rapid increase of patients frequented Katherine's flat. At first it was only women and children who sought help. Clearly word on the street was that Doctor Macpherson was a woman! There were cases of second degree burns, abrasions, boils, carbuncles, whooping cough, measles, typhoid fever, diphtheria, dysentery and most of all venereal disease. Katherine was now well aware of the scale of prostitution. Many of the women from Leith worked on Princes Street in Edinburgh or entertained at home.

A young pregnant woman suffering from syphilis had particularly concerned her. Her baby would not survive. Katherine used calomel ointments and pills, but was well aware of the potential side effects of mercury-based products. With some patients who had already used these concoctions, she witnessed the start of tooth loss and skin ulcerations. For those with gonorrhoea Katherine had to perform delicate injections into their urethra. This was a traumatic experience for girls as young as fourteen.

Katherine had to invest in a doctor's bag as the need to visit patients at their home increased. After checking the lock still operated, she had bought a brown pigskin bag from a second hand shop. She also acquired a local street map. She was already struggling to combine her nightly medical practice with her days at university and had the worry her monthly allowance was not enough to cover costs. Some patients paid whatever they could afford; others gave her homemade produce and some nothing at all.

She had again written to John requesting an increase in her allowance but he had flatly refused. After setting her pride aside she had written to her father in Chicago for some financial support. She had yet to receive a response. Alec and Avril had managed to 'secure' some of the drugs she requested and the aspirin samples, but Katherine was in short supply of the most basic equipment and drugs.

On a cold damp November evening she had a late visitor. It was almost nine-thirty pm when a woman by the name of Jean pleaded with her to call on her husband. Katherine had asked details of his symptoms. 'He is in agony,' was all she could muster. Grabbing her bag she accompanied the woman to a house on Gayfield Square.

The modest terrace house was clean and tidy. An aroma of sweet smelling tobacco hovered in the room. Katherine was introduced to Bill who was seated by an open fireplace. He was a well-built man in his thirties, rugged handsome features and clearly in distress. Jean had told her he was a Leith fireman. Only dimming heat came from the cinders. Bill's face looked drawn and pale.

"This is Doctor Macpherson Bill," Jean said meekly.

He remained seated and they shook hands. "Good evening Mr, um Bill. Can you tell me what troubles you?"

"It was her idea," he muttered staring at his wife, his face wincing.

"You should be thankful. Your wife did the right thing. She is worried. What is ailing you?"

"I think I have the clap Missus, Doctor." He paused and whispered, "I'm pissing pins and needles. The pain is unbearable."

Katherine removed her coat and knelt on the fireside rug beside him. "Do you have any other symptoms? Do you have pus discharging?" Katherine asked clearly.

Bill was uncomfortable having such an exchange with a woman and an attractive one at that. He wished he was somewhere else. His wife was standing behind them listening intently. Bill turned his head. "Jean, go to the scullery." She left the room.

Katherine asked, "Well do you?" He shifted in his seat clearly in discomfort.

"Aye, it's horrible."

"And do you have testicular pain?"

Katherine could hear and smell Bill had a throat infection.

"What?" he asked. He then grasped the question, "Aye, my ballocks are raw and a dull ache is making me feel sick. It's getting worse by the minute."

"Have you any pain in your rectum?"

He nodded, "Aye, its tender and a wee bit of bleeding."

Katherine opened her bag, retrieved a magnifying glass and turned to Bill. "It sounds as if you have gonorrhoea. Have you had intercourse with your wife since you had these symptoms Bill? You must be honest because your wife might be infected."

Bill thought for a few moments. "I don't think so," he replied with embarrassment.

"Bill, are you sure, otherwise I will insist on checking your wife!"

"I'm sure," he said firmly.

"Okay, let's have a look. Drop your breeches please."

"Jesus Christ almighty," was all he could curse as he reluctantly got to his feet.

Back in the scullery Jean listened at the door. A few minutes later she heard her husband yell as the doctor delivered the injection.

CHAPTER 44
January 1901, Leith, Scotland

Katherine arrived at her flat during mid-afternoon. Her festive visit to Ballindalloch had predictably stretched her patience. Christmas was a non-event and Hogmanay the same story. The only reward was spending time with Alexandra. Her daughter was blossoming into a clever and tenacious girl. She would be five later in the year.

She opened the door to a scattering of notes and letters scribbled in multiple types of paper. Dropping her luggage she gathered the papers and laid them on the table.

I am so tired. She'd had a major delay in Perth and the multiple changing of trains had increased her frustration. The flat was cold. Katherine shivered, *Thank the Lord, university doesn't start until Monday.* Lighting the fire she had a sense of relief she had prepared the coals before she left. She went into the scullery and turned on the gas stove.

Fifteen minutes later she was sitting comfortably by the table trying to read the messages that had been delivered in her absence. Many were written by children whose parents were illiterate. Katherine planned to go to Joppa tomorrow and collect some personal items. A long hot bath would be so welcome.

John and Victoria were due to arrive at Joppa on Monday. They were invited to an opening ceremony of some new building in Edinburgh. She forgot which one. She would make sure the villa was tidy. Katherine had informed John she would not be there on Monday due to a prior engagement.

Rising at six o'clock the next morning, Katherine quickly washed and dressed. She was descending the stairs when Mrs Duncan appeared. The old lady was dressed in a cotton housecoat and worn slippers. Her eyes peeked through her dishevelled grey hair.

"Good morning Katherine."

Katherine stopped in her tracks. "Good morning to you Mrs Duncan. Are you well?"

"To be honest dear, I don't feel well."

Katherine was taken aback when she noticed a large bruise on her face. "What happened to you?"

"I had a dizzy spell hen. I fell against the scullery sink. I'm sorry to cause you any trouble."

"Not at all, come with me."

Katherine checked Mrs Duncan's temperature and blood pressure. Her diagnosis was concerning. Both were high. She told Mrs Duncan she must stay in bed. As Katherine placed her sphygmomanometer back in her bag she asked, "Do you have any relatives close by Mrs Duncan or a friend perhaps? I think it would be wise if someone stayed with you today."

"Maybe Mrs Turnball at number 28." Katherine accompanied Mrs Duncan back to her flat and helped her to bed.

She quickly went to fetch Mrs Turnball, who was only too eager to assist. Katherine instructed Mrs Duncan to drink as much water as possible and left the two elderly women chatting in the bedroom, promising to look in later.

During the night Mrs Turnball came knocking on Katherine's door with the shocking news Mrs Duncan had passed away. Devastated, Katherine somehow felt responsible, despite knowing there was nothing she could have done. There was no known treatment for high blood pressure or hypertension other than rest and diet. But still. This was to be the beginning of a six-month period, which would change Katherine's life forever.

***

On the twenty-second of January, Katherine together with the majority of the nation was mourning the death of Queen Victoria. She felt no genuine grief. She had too many other problems close to home. Her bogus medical practice was now overwhelming. The volume of people seeking help grew to an uncontrollable level. The child mortality rate was the most distressing aspect. When a child was terminally ill, many parents would look to Katherine for some divine intervention. Often, prayer was the only medicine left. Katherine on many occasions would tend to dying children through the night.

Tuberculosis remained the main killer. Katherine was thrilled to discover a British Congress was planned in July on how best to combat the disease.

She struggled with the administration demands and the stock control of the drugs and wished a full time assistant could be employed. She was however running out of money. She had sold all her jewellery, except a locket inherited from her mother. Katherine's personal appearance had deteriorated. She hadn't bought any new clothes, under garments or shoes for almost a year. Her grades at university had slipped dramatically. Many teachers and students alike had expressed concern. Katherine Macpherson was exhausted and knew in her heart the situation was not sustainable. She did not want to betray the people of Leith either. After all she was now one of them.

Everything was to change one Friday evening in June.

A short taxi ride from Morningside to Holyrood Road took John and Cathy to Barclay House, home of the Scotsman newspaper. Nothing more had been said on their brief escapade of the previous evening. Cathy went with the flow.

When they arrived, John's friend Davie Deaking took them straight to the archive department. He sat beside them in a long narrow area of the room beside a microfiche machine. The unit was one of six available. Unlike Bobby Bell's office at the university, Deaking's workplace was immaculate. The three of them huddled around a machine, Davie in the centre, showing the visitors how it operated. "We have many archives on digital, but the period you are researching is only on fiche." Demonstrating how to use the equipment he said, "There is no search button, you can only scroll backwards and forwards like this, so it is a bit tedious." Davie showed them how to zoom in to images and capture the index number of any pages they wanted to have printed.

"Good luck, give me a shout if you need any help."

Cathy and John split up, so they could use two separate microfiches. You had to load a reel of film on the machine, each reel covering the daily newspaper for a specific time period. They agreed to start searching 1901, starting in November. It didn't take them long to find what they were looking for. It was John who made the first strike.

"Cathy, come look at this," he whispered. It was a small column on the right hand side of the front page;

Friday, 13th December, 1901.

UNIVERSITY STUDENT FOUND GUILTY OF ILLEGAL PRACTICES

Judge, the R.H. P.D. Houseman, in yesterday's Sheriffs Session, Edinburgh University medical student Miss Katherine Macpherson, age 22, residing at Brunstane Road, Joppa, was fined £100. She had been arrested and charged of conducting medical practices in Leith without the appropriate license from approx. September1900 to June 1901. It appears Miss Macpherson had over some time built a 'surgery' in Leith and prescribed treatment and medicines to the local community. The Reverend Martin Buchan of St Philips Parish, Joppa, spoke at length as a character witness for Miss Macpherson. The judge, in his summary, provided Miss Macpherson some leniency as she pleaded guilty as charged. The courtroom was disruptive throughout the hearing with constant abusive shouting from the public gallery by a group of Leith residents, in support of the former student, who has been expelled by the university in November. Miss Macpherson left the courtroom with a Mr John Macpherson, thought to be her brother and it is believed she has returned to her home near Inverness.

Cathy looked at John. "What do you make of this?"

"She was quite a girl, reminds me of you," he said, patting her knee.

They spent a few hours looking for more, but found nothing else. After retrieving a printed copy of the report, they thanked Davie for his help.

As they left the building Cathy said, "It's a bit of a let-down. The poor girl must have been devastated."

John scraped his throat. "Excuse me, not half as much as it must have been for the family at the time. I wonder how they explained it away to their friends." John laughed. "The story must have been published in the local press. Can you imagine how my Dad would have reacted had it been his daughter? If you want we can search for more articles in the local rags."

"No thanks John, I've seen enough." Her disappointment clearly showed. "Darn, I was hoping I could have searched for a *Doctor* Katherine Macpherson in the States," Cathy said, punctuating the air. "It would have made it a whole lot easier. Maybe she did practice illegally in the US. By the way Davie seems a nice guy. Where did you meet him?"

"He is one of my golfing and squash buddies at weekends. We regularly book tee-times at Bruntsfield Links. We are both members."

"What is your handicap?"

"Women, Cathy, women," John said jokingly. "Oh I should inform you I have had a change of plans. I'm coming back with you. We're driving, so you can forget the train."

CHAPTER 46
Friday 21 June 1901, Leith, Scotland

It was almost eleven o'clock in the evening. Katherine clutching her bag was making her way home from a house call. She was upset. A newly born baby she had treated surely had syphilis. An earlier house call had also haunted her. Sandy, a sweet four-year old boy had scarlet fever. She hoped the Jeyes Fluid in a daily hot bath would help, but she worried the parents couldn't afford to heat enough clean water.

The street was dark. The only sound was Katherine's quickening footsteps. Her breathing was heavy, anxious to get home. When she turned towards St James Square, four men appeared from the gloom some twenty yards ahead. Their staggered walk and loud voices frightened Katherine. They drew closer. She noticed one of them was holding a bottle. Concentrating on avoiding eye contact, she tried to pass. A heavily built man stepped from the group, grabbed her arm and pulled her body against his.

Katherine stumbled trying to push him away. "Leave me alone you lout," she cried out.

He looped an arm around her waist, squeezed her even closer and tried to kiss her. She turned her face away catching his boozy breath. The smell made her choke.

Still clutching Katherine he shouted, "Lout am I?" looking at his friends with a drunken smirk for approval. "I'll show you what I am." He pushed Katherine towards a narrow close. The others were laughing.

"Give her one Jim," shouted a younger voice.

In the struggle to break free Katherine dropped her bag. The man was too strong. "I am a doctor, please ..." Katherine's words were smothered by Jim's large hand pressed tightly over her mouth. He kicked her bag onto the road.

With one hand he held Katherine against a wall. He ripped open her coat, found her breasts, squeezed hard and shouted, "Nice tits lads! Who wants a feel?"

"Get her down Jim, we'll hold her," another shouted, clearly excited.

Within seconds Katherine was pushed violently to the ground, her head crashing on the cobbled stones. She felt nauseas, bile rising in her throat. Many hands were now gripping her legs, tugging violently on her skirt and petticoat. Her blouse was torn open. A man was kneeling beside her head pinning her shoulders.

Her eyes closed, Katherine mumbled, "Please don't, please stop."

The group of men surrounded her. Writhing on her back, her skirt and petticoat now above her waist, she felt hands gripping her inside thighs pushing her legs apart, other hands fondling her exposed breasts. One of the thugs whispered, "Fucking bare legs Jim! Look at that muff."

She sensed someone kneel between her legs, "I'll get her in the mood."

Katherine squeezed her eyes closed. Fingers were clumsily trying to push inside her. Now sobbing, Katherine urinated.

The fingers disappeared almost immediately.

"You dirty fucking bitch." A solid punch smacked the side of her face.

Katherine, close to being unconscious, faintly heard shouting echoing around her. The hands that had been gripping her body had gone. She opened her eyes, to see the outline of a man land a punch directly on the belly of the fat rogue called Jim. Somebody in the distance was running, maybe chasing the scampering accomplices. Katherine closed her eyes, listening to the screams of what she hoped was the man called Jim, being thrashed by her rescuer. Apprehension and humiliation overwhelmed her. Then she passed out.

***

Katherine slowly opened her eyes. She was lying on a sofa. A quilted cover had been tucked around her. The room was dim, the aroma of sweet tobacco hung in the air. Her head and neck ached. She blinked rapidly in the attempt to focus. Sitting by the fireplace smoking his pipe, Bill said softly, "Welcome back Doctor. Let me fetch Jean."

CHAPTER 47
Friday 14 October 2011, Edinburgh, Scotland

The car cruised at seventy mph along the M90 motorway in the direction of Perth. The road was quiet and the cloak of darkness was slowly falling. BBC Scotland was on the radio, but John had turned the volume so low it was impossible to hear what was playing.

John had been rather subdued since they left Edinburgh. Cathy wondered what could be going on. *Was it last night?*

"Katherine must have been quite a character, a true feminist. I wonder how the family handled the situation?" she said, in an effort to make some kind of conversation.

Her comment raised a smile from John. "Oh, I am sure the Macphersons would have swept it under the carpet. They might have thrown her into the dungeon. Maybe you should hire a JCB and check it out?"

Cathy laughed before returning to a more serious look. "Is everything okay John? Are you worried by Mrs Cox's claim?"

John kept his eyes on the road. "No, she's not a problem I assure you. I just have a few things at work to be sorted out."

Silence returned to the Mercedes.

A few awkward minutes passed before John spoke. "I listened to what you said last night as to why you are staying on. Why are you researching this Katherine?"

"It's just a hunch. From the beginning the Alexander Stewart and Katherine story fascinated me. It's almost like a romantic novel. I just want to know more about them and William."

"William? You need to remind me, who was he?"

"Gordon's younger brother, Katherine's uncle who lived in the States. Uncle T told me he met Katherine once when he was a young boy and she had such a different accent. She must have lived in the States for a while."

John had doubt written all over his face.

"I've never been interested in all the family tree stuff. I do admire your tenacity."

"John, I will make it up to Angus. He has never asked me for a penny and supported me through everything …"

"He must be fond of you Cathy. Surely your husband cannot be happy with the situation though. If it was my wife …"

"David's coming over later this month."

"Oh right," was all John said. He shook his head. "I find it all so bizarre. Can you imagine if the media latched on to this, the Stewarts and Macphersons? What a scoop."

Cathy went silent. *He's right. It's unbelievable.*

John's mobile chimed. It was lying on the rest between their seats. Cathy picked it up, "Do you want me to answer for you John?" Looking at the display she said, "It's a Walter."

"Leave it," John snapped, immediately regretting his tone. "Thanks Cathy," he corrected himself, "I'll return the call when we get home."

With a straight face John switched off the phone.

"You can tell me it's none of my business, but how come you and David do not have children?"

"I would love to have kids, but I can't. Have had all the tests, second opinions the lot."

"I'm sorry. I hope you don't think I was prying."

"Well now you know. My turn, where is Ghislaine? She obviously doesn't spend time at Morningside going by the décor of your apartment."

John cast a quick glance. "Touché! She is a beautiful French woman I meet whenever she is in the UK."

"You meet?" Cathy laughed. "You mean for dinner and breakfast?"

John sniggered. "Let's pull over for a coffee at Newtonmore. I know a pub there."

CHAPTER 48
September 1901, Edinburgh University, Scotland

"Katherine, Katherine, Katie, please have some patience!"

It was thanks to the unwritten rule, students were not allowed to run inside the university building, that Alec Boswell Timms was having problems keeping up with the long strides of his fellow student. The tails of his waistcoat fluttered behind him as he marched through the corridor leading from the medical museum to the main campus building, one arm forcefully swinging up and down, while the other clumsily clutched a couple of books.

"There's nothing more to say," Katherine called out over her shoulder, not diminishing her speed in any way. She didn't want his pity or comforting words. Katherine had brought this upon herself and had to bear the consequences.

Having no other choice, Alec made the decision to quicken his step.

"Don't be foolish," she said, when he finally caught up with her. "If they catch you with me, you will get suspended as well. They are just looking for a reason to get rid of me."

"Will you stop and listen...*please.*" Alec forced his request by grabbing her arm. "The editorial was impartial. Your name was not mentioned."

"As impartial as the Pope is Catholic," Katherine retorted. "Alec, you have been a great friend, you've taught me a lot and thanks to you we have been able to give help to a few people in Leith. I appreciate all you have done, but *don't* tell me the lecturers are not discriminate against women. They will use this to expel me."

"Standing here screaming at me won't help. Come on Katie calm down, let's go to Leslie's. It will be quiet this time of day. We can have a drink and talk this over."

With a deep sigh Katherine complied. Reluctantly she accepted his arm and they strolled towards Ratcliffe Terrace which gave Katherine a chance to vent more anger. By the time they'd found a secluded table off the island bar in Leslie's, she was more composed. Alec ordered a beer and Katherine tried a new beverage, Iron Brew.

"You'll never find out who informed The Student," Alec said, "and even if you did it would make no difference."

Katherine looked worried.

Alec went on, "Why let this defeat you? Do you really think they will send the police to knock on your door and put you in prison?"

"They might, but I'm not scared of that."

"Then what is it? You have done an amazing job Katie. Are you going to forsake everything because of one lousy article?"

The students who ran the weekly rag of Edinburgh University were usually conservative in their editorial. What they had now published was an attack on illegal medical practices conducted by a student from their university."

"I wonder who the Judas was," Alec said, scratching his hair. "I am the only person you confided in, and it sure wasn't me."

"At least they only mentioned the medical practice. Nothing about where I actually obtained my supplies." She stroked her chin. "It's Dufferin, I'm sure. He vets everything before the rag goes to print. The previous Rector had far more liberal politics." When Malcolm Durie had introduced Katherine to the university Board, Lord Balfour had been the Rector. Durie had an excellent relationship with Balfour. Together they had convinced the Board to accept Katherine's placement. Two years into her studies it soured, when Balfour was replaced by the Marquis of Dufferin. The Marquis made no secret of his stance that women should not be encouraged to study medicine.

Katherine shook the rag in her hand and then recited an extract; "It is common knowledge in the Quad, a female student not yet qualified, has been providing residents of Leith with medical advice and medicines. This has been brought to the attention of the university staff as The Student fears our fine faculty reputation will be tarnished."

"Katie, it will all blow over."

Despite this latest crisis, compared to two months ago, Alec thought how Katie was looking well. In June, she had horrific bruising on her face. Katherine had told him she had an accident; hit by a horse and cart, entirely her own fault.

They finished their drinks. Alec offered to get another. "No, I want to check if Mr Durie is available and have my say. I'm leaving Alec, and that is my final word."

"Katie, I think you should wait. The General Medical Council will …"

"No Alec, it's something I must do, I have no other choice."

Alec leaned back in his seat observing the enigmatic Katherine Macpherson, leaving the bar and ordered another drink.

CHAPTER 49
Friday 14 October 2011, Ballindalloch, Banffshire, Scotland

Cathy and John arrived home shortly after ten. The only person around was Billy. John made his way directly to his bedroom and Cathy went to the kitchen to make tea. She thought about calling Uncle T's room, but it could wait until morning.

"Catherine, welcome back," shouted Angus, as he walked into the hall. "How was Edinburgh? Where is my boy? Did he look after you?"

The question made her face flush a little. "John has gone to bed. Edinburgh was wonderful. What a beautiful city and your son was the perfect host."

"Did you discover anything of interest?"

"Yes, if you consider the fact Katherine Macpherson was kicked out of university interesting."

Angus raised his eyebrows. "Well I never. Expelled, for what reason?"

"She was practicing medicine without a license."

"Oh dear, oh dear," Angus mumbled. "What business did women have studying medicine in those days anyway?"

"You're on dangerous territory Mr Macpherson," Cathy said flippantly. "You're lucky I'm tired and need my bed."

In her bedroom, she tossed her case on the bed and switched on her laptop, hoping Billy had not switched off the router, as he often did. She stared at the computer waiting for a connection, letting her mind reflect on everything that happened in Edinburgh. The Windows jingle snapped her out of her thoughts.

She opened the browser and Googled; 'Ships Passenger lists Glasgow to USA and Canada 1901-1905, Macpherson K.'

The computer responded; 294 hits, with a wide variance in the spelling of the surnames. She narrowed the search by gender; 114 hits. She quickly reviewed the returns and sighed. There were a lot of female Macpherson K's listed, travelling alone, but only seven in the age group she was looking for. Five were bound for New York, one to Boston and the other to Quebec in Canada.

Cathy gave up on the passenger quest. *Let's try and find her Death Certificate.* Cathy recalled Uncle T's recollection of Katherine's visit to Ballindalloch when he was a young boy. This was during the 1930s. Logging on to Genes Reunited, a highly recommended website for tracing births, deaths and marriages, Cathy entered Katherine's full name, gender, origin; Scottish or British as well as deaths from 1939 to 1950. A list of six names appeared, all the wrong age. Cathy noticed once again, the many variants on the spelling of 'Macpherson'. *Maybe she married and registered under a different surname.*

Cathy tried 1951 to 1955, in the effort to narrow the window. Four names were displayed. One in particular looked very promising. Cathy clicked on 'view document' and then hit the 'pay' button. She gazed at the screen; the digital image of the document slowly appeared. The certificate, numbered 4712, was busy. She enlarged the font. This *had* to be her Katherine. Cathy's eyes moved to the 'Personal and Statistical Particulars'.

Date of Birth; July 1877

Origin; Scotland

Color of Face; White

Marital Status; Spinster

She scrolled to the section, *'Medical Certificate of Death'* …

Date of Death; August 4th 1954

She then read the declaration below;

I hereby certify the cause of death on the date stated above was as follows:

Cardiac arrest caused by an arrhythmia attack.

It was signed by Doctor Wilfrid Bannerman.

Cathy scrolled back to the top of the document to discover 'Katherine MacPherson' died in Palos Park, Palos Hills, Cook County, Illinois. After a quick search on the net, Cathy smiled when she discovered Palos Hills was only just over twenty miles from Chicago.

She began a fresh search; 'Alexander Stewart, Boston Globe 1900 to 1916'. Google returned pages of hits. Cathy tried to absorb what was mainly the headline details of articles Alexander had written. She clicked on one at random. *Shit.* A subscription was needed to access the full article from the Boston Globe archive. It could wait until morning. Cathy was about to log off when she noticed;

Click, the full article was displayed without charge.

OBITUARY

January 15, 1916, Boston, MA

STEWART, ALEXANDER; Correspondent, killed January 5, 1916 at Gallipoli, Turkey, age 41, of Boston Mass.

Our much valued colleague at the Globe. He was born in 1873, Scotland, the only son of Robert Stewart and Jane Black. He joined us at the Globe in 1896. Alexander enjoyed a variety of journalistic achievements ranging from sports events, local and international news, in particular Europe. He was a people's writer who was not afraid to report on controversial topics. He will be remembered for his daring written words on woman's suffrage and racial discrimination as well as his much recognized charitable work. In addition his remarkable coverage of the survivors of the RMS Titanic disaster was used nationwide. Alexander progressed into his desire to be a War Correspondent covering many conflicts in his unique and honest ways. He will be sadly missed by all. Mr Stewart is survived by his loving wife Sarah and his two sons Michael and Robert.

Go To: Alexander Stewart Inquiry, Boston Globe, MA

She opened the Inquiry.

MR MICHAEL DEVANE DEMANDS INQUIRY INTO STEWART'S DEATH

February 18th, 1916, Boston, MA

A well-known and respected Boston business man, Michael Devane has demanded the Globe request an official inquiry into the death of their employee Alexander Stewart. Mr Stewart, a correspondent for the Globe, was killed in Gallipoli last month ... if you want to see this full article, join us now...

Shit! Cathy recalled the family name Devane from the Alexander letters. She flopped on the bed, hands behind her head and closed her eyes.

Where am I going in all of this? What did Katherine do in the States? Did she track down Alexander? Not the uncle, I would go to James. And Alexander, an inquiry no less, I wonder why? Will read the full report tomorrow and share this with Uncle T ...

Cathy was vaguely aware she was slipping into slumber. She tried to fight it, but eventually surrendered to the inevitable.

***

Cathy heard music and was dancing with John. It was a quick-step and gradually the tempo of the music increased. They were spinning and trying to keep up with the rhythm, until finally he let go and Cathy slipped into an abyss, falling and falling what seemed forever. She plunged into water that didn't feel wet and she could still breathe. It made her realise she was in a dream. Her father stood on a bridge and was clearly annoyed. He shook his fist from above.

When she awoke, Cathy needed to shake off the feeling of trepidation. Although fully clothed, she shivered, got up and cranked up the heating valve of the radiator. It was 04:35 am when she switched on her laptop and the kettle. Her mouth felt as dry as dust and tasted strangely salty. Sipping Earl Grey a few minutes later, she was busy on the web and used her Amex to sign up for membership of the Boston Globe Archives to retrieve the full article regarding the inquiry on the death of Alexander;

MR MICHAEL DEVANE DEMANDS INQUIRY INTO STEWART'S DEATH

February 18th, 1916, Boston, MA

A well-known and respected Boston business man, Michael Devane has demanded the Globe request an official inquiry into the death of their employee Alexander Stewart. Mr Stewart, a correspondent for the Globe, was killed in Gallipoli last month. His family received little detail as to how he lost his life. Mr Devane, the owner of one of Boston's largest construction companies also lobbied and received the support of the Boston Republican Senator, Henry Cabot Lodge. Mr Devane has offered to pay all the costs to have the body of Mr Stewart returned to Boston and Senator Lodge has pledged he will take up this cause directly with the British Consulate. With some words of caution, Mr Devane commented he understands the British are fighting a War and facing many problems in Ireland, but trusts their government will support the inquiry and return of said remains.

A spokesman from the British High Commission when asked was unable to pass comment.

CHAPTER 50
April 1902 Ballindalloch Grounds, Banffshire, Scotland

The white mare snorted intermittently. They were tracking shotgun blasts, disturbing the otherwise peaceful morning. Katherine dismounted her horse. Gripping the reins she walked into the woodlands. She approached a small clearing and saw the gamekeeper some twenty yards ahead reloading his firearm.

"Good morning to you Mr Gunn," she called out.

The man turned and tried to focus through the shadows of the trees. He smiled when he recognised her, admiring the young woman in her riding jacket, tight breeches and boots, her hair tied in a bun. He un-cocked the shotgun and walked towards her. "Good day to you Miss." He took the reins from her and looped them on a branch.

"What are you hunting?"

Gunn smiled and removed his hat. "I was just getting in some practice Miss. How are you this fine morning?"

Katherine had to think how best to respond to the simple question. In January, she had returned from Edinburgh to face the wrath of John and Victoria after the court case. Provided she would cease her activities immediately, there would be no further investigation. This had left Katherine with little choice. The reputations of Alec and Avril could be compromised as well. John had managed to persuade the local press in Elgin and Grantown to publish only a small article on Katherine's trial. With great difficulty he also convinced the editor of the Strathspey & Badenoch Herald, to relegate the report to page four. However, he had little influence on the newspapers in Inverness and Aberdeen. John had threatened to write to William explaining her exploits, but Katherine insisted she should be the one to inform him. Too fed up with the whole situation he had backed down.

Donald, Mary, MacLean and the other house staff had extended their support. 'Being expelled for doing charity work,' Mary had muttered, 'what is the world coming to?' Katherine had not commented much. Only she had known the real reason why she left Leith. What troubled Katherine was how it would affect Alexandra. She was too young to understand now but Katherine wondered what she would think later in life of her 'aunt's' behaviour. The traditional upbringing John and Victoria gave her could well leave its mark.

"I'm perfectly well Mr Gunn," Katherine finally answered. Even though he had been the gamekeeper for nearly five years, she didn't know him very well. Katherine guessed he was close to forty. A handsome man with an athletic build, he towered above her. She stared at his face and noticed he hadn't shaved for a few days. For a brief moment their eyes met. "It's such a beautiful morning for a horseback ride."

"Well I'm sure you have a lot on your mind but I had better get back to work."

"A gamekeeper's work is never done Mr Gunn. There is always something to do."

He turned and gave her an awkward glance. "Aye but I'm roped into doing things which are not in my job remit Miss."

"Mr Gunn I'm sorry, you should complain to John."

"Maybe you could have a word in his ear?" he replied with caution.

Katherine gave a sardonic grin. *As if John would listen to me.* "What tasks are you referring to?"

"I have to supervise the demolition of the Monk's Cottage Miss."

Katherine couldn't hide her shock. The image of Alexander and her making love sprung to mind as if it was only yesterday.

"I'm sorry Miss. I shouldn't have asked."

Katherine walked to her horse, untied the reins and mounted. "I can't help you Mr Gunn. You'd better address this matter yourself."

She wondered if Mr Gunn knew anything of her and Alexander.

CHAPTER 51
June 1902 Ballindalloch Castle, Banffshire, Scotland

Wearing a long pale blue cotton dress with short sleeves and flat shoes, Katherine sat by her bedroom window to capture the summer daylight and read the letter she had received from Alec Boswell Timms. The gentle chime of the grandfather clock in the upstairs hall added to the tranquillity of the morning. She was enjoying Alec's news. Having graduated from university, he was planning his return home. As she moved on to the second page a small shock awaited her.

I have to inform you Katie the person who notified the university on your practices in Leith was not a fellow student, but a Doctor Carmichael. A letter from the gentleman was recently published in the Scotsman newspaper. I have enclosed said article. You will observe Carmichael states he regrets the state of healthcare in Leith and recognises more help is needed but argues what Leith needs is another qualified male practitioner rather than a woman.

It now made sense to Katherine. Bill had carried her to his house after the assault. Carmichael had been the doctor who treated her there. He had examined her and tended to her wounds. Carmichael had been compassionate but stern. 'People are not ready for women practicing medicine,' he had said. 'Not among the poor, nor the rich for that matter. I think it's time you find yourself another occupation. What you are doing is illegal,' he had said firmly. Perhaps in his heart he admired her bravado and her care, but he also understood his professional position.

A knock on the door interrupted her ponderings. "Who is there?" she asked rather annoyed.

"It's Mary Miss, to strip your bed."

Katherine smiled, "Come in."

Mary Montgomery entered the room, carrying a linen basket leaving the door ajar. She looked at the letter Katherine was holding. "Good news I hope?" Mary had been keeping close to Katherine during recent events, the vow to her Lady Elizabeth always at the back of her mind. Feigning disinterest for the answer, Mary pulled off the bed sheets, vigorously stuffing them in the basket. Casually she remarked, "Did you hear they are starting art classes for adults at the Grantown Grammar School in August? You have always had an interest in painting and drawing since you were a wee one. It might be a nice way to get your mind off things."

"Thank you Mary, I'll think about it. Can I join you for tea today?" Katherine avoided meals with John and Victoria. She either ate in her room or would join Mary and Donald.

"Our pleasure Miss. Tea will be ready in the kitchen around half past twelve." A look of concern appeared on Mary's face. "Did you hear of Bertie Miss?"

"Bertie? Oh you mean the King. He's not dead is he?"

"Nearly. MacLean told me he was diagnosed with appendicitis, King Edward that is, not MacLean. The coronation has been postponed."

"Appendicitis can be a killer Mary, though they have made a lot of progress on anaesthesia and antisepsis over the years. I'm sure he will be treated by the best surgeons. She wondered if Joseph Lister from Edinburgh would have been summoned to London."

Standing in the open doorway unnoticed, Victoria had been eavesdropping on their conversation. Catching Katherine and Mary by surprise she said, "Mary would you be so kind and leave. I need some time with Katherine."

Katherine glared at Victoria. "You may finish your chores first Mary," she said holding Victoria's gaze.

With some help from Katherine, Mary finished her task and scurried out of the room closing the door behind her. Without invitation Victoria sat down on the edge of the bed. "You do know your brother Donald will be returning from Africa?"

"No I didn't, when?" This pleased Katherine though it irked her John had kept the news from her.

"The war is over apparently," Victoria continued, oblivious to Katherine's thoughts or feelings. A treaty has been signed a few days ago so we assume he will come home soon."

"If he has any sense he should stay in Africa."

Victoria eyed her sister-in-law. "Which I may say is the point of my visit Katherine. I'm here to suggest you leave Ballindalloch. You are clearly uncomfortable here. It is causing distress for Alexandra." She pouted her lips. "She is a sensitive wee girl and the atmosphere you create when you are in my company or John's is ..." Victoria paused.

"And I am the only one to blame? It's nothing to do with you or John?" Katherine suppressed her anger. Deep down, she knew Victoria was right. She ought to leave and start a life of her own, but found it a hard decision to make. "Don't you dare tell me what I should or should not do! You and John are not exactly the perfect couple. Where is he now, in Inverness with his mistress? You thought I didn't know, well everybody knows."

Victoria's face turned crimson. "What you say has absolutely nothing to do with Alexandra!" She stood up and walked to the door. "You can be so cruel and uncouth Katherine. I'm only concerned about the welfare of *our* daughter.It would be best for her if you left. Think of her for once, rather than yourself."

Victoria left the room slamming the door behind her, leaving Katherine to ponder on her closing remark.

CHAPTER 52
August 1902 Ballindalloch Castle, Banffshire, Scotland

The tension with John and Victoria was increasingly unbearable with John spending more and more time in Inverness. Throughout the summer months Katherine had squandered her time, horseback riding, reading, sketching and occasional trips to Elgin and Grantown. Her bond with Alexandra was strong. Intuitively the girl sought her company backing away from the atmosphere between her parents. Still, Katherine saw little of her. Victoria used all sorts of excuses to keep her away. Alexandra, now six-years old, was attending Inveravon School. Mrs Roxburgh, a tutor who had served the family for many years, was also teaching her. The same woman taught Katherine as a young girl as well.

John had reduced Katherine's allowance considerably. She was restricted in what she could afford. This changed on a dull, damp Friday when she received a letter from William, announcing he was coming over for Hogmanay and responding to a request she had made. He instructed her to keep both matters quiet.

"I must go to Grantown John. Can McLean take me?"

John was seated in the study. An electric desk lamp shone on the multitude of papers in front of him. He stared angrily at his sister. "Can't you see I'm busy," he barked, "but since you are here I might as well inform you the Grants are visiting tomorrow evening to celebrate our success in America. Uncle William is doing a wonderful job out there. The dollars keep rolling in." John forced a laugh. "*You* are not invited. Gossip on your behaviour in Edinburgh is still rife. I don't want you around. I don't want it to overshadow the achievements of our family. You are an embarrassment and your absence at the Kirk doesn't go unnoticed either."

"Yes John. Now can I ask MacLean…?"

"Do what you must Katherine, now go," he said, impatiently waving his arm. "I have a lot to get on with."

Katherine calmly opened the door and left with a smug look on her face.

***

Like many towns in Britain, Grantown had changed a great deal in a short time. The town had a courthouse, schools, banks, shops of all kinds and a thriving market. Somehow it seemed bigger now, busier and more alluring. The social scene was also thriving. Posters dotted around the town advertised dances, youth clubs, choirs and reading groups. Katherine had much to do today. She was dressed appropriately for the tasks she needed to complete. An ivory coloured puffed frilly blouse with a lace collar, her black skirt fitted at the hip and fluted to the hem. Her hair was parted in the centre, pushed back, partly covered by a broad brimmed hat, adorned with ribbons and feathers.

Gracefully she made her way down a busy High Street towards the Royal Bank of Scotland. Gentlemen tipped their hats as they passed her and ladies smiled. A few looked away aware of who she was and what she had done.

At the bank she was ushered into a stuffy oak panelled room and offered the most uncomfortable wooden chair imaginable. From an open window she could hear the noise of people passing, the rattle of carriages and in the distance, the shouts of market traders.

A young man entered the room. He was smartly dressed in a three-piece tweed suit with small high lapels, an upstanding starched shirt collar and knotted tie. His dark hair shone and his face was pleasant, sporting a neat moustache. Not handsome but nonetheless appealing.

"Miss Macpherson, please sit down. I am Mr Unsworth, the Assistant Clerk." He proffered his hand, pulled a chair close to her and sat down holding a small account book.

"I am pleased to meet you Mr Unsworth." She eyed the young man who seemed much younger than she, making Katherine feel quite old.

Clearing his throat he opened the book. "You have had a remittance of £200 Miss Macpherson, from a Mr William Macpherson in Chicago." He looked at Katherine. "Chicago is in America."

Katherine smiled lazily at his innocence. "Yes Mr Unsworth, I believe in Illinois."

"Exactly," he said, glancing at Katherine before returning his attention to the book. "You now have a balance in your favour of two hundred and twelve pounds, eighteen shillings and four and a half pence."

Katherine gave a sigh of relief. She stood up gratefully. "Thank you. If you please I would like to withdraw five guineas."

"Anything you want Miss Macpherson. You must know, The First National Bank of Chicago confirmed you can expect one hundred pounds on the first Monday of each month to be deposited."

"Thank you Mr ... what is your first name?"

"Terence Miss Macpherson," he answered, feeling slightly embarrassed with her informal approach. "Let me get your money."

"I'm Katherine."

He gave a tremulous smile and nodded, turned and left the room.

Katherine's next call was with the family solicitors, Cooper and Waddell of Inverness. Their premises on High Street, a short walking distance from the bank, were modest. An elderly gentleman tipped his top hat and took Katherine by the arm to escort her across the busy street. At the solicitors she had a brief discussion with an efficient Mr Cameron regarding her inquiry to rent furnished property in Grantown. She outlined her requirements and budget. The lawyer seemed confident he could meet her demands and said he would contact her within the week.

Katherine then walked north towards the Square, briefly delayed by a small crowd who had stopped to watch a horseless carriage pass by. She wondered who the owner was. She made a brief visit to the Grammar School and enrolled for adult art classes, thinking gratefully of Mary's advise. After glancing at the Town Clock tower, she crossed the street. *Still time before MacLean arrives.* She continued walking setting course for the orphanage. Many locals referred to the institution as the Charity School. The orphanage had been in Grantown for many years and housed boys and girls, not only orphans but children who had been abandoned by their parents who were unable to feed and clothe them. Inside she met two patrons, Mrs Peters and Miss Caldow, who had already been around in the days her mother would visit the orphanage. Both women were now in their forties and neatly dressed in modest attire suitable for their work. Mrs Peters was delighted to see Katherine and happily brought up her fond memories of the late Lady Elizabeth Macpherson.

One hour later Katherine left the building. She had been accepted as a nurse and teacher. She would dedicate three days a week to the orphanage and work eight hours each day.

She had just enough time to buy a gift for Alexandra and something to please Mary; her favourite haggis and black pudding.

Pleased with the results of her actions, Katherine felt a sense of relief she had not encountered in a long time. Soon she would be free.

Katherine was one of twelve students seated in the examination hall in Grantown Grammar School. You could hear a pin drop as everyone was focused on a crystal bowl of mixed fruit sitting on the centre of a table positioned close to a window. The majority of budding artists were adult women of various ages with the exception of two young gentlemen, one of them, Terence Unsworth. Katherine had been pleasantly surprised to see the clerk attend the art class. 'Quite an achievement for a banker,' she had quipped at their first evening of class.

"Time to give some colour to my life, don't you think?' he had responded, admiring how Katherine's simple outfit of a plain white blouse, grey pleated skirt and black ankle-high boots, still gave her the appearance of a lady.

The teacher, Mrs Penny, slowly walked between the students, eyeing their efforts. "Remember the value of tone," she said, her voice echoing around the huge hall. "See the shapes ..."

This was Katherine's sixth class and her progress had been steady. Mrs Penny had commented she had a lot of potential. When the session finished, Katherine approached Terence. "Let me see," she said, gently pushing him aside.

They had quickly become friends. Katherine had learned over the past few weeks that Terry was the youngest son of a banker in Forres, being trained in all aspects of the industry. His time in Grantown would end in January next year, and then he would return to Forres. Twenty-two years of age, he was the youngest of three sisters and two brothers. All of his siblings were married, with the men also working at the bank. Terry was keen on shinty and played for Inverness.

Terence stood back and proudly waved a hand at his painting.

"Mm ..." Katherine rubbed her chin with one hand, folding the other arm around her waist, mimicking Mrs Penny, who was never easy to please. "I suppose it will look better when it is finished."

"I *don't* want to see your painting," Terence jested.

Katherine walked over to her easel and held up her portrait with both hands.

"You definitely have the talent Katherine, well done."

Katherine and Terence were the last students to leave the hall. Pulling on their coats, Terence peered out at the darkness. "The usual drink in Grants?"

Katherine was busy reading the notice board. The local Temperance movement had posted details of their next meeting. There were also leaflets of various charitable societies. She turned to Terry. He was wearing casual clothes which gave him a relaxed aura. "Not tonight, I've just moved into my new home and am enjoying my newfound freedom so much. Do you want to come and have a look?"

Slightly taken aback, Terence hesitated. "I'd … I'd love to… I think. Are you allowed visitors?"

"I would hope so," Katherine said firmly. *I pay the rent and will do as I please.* She looped arms with Terence. "Follow me, it's only a short walk."

A few minutes later she was opening the door to her flat on Church Street. They stepped into a small hallway. The building had four dwellings, two up, two down. Katherine's home was on the ground floor. The flat was modest, neatly furnished and spanking clean. The drawing-room overlooked the street.

She pulled off her coat and tossed it on a recently upholstered armchair and drew the drapes. "The toilet is shared I'm afraid, out there …" she commented pointing to a back door. "Let me take your coat."

"Have a look around my castle," Katherine suggested, "and I'll make us some tea."

It took Terence only a few minutes to view her bedroom and scullery. "Katherine you have made this house into a real home." He lit a John Players Navy Cut cigarette and sat on a small sofa. "Do you want one?" he asked, holding out the five-pack.

"No thank you, I'm trying to cut down." Katherine had picked up the habit of occasionally smoking during her student days.

"What are your neighbours like?"

Katherine joined him in the lounge with two mugs of piping hot tea, placing one on the table next to Terence, cradling the other. "Come on move over." She squeezed in beside him on the couch. "Next door is a young couple. They both work, so I rarely see them. The flat directly above is vacant and the other is occupied by the local ironmonger, Mr Winchester. He seems pleasant enough."

"I admire your spirit Katherine. You're very different from most women I know."

Katherine gave Terry a friendly look. "How long have we known each other? Six, seven weeks, is it not?"

Terry looked back at her. She seemed comfortable, content. "What makes you ask?"

"That's a bit hard to explain. My life has taken many different turns over the years, some for the worse I'm afraid."

Terry nodded. He'd heard the gossip about Katherine being expelled from university, which in turn had stirred up older rumours of the laird's daughter and a gamekeepers' son. "I've heard some stories," he admitted.

Katherine looked down at her mug of tea as she went on, "It has made me somewhat distrusting, although I try and stay positive. I have turned into a bit of a recluse." Looking up at Terence, she continued, "When I'm with you, I feel very much at ease … and actually even more than that."

A little shy, Terry looked away for a moment. Returning her gaze he braved what he'd been meaning to say since the day he met Katherine at the bank when she'd bluntly asked for his first name.

"You're a courageous woman Katherine. As you know, I grew up with older sisters. It gave me a little advantage over other men, I guess, on the subject of women. I've never met a woman as forward as you. I try to embrace it, but don't want to take advantage of it."

"Your chivalry suits you Terry, but you can come off the white horse. I have neither expectations nor inhibitions."

Terence needed no further encouragement. He had wanted to kiss her from the first day they met. He stubbed his cigarette in the ashtray, took her mug and placed it on the table next to his. Apprehensively he put an arm around her shoulder, leaned forward and looked into her sparkling green eyes. It was Katherine who took the initiative and gently kissed him on the lips. Terry naturally responded. Their tongues touched in a long, lingering sense of being together. They stopped and stared at one another.

Katherine felt tremendous relief. She had feared the assault in Leith would prevent any new experiences, but it didn't. Kissing Terry felt surprisingly natural. Katherine pulled away. "Wait, I want us to do this properly Terry."

***

Katherine awoke around seven. Terry was lying on his side. She moved the bed sheet so she could watch her finger slowly and gently stroke his back, all the way to his buttocks, a smile of satisfaction resting on her face. It had been Terry's first time. He had ejaculated within seconds before they had done anything other than touch, but had more than made up for it later.

She felt her body respond when he stirred. They still had an hour before he had to leave.

CHAPTER 54
Tuesday 23 December 1902, Ballindalloch Castle, Banffshire, Scotland

William Macpherson had arrived late in the evening of the day before. His journey had encompassed the normal chaos due to the foul weather conditions. He hadn't slept well and had fallen into a bad tempered mood. He was seated by the fire in the main sitting room together with Victoria, who was standing anxiously by the window. William droned on about the staff of Ballindalloch. They were in his opinion, too old and no longer capable.

The room was silent apart from the crackle and sparking of the coals. "These trips from Chicago are killing me Victoria. It is MacLean's doing. The most dangerous part of the journey is in *his* carriage from Grantown to here. The man should retire. Don't let him anywhere near that automobile out there." William glanced at his pocket watch.

Victoria peered out of the window. "Well you had better suggest this to John, not me."

"The man is a lunatic, his mind must be going. And here we are waiting on him bringing Katie from Grantown. We must all be mad." He looked at his watch again.

William had been disturbed to discover Katherine had in fact moved out. His worries had increased when John informed him she was working in the orphanage. He had wanted to see Katherine close to Alexandra to compensate for what he feared John and Victoria were unable to supply in the girl's life. She was after all his granddaughter. He had failed her grandmother and Katherine and did not want to see this mistake repeated with Alexandra. The morning after his arrival he had gone to MacLean and in no uncertain terms had told him to bring Katherine. 'No matter what she is doing,' he had barked, 'tell her to pack plenty of clothes. I want her here for Christmas and Hogmanay.'

His mood had only softened when later he spent some time with Alexandra before she left for school. She had been so sweet calling him, 'uncle'. 'In future young lady, call me 'Papa William' he had said. She had giggled at the name.

"A carriage is approaching, it must be them," Victoria said, turning to face William. "I will go and arrange some tea."

Katherine came into the room, her face flushed with the cold. William stood up and hugged her. "Sit by the fire Katie and warm yourself. Let me look at you."

Katherine removed her coat and hat and sat down adjacent to William. "How was your journey?" she queried.

"Don't ask." He leaned forward and whispered, "What do you think of MacLean's handling of the carriage? It is a miracle you are here in one piece."

Katherine jumped to MacLean's defence. "William, the road is a quagmire. It's not *his* fault ..."

William got up and walked to the door and bawled in his loudest voice, "MacLean bring the box. Are you there? Bring me the box."

"What news of James and his family?" asked Katherine.

William sat back down looking pleased. "James by all accounts is doing well. We exchange correspondence on an infrequent basis. Now lady, what's going on? I'm told you live in Grantown." Leaning forward and in a low voice he asked, "Why have you left your daughter?"

Katherine leaned back in her chair. Keeping her voice down she replied, "I had no choice. Living with John and Victoria was simply impossible and they can't be parents when I am around. My presence was confusing Alexandra. She could sense we did not get along, and anyway, I needed a life of my own."

"You call working in an orphanage a life?"

"No, the orphanage is just part time," she snapped. "I work with a lady who knew mother. The children are adorable and one day I might even adopt."

William remained quiet.

"Having my own home and not being held accountable to anyone but myself gives me my life back. You must see this, and it's thanks to you."

Without announcement MacLean appeared, clumsily carrying on his shoulder a large wooden crate. For a fleeting moment William and Katherine thought he was going to fall over. He was gasping. "Where do you want this sir?"

"Just put it down man before you have a seizure," William bawled. "The crate has survived all the way from Chicago so don't you dare drop it."

MacLean looked around as if unsure where to place the crate.

"Put it down!" shouted William.

Finally, MacLean went down on one knee and slid the crate onto the wooden floor. William extended a hand to help him back on his feet. "Thank you sir," MacLean said, trying to catch his breath.

Katherine held a hand over her mouth to hide her giggle. They both watched an out of breathe MacLean leave the room.

Katherine was intrigued. "What's in the box if I might ask?"

Victoria came into the room carrying a tray with a pot of tea, cups and saucers, sugar and milk. "What was the commotion?" she said staring at the wooden crate.

"It's a doll's house for Alexandra," William said proudly. "I had it made especially for her and a lot of miniature furniture and other stuff. I hope to God it is still in one piece after MacLean's exploits."

"Thank you William, I am sure Alexandra will adore it," said Victoria, placing the tray on the table.

Katherine smiled. William *was* smitten with Alexandra.

The three of them chatted over tea. After a while Victoria excused herself. She had to get ready for John's return. He had spent most of the morning with the gamekeeper reviewing the accounts and planned expenditure for the coming year.

"Now where were we Katie?"

Katherine shrugged her shoulders.

"You are staying here until Friday and will spend time with your daughter. I told MacLean …"

"Yes, I will. How long will you be here?"

"I depart on January fifth weather permitting. As for you living in Grantown, you should make sure you are here at least one day a week Katie."

"I will, weather permitting."

William grunted. He moved closer, "I don't trust John. I need you to keep an eye on him. One more thing, I want you at the Kirk on Thursday."

Katherine sighed with exasperation. "I haven't been to church in ages. Reverend MacDonald is so old fashioned and he doesn't like me …"

"Unlike the minister in Joppa you mentioned in one of your letters? I want you there Katherine, by my side. You need to show yourself in church whether you like it or not."

Reluctantly she nodded in agreement preparing herself. "I do have to inform you of another suitor."

William stood up, grabbed the scuttle and poured more coals on the fire. He turned his head, "I'm listening."

"I am in a relationship with a young gentleman. Sit down for a moment," Katherine said, patting the seat next to her. William sat with a grunt and listened intently as his daughter spoke of Terry with great enthusiasm.

"For a banker he seems like a decent fellow Katie." He paused and asked, "If Terry plays shinty he must have a few bruises on his legs."

Katherine's face reddened.

"You be careful. You of all people should know. No more babies. You are a grown woman, so if you must indulge, take precautions."

Katherine appreciated her father's frankness. She could never have had a conversation like this with Gordon.

"Come on then," William said, slapping Katherine's knee. "Let's wrap up, brave the snow and go meet Alexandra coming out of school."

CHAPTER 55
Thursday 15 January 1903, Grantown-on-Spey, Morayshire, Scotland

The winter cast one of the worst snow storms in living memory. Eighty mile per hour gales swept in from the west. After two days of wind and drifting snow, towns and villages were cut off completely. The roads between Grantown to Forres and Elgin were no exception. When the snow finally ceased, temperatures plummeted to minus sixteen degrees. The landscape was a vast frozen mass. Food and fuel supplies were becoming scarce. Many people were forced to burn furniture, in an effort to keep warm. The highland counties were in total disarray and the young and elderly especially vulnerable. In the farmlands, livestock loss were a catastrophe.

Katherine, wrapped in a quilt, sat close to the fire. Her stock of coal was low. She looked around the room thinking the mahogany table will be first to go. She didn't like it anyway. Her mind wandered to Terry. He had returned to Forres just after New Year. They had corresponded almost daily, but the storm now prevented any mail. She didn't have many concerns on Alexandra's well-being. The castle was prepared for anything Mother Nature could throw at it. They had an abundance of fuel and food.

The couple next door had escaped the nightmare. A week earlier they had travelled to Dundee. Mr Winchester had been an angel. He and many volunteers had been busy moving desperate people into the Grammar School. This included the complete evacuation of the orphanage when their supply of coal had run-out. This morning, he had come to her back door, to make sure everything was in good order. 'The biggest danger is burst water and gas pipes, Miss Macpherson, especially when the thaw arrives,' he had warned.

Around mid-morning, Katherine thought the best method to keep warm was to go and join the volunteers.

CHAPTER 56
February 1903, Grantown-on-Spey, Morayshire, Scotland

The aftermath of the January blizzard had been devastating to the local community. Grantown had suffered over thirty deaths, including two babies and two young children. There had been severe flooding and concern had been raised on the water level of the Spey and Avon, but the banks of the rivers held firm. Skeletal remains had been washed up by the Spey downstream, close to the Burn of Mulben. Katherine felt anxious when she heard local gossip speculate it could be Gordon Macpherson. She hoped it wasn't true. She couldn't bear the story being resurrected in the newspapers.

Terry turned out to be a faithful correspondent. The most recent letter suggested he would come to Grantown at weekends on the condition she planned a visit to Forres, so he could show off his home town. Katherine pondered over her reply. In response she wrote, 'I will welcome you with open arms,' avoiding any mention of Forres. Normality returned. Although even more snow had fallen, it was nothing compared to the January storm. Katherine had made a couple of trips to the castle, hiring a horse-pulled carriage. She had been informed that her brother Donald had no firm plans to return home as yet. John had scoffed, 'Apparently he is busy in Edinburgh helping establish government aid for war veterans.'

Meanwhile, she maintained her commitments at the orphanage. She worked on Tuesdays, Wednesdays and Fridays. The children she taught were between the ages of five and ten. The older boys and girls would be working, mainly on the farms or the linen and wool factories. She would teach English from ten o'clock until mid-afternoon and use the last few hours to nurse the children in the sickbay. Katherine was also an active player on their fund raising committee. She had managed to convince Mr Gunn to provide salmon and game to sell at the Saturday market. Katherine also offered adult reading and writing classes, two evenings a week. The response had been overwhelming. Her 'students' paid whatever they could afford, either in money, produce or anything which could be sold.

Her weekends had become precious. Since the beginning of March, Terry would arrive in Grantown either on a Friday or Saturday evening, depending on whether he was playing shinty. He would normally catch the last train to Forres on Sunday.

Katherine looked forward to the summer months so she and Terry could spend more time to enjoy the local countryside.

CHAPTER 57
May1903, Morayshire, Scotland

The train steamed towards Forres. The morning had brought a mixture of bright sunshine and occasional cloudbursts. The carriage was quiet. Katherine sat by the window with Terence beside her. Only two others occupied seats, a young girl in the company of an elderly gentleman.

Terence had arrived at Katherine's the evening before so they could spend the night together.

"I am so happy you will finally see Forres. You will be impressed Katie. It is a tidy wee town. Around five thousand people live there."

"It's a lot bigger than Grantown. I have faint memories visiting when I was a young girl. I remember being on a boat on the River Findhorn."

"Good salmon-fishing there, a bit like the Spey I guess. We can enjoy a lovely walk along the river if the weather holds up. The Cluny Hills is also a beautiful walk. You can get right to the top on a good day and see Nelson's Tower."

Katherine smiled at him and saluted, "Aye aye, Admiral."

He returned a grin. "I don't think we will have time to go there today, but we could go to Brodie Castle?"

"No thank you, I've had my fill of castles. Are there any distilleries in Forres? My f ... uncle imports whisky in the United States. I could perhaps improve my knowledge on how the beastly drink is made, and buy him a gift."

"There are quite a few in the area but not in Forres itself. We did have one, but it didn't last long. It was owned by a spirit broker from Leith." Terry paused. "Benromach I believe."

"Never heard of it," said Katherine now losing interest in the topic.

They sat in silence for a while. Terry was the one to break it. "Katie, I do love you. You know this, don't you?"

Katherine nodded, but remained quiet. She couldn't bring herself to reply. She'd rather not think about how their relationship was developing, content with the way things were.

"There is something you need to know," he said softly. "It's something we have never discussed."

Katherine shifted slightly. "What?"

"I'm Catholic. All my family are devout worshipers."

Katherine couldn't hide her surprise. He was right. It had never crossed her mind. Searching for a reply, the best she could come up with was, "So, what does it matter?" The moment the words left her mouth, she realised it did matter. It mattered a lot.

"My family is quite well known in the area. They have a reputation to maintain."

Katherine felt her eyes fill. In a soft voice she said, "And of course with *my* reputation it would tarnish the bank's name, is that it?"

"Oh Katie please don't say that. I love you, you know I do and I'm willing to face those problems." His eyes were dancing. "If I can't work for my father I'll go and find a job somewhere else. We're almost living together and you know I'm not hiding you from anyone. The whole world can know I love you."

Katherine didn't answer. She glanced out of the window knowing her fantasy world was about to come to an abrupt end. Suddenly, she couldn't fathom why she had allowed the situation to get this far. Their love making over the months had become increasingly satisfying and exciting. For the first time in her life, togetherness, a sharing, a longing and love for a man had clouded her judgement, yet deep down she'd known this would happen. He deserved better.

"Katherine? What is wrong?"

She turned and faced him. "Terry, I think you should be wise and marry a nice Catholic girl from Forres. Family is important. It is very difficult being an outcast, believe me, I'm saying this from experience."

"But Katie…I…we…"

"Hush," she said placing a finger on his lips. "There is so much you do not know about me and never will." Tears were now rolling down her face. "I am truly sorry I've hurt you. We did this together and perhaps we shouldn't have, but think of the beauty of what has simply happened. Look at how close we have become, best friends to one another. In a strange way you're like a brother. I know brothers and sisters don't do …" Katherine struggled to look at him, he was clearly distraught. "What I mean is we've been bound by our independence, rather than a church that keeps couples together for better and for worse. I will never forget what we had. I'm so sorry to have caused you grief and I think it's time I should leave."

"Leave? Leave where?"

"I've been contemplating to spend some time with my Uncle William in Chicago, do some travelling. I'm not cut out to be someone's wife Terry. I need more out of life."

The guard appeared in the carriage, "Next stop Forres," he called out.

"I don't understand," Terence said. His face was now sallow, his eyes filling.

Katherine stood up to retrieve her bag. She looked at him leaning forward in the seat holding his head in both hands. With a tremor in her voice she said, "I think it best I take the next train back to Grantown."

CHAPTER 58
October 1903, Grantown-on-Spey, Morayshire, Scotland

Katherine stood on the Spey Bridge on the edge of Grantown looking down on the river. The fast flow and darkness of the water transfixed her. Low hanging clouds swirled and gusty blasts of wind made her shiver. The summer months had passed slowly. She had been dejected, unable to act normally. Her break up with Terry had suspended her life and left her bereft of how to continue. Even her treasured work at the orphanage had suffered. The Governess had shown sympathy and had instructed Katherine to take a month away from the institution. She did! Her visits to the castle became infrequent. When she was with Alexandra on her seventh birthday in July, even Victoria had genuinely expressed concern on her unusual lacklustre demeanour.

In August, she returned to the art classes, but the memories overshadowed enjoyment. After one class she simply stopped going.

Katherine had asked Terry to promise not to write and he'd kept his word. She now wondered if he yearned as much for her as she did for him. She felt so lonely.

Pulling the collar of her coat around her neck, she walked towards town. She needed to make a few decisions. She would write to William. He had stopped visiting Ballindalloch. He was getting older and the strain of such a journey was now more difficult. Then she needed to inquire into the cost of a ships passage to New York and Boston and how to buy a ticket. Her father would be thrilled to know she was finally coming. She also needed to talk to John and Victoria about allowing Alexandra to come with her for a summer holiday next year. Her brother and sister-in-law had resorted to sending Alexandra to summer retreats. They never embarked on a proper family holiday. It was time Alexandra had some fun in her life.

Finally the most trivial of all; she had purchased a novel some weeks ago but had been unable to concentrate on reading. *I need to curl up on the couch and start.* She recalled the dust cover, The Call of the Wild, by Jack London, a Tale of Survival.

CHAPTER 59
Saturday 21 May 1904, Ballindalloch, Banffshire, Scotland

"Yes please, can you move a little to the right ladies and just a wee bit closer together please?" Alex Ledingham carefully repositioned the wooden tripod on the white cobblestones beside the river. He would not want his expensive Thornton-Pickard camera, which served as his main source of income, to topple over.

"Now look at the camera please and hold it … yes … here it comes …" Ledingham had to raise his voice to overcome the noise of the rapid rush of the River Spey. A blue flashlight of magnesium exploded, for a moment illuminating the grey highland surroundings.

"I think we have it," the courteous photo artist said, slightly bowing his head to his subjects in acknowledgement. He'd enjoyed making the picture with the patient ladies. Even though photography assignments had brought him to Ballindalloch on other occasions, Mr Ledingham could not remember seeing the girl before. The likeness with her aunt was striking.

"You're definitely a Macpherson," he said to Alexandra, and in an attempt to discreetly charm them, "you and your aunt could be sisters."

The younger sister of the laird intrigued him. She had studied medicine he knew; one of the first women in Scotland. Ledingham had to admit he admired the lady's zest for learning, although he wouldn't want *his* daughter to do the same.

"Thank you Mr Ledingham, make three copies of the picture please so my niece can have her own copy and I have one spare."

"I don't mind sharing Aunt Katie, it will be our picture." The young girl's voice sounded happy at the prospect.

"Yes, my dear, but I want to have my own copy when I'm travelling."

The happy expression on the girls face fell. "Mother said you would never be going back to Edinburgh."

"No sweetheart, not Edinburgh."

"Where will you be going Aunt Katie?" she asked.

"On a ship and sail to the other side of the Atlantic."

"America!" Alexandra screamed, showing her quick learning. "What will you do there?"

"I am going to visit Uncle William."

"Have I met him?" Alexandra asked, probing her mind. To her, the Macpherson family was extensive, many only visiting on rare occasions.

"Oh yes, he visited at Christmas a few times. Do you remember? He brought you that beautiful doll's house you have in your room."

"Why doesn't he come *here* again? Why do you have to go *there*?"

Katherine felt a twinge of guilt. How was she to explain to her eight- year old daughter why she couldn't bear to stay?

"Tell you what," Katherine said, taking the girls hand in her own. "I'll give you a photograph album for you to put the picture in. From now on we will take pictures. You can keep them safe and look at them when I am away. I'll be back for Hogmanay and we can look at the stars together and make a wish."

"Promise?" the girl asked, suspicious of the aunt who had proven she could easily change her mind.

"I promise! I'll be back, cross my heart."

CHAPTER 60
Saturday 15 October 2011, Ballindalloch Castle, Banffshire, Scotland

Angus and John were sitting opposite each other at the study desk. The laird's face was lined with concern. They planned to accompany the gamekeeper later in the afternoon to inspect the locations of recent attacks on game birds, but the rain battering against the window was not encouraging, nor the atmosphere between father and son.

"Why didn't you inform me of your investment in Glen Fraoch John?"

John leaned forward. "Dad, I didn't feel it was necessary, it was such a small amount initially. The stock accumulated over many years. I never expected the share price to grow the way it did!"

Angus frowned. "I must be honest I am extremely disappointed you kept this from me. I don't like family secrets, especially by my eldest son and future laird."

John smiled ruefully at his father's comment. "You wouldn't have approved. Admit it, you would have wanted me to invest in Grants."

Angus knew this to be true. "So, I assume Doug Stein knew you were Broadside whatever. Who else knows?"

"The Grants," John said softly.

"My God!" was all Angus could say. "I feel such a fool. Stein knew and even the Grants, but not me, your own father who now has to act as executor for Doug." Angus leaned back in his chair. "To make matters worse you are now caught up in a bloody murder. Did you see the news? International espionage suspected."

"I am not involved in Doug's murder," John shouted, pushing away from the desk, his chair scraping noisily over the floor.

"Then why is bloody Duckett coming to see you?" he cried out, throwing both hands in the air. Angus gave a sarcastic laugh. "He must love this. Yet another reason to hound the Macphersons!"

"Dad, for the last time I had nothing to do with Doug's death. I simply wanted to sell my stock to Grabowski and Doug knew this. Their offer was subject to Doug selling a proportion which would give them ownership. I could have made a small fortune."

"Listen to you," Angus fumed in contempt. "Working in the bank has turned your head. Why do you need money? Look outside, all this is yours."

"It's called independence father, but maybe you don't understand the meaning of that. Besides as you well know, 'all this'," John gestured towards the window, "costs a bundle to maintain."

Angus glared at his son. He would never have talked this way to *his* father. "As executor of Doug's wishes I'm telling you, you'd better find another buyer, because the Grabowski offer will never ever be accepted. Over my dead body! Please leave me be. I need to be on my own for a while and I think *you* need to go and prepare for Duckett's questions."

***

DI Duckett was always punctual. At five minutes to three he arrived at the tourist entrance. John had made sure someone was there to open the gate. The rain had stopped and the skies were clearing. At exactly three pm he climbed out of his car and was met by the autumn aromas of the Ballindalloch estate. He looked around at the lush manicured lawns stretching out before him. In the distance, a mild breeze gently brushed the trees which hid the river.

"Good morning," greeted John Macpherson, startling Duckett out of his observations. "Could we enjoy the fresh air and have a walk inspector?" They shook hands.

"We meet again Mr Macpherson. I don't mind a stroll. Let me get my coat from the car."

"Call me John, please. Come on, let's take the river walk."

The grey gravel path meandered its way towards the river. "How well did you know Mr Stein? I know it's Walter Brodie who represents Broadside on the Board. So I am guessing you didn't meet up with him often?"

"Correct. Can I call you Peter?"

Duckett nodded.

"We rarely had any formal communication. We bumped into one another at social events. In fact, the last time I saw him was at the castle, after Gordon's funeral. I really didn't have many direct dealings with him."

"Did Brodie inform you of problems at Glen Fraoch during the past few months John?"

John stopped walking. "Oh, you mean the water contamination? That was a nasty piece of work."

"As well as a fire in the loading bay and losing major customers," Duckett added. "Strange isn't it, losing loyal customers for no apparent reason?"

"I wasn't aware of any fire. The lost clients were my biggest concern and I did request Walter get to the bottom of this. I do get copies of the board meeting minutes so I know most of what goes on."

201

As they continued their walk John asked, "Are you heading the search for Doug's killer?"

"No, it's at the highest level. My role is to investigate a motive."

"I assure you I had nothing to do with Doug Stein's death, you surely know this?"

As they approached the wooden fence that prevented cattle from straying towards the river, Duckett asked, "Broadside Holdings and its relationship with the Grabowski Group. Can you enlighten me?"

"Relationship! What relationship?" John exclaimed. "I don't think so! They have been offering serious cash on behalf of their client to buy out Glen Fraoch. Doug always refused …"

"Did you agree with Mr Stein not to sell to the Ukrainians?"

"What a strange question. What on earth has this got to do with anything?"

John unlatched the gate. After they both stepped through, John turned to secure it.

"You would make a bundle of money wouldn't you?" Duckett suggested.

"Yes, along with many others I may add. But inspector your question is hypothetical."

"So, you had no direct contact with Grabowski or any of their clients?" Duckett continued.

Without hesitation an irritated John responded, "None whatsoever."

They continued on a dirt path that followed the river. The noise of the rapids changed the atmosphere.

"I believe you work for RBS, in the foreign investment branch. I've seen your profile on the company website."

"What of it?"

"Tough time for banks," Duckett said, stopping to stare at the river. "Especially RBS, they have made thousands redundant. How is your department doing? They must be struggling as well."

"We are keeping our head above water Peter. Get to the point."

"I will. Do you travel in your line of work? I believe you have responsibilities for Eastern Europe?"

"Yes, but I never visited the Grabowski Group if that's where you are going. My business trips are mainly to Moscow, Kiev and Tbilisi."

"Kiev is close to the Grabowski office. I am going by memory here. Does Berezan ring a bell, John? It's close to Kiev."

John stopped in his tracks and glared at the policeman. "I told you I have no direct dealings with the Grabowski Group. I'm done with this talk. Can we go back to the house?"

"One more question," commanded Duckett holding John hostage. "Where were you last Monday the tenth of October?"

"I would be in the office," John answered curtly.

"And you can prove that?"

"Yes, ask my colleagues and check my meeting schedule. I have nothing to hide."

"Oh don't you worry, I will check." Duckett looked at the angry waters. The confluence of the Spey and Avon looked menacing as if the rivers were battling for control. "Isn't this the exact spot where they said Laird Gordon was fishing the day he disappeared?"

"Inspector, Peter, I don't know. Why are you asking me my whereabouts on the tenth of October?"

Duckett gave a thin smile, knowing John was rattled. "Mr Stein had a meeting with Grabowski representatives in Edinburgh on the tenth. Stein's secretary, Linda, confirmed this, but she has no idea where the meeting was held. I have the names of the two Ukrainian gentlemen who attended. I just wondered if you were there to help convince Mr Stein to sell up. Or did you send Walter Brodie? Maybe the meeting was held at RBS or at Broadside Holdings' office?" Peter Duckett stared at an angry John Macpherson. "Well, answer me."

"No, I wasn't there and neither was Walter. They certainly did not meet at RBS. As for Broadside Holdings, the so called office is my apartment."

"I checked the company registry in Edinburgh and couldn't find Broadside Holdings." Duckett looked at John.

"Because it's registered in Jersey," John responded raising his voice. "The Channel Islands, in case you didn't know."

Duckett smiled slyly at John's remark. "Let's head back John. I'm finished for now until I confirm a few things."

"Like what?"

"Oh making sure you were at work on the tenth. No missing hours. Our legal guys will look at Broadside Holdings, to make sure all is above board. You know tax, financial transactions, salaries drawn and the like. Is your father involved with Broadside? I understand he is the executor of Mr Stein's will."

"You fucking leave my father out of it." John had lost his patience. "Ever since the incident in August you have been hounding us. All you are doing is wasting the taxpayer's money. It's people like me who keep you in a job."

Duckett was not deterred. "Aye, the Macphersons have excelled in keeping me busy. I'll be in touch." John was flabbergasted as Peter Duckett made his way back.

CHAPTER 61
Saturday 15 October, 2011 London, England

Smartly dressed in a dark blue suit and appropriate shirt and tie, Thomas Macpherson walked in to the cocktail bar of the Richmond Hill Hotel near Dew Gardens in the west of London.

He glanced at his watch and sat down on a plush sofa positioned close to a window overlooking the hotel car park. A young waitress approached him. After a welcoming smile she asked, "Can I get you anything sir?"

"I'll have a bottle of sparkling water please, no ice or lemon." As he glanced out of the window he saw Hugh Millar make his way across the car park with the aid of a walking stick. Macpherson's mind returned to Belfast in October 1974. It had been late evening, the day of the Long Kesh fire and subsequent riots. His squad had been directed to the Ardoyne district to quell a Republican mob. No sooner had they arrived, shots were heard close to a derelict petrol station. Together with three soldiers he went to investigate. In the station courtyard some twenty yards in front had been a wounded officer on his knees and a man aiming a pistol at the stricken soldier's head. Without hesitation Thomas had pulled his handgun and shot the terrorist dead. The sergeant he saved was Hugh Millar. Some years later Hugh was discharged from active duty and was given a senior administration role in the army National Archives headquarters.

Thomas looked around the bar. Only two other people were present. On seeing Millar come in, he stood up.

Hugh walked towards him with a huge grin on his face. "Tam Macpherson, I'll be damned." The men shook hands with vigour.

Millar removed his coat and sat down. "It's good to see you Tam, you are looking well. It must be the highland air and the porridge man."

Thomas Macpherson wished he could return the compliment. Hugh, although of similar age, looked older and his skin colour was like an old newspaper. "Hughie thanks for seeing me I really appreciate it."

"Tam for God's sake, you are speaking as if I had to reschedule my appointments." Millar leaned back in his chair, "So how the hell are the Macphersons? Are you still living in the castle?"

The young waitress interrupted, put a glass on the table and poured Thomas's water. She asked Millar if he wanted anything. He asked for a large Glenfiddich, neat.

"I'm on my own now, Betty passed away five years ago," Hugh volunteered.

Thomas eyed the ex-soldier loosening his tie. "I'm sorry to hear that Hugh. Betty was a fine woman."

Hugh's eyes held a watery glaze. "I saw the news on the telly, was it August? Couldn't believe my ears, Thomas Macpherson detained along with some American woman. Christ you could have knocked me over with a feather." He leaned towards Thomas and said, "What the hell was going on?"

"Well it might be connected to the favour I asked you on the phone."

Thomas only smiled and Millar shook his head. "You are a secretive one at times aren't you?" He pulled some papers from the inside pocket of his blazer. "Here, this is all I could get."

Thomas straightened out the papers and read with Hugh watching him. The waitress set Millar's whisky on the table.

"You can see a file was deemed classified. Even with my contacts I couldn't find out anything more on Munro. Mind you the Alexander Stewart guy was on his ship for sure."

Thomas looked up. "Munro and Stewart's death certificate's both state 'killed in action' on the exact same date, but zero casualties were reported during the evacuation."

Millar looked at Thomas. "That struck me too Tam. The evacuation in 1916 went peacefully. The Turks never fired a single shot."

Thomas sipped his water while Hugh downed his whisky in one gulp.

CHAPTER 62
Wednesday 3 August 1904, SS Caledonia, Atlantic Ocean

Katherine stood on the first class deck of the SS Caledonia. She could feel the warmth of the morning sun on her face. The sea was tranquil. Even though it was still early, the world around her was already wide awake.

Seagulls were squealing and artfully manoeuvring their wingtips in acrobatic attempts to catch the remains of breakfast the cook's mates were casting overboard from the poop deck. Katherine noted the huge numbers of seagulls gathering even though land must still be a day away. She wondered what made them abandon their natural food resources closer to home, and go to such length to fly all the way to the ship for scraps of food. It seemed such a useless practice, yet she could relate to the gulls. Giving birth to her daughter, studying medicine, practicing her profession, all the intention and effort she had put into her enterprises had been burned up in the process of it, leaving her nothing to go on with. It could make life feel utterly useless. Why go through the motions when in the end nothing is gained, yet sooner lost. Why bear a child when she could not raise it? Why study medicine when women were not considered suitable doctors? Why start a medical practice when it is inevitably closed down? Why make love, when the love has no future? To Katherine, life had become one big string of ponderings.

She had questioned what had made her put in yet another attempt to change the confines of her world. Sometimes, she wished she had married a Grant, like Gordon had wanted her to. She could have been comfortable in a life of luxury. People would have accepted her, rather than denounce her. She wouldn't have had to fight over her future or being a woman. Life could have been so much easier. Yet, like the seagulls, she had chosen to go to great lengths to find elsewhere what nourished her in life, outside of her natural habitat.

Katherine retrieved her cigarette case from her purse and stepped aside out of the breeze to adjust a Phillip Morris into a holder and light it.

There was no way Katherine could ever go back. She had contemplated at length telling Alexandra the truth and take her to Chicago, but had decided against it. It would have caused a huge family eruption. She had already caused enough. Gratefully Katherine allowed the cigarette smoke to flow into her lungs, bracing herself for what Fate would have next in store.

Impatiently Katherine elbowed her way through the crowd. Even though first and second class passengers had their medical check aboard ship and could go straight to customs at the pier, the whole process of entering the United States was arduous. A porter carrying her luggage had difficulty keeping up with her.

"No lady to fool around with," he muttered in an Irish accent; and he'd seen a few of those in his days. "Excuse me ma'am," he called out to Katherine. "Make way to your left."

A frown creasing her forehead Katherine looked around anxiously. The ship had been almost a day ahead of schedule. She'd sent a telegram and hoped William had received it, otherwise she would have to find a suitable hotel. They had arranged to stay in New York for two days to do some sightseeing before taking the train to Chicago.

A woman's shriek made Katherine turn. A girl in her twenties was trying to step away from a child who was vomiting over her skirt. For a moment Katherine's instinct prompted her to assist but she stopped in her tracks. It was probably the combination of the heat and excitement.

William had warned her to stay clear from any medical practice in America. 'Doctors are not well regarded in the United States' he'd written. 'Many don't even have a degree and have not the slightest notion what they are doing. They are often paid in goods and generally treated as scoundrels.' Katherine had scorned the remark and in her reply she hinted that maybe it was time for change. William had been stern, promising he would introduce her to friends who could help her settle in her new surroundings and help her decide what she wanted to pursue. He had suggested she could explore her talent in the arts, painting perhaps.

The jostling of crowds, the noise of nervous horses, streetcars, people shouting out names of loved ones or business associates made her feel she was back in Edinburgh.

"Katherine, Katie." The familiar voice of William Macpherson was most welcome. Within moments they were hugging. She enjoyed the feeling of being welcomed.

"Let me look at you." William stood back, his eyes dancing at the delight standing before him. "You look as pretty as a picture Katie. How was your journey?" Katherine was wearing a long cotton dress with a high collar, edged with lace and a matching ornate hat trimmed with ribbon. Her leather fawn handbag dangled from her elbow. The porter gave a sharp whistle to draw the attention of a cab driver.

"Come, this way," William said, taking her hand. The porter followed pulling a cart holding Katherine's luggage.

"The journey was boring, a lot of toffee-nosed snobs who did nothing but complain. Thank heavens I had my books."

William gave a grateful porter a dollar. Soon, they were sitting inside the back of a taxicab. The driver was mumbling to himself as he secured Katherine's travel trunk to the front of the carriage. He clearly disliked the physical aspect of his job and cursed when he almost lost his top hat to the coastal breeze. A metal plaque inscribed, 'The Electric Carriage & Wagon Co.' was displayed on the side of the vehicle. Katherine was intrigued by the automobile. Two enclosed passenger seats to the rear with space in front for luggage. The driver sat behind the passengers elevated to a height where a clear view of the road was possible.

"Hotel Wolcott and don't spare the horses," shouted William laughing at his own jest. "It is called an Electrobat," William whispered, observing his daughter's puzzled expression. "I cannot steer one of these yet. It looks too complicated."

"We will learn together, it will be fun."

"We will indeed Katie, but not in this little carriage. I have my eye on a Studebaker – Model C."

Katherine had no real interest in automobiles. "How are you father? Even after all these years it still feels peculiar calling you father or do you prefer pater?"

"I'm keeping well and good God girl! William will do fine. How is my wee granddaughter?"

"Alexandra has just turned eight now. It is difficult to believe at times." Katherine was searching inside her handbag. "She is such a clever wee girl and has been doing so well at Inveravon. Next year, she will be going to St George's School for Girls in Edinburgh. Have a look." Katherine handed William the photograph taken by the Spey.

"Aye well she takes her brains after her grandfather," William said, peering at the photograph. "I hope John and Victoria are looking after her well and have inspected the school in Edinburgh? I never receive any correspondence from John or any of your brothers. Not even from James in Carolina. She is a bonnie lassie," he said proudly handing back the photograph. "You will miss her Katie."

Katherine remembered her daughter's face before she left. "I do. She finds it hard to get used to her 'Aunt Katie' travelling. I've spoken to John about bringing her here for the summer."

"You must find the pretence difficult at times, I know *I* do. I would like nothing better than to acknowledge Alexandra as my grandchild. When the time is right you and the wee one will be my benefactors."

"Yes, it is trying. John and Victoria do look after her but I'm sure they will be happy when Alexandra goes to Edinburgh and so am I to be honest."

"Well, I will enjoy each moment she is here," William said gleefully.

William edged closer to Katherine and put an arm around her shoulders. The vehicle was making its way slowly through the broad roads. Katherine had to admit the ride was extremely comfortable. She looked out the small side window admiring the buildings but was aghast at the congestion. Each passing minute seemed to add to the number of horse drawn and horseless carriages, omnibuses, some with two or three wagons and people of all ages riding bicycles.

Pointing out the window William said, "Broadway's out there."

Katherine had never seen anything like it. It was nothing like Edinburgh, this was a metropolis. Many of the buildings were gigantic and they passed theatre after theatre, the sidewalks bustling. She was struck by the number of dark skinned people. There were street acts of all types doing their tricks and an abundance of food stalls.

"I happened to acquire two tickets for tomorrow evening Katie, at the New Amsterdam. Guess what the stage play is?"

"What? Stop teasing me." Playfully she slapped him on the arm.

"Dr Jekyll and Mr Hyde, it opens tomorrow night."

Katherine released a shriek, almost causing the automobile driver to swerve off track. "Robert Louis Stevenson, I've read the book and it is ever so frightening."

"And while you are here," William said, moving closer to Katherine, "I want you to find a handsome, American gentleman, get wed and give me more grandchildren. You are now twenty-seven years old, time is running out. You don't want to be an old maid do you?"

Katherine pushed his arm, "You are one to talk, old man. It's time *you* had a woman in *your* life."

William gave a set smile. "I do in fact. Clementina Dorrington is her name. A good woman, you'll meet her. She has actually accompanied me on the odd business trip."

The automobile slowed, as they approached their three hundred guest room hotel on West 31st Street. "I will tell you more about her later."

***

The hotel was in the perfect location between Fifth Avenue and Broadway. Katherine was impressed with the scale of the lobby. It extended all the way under a musician's gallery and continued into a dining room at the rear. The polite male receptionist explained the ground floor had a ladies reception room, café, smoking room, a children's dining room and a palm court. French mirrors lined the Louis XVI-style lobby. Mahogany chairs, upholstered in green velvet, carried the hotel's embroidered crest. The palm court ceiling had stained glass over a trellis of vines giving the effect of being open to the sky. Ornamental iron, rich moulding and mosaic floors decorated the lobby.

William and Katherine found the guest rooms were executed with artistic taste and the appointments were perfect to the last degree, including all the latest improvements for the comfort of hotel patrons.

They enjoyed a busy two days in New York. The stage play had been a sell-out. The hotel concierge had given them a bundle of calling cards and recommended the most convenient way to see the town was to board the electric omnibus at the Flatiron Building on Broadway and Fifth Avenue. He also suggested the Steam Yacht excursion boat. 'And mention Kenneth sent you', he'd said. 'Just look for the Seeing New York signs'.

They visited the Statue of Liberty, using the steam yacht and spent a lot of time in Manhattan. Katherine tried to seek out the more obscure buildings, but her first call was to The Metropolitan Museum of Art on Fifth Avenue, where they spent a few hours absorbing the collections. In Manhattan they explored, The Third Judicial District Courthouse, St Paul's Chapel and the Bridge of Sighs, a small bridge connecting the Manhattan Criminal Courts building to Tombs Prison. In the Morningside area of Manhattan they visited Grant's Tomb. "Aren't the Grants everywhere," Katherine had remarked.

She had particularly adored Times Square, formerly Longacre Square. It had been renamed in April after The New York Times moved its headquarters to the newly erected Times Building. William revealed to Katherine how on last New Year's Eve, The Times, to promote their new building, had staged a fireworks display at midnight, set off from the roof. The event had been a huge success attracting 200,000 spectators.

They finished their sightseeing exploits by using a horse-pulled taxicab. William wanted to show Katherine the Andrew Carnegie Mansion.

"Andrew is probably the most successful industrialist ever known," William informed Katherine. "He was born in Dunfermline you know. He is out of the country right now otherwise I would have arranged for you to meet him." William chuckled.

"Why are you grinning like a cat which got the cream?"

"Some years ago we received a letter from Carnegie requesting we send the President, it was Benjamin Harrison, a keg of nine or ten gallons of our best whisky. It was a simple letter, at the end he had written, 'send the bill to me'."

"And did you?"

"Sure! And it's not only how I got to know Andrew, but when word got out it helped boost our sales. He is quite the genius. He taught me a few things Katie. I always remember his advice on getting products into the market: 'the first man gets the oyster; the second man gets the shell.'"

"He must have learned through trial and error. How old is he?"

"I would guess he must be around seventy."

Katherine pondered, "Did he arrive here after the Civil War?"

"No," William replied impressed by his daughter's historical knowledge. "He was here during the war. Like many of the rich he avoided fighting by paying a replacement to fight for him."

The comment disgusted Katherine. She turned and glanced out of the window.

***

Saturday 6 August, 1904, New York, 5:35 pm

On Saturday late afternoon William and Katherine arrived at Grand Central Depot and had their luggage deposited with the porter. They were walking on the lower level towards the platform to board the express passenger train to Chicago.

"Just wait till you see this locomotive," William said, in an excited tone to Katherine. It's even faster than the Royal Scotsman."

Katherine, who knew about William's love for trains, had never quite understood men's infatuation with anything mechanical that could go fast. She had to admit though, the engine looked impressive.

The railroad company, 20th Century Limited, had a reputation for style. The Century ran as a luxury sleeper train of Pullman Company coaches.

"How long will it take us to reach Chicago?" asked Katherine.

"Twenty hours give or take," replied William. "You will have many amenities to pass your time Katie. I have arranged some secretarial services on board as I have a lot of catching up to do. Meanwhile, you can get pampered in the Ladies Lounge. We can enjoy a drink in the observation car where we get a wonderful view of the Hudson."

"Twenty hours, my goodness, I never thought for a moment it would take this long."

"Katie, it is almost one thousand miles to LaSalles Street Station," William said, and shook his head. This is probably the most famous and fastest train in the world!"

On reaching the platform they were greeted by two attendants and directed to their specific carriage. They entered the train ready to be serviced by stewards, conductors and bar tenders. It surely was the train of tycoons.

CHAPTER 64
Sunday 7 August 1904, Chicago, Illinois, USA

"Katherine, have a look," William called pointing at a luxurious electric automobile purring its way along Maxwell Street. "There's the kind of vehicle I have set my mind on, a four passenger." Katherine was standing in front of the steps leading to William's terraced house on Near West Side. It was to be her home for the foreseeable future. She turned and glanced at the road. The footman who was busy unloading Katherine's travel trunk stopped to follow her gaze. The driver of the passing automobile courteously doffed his hat to his audience making Katherine laugh.

"The gentleman's new pride and joy no doubt," she jested. "I still prefer horses. They are more fun."

William smiled like a Cheshire Cat. "I'd advise you to embrace the mechanics of modern transport. An electric automobile would be ideal for you, no cranking needed on those. Much better than the dirty gas powered engines."

Katherine looked unconvinced. "I'll let you try all the latest inventions," she jested. She did notice the automobile's high roof and thought how convenient that was when wearing a hat.

"Katherine, this is Danaher." William drew the attention of the man servant who was still staring at the Studebaker. "Anything you need, anything at all, just ask him."

Richard Danaher assembled himself, "Yes sir." His eyes briefly inspected Katherine. "Miss Dorrington is waiting in the lounge, she arrived thirty minutes ago."

William frowned. He'd hoped she would have waited until tomorrow. He wanted Katie to get familiar with her new home first.

"Ah the mysterious Miss Dorrington," Katherine remarked. "I get to meet her."

"I told you Katie it is not what you think. We're just good friends."

"Acquaintances who regularly go on vacation together! William why are you so coy? It is obvious you are fond of her. I have seen it in your eyes when you talk of her." Katherine wiped her forehead and wished she had dressed more appropriately. It was hot and humid.

William seemed embarrassed. Katherine was not the kind of daughter he could instruct to shut her pretty little mouth and mind her own business. She'd mock him.

Feeling a little apprehensive he ushered Katherine inside. With a sigh of relief to be out of the heat she looked around the modest hall. *A typical gentleman's house.* A small circular table, two high backed chairs, a coatrack and a landscape painting which looked desolate on a spacious wall, failed to provide a welcoming ambience.

"Darling, it's wonderful to see you!" The greeting made Katherine turn and observe a woman appear from the sitting room. She seemed to glide rather than walk. Katherine had not busied herself imagining what Clementina Dorrington would look like, but the woman who stood in front of her was far from what she expected. If anything, Katherine had pictured her to resemble her mother. Clementina emanated the total opposite. Looking her up and down shamelessly, Katherine peered at a woman dressed in a purple skirt of thin velvet showing part of her shins covered in silk stockings and shoes tied with laces around the calves and ankles. A small sleeveless body exposed much of her neckline as well as her shoulders, only covered by a wide silk shawl hanging loosely over her arms, reaching almost to the floor. A small hat decorated with skilfully draped folds and feathers, tilted over her left ear. The finishing touch was her makeup, giving her face an artistic look. Katherine guessed this flamboyant lady was in her early forties. Eyebrows pulled up in surprise, Katherine turned to her father who had followed her two steps behind.

"Told you it wasn't what you thought," he said sheepishly.

Laughing, Katherine embraced Clementina.

"Thought I'd give you the whole story upfront," Clementina said, hugging back. Her smile revealed dimples at the corners of her mouth. "I'm due at the theatre soon. It takes a lot of time for me to look like this."

Hooking her arm through Katherine's, Clementina guided her to the sitting- room. "I'm so excited to meet you Katherine. Will talks about nothing else but you and Alexandra. I trust you had an enjoyable time in New York?"

She gestured to Katherine to sit on a fawn leather sofa next to a horn gramophone.

"Yes, it was wonderful to spend time with father and see the city."

Clementina sat beside her. "Will is such a sweet man but he works too darn hard. I am delighted he actually had a few days off. Did you enjoy the train ride? It's marvellous, isn't it? I have used the Century a few times myself. Mind you I much prefer Chicago to New York."

"The train was quite luxurious but it is going to take me some time to get used to big city life. The congestion on the roads from LaSalles to here was awful. It was even busier than New York."

"You will adjust in time. We have over two million people in the wider Chicago area, almost one-third foreigners. You will find Germans, Italians, Irish and blacks. It can be a dangerous place

Katherine. Anyway, the good news, honey is the population where we live are all white."

Katherine was lost for words.

"Oh you probably don't agree with me just like your father, but let me tell you this, you have no idea what it is like to be born and raised here. I don't want more problems than I can handle. We have the highest homicide rate in America, so you'd better listen to my advice."

So far all Katherine's experience in the USA had been nothing but pleasant, with no trace of anything Clementina had just implied. To distract them from the topic she asked, "Where has father gone?"

"He will be with Danaher to get all the latest gossip and go through his messages. I know the Mayor was asking for Will yesterday. He doesn't like me you know, Danaher. I do think Katherine he doesn't like women in general."

"It seems father is acquainted with a lot of well-known people. He's mentioned a few."

Clementina gave a brittle smile. "Your father is acquainted with many people. Carter Harrison Jr is the Mayor like his father before him. He talks a lot and although a Democrat, he can be quite the gentleman. Carter is useful to your father in many ways."

"Useful, what do you mean?"

Clementina glanced at the door. "He helps William sell his spirits to all sorts of establishments, including the brothels." Without needing encouragement she continued. "We have a whole darned tourist trade built around brothels Katherine. You can pick up maps downtown on how to get from one to the other. Carter would say Chicagoans desire is to make money and spend it and what better way than in a brothel."

Katherine observed Clementina for a moment. She was warming quickly to this lady the likes of whom she had never encountered. "I guess I have a lot to learn. What's the perfume you are wearing? The scent is heavenly."

"Francois Coty, La Rose Jacqueminot, it is French. A close friend purchased the bottle in Paris. You cannot find it anywhere in Chicago. Now tell me, how is Alexandra? You must miss her terribly."

Katherine retrieved the photograph from her handbag and handed it to her. Clementina walked to the large window and drew the drapes fully open to inspect the photograph. "She is a pretty little thing, as cute as a button just like her mother," she said, re-joining Katherine on the sofa.

"So how long have you known father?" Katherine asked.

Clementina gave a short smile. "We met at the house of a mutual friend a few years ago. I have helped him appreciate some of the finer things in life and he certainly has given me a taste for your Scottish whisky. I have never been to your wonderful country. Maybe one day I will."

Katherine glanced around the sitting room. "I think it is wonderful he has a woman in his life. Perhaps you should try and influence his ability to furnish the house."

"We do not live together Katie and I do try with utmost patience not to interfere in his personal world of work and how he lives in this abode. Will can be such a private man and I know my place. I admit I often wonder why he bought this house. Nearly all the residents on this street are Jewish."

Katherine was intrigued by her opinionated openness.

As if guessing her thoughts, Clementina placed a hand on Katherine's knee. "I was married once. It was a long time ago and all I kept was the surname. My maiden name is a tad too German for the theatre. I figured Dorrington was a more attractive stage name. I'm a dancer and an actress Katie. Once you're settled you must tell me *your* aspirations my dear. I admire young women like you. Will told me you are a gifted artist. I'm sure you'll have no problems adjusting to the Windy City, even though it is too warm in summer and darn cold in winter."

William entered the room and a sigh escaped his lips. "Clementina, I'm sure you are pressed for time. Let me show Katie the house and garden." He wasn't sure if meeting the vaudeville of Chicago was the best of starts for his daughter. But then again, life was what it was. Even though he had learned to portray himself in a different way, he had been dealt too many disappointments to stick to the cultural norm he had been brought up with. He knew Katherine might be in for a surprise or two.

216

CHAPTER 65
Thursday 20 October 2011, Ballindalloch Castle, Banffshire, Scotland

Cathy and Thomas Macpherson were strolling in the walled garden within the castle grounds. They were wrapped in warm clothing. The autumn air was crisp and the trees in the distance were a whirlwind of colour. Two gardeners were busy working on the plants and shrubs in preparation for winter.

"How was your visit to Edinburgh? Angus told me Katherine was expelled from university."

Cathy chuckled. "She was illegally practicing medicine, summoned to court and fined. It is a blot on the Macpherson family Uncle T, but I'm sure you can live with the shame."

"You are quite a detective." Thomas stuck both hands in his jacket pockets.

Cathy looped arms with him. "It was quite easy actually. I got the lead from Mr Durie at the museum. A picture of one of his descendants at Edinburgh University was hanging there and our Katherine was in the picture. So it was just a matter of following up. John was a great help."

"You and John seem to get on well," Thomas said, with just a hint of teasing.

Cathy's face flushed. "We do, but not in the way you are thinking Uncle T, so please remove the smirk. How was London? Were you visiting Her Majesty?"

The old man just smiled. "It was interesting. I had a reunion dinner to attend, you know some old pals of various regiments. Before you went to Edinburgh you asked me if I knew anything on Gallipoli, remember?"

"Yeah right, where Alexander Stewart died."

"Catherine, did you research Gallipoli or Alexander?"

"A little, have had other things going on but I plan to spend more time on the web. Right now, I am more interested in the Macphersons and this Mrs Cox."

Thomas Macpherson smirked. "Angus has his knickers in a twist. I wouldn't give her the time of day."

"Morning," the gardeners said simultaneously as they passed. "What do you think?" Thomas asked. "Should we take this Mrs Cox seriously?"

"I think so, but John seems confident he will sort it out." After a brief pause Cathy continued, "Did you find out anything of interest on Gallipoli?"

"I did some research in old War Office records from 1914 to 1916. Alexander was in Gallipoli at the time of the Asquith Letter Scandal. In fact it was he who first published an uncensored report in the USA on what was *really* happening."

"Uncensored? Do you mean somebody vetted their reports like prisoners letters?"

"Exactly, a lot of the factual information was removed. The British and allied troops in Gallipoli lost thousands of lives, but the general public were not aware because of the censorship."

"How did Alexander manage to do that?"

"He got a little help from his colleagues."

"It must have upset a few people in the States I guess?"

Thomas smiled broadly at her question. "Not as much as it did here. It's quite a story. Alexander was part of a group of correspondents who managed to get uncensored dispatches to the Prime Ministers of Britain and Australia. The Generals were not providing accurate feedback on their casualties and the true status of the campaign."

"Mm ... interesting," said Cathy, not sure what to ask next.

"I will try and find out more for you my dear, just give me some more time."

"I don't have any drawing materials," Katherine said to Clementina, who had stopped by at Maxwell Street to accompany her.

"You don't need anything my dear. All we're going to do is have a look so you can decide if it's for you. Brandon will be the model, you'll enjoy the view. He has the body of a Greek God and might even be posing as one. If you want to stay, the tutor will have charcoals."

Clementina had suggested they take the omnibus. This was the first time Katherine had used public transport in Chicago. "I used it when I was studying," Katherine said, "but more often than not, I found it was quicker to walk."

"I believe Chicago is much bigger than Edinburgh," Clementina commented.

With the evening rush being over, they found two seats side by side quite easily.

"Do you miss home?"

"I miss Alexandra terribly, but I am sure in due time Chicago will feel like home. I never liked Ballindalloch you know."

"Oh darling, that is such a European thing to say! I don't like my home. It is only a castle," Clementina mocked. "Well I know what I'd do if I was born and raised in a castle."

Katherine gave the woman she had grown to appreciate, a benevolent smile. "What? Tell me Clementina; what *would you do* if you were living in a castle?"

Clementina looked at Katherine in a flirtatious way. "I'd throw party after party after party. I'd invite musicians, actors, poets, authors and artists. I'd organise a life drawing studio like the one we're going to and fill my summers painting models, landscapes and whatever comes to mind. And my dear, we would sip whisky along the way and enjoy the pleasures of life."

Katherine laughed out loud, her mind's eye producing an image of a nude male model standing on a pedestal in the library of Ballindalloch.

"It's a pity my father didn't inherit the estate. Would you have married him if he had?"

Clementina's demeanour changed slightly. She seemed distracted by a thought. "Oh, I don't know Katie. It is not what you think, between your father and I. We are simply good friends. Abruptly she added, "Let's get off at the next stop, Adams Street. It's only a short walk from there. The Art Institute is such a beautiful building, but one could get easily lost inside. Remind me to show you the view of Lake Park, sorry Grant Park, when you are finished."

***

With a pensive look on her face Katherine stood behind the easel, her hands blackened by the charcoal blocks. Clementina had left, after introducing her to Gregory Hamilton, a dark haired, somewhat grim looking lecturer in his forties. She was one of eleven budding artists; a mix of men and women of all ages.

Brandon, the model, was standing with his back to his student audience. A white string of cloth was draped over his left shoulder, his buttocks seductively protruding from underneath. Katherine wondered how he could stand still for such a long time. She'd only seen him move slightly once or twice during the past twenty minutes.

The silence in the room was palatable. It was also quite warm in spite of the September wind moving the treetops outside. Hamilton, who had pointed out where she could find blocks, had advised her to come lightly dressed next time as the room was being kept warm for the model. "Nude painting is the most challenging," he explained, when Katherine asked why they didn't use still art, like a bowl of fruit. "Learn and see muscular structures. Know what is joined with what. You can't sketch or paint what you simply see if you don't know how anything works," he said, in a somewhat condescending way.

"I've studied medicine. I know how the human body functions."

Hamilton threw her a doubtful look. "Examining bodies is one thing Miss Macpherson, sketching them is a totally different matter. It's all outline, shape, proportions, light, shade, tone, colour, texture, form and composition. Imagine you are the model and ask where your weight would fall. Feel it and improve your work." At that he walked away leaving Katherine somewhat deflated.

Feeling a trickle of perspiration run down the nave of her back, Katherine tried her best to capture the posture of Brandon's body. She did feel her medically trained eye served as an advantage. She noticed a rash at the back of his knees and was tempted to include it in her drawing, but thought it best not to challenge Hamilton's patience which seemed in short supply. He had given the impression he doubted her abilities. It motivated Katherine with the need to prove him wrong. She wasn't here due to some immature whim, she wanted to learn.

"I must say." Hamilton's sudden interruption, almost made her drop the charcoal. "Not bad at all. There might yet be hope for you Miss Macpherson."

220

She turned and smiled. "Call me Katherine please. I would like to register for the evening class if you have a vacancy."

The dour teacher nodded. "Next week bring a mirror. Reversing the image helps you see the balance of the composition. Mr Leonardo Da Vinci would tell you this," he said, pointing a finger at her.

When Clementina returned, Katherine was excited, her green eyes sparkling. "I had no idea it was this late," she said, "can't wait to come back next week."

The women strolled towards Grant Park opposite the Art Institute. Katherine observed that it not only housed education but exhibitions and collections.

"If you want to sketch at home I can pose for you. I've modelled here a lot. It's how I know Gregory."

For a moment Katherine didn't know what to say. She was not surprised to hear Clementina was a model. In the burlesque shows Katherine had seen her and her fellow entertainers reveal parts of their bodies most women wouldn't dream of showing. What surprised Katherine was her father's lady friend should offer to pose nude.

"I'm not sure Clem, it seems a bit improper don't you think? I wonder what father would say."

A secretive smile curled Clementina's lips. "There's a thing or two you don't know regarding your father Katie, or me. But if it doesn't feel comfortable by all means I understand and will not feel rejected. Forget I ever suggested it."

"I'll give it some thought," she said, observing Clementina. "Thank you for the kind offer."

"Good, it would be so much fun having *you* capture me."

CHAPTER 67
Thursday 20 October 2011, Ballindalloch Castle, Banffshire, Scotland

After her talk with Thomas, Cathy went directly to her bedroom. On entering she distinctly sensed someone had recently been in the room. A parcel propped against the pillows of her four-poster bed confirmed her feeling. It was rather large, wrapped in brown paper and loosely tied with string. The words 'HANDLE WITH CARE' had been written on the paper, in black old-fashioned lettering. Slightly hesitant, Cathy picked it up and removed the string. Carefully, she un-wrapped the parcel until she was holding a leather-bound album of an exceptionally beautiful auburn colour. Two thirds of the front cover was cushioned with soft pink silk, decorated with small faded red and gold-coloured beads, bordered by flower patterned embroidery.

She sat on the edge of the bed, kicked off her shoes and opened the album. A leaf of tissue paper covered the first page, but she could already read the words: 'Memorable Moments of Alexandra Macpherson.'

Excited, Cathy turned the page. What appeared made her hold her breath. The single picture positioned in the centre was of a young woman and girl holding hands standing by the bank of a river. It was the same picture John had shown her in August and more recently, Diane Cox. Again, it gave her the creeps as it felt as though she was staring at her own face. 'I'd say you resemble her.' Diane's words echoed in her mind.

In the same neat handwriting was an inscription in ink below the picture: 'Me and Aunt Katherine'. The familiar feeling of déjà vu crawled up her back and made her shiver. Eager to see more she turned the page, then to the next page and the next. Wrestling at times with the tissue paper separating the images, picture after picture passed her wide-open eyes.

Cathy struggled with the overwhelming information the images provided. For the first time it dawned on her, she had been fixated on Katherine and to some extent Alexander. She hadn't really considered Alexandra in her research as a way to unlocking the past. Holding the album, Cathy heard herself say, "Alexandra, this really is a blast from the past." It seemed too good to be true, a gift landing on her lap through the annals of time.

After leafing through the album one more time, Cathy took a deep breath and closed it. Her mind was racing as she tapped her fingers on the cover. She re-opened the album.

Many pictures of Alexandra were with Katherine, some with others. There were a few school photos stamped, 'St Georges of Edinburgh' showing Alexandra with fellow pupils. To Cathy's surprise some of the later pictures were in colour. All photos were dated, showing a month and year spanning 1904 to 1915. Cathy gawked at the sequence of pictures showing Alexandra develop from a young girl to womanhood. She was quite a looker. *No wonder she became an actress!* Cathy felt herself become a tad emotional as she wondered about Alexandra's short life.

Most of the photographs seemed to have been taken in the States. Flicking through the album, Cathy paused at a pic of the Chicago Theatre. In front of the building stood Alexandra and an elderly gentleman, both smiling at the camera. The inscription below disclosed it was 'Papa William.' He was holding a hat, his other hand placed on Alexandra's shoulder. Another picture was for sure taken in Chicago. Alexandra and Papa William posing beside a wall poster; 'Comiskey Park Opening - Home of the White Sox.' Beneath the picture was written; 'We lost.' It was dated 1st July 1910. Some photos had a brief story written, describing where she had been or what she had done. The same names popped up: Papa William, Aunt Katherine, Clementina and Danaher.' A few pictures showed Alexandra with a dog, a blonde Labrador.

Abruptly Cathy closed the album, grabbed her laptop and switched it on. While waiting for a connection, she retrieved her family-tree papers. Her mind was racing. Only a fleeting moment, did she wonder who had delivered the album. *Was it Uncle T? Maybe he talked with Maggie and Euphemia?* For now, it was of little importance, although she would eventually like to know. Eager to process the new information, she started scribbling notes on the family-tree documents. The Edinburgh school pictures proved Alexandra initially had been a visitor to the States and not a resident.

The Windows jingle announced the computer was ready to go, but Cathy first picked up the picture book again and leafed to the last page. The entry beside a picture of Alexandra and a group of trendy young people highlighted it was the summer of 1915. Cathy went to the beginning of the album and methodically worked her way through it, taking notes of the date and location of each picture.

When Cathy was done she placed the album on the writing desk and uttered a deep sigh. She got up, walked towards the window to take in the scenery of the estate. *Why* Cathy wondered, *did Alexandra spend so much time in the USA? Why is there not one solitary picture of her parents? The name John and Victoria occurred nowhere in the album.* A fleeting thought, that had presented itself before, began to return. Cathy smacked her forehead with the palm of her hand. *Alexandra, Alexandra, Alexander.*

Intrigued, Cathy returned to her laptop and logged-on to the now familiar genealogy database, Scotland's People. Using the Macpherson family tree details she searched for the marriage of John Macpherson and Victoria Galbraith, keying in their names and the year 1889.

One match was highlighted.

<u>1889</u> MARRIAGES IN THE DISTRICT OF <u>Inveravon</u> IN THE BURGH OF <u>Banffshire</u>

Cathy clicked on the 'view document' button.

WHEN, WHERE	SIGNATURE OF PARTIES	PARENTS
1889	John Macpherson (age 25)	Gordon Macpherson
7 May	(Landlord)	(Laird)
Inveravon	Ballindalloch Castle	Elizabeth Macpherson
Church		m.s. Douglas
According		
To the	Victoria Galbraith (age 22)	Archibald Alexander
Forms of	Lockwood,Aberdeen	Galbraith (Deceased)
Church of		(Retailer)
Scotland		Ellison Galbraith
		m.s Law (Landlady)

She stared at the digitalised document noticing Alexander was the middle name of Victoria's father. She smiled at the irony, *pure coincidence,* and discarded any possibility of Alexandra being named after him. Feverishly she went through her notes. John and Victoria married in 1889. They had only one child, Alexandra, born June 22nd 1896, seven years after they married, eight months after Alexander left Scotland, three months before Katherine went to university. A possibility started to form in Cathy's mind, still incoherent, but it gave her that familiar tingling at the back of her neck. *If only I knew what Alexander Stewart had been up to.*

CHAPTER 68
Wednesday 21 September 1904, Boston, USA

"Harry, please tell me you have photographs." Twenty-nine year old Alexander Stewart leaning with both hands on the edge of his desk was facing Boston Globe photographer Harold Williams.

Harold tossed his hat on a chair, removed his jacket and hung it on the back. "No problem Alex, they are being developed as we speak. Those guys are something else!"

Alex sat down. "Well done! I've almost finished the report. I'll give it to Sam once we agree which photographs to use. I think we should have at least two.

Harry nodded in agreement.

"How was Ohio?"

"Muddy." Harold lifted a foot showing a dried mud covered brogue. "Huffman Prairie is in the middle of nowhere."

"Were there many journalists and photographers there?"

"Quite a few, but not as many as I thought there would be."

"This has to be big news, navigating without a balloon!" Alexander felt a tinge of excitement.

The Boston Globe had been following the two brothers from Dayton, Wilbur and Orville Wright and their flying machine. After their successful flight in December 1903 over North Carolina Sands, they flew a complete circle over the Ohio prairie. Although not part of his official remit at the Globe, Alexander had insisted he took the lead in reporting this remarkable achievement.

Starting with the Globe as a junior journalist in 1896, Alexander had risen through the ranks in the organisation. Within three years, he was the Deputy Chief Journalist of Foreign News, specifically Europe. In January of 1904 he accepted the role of War Correspondent. He had not yet any field experience even though the world was full of unrest. Alexander was not short of material. Using the media agencies of journalists around the world he had reported on the horrors unfolding in German South-West Africa. Germany had faced an uprising of the Herero people against colonialism. General Lothar von Trotha, had successfully driven the Hereros into the desert. Reports were now surfacing that tens of thousands had died of thirst and hunger.

Alexander and his colleagues were also covering the Russo-Japanese War. Russia had infuriated Japan by leasing Port Arthur from China, on the tip of the Liaotung Peninsula in Manchuria. The Empires went to war in February. Alexander had received dispatches from their London contact, reporting the Japanese General Nogi had attempted an assault on the port. Early indications given, the Japanese had failed and suffered heavy casualties.

The exploits of the Wright brothers made a welcome change from the horrors of war. Together with Harry, Alexander selected two photographs. After that he was eager to exchange the office on Washington Street for family life and headed home by streetcar to Back Bay. They had been going through a frightening episode, when two weeks ago, Robert his four-year old son, had been diagnosed with scarlet fever. Thanks to Doctor Lyons and his wife Sarah the boy was now recovering.

Alex had first met Sarah Gibson and her husband on the passage to the States in late '95. Sarah's husband had been unwell and disappeared at sea, a probable suicide. By chance, nine months later Alexander and Sarah had met again at an open air dance held at the church Alexander attended. A courtship blossomed. Two years later they married.

In November '99, despite the unsolicited advice, they fostered Michael, a six-year old black boy from the orphanage where Sarah was a volunteer worker. The following year, in September, Sarah gave birth to their second son, Robert. Over the years they had faced racial slurs from neighbours, the church and school, so called friends and random hostile occurrences from total strangers. The family had learned to cope, including Michael, who would soon be eleven. Although the abuse had subsided, it had been especially difficult on Sarah, as Alexander's occupation often involved travelling. What pleased him and Sarah, was Michael and Robert had bonded. Alexander and Sarah knew it was difficult for Robert. He was being taunted at school about his black 'brother' but always defended Michael.

Alexander was looking forward to the holiday in Texas. The Stewart family planned to make the 1800-mile sail to spend a month long vacation with Alexander's dearest friend, oil tycoon Sean Devane, his wife Colleen and their four-year old daughter Mary and two-year old son Sean. Alexander's bond with the Devane family was based on a deep felt gratitude. He and Sean had befriended on a train journey from New York to Boston after Alexander had just arrived in the States uncertain of what the future held. The first few crucial months he took residence with Sean and his father Michael Devane. This turned out to be an important factor in Alexander settling into Bostonian life. In fact, it was Michael Devane who helped Alexander secure a job with the Boston Globe. Alex held the Devane family in deep regard.

The young Devane family had been in Beaumont, Jefferson County since the turn of the century. Sean, together with other investors and experts, established an oil exploration company. Sean made a fortune from the Spindletop Lucas Gusher in 1901, gifting Alex a company bond in 1899, which had now matured into a substantial premium, making him a wealthy man, on paper at least. Alex and Sarah had promised Sean they would watch over his father, who remained in Boston running a successful construction company. Mr Devane had now become part of the Stewart family.

Alexander's life *had* changed. He had never imagined he would be so content leading a city life and being settled with a wife and children. It had been a while since he thought of Katherine, but for some reason, tonight staring out the streetcar window, his thoughts drifted to her. She would be twenty-seven years old now. He hoped she was happy and wondered what she was doing right now. For sure he guessed, the Katherine he remembered would not be in Ballindalloch.

CHAPTER 69
Saturday 15 October 1904, Chicago, Illinois, USA

"Father, I need your help."

With long strides, Katherine barged into the room where William and Clementine were enjoying a late breakfast served by Danaher. Clementina looked up in surprise. It was not often Katherine displayed concern and now it was written all over her face.

"What's wrong my dear, tell me?" William asked.

"It's John."

William dabbed his mouth. Thoughtfully, he placed the napkin back on the table.

"What's he done this time?" he spoke softly.

"He won't permit Alexandra to come here for the summer, even though I promised I would come and collect her!" Katherine fumed. "He wrote, she's too young for such a long journey and that with her going to boarding school, she's away from Ballindalloch enough as it is!" With a forceful grunt Katherine plunged herself down on a chair and threw John's letter on the table for William to read.

A sympathetic Danaher approached carrying a teapot.

"Sometimes I just feel like exposing us all!" Katherine shouted, "He promised I could see her as often as I liked. If he doesn't keep his part of the agreement why should I?"

"Because it would involve compromising your child my dear," Clementina cut in. "Just imagine the gossip at her school if it became public knowledge that she's not John and Victoria's daughter."

"And John knows!" Katherine exclaimed, swinging her right arm up in the air in an angry gesture, oblivious to Danaher who was now standing behind her.

"Calm down Katherine," William said, indicating the butler to leave the room. "You know well, talking this way is useless. I will write to John and you can personally deliver the letter at Christmas. I take it you are still going back to Scotland to celebrate Hogmanay?"

"Of course, I want to see Alexandra and I promised her. I will not let her down again."

An awkward silence fell over the breakfast table. All were absorbed in their own thoughts. The only sound remaining was the wall clock ticking in the corner.

"I should have listened to you when I was pregnant; to you *and* James." Katherine's voice sounded remorseful.

"Yes, well it is too late to bemoan," William said, "and to be honest in retrospect I think you wisely made the right choice."

"And my dear Katherine," Clementina contributed, "all is not lost. I'm sure William can change John's mind. Your father can be persuasive when he wants."

Sunk in dour thought, Katherine missed the exchange of meaningful glances between Wiliam and Clementina.
She hoped her father would indeed be successful.

CHAPTER 70
Wednesday 21 December 1904, Ballindalloch Castle, Banffshire

"You have no inkling what you have stirred up," John shouted at his sister, waving William's letter in front of him. Katherine had only arrived the previous day at Ballindalloch, after what had been a trying journey over a freezing cold Atlantic and snow-covered land. The trains had been delayed many times as a result of the tracks being impassable and in the end she saw herself forced to hire a horse-drawn sleigh for the last stretch from Grantown to Ballindalloch.

The following morning before breakfast she had given the letter to John. She wanted to be able to tell Alexandra of the adventures they were to undertake. Without ceremony, John had summoned his sister to the study.

"Explain yourself John." Katherine retaliated. "I do not have the faintest idea what you are trying to say. All I asked William was to support my request." Katherine was careful to remind herself not to refer to him as Father.

"To which I had given you my answer! John exclaimed. "We have done enough for you, little sister. You and your insistent demands are becoming a burden."

"If you would stick to our agreement, we would not be arguing. Let's be honest John, in all the times I returned to Ballindalloch, either from Edinburgh or now from America, you and your wife have been extremely distant. If that's how you want to behave, I can live with it! I can't help but worry over your attitude towards my child. I've never heard Victoria speak a kind word to her or seen her make a loving gesture."

His sister's remarks deflated John. For a moment he felt remorseful and helpless. He'd never understood his sister's zest or unladylike ventures. In retrospect, he felt for his father having been obliged to raise a daughter like Katherine.

"I have no intention of allowing Alexandra grow up the way you did," John snarled. He sometimes regarded his sister's ways with jealousy, wondering how she summoned up the courage to live the way she did. In his view it certainly did not agree with the values the Macpherson children had been raised with.

'So?" Katherine said, her arms folded over her stomach. "Explain what I supposedly caused this time?"

John only stared at his sister. She would never understand. There were too many differences between them, just like she never understood their father's reasoning. And yet, both men had only done what they had thought was proper. With a sigh of frustration, John plunged himself down on the chair and stared at the letter as if it would speak differently this time. He wondered why life had to be so complicated.

"And what will I tell Victoria?"

Katherine raised her eyebrows. "The truth! Remind her of our agreement! I am to see Alexandra as often as I want. I will come and collect her and accompany her back to Scotland."

"Why make it all so difficult? Why don't you just come and stay here during the summer months?"

"Because I've done that for years and I'm bored with it. Alexandra is old enough now to see more of the world."

Katherine and her daughter had made the occasional trip to Edinburgh, Glasgow and even to London when Alexandra was only six-years old, to take part in the coronation festivities surrounding King Edward. While John and Victoria had been guests at Westminster Abbey, Katherine and Alexandra had roamed the city to watch the performances of the street artists and sample the local treats.

"It was part of the agreement John. Victoria knows this and honestly I would not be so insistent if I knew Alexandra was happy here. As I said, I'm sure a change of scenery will do her good."

John threw his sister a dark look. There was no way he could refuse. William was a gentleman and a rogue, who would certainly carry out the threat written in his letter, unless Alexandra was permitted to travel. John knew well enough.

"Have it your way. I have no choice. Alexandra can go with you to America this summer."

For the first time Katherine wondered what William had written to evoke such response from John.

Part III

 I saw a man this morning
Who did not wish to die:
 I ask and cannot answer,
If otherwise wish I.
Fair broke the day this morning
Against the Dardanelles;
The breeze blew soft, the morn's cheeks
Were cold as cold sea-shells.
But other shells are waiting
Across the Aegean Sea,
Shrapnel and high explosive,
Shells and hells for me.
O hell of ships and cities,
Hell of men like me,
Fatal second Helen,
Why must I follow thee?
Achilles came to Troyland
And I to Chersonese:
He turned from wrath to battle,
And I from three days' peace.
Was it so hard, Achilles,
So very hard to die?
Thou knewest, and I know not---
So much the happier I.
I will go back this morning
From Imbros over the sea;
Stand in the trench, Achilles,
Flame-capped, and shout for me.

Patrick Shaw-Stewart, who survived Gallipoli
only to die in France during 1917.

CHAPTER 71
Friday 27 August 1915, Helles Beach, Gallipoli, Turkey

Forty-one year old Alexander Stewart and two companies of Royal Hampshires scurried quickly and silently across 'V' beach, the main landing point protected by the navy on three sides. Alex felt he had been launched into a nightmare. The Turks were rumoured to have machine guns, pom-poms and rifles guarding the beach. It could have seemed a normal August sunset, the sea glassy, the sun a blood red orb over the Asian coastline. Normalcy was not the case.

Corpses and military debris littered the beach. Twisted bodies were lying like dead fish washed in by the sea. Lines of barbed wire were visible across the beach. Not a Turk to be seen or heard. Like many, Alex hoped they were all dead or had fled. He was thankful to be at the rear of the group and not carrying the weighty backpacks of the troops. Wire cutting caused short delays in their progress as they continued to make their way towards the bank. Alex repeatedly passed dead soldiers in the sand. He glanced at the corpse of a young soldier crouched against an empty ammunition trunk, as if he was resting. A hole, the size of a tennis ball, was gaping from the side of his head.

When they cleared the beach, the troops, four abreast, continued climbing up through a narrow gulley into the darkness. A distant rumble of heavy artillery could be heard as they approached the summit. The whizzing of a hailstorm of bullets filled the air above.

An officer ordered Alex to the trenches dug deep behind the hill. Alex watched the soldiers row by row disappear over the brow. His breathing was heavy as he tried to calm his nerves. The stench hit him like a hammer. It smelt of sage, decaying flesh and death. Alex choked and vomited effortlessly.

It had been the troopship RMS Alaunia that brought him. During the voyage, rumours had been rife that the British and Allied Forces were going to completely evacuate Gallipoli. Losses had been substantial, although reports varied widely on the actual numbers of casualties and wounded. After almost seven months of fighting, Churchill's new war front in the Dardanelles had come no further forward.

Alex had exchanged a series of communications with London-based Ellis Ashmead-Bartlett, a seasoned Fleet Street journalist working for the Daily Telegraph. He had been reporting on the campaign since the beginning of the conflict. He had informed Alex that all dispatches were vetted and if deemed necessary part censored before being released. Bartlett was in Gallipoli.

Stooping, his left hand over his mouth, Alex made his way to the trenches. The chaotic surroundings made the trudge difficult. He was looking forward to meeting Ellis in the flesh. Ashmead-Bartlett had a reputation as a scandal monger, always broke because he lived above his means. Alex had been shocked to learn the rumour the man had his own personal chef from Malta on Imbros, the base of the GHQ of the Mediterranean Expeditionary Force. He was a few years younger than Alex. Amazingly, at sixteen-years old, he had accompanied his father with the Turkish army in the Graeco-Turkish War. Bartlett had also served in the Bedfordshire Regiment during the Boer War. He was undoubtedly an experienced War Correspondent.

It took Alex much longer than anticipated to reach the trenches. His mouth felt dry. Exhaustion was setting in. A scattering of wounded soldiers dotted the vast line of dugouts. Some were huddled in small groups, others walking aimlessly, some with makeshift crutches. Their bandages and dressings looked as though they hadn't been changed in weeks.

An adjutant stepped forward to greet Alex. His combats were covered in dried soil, his face displayed several weeks of growth. His left arm was heavily strapped from the elbow to shoulder. The soldier introduced himself as Staff Officer Barker. When Alex explained he was a correspondent, Barker immediately recited the standard journalist house-rules; "You are a subordinate to each soldier no matter the rank. You will remain behind the battlefield at all times. You can converse with any soldier up to the rank of corporal. You must obey all orders. All dispatches must be given to me for inspection. You will conduct yourself at all times in the manner befitting King and country"

Alex looked at Barker in disbelief.

"I know this will be difficult for you," Barker continued, oblivious to Alex's confusion. "Correspondents are nothing but dangerous meddlers." Barker saluted as if the King himself was present, slumped on a sandbag and blurted, "My commanding officer is dead you know."

"When did he die?" asked Alex, recognising the man was totally unstable.

Staring at the ground he replied, "A week ago."

Alex peered at the broken soldier. "Do you have orders to evacuate yet?"

Ignoring the question, Barker muttered, "We did try you know. We found men lying on the ground moaning, crying in agony. There was no one to attend them, no one to carry them back to the beach. Everyone was demoralised, sick, waiting for stretcher bearers who never came." Barker's eyes were dancing. In a louder voice and

236

waving his good arm he continued, "Dysentery and fever is everywhere. Mr Stewart, welcome to Hell. There is not so much sudden death here like the front, but death is everywhere. Not bullets, but germs."

Although concerned for the man, Alex knew he was unable to help. He made his way to find a vacant dugout and quickly discovered there were many available, all similar in size. They were like huge rabbit burrows, heavy with the dank smell of decay. He chose a dugout with earth piled on a galvanised roof as protection against shrapnel pellets. A canvas sheet shielded the entrance and the walls were sandbagged. Unlit candles made of rancid butter were scattered on a floor of random wooden planks. Alex made himself as comfortable as possible on a torn mattress speckled with dark stains. His mind struggled to come to terms with what he had witnessed. The continuous drone of bursting shells made him shiver. The sound seemed to be getting louder. He wondered who else had used the dugout. Thoughts of his own mortality, Sarah, Michael and Robert overwhelmed him. *Would he live long enough to meet Ashmead-Bartlett?*

***

Night-time had set completely, his dugout pitch dark. Alex fumbled in his kitbag searching for chocolate. He heard voices in the distance, but the rumble of the Krupp guns smothered the words. He felt clammy and cold at the same time, as if his life energy had been sucked from him. He tried to picture Sarah and the children, but couldn't remove the images of the horror he had seen. He pondered when and how he could venture to the battlefront.

The canvas was pulled to the side. A lantern dangled from an outstretched arm.

"Mr Stewart, I presume?" A startled Alex looked up. A tall well framed man dressed in khaki combats climbed into the hole, removed his helmet and sat. In the sparing light, Alex observed the pale confident looking features scrutinising him. Its owner appeared to be somewhat younger than he.

"I'm pleased you made it in one piece Mr Stewart. I am Bartlett," the man said and extended a hand. They shook firmly. Bartlett offered Alex a silver hip flask. "Have a shot old man it will warm you, if only for a few seconds."

Alex was too numb to ask how Bartlett had found him. He lifted the vessel to his lips as Bartlett asked, "Why are you dossing here man? We are expected at Imbros. We cannot afford to stay here too long. Disease is rife."

Alexander coughed loudly. The impact of the brandy surprised him. Recovering he returned the flask to Bartlett who took a greedy gulp.

"I guess I just wanted to go to ground as soon as I arrived," Alex responded. "I know we should be at the island. When can we get to the front line?"

"Be patient. I hope you have packed a good book. You will discover we have a lot of waiting time. Within the hour we will be taken to HMS London. So tell me Alexander, are the good people of Boston being told all here is under control?"

Alex grimaced. "As you well know even the folks in London, let alone America, don't know the extent of casualties. We are losing the battle, Mr Bartlett? By the way call me Alex."

"Aha losing the battle," Bartlett laughed, shuffling with discomfort. "You are indeed the master of understatement. This campaign was lost before it began. Thousands of families will be without their fathers, sons, brothers and the like after this is all over."

"Have you managed to get dispatches out?" Alex asked.

Bartlett frowned. In a soft voice he answered, "I keep trying to bypass the bloody censors even if it does bring down Hamilton. You signed the declaration?"

"Had no choice otherwise I wouldn't be here."

"Bastards, all of them," muttered the Englishman. He quoted verbatim, "Not to impart to anyone, any military information of a confidential nature unless first submitted to the Chief Field Censor. Well let's wait and see. We need to be determined correspondents, make our protest heard," he said, squeezing Alex's shoulder.

"Does the London have a Marconi?" asked Alex.

"It does, but there is no way we could get near the communications deck. I am working on a letter to Asquith. The content will be explicit as to the truth of our casualties and the arrogance of the senior officers. I will show you the draft later. There is someone else I would like you to meet, a young Australian, Keith Murdoch."

Intrigued by Bartlett's enthusiasm Alex asked, "How will you get the letter to London?"

"Keith," Bartlett simply said, "he will deliver it personally. He is a young eager correspondent and like me, desperate to let the world know of this bloody mess. He is going to hand carry the letter."

"What if he is captured? Is he aware of the consequences?" Alex asked with concern.

Bartlett smiled, "He is, but he is a determined fellow. Keith's family is well connected in Australia. If captured by the Brits, they would not dare harm him in any way. His bravado must stem from his Scottish blood." He slapped Alex on the shoulder. "His parents are Scottish you know. You'll like Keith."

"With a name like Murdoch, I would have thought as much. When will he set off?"

Bartlett gave a thin smile. "We are working on figuring out the best route. I would guess sometime next month. You must never mention this to anyone, including other correspondents. I trust you Alex." Bartlett gave Alex a terse look. "I checked you out old man. I have heard good things of you Alexander Stewart." He paused, still staring into Alex's eyes. "I know you have a family."

Alex's eyes lit up. "Yes, a wife, Sarah and my son Robert in Boston. My oldest boy Michael is at Glasgow University in Scotland."

Bartlett observed the pensive look on Alex's face. "Glasgow is a fine town Alex. I must say, you have not lost your Scottish lilt. Why did you send your boy to Glasgow? There are fine universities in Massachusetts."

"Well it's a long story. The bottom line is they wouldn't accept him because he's black."

"Black!" Bartlett gasped.

Not surprised by the reaction, Alex went on, "Yes, black. We adopted Michael. He was four-years old. As I said it is a long story."

"You must be a courageous person as must your wife. A black son, I just cannot imagine." The Englishman shook his head. "Which part of Scotland are you from? I am certain it's not Glasgow."

Alex gave a short laugh. "I am from up north, Ballindalloch. It lies between the towns of Grantown-on-Spey and Elgin. It is a beautiful part of the country."

"The highlands produce fine whisky. I have a few malts in my cabin I keep for medicinal purposes," Bartlett said, winking. "Why did you move to Boston?"

"Also a long story," Alex replied, uttering a deep sigh. "Maybe I'll tell you some other time." Keen to change the topic Alex enquired, "How many correspondents are here?"

Bartlett laughed cynically. "Not as many as a month ago. There are a few from England, Australia, New Zealand and France. Don't trust any of them, especially Nevinson of the Guardian. Keith Murdoch though, can be trusted. Number one, he has no love for the British and number two, as I mentioned earlier, his family is well connected. To the Australian PM, Andrew Fisher."

Alex whistled. "Fisher! Surely that will be in his favour."

"Fisher is another Scot, from Ayrshire I believe."

Bartlett's passion for honest journalism was familiar ground for Alex. His educated accent was not a surprise. Although Bartlett was perceived as somewhat aloof, his reputation as a war correspondent was impeccable. Alex quickly warmed to the man and would not allow gossip to be his judge.

Bartlett asked how Alex's journey from the USA had been, but before he could answer, Bartlett continued with conviction, "I hate bloody ships. My advice when we board later, sleep on the deck, not in your cabin. I was on board the Majestic last May when it went down. We were anchored off 'W' Beach. A bloody German U-21 torpedoed us. Sleeping on deck saved my skin."

Alex gasped, "My God! You were one lucky fellow."

"Nothing to do with luck old man," Bartlett replied with some disdain. "Weeks earlier, I had seen the Triumph suffer the same fate. Take your mattress on deck Alex."

"Why are we still here?" Alex asked. "They are going to evacuate Suvla and the Anzac Cove, why not Helles?"

"Helles is a face saver Alex. From the beginning the generals knew they had to take Achi Baba. It had been the goal from the start, even though they knew it couldn't happen, not before and not now." Ellis sighed. "Achi Baba was *never* the key to the peninsula and Helles has *never* been the place to land. It is too far from the forts, not in miles but in terms of hills, gorges and plateaus, which would need to be taken first. My God! And they call this a strategic front. How the so-called First Lord of the Admiralty Churchill sleeps at night I will never know. The bloody Boers should have shot him when they had the chance."

Alexander now witnessed Bartlett's emotions running high. His voice was of a sour and hostile nature. His comments almost made Alex chuckle.

"Alex you ask any soldier here and they will tell you the Turks did not beat us. We were beaten by our own High Command."

A voice bellowed into their dugout, "Gentlemen, make haste, time to go."

Both men stepped out into the cool air. Alex pulled his balaclava over his nose and mouth in an attempt to smother the stench. Their guide was a young wispy snowy haired lad. Going downhill proved easy. Within a few minutes the beach stretched out before them. The Aegean Sea was flat. The moonlight reflected on the glassy water. Silhouettes of gunships were clearly visible as they moved at pace over the sand, following the boy who was creating a pathway between the debris and dead. In an instant, hell seemed to break loose. The

240

deafening sound of six-inch shells being pounded by the ships terrorised the correspondents. They gathered pace, trying to keep up with the young soldier.

Out of the smoke drenched sky, a stray shell engulfed the earth some twenty yards in front. With deafening noise, the vibration of the explosion fired sand and shrapnel through the air, completely catching the men by surprise.

CHAPTER 72
Saturday 28 August 1915, Gallipoli, Turkey

In a stuffy surgery cabin on the hospital deck of the cruiser HMS Edgar, Alex and Ellis were waiting for a doctor. Side by side, both men were perched on a bench dressed only in their under garments. Alex peered at Bartlett's gold Saint Christopher pendant nestling in his dark chest hair. They had been knocked unconscious by the beach explosion and suffered minor shrapnel wounds to their legs. The intense heat of the blast had singed their hair. It was Petty Officer Brook and two crewmen who had rescued them and got them back to the ship. They found both men in shock. Alexander was almost unrecognizable. His face had been splattered with a mixture of sand, flesh and blood from the young lad, who had been blown to smithereens.

Both men now laughed nervously at their missing locks and scorched foreheads. With the ship still pummelling her shells, the cruiser was constantly vibrating. The two correspondents were staring in disbelief at the fragments of metal puncturing their legs. Both winced in pain as the shrapnel continued to cool. Bartlett chirped, "Six inches higher old man, we would be eunuchs."

A loud rap on the door disturbed the men. A small round-shouldered man entered the room. The thick lenses of his spectacles made his eyes seem enormous.

"Doctor Ernest Proctor at your service gentlemen," he said, wiping his hands on a blood stained apron, dangling way below his knees. Looking at the four limbs dangling in front of him he added, "Now please tell me you have not touched any of the wounds or even worse removed any of the little mites."

Both men just shook their head.

"Lucky buggers you are," he uttered, snapping tweezers in his right hand. "This will take a while, but don't worry you won't feel a thing."

***

In the early afternoon, Alex and Ellis were back on deck after sharing a can of boiled beef. The shelling had stopped. On the port side of the cruiser both men were deep in dialogue. Sailors were noisily scurrying around the deck making it impossible to find any privacy. Despite this, Bartlett refused to go below.

The Englishman had slipped into a pessimistic mood. Bartlett was whining on and on regarding the young officers at GHQ. He had become unpopular with them because of his constant predictions of disaster.

"There are now at least four censors Alex, all of whom cut up your stuff. Maxwell starts it, Ward, General Braithwaite and finally Sir Ian fucking Hamilton. All hold different views and feel it their duty to take out scraps. Only a few dry crumbs are left for the wretched public." Handing Alex a bulky document he said, "Here, take this. It is the draft letter to Asquith."

Glancing around him, Alex tucked the paper under his jacket. "Who is the Major on the Edgar?"

"He is a right bastard. Major Crawford Munro, a bully, full of self-importance. Alex, you have witnessed the horror of what's going on here. Wounded and dead are left behind. You have seen how poor the medical facilities are on this ship. Well believe me, there is next to nothing at the battle fronts."

Alex observed the tranquillity across the bay, only disrupted by occasional rumbling of distant shelling. Leaning over the ship's rail, the correspondents were now whispering and discussing the content of the letter to Asquith.

A strong Aussie accent sounded behind them. "G-good afternoon Ellis." A young man squeezed between them.

"Keith, good to see you, glad you made it," responded Bartlett.

"I heard you and ..." The young Australian turned to Alex, "...Mr Stewart had been w-wounded. I am Keith Murdoch of the Melbourne Herald by the way," he said to Alex. They shook hands.

Alex studied him. Keith was not even thirty he guessed. He was dressed in khaki combats and sturdy boots. His neck was covered with a large neckerchief and he was holding a slouch hat. Although a tall well-featured man with a full crop of groomed brown hair, his obvious stammer emanated a lack of confidence. "How are you both?" Keith enquired tamely.

Ellis was quick to respond. "We were lucky, unlike the lad who was with us." Tapping his legs he went on, "Shrapnel wounds, we should be okay." Bartlett dropped his voice, "I have told Alex of the letter. He works for the Globe. He is returning to Boston next month and will publish it."

Murdoch looked a little perturbed.

"I know what you are thinking Keith. The content of the letter will be safe."

The Australian responded, "Well the f-fewer the better," with a doubtful glance.

"Listen, both of you," Alex commanded. "There are a lot of sympathisers in America, both for and against Britain. In Boston alone, the Irish community is more interested in fighting Britain to get a Free State for Ireland. When I publish Ellis's account of what is happening here, it will stir up emotions in America and can only be of beneficial consequences later. I will make sure the New York Times run with the story as well."

"Your accent r-reminds me of my father," Keith said, changing the seriousness of their conversation. "He was from Cruden. It is n-north of Aberdeen, near Peterhead."

"Aye, I know of Cruden. It is not so far from where I was raised, Ballindalloch."

"D-don't know of it," Murdoch responded. He switched to a more serious tone. "Well let's get this l-letter to London as quickly as possible. The whole Dardanelles has been a series of underestimations. The c-conceit and self-complacency of the Brits is equalled only by their incapacity. They have countless high-ranking officers and conceited young cubs who are only p-playing at w-war. Even appointments with the general staff are made from motives of f-friendship and social influence. This h-has to stop."

Ellis looked pleased with his protégé but added, "Calm down Keith, you are drawing attention to us."

"S-sorry, I can get ahead of myself."

"One day, I'm telling you," Bartlett said pointing a finger, "we will bear witness that those accountable for this atrocity, will be brought to justice. Right, I need to get on my way. I'm heading back to the front. Alex, join me when your leg is better."

Despite his injuries, Bartlett was walking freely. Alex on the other hand was not. Severe jolts of pain in his left shin prevented him from joining Bartlett on the bay. The men all shook hands. As Bartlett walked away, he teased, "Good day chaps, let's all meet up for a drink in London, soon I trust."

***

Alex wished he could get something to relieve his pain and went looking for a doctor. Inside the makeshift hospital there were many casualties. The ward was humid, the stench like rotting food. Only two medical attendants were present, a doctor nowhere to be seen. He overheard a well-recognised accent. With the aid of a walking stick, Alex limped towards the bed of a stricken soldier. He had lost his right arm and the right side of his face was heavily bandaged. His appearance was so skeletal it was difficult to determine his age.

"How are you doing sir?" asked Alex.

"Not as well as you," he replied, his voice barely audible.

"You're an east coaster," Alex said. "Where are you from?"

"I'm from Leith, but usually I say Edinburgh." The soldier rubbed the bandaged stump below his shoulder. "I'm Charlie Jeffries, a sapper with the First." His watery eyes stared at Alex. "I don't think I will make it home."

Alex looked with compassion at the frail soldier. "Have you family in Leith?"

"Only my darlin' Jeannie," Charlie said, and pressed his head deeper into his pillow. "We don't have any bairns." He closed his eyes.

"You must get well for your wife Charlie," Alex said, trying to be positive.

"Years ago, Jeannie lost a baby." He opened his eyes and asked, "Are you a doctor?"

"No I'm trying to find one though."

"Well you'll wait a while here. Mind you, I have a lot of respect for doctors." The soldier shuffled in his bed trying to get more comfortable. "Our doctor saved Jeannie's life. I thought she was going to die along with the child. Poor Doctor Macpherson, she was in tears." He sighed and closed his eyes again. "We can't have children you know."

"I'm sure the doctor did all he could Charlie."

CHAPTER 73
Friday 3 September 1915, HMS London, Ibros Island, Aegean Sea

Back at the Wardroom in GHQ, dinner was served at seven o'clock and the officers of the formidable class battleship London did the Australian officers proud. Whatever their destiny, at least their last night was made as lively as possible. Many had not tasted alcohol for a long time. They were served cocktails, champagne, whisky and sodas. Alex and Ellis readily gave up their cabins to the officers in order they were comfortable. They turned in around half past ten and snatched a few hours' sleep on the deck. At sunset all lights on board had been extinguished and they steamed slowly through the night to their unknown destination and to an unknown fate.

"It's a fine night for a sail," muttered Bartlett. He was standing over his colleague, stretching his arms. Alex was lying on the deck, half wrapped in a makeshift blanket.

"What time is it?" he asked, without moving a muscle.

Ellis looked around at other men dotted around the deck pretending to be asleep. "It's after midnight. Not long now I would guess before we reach our destination. Taking or attempting to take a beachhead my friend is going to test your resolve and mine."

Bartlett yawned and helped Alex to his feet. Alex caught a whiff of brandy from the Englishman's breath. Both men were dressed in combats. They had been given an outline of the mission without the actual name of the targeted beach. They were the only correspondents on the ship, which pleased Ellis, although they had no official pass to accompany the troops.

Alex was surprisingly calm.

"Whatever happens, remember and stay close at all times," Bartlett said for the umpteenth time. "We had better get some food in our belly soon."

Bartlett was now squatting on the deck writing notes in his diary. Alex continued to update his log and write a letter to Sarah. Both men sat in silence.

***

At 1 am the Fleet stopped and all on board were roused. The Australian troops were having a final hot meal before falling in. For the officers, food was being served in the Wardroom and both correspondents were present.

"They certainly keep their distance," Alex whispered.

246

Bartlett muttered, "It's because they don't trust us."

They were seated in a corner of the room away from the main body of officers. The atmosphere was tense and there was little conversation.

Bartlett was wiping his mouth with his handkerchief. "Bloody awful," he said, pushing away his plate. He glanced at the large group of officers and without looking at Alex commented, "Poor bastards, it must be impossible to provide leadership in something you don't believe in."

"I hope Keith is successful Ellis, and maybe, just maybe, put an end to this."

"I am sure, he will one way or another."

At two o'clock the troops were ready. The boats had been lowered, together with the steam pinnaces that were to tow them. There was only faint light from the moon. The scene on the deck was surreal. The huge contingent from Australia stood there in absolute silence; the men receiving their final instructions from officers. Around them stood the beach parties from the ship; they were to put them ashore. Lieutenants in khaki, midshipmen not yet out of their teens, in old white duck suits dyed khaki. They were carrying revolvers and water bottles almost as big as themselves.

Alex was stirred and inspired when at two o'clock the pinnaces towed the boats alongside and the men immediately embarked. There was no confusion, no overcrowding and no mishaps. At three o'clock steam was again raised as the soldiers moved slowly towards the shore until almost four o'clock. The dim outline of the coast became visible for the first time. Thirty minutes later, Alex noticed four battleships were in line approximately three thousand yards from shore. The signal was given for the tows to be cast off and make their way to the beaches. It was still dark. The pinnaces and their trail of boats looked like giant snakes as they slowly made their way inland.

As soon as all the soldiers departed Alex and Ellis made their way to the bridge to join the Captain and his Staff. This was the most captivating moment Alex had ever known as he watched the boats slowly make their way towards the land.

***

Fighting continued throughout the afternoon. The ship received ongoing orders to fire on various positions, where the Turks were pushing the Australians back to the first line of hills they had seized. It was obvious to Alex they were extremely hard pressed. The wounded never ceased to come off the shore in an endless stream. The accommodation on the hospital ship quickly gave out. Ellis highlighted to Alex the medical arrangements, which as usual, were a shambles. There was no single officer with authority to direct the wounded to a specific ship. There were not enough surgeons. Alex was horrified when an order was released that the wounded be sent to empty transport ships. Doctors would be sent on board to look after them until they reached Egypt. The pinnaces were so busy Alex and Ellis had to wait until after five o'clock before getting a boat to go on shore.

From soldiers returning from the front, the correspondents had collected reports from all ranks. They suffered enormous casualties, the beaches piled up with wounded who could not be moved as the enemy shell and sniper fire was heavy.

Alex struggled to contain his emotion as many were in an obvious state of shock. He could hardly read his own writing as he struggled with the enormity of what was happening.

"Alex! Come on let's get ashore," Bartlett screamed amidst the chaos.

The adrenalin in Alex's body was pumping. Taking a deep breath he followed the Englishman.

***

Alex and Ellis were steamed to the shore under a hailstorm of bullets coming from the hills. Fortunately the fire was high. They reached a narrow beach some thirty yards wide and stumbled ashore over some barges. Alex found himself in semi darkness amidst a scene of indescribable confusion. He tried to comprehend what he was witnessing. The beach was piled with ammunition stores among which lay dead and wounded men. Some were so exhausted they had fallen asleep in spite of the noise and excitement around them. There were groups being directed by officers to climb the hills. The ascent was made treacherous by loose sandstone and shrubs. It was continuous, soldiers going up and others coming down.

Alex was in a state of panic.

"General Birdwood," Bartlett announced, pointing to an officer who was giving instructions to a small group of soldiers.

When they approached the general, a nervous Colonel from behind them shouted, "Who are you? What are you doing here?" He didn't wait for an answer and commanded, "Seize those men, they are spies."

The correspondents were quickly surrounded. Ellis blurted, "I am Ashmead-Bartlett and this is Alexander Stewart. We are War Correspondents attached to the Expedition." Captain Armstrong had given them a pass giving permission to go ashore. This did not seem to satisfy the jumpy Colonel as they lacked official army identification.

"How do I know you are who you say you are? Does anyone here know these men?"

Alex now feared for his life. He was shaking and stepped closer to Bartlett. Out of the darkness a gruff voice replied, "Yes, I do."

Alex and Ellis had no idea who the voice belonged to. They were released immediately. Their relief was overpowering.

The correspondents were ordered to return to the battleship HMS Queen. On board, Alex was recovering from the experience on the beach. He was now beginning to envisage his account in the Globe and Times.

***

Five days later on Imbros Island, Alex said his farewells to an ecstatic Bartlett. Alex was preparing to return to London and on to Scotland. Keith Murdoch had left earlier in the morning enroute to London with the letter.

Alex recalled his horrific experience on the beach. The frightening moment when he thought he would be shot. He had asked Bartlett who vouched for them on the beach. Ellis had only shrugged his shoulders.

Yes, I do ... the voice still ringing in his ears, made him forever grateful.

CHAPTER 74
Tuesday 7 December 1915, Boston, USA

"Why do you have to leave now? It will be Christmas in less than three weeks!"

Alex and Sarah were in the kitchen of their Boston apartment. Sarah Stewart did not often speak up against her husband. Most of the time, he was a thoughtful partner and father, always taking the needs of his family into consideration over his own. Gallipoli had changed him.

"It's so unlike you Alexander," Sarah said cautiously. The use of his full Christian name always made him attentive. "You already missed Robert's birthday. You told me the troops are evacuating, so why is it important for you to be there?"

Alex felt himself retreat emotionally. He had felt guilty breaking the news, and a cold almost mechanical bitterness now took over. *How could I describe what the gulf was like?*

"You've read my articles. Don't they tell you enough?"

Sarah sighed. "Don't you see," she cried out, "I'm married to the correspondent who wrote the words. Yet, even I have to read the newspapers to find out what you witnessed. Why won't you talk to me Alex? Why can't you *tell* me why you need to return? I don't understand why anyone would want to go to such a wretched place rather than be with their family at Christmas. It's not *your* war Alex! There'll be men there wishing they were home!"

Alex stared at his wife, lost for words. He had never seen Sarah so angry. Her face was taut, her eyes glistening.

"I can't," he finally cried out, tossing his arms in the air. Alex was totally frustrated. His published articles had a huge impact on public sympathy, but to Alex they seemed insufficient. The injustice, conducted by pompous government cabinet ministers, needlessly sending thousands of men to certain death, ate into his soul like a disease. It was old hurt, upper class arrogance and conceit. Alex couldn't forget a dispatch from the front line requesting reinforcements; 'I have only three hundred bayonets left,' it had read. Not men, but bayonets!

Alex let out a heartfelt sigh causing Sarah to frown. In the twenty years they'd been together, she had never seen him this restless. Gallipoli was taking its toll on her husband. The reports written by Alex had received mixed reaction from the public. She knew he was a respected and competent journalist. Yet his graphic articles, along with his bitter criticism of the British Government, many found hard to believe, including Sarah.

Her disbelief had caused tension. She knew Alex's writings did not reflect his full involvement. Alex had said the less she knew the better. Sarah had been distraught. She needed to know what occupied her husband's mind.

Then, there had also been that unexpected visit from a James Macpherson, one of the siblings Alex had grown up with at Ballindalloch. After twenty years he'd shown up out of nowhere. Alex had been vague on his discussion with James at the Globe office. Sarah felt insecure as she sensed he was hiding something.

"Sarah, I'm sorry, but I *don't* have a choice," Alex exclaimed. "I just need to go back one more time." He hesitated as Sarah's expression of utter sadness made him nauseous. "I feel it's my duty Sarah. I must finish what I started. I owe it to Bartlett and Murdoch. They have been banished and cannot go back. Many more would have died had it not been for those two." Alex couldn't bear to watch his wife's contorted face a moment longer and turned away.

Nervously she tied on an apron. A weary feeling overcame her. Unable to prepare dinner, she rested both hands on the counter top. A random thought took her to the ship which had brought her to America. Then, she'd been a twenty-six year old Mrs Gibson. Her first husband had disappeared on the voyage. Alex had been there as well. Her mind's eye recalled the hapless look on his boyish face when he had tried to console her.

A loud sob made Alex look up. He knew Sarah was crying, but he couldn't bring himself to comfort his wife. They would have to talk. He would have to reveal what James Macpherson had told him and why Gallipoli was not the only reason he had to go back, but he couldn't, not yet.

CHAPTER 75
Thursday 9 December 1915, Boston, MA, USA

Alex had been waiting patiently for almost an hour. He had booked two telephone calls, one to London the other to Jefferson County. He glanced at a small desk timepiece and sighed. With a deep frown he continued reading a report on The Superior Court in Fulton County, Georgia, accepting the charter for the establishment of a Ku Klux Klan organisation.

Sitting on the edge of his desk he glanced out the window. The snowflakes were dancing in the morning breeze. He was alone in his second floor office of the Boston Globe Headquarters. Using his foot, he gently closed the door. Finally the telephone rang snapping Alex out of his despondent thoughts. He snapped the phone from its cradle and found he was connected to Beaumont.

"Alex, is that you? How is the Stewart gang doing?"

Alex gave a broad smile on hearing his friend's unmistakable Irish twang.

"Good morning Sean. We are well. How are all the Devanes?"

"We are just fine Alex. Colleen and the kids are looking forward to the Christmas break in Boston."

Raising his voice a notch Alex said, "Sean, the Globe is paying for this call, so can I be brief?" Alex heard him chuckle and continued, "When are you due to arrive in Boston?"

"I'm not sure. We are all so busy here, but we will be in Boston for sure by the Friday, Christmas Eve. I'm looking forward to seeing you and Sarah and the boys."

"Michael will be staying on in Scotland this year, but Robert will be here. I have a favour to ask though. Could you try and get here earlier? I need to see you way before the twenty-fourth."

There was a pause. "Sean, did you hear me?" Alex shouted.

"Yes, hold on, let me think. Maybe the 18th or 19th might be possible. I don't know, I will cable you Alex. Why the urgency? What's going on?"

"I'll explain when we meet up. Thanks Sean, safe passage and let Colleen know I have complimentary tickets for The Birth of a Nation. Apparently everyone is taken by the actress Lillian Gish."

Back in Beaumont, a perplexed Sean Devane placed the telephone on the receiver. He was concerned about the behaviour of his most precious friend.

CHAPTER 76
Friday 17 December 1915, the Plaza Hotel, Copley Square, Boston, USA

The array of lights and a huge Christmas tree brightly lit the lobby. The hotel was busy. A line had formed an orderly queue at the checkout desks. Porters were busy shuffling baggage to waiting automobiles. Sean Devane sat in the corner furthest from the main entrance. Smoking a cigarette, he observed people coming in from the morning cold. Sean had arrived in Boston only twelve hours earlier and was still feeling the effect of the long journey. His venture into the oil business was challenging. He always felt guilty when he was on vacation. It was as if he was deserting the company. He picked up the complimentary morning edition of the Globe and turned to the sports section:

'Boston Red Sox purchase catcher Sam Agnew from St Louis Browns.'

"Sean, I would recognise the hair anywhere," shouted Alex, as he walked towards his friend.

They hugged and back-slapped affectionately for a few moments. Alex removed his coat and sat down opposite Sean.

"How was your journey?"

"It worked out fine. We arrived around eight last night. You are looking tired my friend. Is everything in order Alex? Are Sarah and the boys in good health?"

"Yes Sean, they are all in fine spirits. How are Colleen and the kids?"

"They are doing great, all sound asleep this morning when I left."

"And your father?" asked Alex. "I'm sure you had a lot of catching up to do."

Sean made a face. "He is of the usual frame of mind. Nobody does anything right other than him and Breen continues to get on his nerves."

Alex smiled affectionately at the thought of Breen who it seemed to Alex had been the Devane's butler for a lifetime.

They sat down and Sean asked, "Why the cloak and dagger meeting?"

Alex sat back and sighed. "I won't be here at Christmas Sean. I'm going back to Europe on Sunday."

"What! You must be jesting man. You surely don't mean Turkey again?"

Alex nodded his head. "Yes, it will be my last visit ..."

Sean interrupted, "You are crazy Alex. Sarah, she ..."

Alex leaned forward, "Sean I do not want to discuss Turkey or Sarah. I am going to Scotland after I'm done at Helles." Alex glanced at his pocket watch.

Sean placed a hand on his friend's shoulder, "Are you in a rush for another appointment? What is going on Alex? Scotland? Is it Michael, is he in some trouble?"

"No, Michael is fine to the best of my knowledge. I *will* go to Glasgow and spend time with him." Alex paused, his features tense.

"Sean, I received some news from Scotland I want to share with you. Promise me you will not divulge this to anyone, not even your father."

The Irishman was as much intrigued as concerned. "Alex you know I will always respect your wishes. Tell me, what is going on?"

Alex leaned closer and whispered, "Sean, I have a daughter, Alexandra. She is nineteen-years old." He waited on a reaction.

Sean looked at the Scot, with his eyes wide open. "My God and Katherine is the mother?"

"Who else could it be?" Alex said, leaning back feeling a sense of relief for having finally shared this.

"When did you discover this? Who told you?"

"A few days ago I had a visitor, someone from my past in Scotland."

Sean stared at Alex and shook his head, "Have you told Sarah?"

Alex raised his voice, "No! She must not know of this and certainly not Michael and Robert."

"But Alex, your children have a sister..."

"Sean, listen, I don't have the time. You are my dearest friend and the only person I dare confide in. Please let me sort this out my own way. I know I am asking a lot, especially as you will be spending time with Sarah and Robert ..."

Sean raised his right hand, "Why in God's name are you telling me all this?"

Alex paused and retrieved an envelope from his coat. "Take this and keep it in a safe place."

Sean took the envelope, gave it a quick glance and looked back at Alex who was now standing. Sean slowly rose from his chair.

"It is a letter to Sarah," Alex clarified. "If anything untoward happens to me, please give the letter to her. I will leave it to your discretion when you do this."

Sean, clutching the envelope in his right hand, just shook his head in disbelief, saddened by what he had just heard.

"Thank you Sean." Alex fastened his coat, "I am sure everything will be fine and you can return the letter to me when I get back." He squeezed Sean's shoulder. "See you tonight," he added and briskly made his way out of the hotel, leaving a perplexed Sean Devane.

CHAPTER 77
Wednesday 5 January 1916, HMS London, Imbros Island, Turkey

The final days of the evacuation of the Helles garrison were in motion. The French troops had departed only a few days before and the remaining British troops, around 19000, were scheduled to leave by the end of the week. There was total disarray within the officer's circle. Alex had discovered with disdain that a Private from the Fifth Battalion, Wiltshire Division had been executed for wilfully refusing to carry out an order. There were mixed emotions on Imbros and tempers were riding high.

Alex was seated in a dispatch room close to the officers' deck, preparing to go to Gully Spur and witness the evacuation. He knew the allies were suffering heavy losses at the ravine as they retreated mile by mile. His kitbag sat on the floor beside him. He had finished updating his war diary and was now busy writing a letter to Sarah. Alex had made all his arrangements on how he would get to Scotland. His thoughts returned to the day he left Ballindalloch all those years ago. Lagmore Stone Circle was still vivid in his mind. He recalled his total despair as he sat on the fallen stone and promised himself he would return one day.

Uninvited, Major Crawford Munro joined him. A bearded man, he stood head and shoulders over Alex.

"I take it you are here to report on the evacuation Mr Stewart?"

Alex looked up at the major. He was in full dress uniform. He looked tense, agitated. Munro was slowly walking up and down the small room and kept glancing out of the open door as if he was expecting someone.

"I wish Ellis was here," Alex responded and returned to his writing.

Munro turned to Alex, "I wish he was here as well but for entirely different reasons. I understand he is forbidden to be on any British expedition. It is abhorrent that Bartlett and Murdoch brought down good men, men with distinguished military careers. He made us all a laughing stock!"

Alex studied Munro and sensed the Major was mentally ill, as if he was having some kind of breakdown. The man was sweating profusely. He continued pacing to and from the door, his right hand covering the butt of his holstered pistol.

"Are you all right Major? Why don't you take a seat?" Alex nudged a chair close to him.

"I am extremely angry. I had for a long time cherished the hope I would leave this inhospitable graveyard defiant, with my head held high Mr Stewart. I'll never admit, even to myself, we have been beaten after the sacrifice of so many men. To desert our comrades and sneak away in the dark without a fight is a revolting thing. The thought of it nauseates me."

Alex tried to ignore Munro and continued writing.

The Major was relentless. "You and your bloody pals Bartlett and Murdoch have caused all of this. Do you realise what you have done? Are you listening to me Stewart?" The Major's voice was now more aggressive.

Alex stood up to face the Englishman. "Listen Major, if it wasn't Ellis or Keith, it would have been someone else. You know deep down in your soul you could never win here. At least you are going home to your family, more than I can say for thousands of others."

"You do not understand Mr Stewart, I cannot go home. The shame, I will be considered a coward, and ..."

Alex interrupted, "Look, I think you need help. Why don't you go to the medical deck and find a doctor. I have things to do, if you don't mind."

Munro sighed and walked to the doorway and looked around. Then he turned and approached Alex. Pulling his pistol from its holster he fired the Webley. The blast echoed around the room. The back of Alex's head exploded, his body jerked forward crashing on the table with a loud thud covering his half written letter. His pen dropped to the floor. Major Crawford Munro saluted, placed the barrel in his mouth and pulled the trigger.

Part IV

Do not be afraid; our fate cannot be taken from us; it is a gift
Diante Alighieri, Inferno 1265 – 1321

The best laid schemes o' mice and men gang aft agley (often go wrong)
Robert Burns 1759 – 1796

There's nowhere you can be that isn't where you are meant to be
John Lennon 1940 – 1980

CHAPTER 78
Thursday 13 January 1916, Ballindalloch Castle, Banffshire, Scotland

"PLEASE Uncle James, I don't want to sound ungrateful in any way, but I don't want it!" Alexandra looked shocked. Tears were glistening in her eyes. How was she to explain to this man how she felt? James had only been part of her life for a fortnight! Her Uncle James, second in line after her father John, had sailed all the way from America to help Victoria and her, settle family affairs.

James wondered if his brother had ever discussed with Alexandra, her following his footsteps as laird. John Macpherson's sudden death just after Christmas had shocked not just his family, but also the local community. He had been returning from Inverness by automobile together with his driver. The car somehow had veered from the icy road and plunged into the River Ness. The coroner had returned a verdict, 'Death by Drowning' for both men.

A new Laird of Ballindalloch now needed to be appointed. Protocol deemed this should be Alexandra as the only child of John. Victoria had been strangely aloof when the telegram sent from the ship had announced James's due arrival.

"Maybe it's time you had a talk with your Uncle James on your future my dear," Victoria had said to Alexandra. "It may all turn out for the better."

The thin smile following her mother's words was no stranger to Alexandra. Victoria, as usual, made her feel inadequate. It was as if some vital ingredient was missing in the chemistry of their relationship, rendering her incompetent in anything she did.

Fortunately, her Uncle James had turned out to be a reasonable man. In fact, he could well have been one of the few Macphersons she felt recognised by.

Now, her friendly uncle was sitting opposite her at her father's desk in the study. He had explained how, as the only child, she was technically next in line. Alexandra, nor any of the other Macpherson family members, as far as she could judge, considered this a good idea.

"Couldn't you take over uncle? You are now the oldest brother."

"Yes my dear, but my wife and children are settled in America. I have my business and friends there."

Alexandra had to agree even the visits to her Aunt Katie in Chicago during the summer seasons, had been enough to dramatically alter her view of Ballindalloch and its inhabitants. The Scottish environment would be so different from what Americans were used to. Even for her it had been harder to settle, each time she had returned.

With her father now gone and her studies behind her, Alexandra wondered if her mother would allow her to go and stay with Aunt Katie.

She was jolted out of her thoughts by James scraping his throat nervously. When she looked up she found him staring at her intently.

"Maybe it's time I told you something Alexandra," he said, in an almost inaudible voice. After a moment's hesitation James continued, "It won't be pleasurable I'm afraid."

Her stomach knotted in her usual barrier of defence.

James had a hard time himself, not knowing where to start, although he had practiced it in his mind over and over again. What a twist of Fate it had been that he should have visited Alexander only the month before, giving in to the call of his conscience that had been following him for almost twenty years. He'd known about Alexander Stewart's whereabouts for a while, after a controversial article on race segregation had found its way into a magazine published in Raleigh, written by an 'A. Stewart.' A hunch had prompted James to hire a private investigator who had indeed confirmed it was the same Alexander Stewart who had left Ballindalloch in 1895. From that moment on, James had been faced with the possibility of setting straight what he had never supported in the first place. Last December, he had finally given in to the call without ever considering the possible consequences of the revelation. Now that Alexander knew, Alexandra had every need and right to know as well. What if Alexander showed up at Ballindalloch?

"There is no easy way to tell you this," James started. "When my sister was eighteen she became pregnant. She was not married. Much against my will I must say, my sister and brother insisted it would be best for the child to be raised in a stable family home."

Alexandra felt her breath quicken.

"It was agreed after great debate that John and Victoria should adopt the child."

Alexandra looked aghast. "And the child was me," she said with difficulty, her quick mind immediately grasping what she was being told. On hearing James' words, something deep inside stirred Alexandra. She should have known all along.

"So, who is my father?" she managed to ask.

"A certain Mr Alexander Stewart," James answered, struggling to keep long held emotion from his voice.

Alexandra felt a cold wave of realisation run up and down her spine. Her heart raced and with her breath becoming shallow she found she was having difficulty to breathe. She hardly registered James rising from his chair with an alarmed look on his face.

262

Alexandra gasped, struggling to breathe.

"Mary!" James cried out for the housekeeper, "Someone get Mary here...now!"

Feeling faint and nauseous, Alexandra desperately gripped the armrests of her chair, as if it was her last connection to life. Her chest felt as if it was being crushed and she found herself incapable of exhaling. Out of nowhere Mary emerged and gently bent the girl's upper body forward so her head sank between her knees.

"Now you take it easy Miss Alexandra, just breathe in and out, like you would blow out a candle," she said mimicking the blow, her rosy cheeks bulging from her face. "There you go, that's better."

Coughing, Alexandra veered back into her chair, tears rolling down her cheeks. Slowly she felt her anxiety subside.

"I'll get you a nice cup of tea miss. Now you just stay here and calm down." From behind the chair Mary threw an angry glare at James Macpherson. Since birth she had taken care of the girl. Mary had spent more time with the child than Victoria and Katherine combined. She had grown to love Alexandra like family.

"I thought she was never to be told," she hissed between her teeth at James, and without another word, marched out of the room to make Alexandra her tea.

***

"Someone should have told the bairn at birth!" Mary's voice echoed in the kitchen. In her anger, she didn't notice the look exchanged by the old coachman MacLean and stable master Callum MacCallum.

"It's not fair to keep it a secret all her young life and take her security away from her, just like *that*," she added, snapping her fingers over her head. Still upset by what she had just witnessed in the study with James and Alexandra, she angrily scooped far too many tealeaves from the caddy into the warm teapot she had grabbed from the cooker.

"Would be mighty difficult to explain to a wee baby," MacLean muttered from under his breath. He and Callum were sitting at the kitchen table centred between the sink and the huge stove.

"Still remember how I drove the old laird to the police station," he went on, not caring whether or not somebody actually listened. They had heard him tell the story hundreds of times. MacLean still relished it.

"Was early morning it was, still horse and carriage in those days, but just as fast. Give me a good pair of steeds any day. I need the smell of life under my nose. I know what I heard, 'twas the old laird Mr Gordon reporting the theft. Why would he have gone through all the trouble of going to the constable if there wasn't truth to the story? You explain *that* to me!" MacLean summarised the same story all over again.

Mary threw an exasperated glance at the old man. "I've heard this once too often." In her younger days when she was personal maid to Miss Katherine and the Lady Elizabeth, she had understood quite well what came to pass. She herself had always been impressed with the young Alexander tall as he was, with dark wavy hair. His blue eyes always seemed aware of what was going on in the world. Uttering a deep sigh, Mary sat down at the kitchen table and shook her head.

"Will there ever be an end to all this?" she asked to nobody in particular. "Simpson, God rest his soul would have said it is time to let bygones be bygones. Poor man," she reminisced. "He was never the same after Robert Stewart died. This house has never been the same since Mr Gordon disappeared and now Mr John and now this."

When it was announced Katherine was with child, the staff were told by John Macpherson no outsiders were to know, threatening instant dismissal. Mary of course had tended to Katherine during her pregnancy and childbirth. She had witnessed the battle the young woman had fought with herself. Wanting a different path in life than what you were born into, was not easy. With nobody else but each other for diversion, the two women had grown close with the boundaries between the served and the servant becoming thinner and thinner.

After the birth, when Katherine left for Edinburgh and the child was registered as the daughter of laird John and his wife, Mary had sworn to take care of Alexandra as if she was her own. Now, she felt, it was time to keep this promise more than ever, and tell Alexandra all she knew.

***

The next day after breakfast, Mary had requested some time with James. Given this was so out of character, James had no hesitation in meeting her.

"Pardon my bluntness Mr James, but Alexandra is in no condition to make any decisions. The poor girl is in shock." Mary stood her ground holding her formidable body erect as she faced James.

"What do you suggest we do?" James asked seriously. Mary had guarded both his mother and his sister like a lioness would her cubs. He knew she was doing the same now for Alexandra. If there was someone who could give solid advice in this extremely delicate matter it had to be her.

"I suggest Alexandra goes to America and stays with her mother. The two will have enough to discuss. Of course, it is up to them to decide but I think it's high time, beggin' your pardon sir, this family should put some things right. I think the child should be given time to decide whether she wants to leave Ballindalloch or whatever else she wants to do."

James had to smile at the way Mary had made the right assumption. "You are absolutely correct Mary. It would not be fair to have Alexandra make decisions now on her future that she might regret later. I'll see to it that she receives an allowance. In the meantime, I will ask my brother Donald to stand in as laird. The estate and the clan need a laird Mary, we owe it to the people, but I assure you Alexandra will never be denied her part in the inheritance of Ballindalloch."

CHAPTER 79
Thursday 20 October 2011, National Archives of Scotland, Edinburgh, Scotland

John Macpherson was seated in a small meeting room, his tablet open on a small table beside a window overlooking Princes Street. His open business case was beside him and he was busy checking his email. The National Archives seemed an appropriate place for this meeting. He didn't like to use the bank's facilities for matters not directly related to his job. John knew one of the curators at the Archives for many years. He had given him permission to use the room.

There was a gentle tap on the door.

"Come in," said John and stood up to greet his guest.

Two women entered the room. "Hello Mr Macpherson, I am Diane Cox and this is my friend Dawn Boswick. I hope you don't mind if she joins us."

John nodded as they shook hands and suggested they all sit. He contemplated asking if they were enjoying their holiday, but thought better of it. He didn't care and would rather get on with matters at hand. The women obviously had been shopping as they had brought many bags depicting well-known brands.

"My father has updated me on the meeting you had with him and Mrs Stewart."

"Yes. You see ..."

"I know all the details Mrs Cox, so we do not need to repeat. Your claim to the estate is based on one Alexandra Macpherson. Am I correct?"

"I'm not claiming anything, I just want some... Alexandra was ..."

"I know who she was Mrs Cox and she never held any position of authority in the family."

Diane looked at Dawn for support and then faced John. "Exactly my point, I would like to know why she ..."

"Have you heard of King Edward and Mrs Simpson?" John asked.

"Excuse me?" Diane looked at the Scot as if he had lost his mind.

"Edward VIII and Wallis Simpson, he abdicated in 1936. He gave up the throne to marry the American socialite. It was a nasty piece of business," John said.

"Yes, I know the story. What on earth has it got to do with anything?" Once again she looked at Dawn who just shrugged her shoulders.

John retrieved a document from his case and slid it over the table to the American and said, "It's not quite on the same scale as Edward, but nonetheless please read this."

Diane fumbled in her handbag, found her spectacles and picked up the paper:

INSTRUMENT OF RENOUNCEMENT

I Alexandra Macpherson of the Ballindalloch Estate do hereby declare my irrevocable determination to renounce the position of Laird of Ballindalloch, lineage and associated assets. My desire is this takes effect immediately. In token where I hereunto set my hand this twenty-fifth day of January nineteen hundred and sixteen in the presence of the witnesses whose signatures are subscribed.

Signed at Ballindalloch Castle in the presence of;
Alexandra Macpherson

Donald Macpherson

James Macpherson

Mary Montgomery

Colin Waddell - Solicitor

It took Diane only a minute to read. She sighed while handing back the paper to John.

"You keep it Mrs Cox, it is a copy."

"How do I know this is genuine? Alexandra could have signed this under duress. Maybe it was because she was a woman?" Diane was becoming flustered.

John leaned back, "We'll never know will we? But sign it she did. So, if there is nothing else ladies, I have a busy schedule and I'm sure you will want to see more of our fine city."

"I, I could go to the newspapers back home with this you know," stammered Diane.

"Indeed you could, it is your prerogative Mrs Cox and I cannot control what you do. You have proved you descend from our family and we welcome and value all our 'cousins' from around the globe. I leave it up to you whether you embrace this, or tarnish what you have in your hand."

John stood up and closed his briefcase.

Diane gestured to Dawn they should go. Picking up her shopping bags she said to John, "I meant no harm Mr Macpherson. I didn't want to claim anything. I just wanted ..."

John interrupted, "Some recognition Mrs Cox?"

"Yes, because I think Alexandra would have deserved that."

The library door was open. Silently she slipped inside. As expected, he was sitting at the reading table. A spread of newspapers covered the table together with a teapot, cup and saucer. Cathy watched him for a few moments. Often she noticed the likeness between him and her father. Even the way he sat completely engrossed in whatever he was reading was similar.

"Uncle T!" she startled him. "My father, who is around thirty years your junior, always needs to use reading glasses. How do you manage without?"

A huge grin appeared on the handsome man's rugged features. "Laser surgery my dear. What are you doing up so early? Is your husband arriving today?"

Cathy sat down opposite him. "No, he will be here on Tuesday." She placed on the table what Thomas thought was an album of some kind.

"So what are you up to?" Thomas asked glancing at the album. "You have an all too familiar look." Thomas Macpherson folded his newspaper indicating she had his full attention. "Another one of your treasure hunts?"

Cathy waved a hand, her mind momentarily flashing back to the ill-fated sixth of August when she made Uncle T her accomplice. "No, I'm done digging castle walls, but I do have a question."

"Let's hear it."

"Last month, when Duckett delivered the report on Gordon, you talked of how as a young boy you met Katherine Macpherson."

Thomas took a sip of his tea. "I was only eight or nine-years old. It is a long time ago."

"How long did she stay?"

"I'm not sure, I only remember she was there. She made a big impression on me."

'Why?"

Thomas paused and stared into space for a moment. "She brought records," he said and started to hum. Then he explained, "That tune is, 'Thanks for the Memory'. We had an HMV Gramophone in those days. I recall my parents and Aunt Katherine, as we were told to call her, playing that record. I wonder what happened to it." Thomas sat in thought for a few moments with Cathy watching him. "She took me to Grantown in my father's Austin Seven Ruby. Catherine, it's been years since I thought of that car. It was a two-door black saloon. My mind must be playing tricks. I'm sure the number 514 was part of the registration plate." Thomas looked genuinely surprised at his own recollections.

"Just the two of you went to Grantown?"

"Yes. I was the youngest in the house and she probably wanted to spoil me. I have always had an effect on women." Thomas winked. "In fact when I think of it…" Thomas gave Cathy a mischievous smile, "she shrieked a lot, her squeals in the car for example. Apparently, she had never driven on the left. She shouted and cursed all the way to Grantown."

"What did you do there?"

"We had lemonade somewhere and I remember visiting her old house."

"She lived in Grantown?" Cathy cried out in surprise. "For some reason I always pictured her at Ballindalloch? Where in Grantown did she live?"

"I don't remember, it was seventy years ago. I do recall when she showed me the building, a soldier came out of the house. I recognised the uniform."

"Even at eight or nine you knew the uniform?"

"I did," he said proudly. "Even then I was fascinated by the military. The Seaforth Highlanders, they had a Battalion in Elgin for years. Catherine, where are you going with this?"

"I'm not sure, I'm just interested. I am the double of this woman and here I am talking to someone who actually met her. Wouldn't you be curious if you were in my shoes?"

Thomas nodded.

"What year was it, do you remember? Was it during the Second World War?"

"No, I'm pretty sure this was before the outbreak of the war, otherwise it would have been too difficult for Katherine to travel from the USA. It must have been when the Spanish Civil War was going on. Many Scots joined up with the International Brigade to fight against Franco, especially Protestants. Of course I didn't know it at the time, I wasn't *that* smart."

Cathy gave him a shy smile. She recalled how embarrassed she had been when on the fateful night they discovered Gordon's bones he had told her of what had happened to him as a boy in Scotland during the Second World War, exposing her complete lack of knowledge on the subject. She had always thought the Germans only bombed London. Her ignorance on the Spanish War was even worse.

"Why Protestants?" she asked.

Thomas quickly settled into his storytelling. He obviously loved reminiscing on military conflicts. "During the 1930s, Europe had seen a rise of fascism in Germany, Italy and Spain. The Pope back then supported Mussolini and Franco, fascist pals of Adolf Hitler. In Scotland, many groups opposed this, such as the SPL, the Scottish Protestant League and the PA, Protestants for Action. Like many countries in Europe, British men went to Spain to fight against Franco."

Cathy stood up and stretched her arms above her head. "Jeez Uncle T, I have to admit, I know nothing of this stuff."

She picked up the album and handed it to Thomas. "Did you arrange for me to get this?"

Thomas shook his head, "No! I've never seen it before."

"It's a photo album, Alexandra's. Open it, have a look. It is amazing Uncle T."

Cathy could tell Uncle T was intrigued. She sat back watching him flick through the pages and studied his face. He would pause at certain pictures and give off the most radiant of smiles. Half way through, he looked up at Cathy, "I've seen this collection of pictures before, years ago. It's strange ..." He continued turning the pages and without looking at Cathy he muttered, "I had completely forgotten these pictures."

"Aren't they just wonderful Uncle T?"

"Yes for sure, but it's peculiar she didn't have any pictures from Ballindalloch." Thomas was still staring at the album. "Where did you get this?" he asked now looking at Cathy.

"It was left in my bedroom. I have no idea who was responsible. There was no note enclosed, only the album wrapped in brown paper. And yes, I had the same thoughts. You said you had seen it before. It must have been in your family's possession."

Thomas gave a wry smile as he closed the album. "I wonder what people will do in the future. Nobody has albums any more. Will people bequeath their hard drives? We all grew up with old photographs in a shoe box." Thomas's face lit up, "Oh, now I get it, I asked Maggie a few weeks ago if she had any old pictures or letters of Ballindalloch. I thought it might help you, Catherine, in your research. It must have been Maggie, the old devil. This proves," he continued tapping with one finger on the album, "William lived in Chicago. It looks like Katherine and Alexandra must have lived there as well."

Cathy replied, "Alexandra probably did eventually. Many immigrants primarily stayed with family or friends until they found a place of their own. I checked the Census records."

"Did you find them?" asked Thomas.

"I found William Macpherson, Spirit Trader, living in Chicago. The age ties in, as does his country of origin. In his household was a lodger, some woman Dorrington and a servant but no Katherine. He *did* live in one of the most desirable areas of the city. He must have had well-lined pockets. I also found him on another website. He was on the board of a distillery group in the USA. That is what was inscribed on Gordon's silver pencil Uncle T, remember?"

"Chicago," said an intrigued Thomas.

"DCL, Distillers Company Limited, headquartered in Chicago. Anyway, I couldn't find Katherine anywhere in Illinois. I also searched the web high and low in the Carolinas where James and his family settled and still came up with a big fat zilch. She died in 1954 Uncle T."

"Aye, I knew it would be in the fifties, as I was on training in England when I received a letter from my mother. Check out the public records office for Last Wills and Testaments for William and Katherine. Maybe they have a website containing archives and the like. I'll discreetly ask our solicitors to have a look if they have anything. It may be a long shot but you never know what you might find."

"Great suggestion Uncle T, thanks."

Distracted Thomas picked up his cup, sipped his tea and made a face. "This tea is bloody cold," he muttered and looked at Cathy. "I do remember something else from Katherine's Grantown visit, her seeing a man at a bank she obviously knew. In those days banks were scary for wee boys. Big hollow sounding buildings a bit like dentist's waiting rooms and the people working there just as daunting. I remember him patting me on the head before we left. He looked quite old but when I think back, it might well be he and Katherine were of the same age. It's just … she didn't look old to me. Her mannerism was youthful in a bold sort of way, not an elderly lady at all."

"Well," Cathy said, "let's see if there's a little more for me to find out about Katherine and William. Do you happen to have any pictures of her visit?"

"I don't think so. You have stirred up old memories Catherine. I'll have a rummage and let you know. He added jokingly, "Otherwise we can always ask Maggie."

" I wonder why Alexandra didn't take the album when she moved to the States?"

"Perhaps she had no room in her luggage, who knows?"

"Mm … or maybe her departure was similar to Alexander Stewart's."

"What do you mean?"

"From what I read in his letters, Alexandra left Ballindalloch in a hurry, no time to pack." Cathy stood up and kissed Uncle T on the forehead. "Thanks for the talk," she said and walked out of the room, leaving Thomas Macpherson to reminisce.

CHAPTER 81
Thursday 13 January 1916, Stirling, Scotland

The first class carriage was packed with travellers heading north. The train was gathering speed as it left the newly refurbished Stirling Station. Due to the curfew, the compartment was dimly lit. Katherine Macpherson was tired. She fidgeted in her seat trying to get comfortable. It seemed an eternity since saying farewell to her father on the doorstep of Maxwell Street. Arriving in Glasgow had been harrowing. On disembarking the ship, security checks had been severe. Two officers had spent twenty minutes thoroughly searching her luggage, asking many questions about her travel plans and place of residence. Troop ships dominated the harbour and military ground traffic was heavy. By taxi, it had taken almost two hours to get to Glasgow Queen Street. The train station was engulfed in soldiers either making their way to the front or returning home. Most were young boys. Wives, children and girlfriends were cheering or crying as they waved their farewells. Others were waiting anxiously for loved ones.

Passenger services had been disrupted due to unforeseen circumstances. A rumour circulated that a train had been stopped and had blocked the line. Suspected German spies were on board. Katherine had been fortunate as she only had to wait thirty minutes before boarding the train to Perth.

Katherine was deeply worried, to the point where her thoughts made her feel ill when she tried to imagine what she would now need to face. Biting on her bottom lip, her dark thoughts lingered. *What will happen? Alexandra surely can't stay on with Victoria! Should I tell her the truth?*

Katherine found the carriage too warm. She removed her tweed jacket, placing it over her lap. A middle-aged gentleman sitting directly across from her unashamedly looked her up and down and smiled. Ignoring his lures, Katherine closed her eyes.

It was the summer of 1905 when Alexandra first came to Chicago. She was such a pretty nine-year-old and quickly settled with her and William. Much to William's discomfort, Alexandra took to Richard Danaher. She would follow him in the house, always asking an abundance of questions. The first summer William seemed a man reborn. He spoiled Alexandra with new clothes, candies, visiting the Lincoln Zoo and drives in his baby, a brand new Studebaker. He even cancelled business appointments to allow more time with his precious granddaughter. Katherine had never seen her father *and* Alexandra so happy. 'Aunt Katie, can I stay here all the time?' the girl had asked. When faced with such innocent honesty, Katherine had to hide her emotions and respond firmly. 'You need to continue your education in Scotland.' Katherine knew Alexandra's life at Ballindalloch was extremely sheltered. Unlike her childhood, Alexandra had no siblings to teach her horse riding, shooting and other outdoor activities a nine-year old should be enjoying. Katherine managed subtly to determine her little girl's life was made up of schooling and learning domestic skills. Alexandra had also volunteered she was becoming quite an accomplished piano player.

Noisy laughter from behind her seat woke Katherine out of her daydreams. She glanced at an elderly gentleman who was pacing up and down the passageway. He reminded Katherine of her father. She was concerned for William. His health had gradually worsened. Nowadays his appearance was gaunt, his eating habits sporadic and his short-term memory poor. He no longer received many social visits, only occasional business colleagues. Katherine had urged him to stop working, but he refused to listen. Even his closest associates, the Dewars, had pleaded with William to step down. She felt despondent as she knew how it was going to end.

Katherine guessed they would arrive in Perth within the hour. She yawned, closed her eyes again. In summer Alexandra would stay in Chicago. During spring of 1906 Katherine had moved into her own studio. Alexandra would stay with her and at weekends they would go to Maxwell Street to be with William. She had watched her daughter grow and blossom each subsequent summer. Alexandra was intelligent and smart. How Katherine loved those years. A holiday, *was it 1908?*, to Niagara Falls was foremost in her mind. William had insisted on driving the five hundred miles in his brand new Buick-5 Passenger Touring car. After only clearing the Chicago city limits, his pride and joy broke down. William pretended he could get the car going again. He only succeeded in ruining his suit. Oil and grease had been everywhere. She could still remember Alexandra's laughter at William's antics.

The following summer at Katherine's request, William allowed Katherine to drive them to Palos Hills, in Cook County, some twenty-three miles south west of the city. It was here Katherine perfected Alexandra's riding skills. William had surprised them the following year by purchasing a log cabin close to the stables. This modest house often became a retreat for Katherine and Alexandra. Katherine had tried to stimulate some interest in painting, but Alexandra never seemed impressed with the local landscape pictures. She had been shocked when she discovered by accident a life model painting by Katherine. She had recognised the model. 'Aunt Katie,' she had shouted, her face as red as beetroot, "It's … how could you?"

In the summer of 1909, Alexandra told Katherine the housekeeper, Mrs Craddock, had passed away. Katherine received all kinds of gossip from the thirteen-year old, whether she wanted to hear it or not. How gamekeeper Peter Gunn had been arrested for shooting at poachers and Callum had married an English woman who was ten-years his senior. Katherine and William knew her boarding school education was paying dividends. Alexandra adored Edinburgh. It delighted Katherine to learn her daughter was popular with her peers at school. 'Aunt Katie,' she had said, 'you can call me Alex now, all my friends do.' The innocent remark had filled Katherine's eyes.

William took Alexandra to see the Chicago White Sox. Baseball had become a passion of William's. Initially Alexandra was excited, especially being inside a brand new stadium, but quickly got bored not only with the game, but with William's attempts to explain what was going on.

The summer of 1913 was special for Katherine. For a few years, she had been an active member of the Illinois Suffrage Movement. During August, Alexandra accompanied Katherine downtown to a celebration party. In July, Illinois women had won the right to vote in presidential and local elections. They actually met the main speaker, Grace Wilbur Trout.

By the time Alexandra turned eighteen, it became more difficult to entertain her. Often Katherine would remember she was almost of a similar age when she gave birth. To do something different, Katherine had booked sailing lessons on Lake Michigan. They had such fun being total novices and the memory of their laughter rang in Katherine's ears.

It was also the time Alexandra had elaborated on her constant arguments with her parents. If she planned to visit Edinburgh for the weekend Victoria would go berserk. 'My father will load the gun and she will fire the bullets,' Alexandra had said. She always knew she would receive a sympathetic ear from her Aunt. Katherine tried to approach the subject of boys. Alexandra had built a circle of friends in Chicago, both boys and girls. She observed her daughter had grown particularly fond of Todd Evans, who was from the same neighbourhood.

The slowing down of the train told Katherine they were approaching Perth. She shivered, and put on her jacket. Katherine had an uneasy feeling of dread. She had tried to grieve for her brother, even Victoria. But all she could think of was Alexandra.

CHAPTER 82
Tuesday 25 October 2011, Ballindalloch Castle, Banffshire, Scotland

Jetlag was lurking in David Stewart's body. He knew he had to try and keep active until bedtime. Thomas Macpherson was an interesting character to help ensure he stayed awake.

"How is Cathy doing Mr Macpherson?" he dared.

Both men were seated in the castle tearoom, their beverages placed between them on a French-style wrought-iron coffee table. Thomas had suggested David should try the famous chocolate cake, home-baked in the tearoom after a family recipe, but David had declined. The looming confrontation with his wife after an absence of eight weeks ensured he had no appetite.

Apart from the two men the room was deserted, the tourist season as good as over. David had arrived at the Garth Hotel in Grantown-on-Spey the previous night and had been sorely disappointed that Cathy was not there.

"She is doing fine David. She is one helluva girl, but you know her better than anyone. Is she aware you have arrived?" Thomas asked, raising his eyebrows as he sipped his tea.

David wondered how much Thomas knew about the stressful situation he and Cathy were facing in their marriage. His wife seemed to have a strong bond with the Black Watch veteran. "Yes. I let her know I would be in The Garth Hotel. Where is she?"

"I would guess she's out and about in John's car."

Thomas Macpherson wasn't exactly making the conversation easy for David. "And you Mr Macpherson, are you keeping well?"

"I'm hanging together by a thread son," he chuckled.

David managed a smile. "Are you pleased you're having a referendum? Has a date been set yet?" Thomas didn't immediately reply, causing David to add apologetically, "Maybe I shouldn't have asked you. I guess it can be a sensitive topic in Scotland."

"Independence is all codswallop. They are just a bunch of egotistical people chasing their personal agendas. There is no actual date yet, but I would guess it will be in September 2014, which is the 700th anniversary of the Battle of Bannockburn." Leaning towards David he changed the topic, "Are you here to try and convince Catherine to return to the USA? You can tell me it's none of my business, I understand."

"Well … we have a lot to …," David said rubbing a hand through his hair. "I do have some unfinished business. As you know, I left rather abruptly the last time I was here."

"Aye, you did, and maybe you shouldn't have lad. A lot of water has since passed under the bridge. Your wife has been doing a lot of research David ..."

"On the Stewarts?"

"No, no, mostly on Macpherson stuff, though she did ask me if I knew anything about Gallipoli."

"Why did she ask you about that?"

"You look surprised David. Put the question to her."

"It's because I have researched so much on the Gallipoli campaign, trying to find out more information on what happened to my ancestor."

"Did you succeed?" asked Thomas.

"Well, yes and no. I do know Alexander Stewart worked closely with two other correspondents and had a part in the infamous letter to the British PM. One of his collaborators was a Keith Murdoch. He hand-carried the letter hoping to get to London, but was captured in Marseilles. Murdoch went on to send his own version of events to the Prime Minister of Australia. The result is now well documented."

Thomas sat back in his chair. Looking at the American he said, "Do you know this Keith Murdoch went on to have a well-known son?"

"*The* Mr Rupert Murdoch of News International fame," responded David.

Thomas Macpherson was enjoying the conversation. "And do you know the Murdochs have been feuding with the Guardian newspaper to this day?"

"No, I didn't, but I guess it has to do with the journalist who betrayed the other correspondents, Bartlett and Murdoch?"

"Exactly," Thomas exclaimed, pointing a finger in the air, delighted to have a peer on this topic. "His name was Henry Nevinson. In his biography he denied the accusation, blaming an un-named War Photographer who had overheard a conversation with Bartlett and Murdoch. To this day the Murdochs refuse to accept this view. I recommend you read Murdoch's book, The Gallipoli Letter."

"I *have* read most of Bartlett's War Diaries," said David, "and he does mention Alexander Stewart quite a few times. But, I didn't find anything helpful on what actually *happened* to him. He died on the 5th January, 1916, two days before the last troops were evacuated from Helles."

Thomas rubbed his chin deep in thought. "You know, David, it's so strange." Thinking on his discussion with Hugh Millar, Thomas continued, "I am a bit of an amateur military historian and I know for a fact when the troops were being evacuated in 1916, all correspondents were confined to the ships and the Turks did not attack the beach. Their soldiers refused to do any more fighting and let the Brits leave peacefully. Not a shell was fired."

"But his death is recorded as Killed in Action."

"Interesting. What else did you uncover?"

"I would like to discuss this with Cathy first if you don't mind. I hope to see her tonight. I'll try her cell, but if you see her would you mind asking her to contact me?"

"Of course, I hope it works out for both of you."

***

Thomas stood outside and watched David's rental Honda CRV drive off, when Billy came walking towards him, looking rather shaken.

"Mr Thomas, it's Mr Angus. He hasn't been seen all morning."

CHAPTER 83
Saturday 15 January 1916, Ballindalloch Castle, Banffshire, Scotland

"How could you leave me with Victoria while you were living your Bohemian life with vaudeville artists in Chicago?"

Upon her arrival at the castle, James had informed Katherine, that Alexandra had been told, and that Victoria, unable to face the consequences, had fled to her parents. James admitted he should have waited until his sister had arrived and allow Katherine to be the one to inform Alexandra of the truth. Although the friction between Katherine and James was intense, Katherine couldn't help feel some kind of relief that it was finally out in the open and her brother had taken the coals out of the fire for her. Alexandra's rage and pain however, had not subsided.

"You must have known what it would be like to live with *her*. Who were you to decide over my life? *You* were my mother; *you* were supposed to love me, not your brother's wife! Do you know what it feels like, not to be loved?"

Katherine turned away as the stream of emotion came pouring out. During the first day of Katherine's stay, Alexandra had been dangerously subdued, not expressing much by facial appearance or in words. But today the final drop had hit the ocean of reproach and the feared conversation had arrived.

Hands shaking slightly, Katherine lit another Philip Morris. "I... I couldn't... I had no choice, don't you see?" she said, after drawing on her cigarette. "You would have been shunned had it been known you were my child. Neither of us would have had a life to speak of. It would have made us the unmarried mother with the gamekeeper's child. It would have been impossible, but I do love you, you know that! I gave you all the love I had to give."

"If you weren't in Edinburgh, tending your precious patients! You were hardly at Ballindalloch, you never *really* cared!" The pain Alexandra felt over Katherine's betrayal was visible in mature lines on her face.

Katherine swallowed with difficulty and felt her throat hurt. How was she to explain why she did what she did? She could hardly believe it herself now that she was confronted with the anguish she had created.

"Listen," Katherine finally said, looking her daughter straight in the eyes. "I did what I thought was right at the time. When I signed those documents, I was only eighteen. Your father had left me and I had never been a mother. I had no idea what it would feel like. I thought

280

you'd be safer here rather than with me. Your Uncle James tried to warn me. He said one day I would regret my decision, and he has been proved right. I just didn't know. I can understand your anger, but I beg you to forgive me. If there's one thing I've learned, it is to linger in reproach is the worst prison someone can fabricate. I've carried the burden of deserting you and it hurts deeply, believe me. All my life I have been reminded one way or another of what I've done. Give me a chance to make it up to you. You know I loved you dearly as an aunt, let me love you as your mother."

"It's too late," Alexandra rasped. "I'm nineteen-years old. You will *never* be a mother to me. You are my *aunt*, an aunt I used to love, but one whose life has been one enormous lie. How can I ever trust you again?"

Silence hung heavily in the room. Alexandra, now put forward the question Katherine had not wanted to hear.

"Why did you not try and look for my father?"

"I did," Katherine could see Alexandra taking a sharp intake of breath. "Did James tell you who he is?"

Almost inaudible Alexandra answered, "He did." Raising her voice she went on, "And then it turned out everybody in the whole bloody estate knew … except me!"

Feeling her daughter's suffering, Katherine turned away.

"Did you find him?" Alexandra bawled.

Slowly Katherine turned to face Alexandra's rage. "I had him traced and yes, I discovered his whereabouts."

Astonished, Alexandra shook her head. "I don't know if I can take much more of your conceit. I can't believe you never came to me to share any of it."

Her hands fumbling with the fringe of her silk shawl, Katherine took a while to find the right words.

"You see, what I came to believe is my behaviour towards Alexander had been selfish. I seduced him you know. Of course he could have said no, but I don't think I gave him much space," Katherine said, with a hint of a smile on her lips.

"He's a journalist with the Boston Globe, a writer, just what he always wanted to be. He is married and has two sons. I didn't want to ruin any more lives than I already have."

Confusion washed over Alexandra like a tidal wave. "All this time," she hissed at her mother, "all this time you have kept all this from me, even the fact I have two half-brothers. Just *think* of the life I could have had in America, with my real father." Alexandra spat each word at her mother as if she was cursing her, making Katherine cringe. "All the time I have spent in this tomb, because you signed some wretched

281

contract. *You,*" she screamed at her mother, "*You* have ruined my life. I want nothing to do with you anymore, never, ever again. I'll go to America on my own and find him and *I'll* tell him."

CHAPTER 84
Tuesday 25 October 2011, Garth Hotel, Grantown-on-Spey

Cathy walked into the small intimate bar of the Garth Hotel where David, the only customer, sat nursing his single malt.

"Hey Cat, it's great to see you." David felt awkward, like a schoolboy meeting his prom date. He got up and kissed her on the cheek. Cathy seemed distracted, her usual assertiveness absent. She sat down opposite David.

The Garth was quiet, October being late in the tourist season. Though David had not expected a warm welcome, Cathy's demeanour gave off confusing signs. Her drawn expression and watery eyes reinforced his unease. For a moment, he thought of joking that he hadn't expected her to take his return this hard, but thought better of it, sensing something was really wrong.

"Wanna tell me?" he asked in a hushed voice.

To his horror Cathy burst into tears. David froze. His heart wanted him to walk over and take her in his arms, but he knew Cathy often bounced compassion.

"Let me get you some water," he offered, feeling utterly inadequate. A waitress observing the scene was a step ahead of him, already bringing a glass. Gathering herself, Cathy wiped her eyes and thanked her. She then turned to David.

"Don't know whether your timing is good or bad," she said softly. "I have been searching for Angus all afternoon."

David remained silent, encouraging her to go on.

"He's missing. I'm sorry David. I can't do this right now. I really need to go back."

"I'll drive you," David said, picking up his room key, "Let me get my coat and you can tell me on the way."

As David left the pub, Cathy sat quietly in surrender. She felt extremely tired and found herself yearning to be back in Raleigh, wishing she had never left the States. If she hadn't come to Scotland, none of this would ever have happened. Unable to cope with her feeling of guilt, she silently blamed David for ever bringing her here.

**

Thirty minutes later, Cathy and David arrived at the castle. David parked his rental in the courtyard.

In the hall, they met a concerned Billy who gave David a surprised glance. "In the library," was all he said. As they entered, both Thomas Macpherson and Peter Duckett stood up.

"Catherine, David, please let's all sit down," Thomas Macpherson said.

Duckett eyed David with curiosity. They had met before; the day of Cathy's arrest.

David felt his gaze. "Is it okay if I stay?" he asked.

Thomas simply waved his hand and said, "Of course! Peter, go on."

"Well," started the policeman, "Mr Macpherson, *Angus* that is, has not been seen on the grounds since early this morning. I interviewed all the staff working today, including Mr Brocklebank. He told me that he had last seen Mr Macpherson just before breakfast. I believe his routine is breakfast at eight prompt."

Thomas sighed, "Look, let's use first names here, keep it simple. Call me Thomas and Angus Angus."

Duckett nodded in agreement. "Mr Brocklebank, *Billy*, also informed me Angus has left his mobile telephone and diary in the study and there were no appointments listed for today."

Thomas stood up and started pacing up and down. "Angus is religious on making sure the administration office know his whereabouts. Please excuse me for a moment. I need to ask Billy to make sure Kenny is informed. Christie is due back from Glasgow anytime soon and I don't want him finding out by accident."

As the veteran started to leave the room, Cathy called, "Uncle T shouldn't you let John know what is going on?"

"No, not yet. If nothing changes, I'll contact all the boys tomorrow."

Cathy was visibly upset. "What is the law here on reporting a missing person Peter?" she asked.

Duckett harrumphed. "Contrary to what most people think, you can report a missing person within a few hours, especially if the person involved is a child. It does take forty-eight hours for all police constabularies in the UK to be notified. I have already informed the Grantown, Elgin and Inverness stations. Mr Macpherson, Thomas, gave me a picture of Angus earlier this afternoon. Although he is well known in these parts, it will help in our door to door enquiries. I asked Thomas if Angus had any health issues or if he was taking any specific medication. He was not aware of any."

Thomas returned.

David Stewart asked, "Can I join the search?"

As Peter stood up he said, "Thank you David. If you make your way to the Grantown Police Station around eight, tomorrow morning, the full search party will be there. Is there anything else anyone wants to add?"

There was silence.

"I think there is nothing else to be said," Thomas uttered. "If we hear anything Peter, we will of course let you know."

As the policeman left the room, Cathy turned to her husband and whispered, "Will you be going back to the hotel or are you going to stay here?"

Thomas overheard. "No question, you're staying here David. It's late, there's no moon and the roads are dark." Without waiting for a response he called for Billy and requested extra towels and toiletries to be taken to Mrs Stewart's room.

Wearily Billy limped out of the library to set to his task. He was deeply worried. He felt a strong grudge towards the American couple. Nothing but trouble had come since the first time they set foot in the castle. Billy knew he would have a restless sleep. After supplying the Stewart room with the requested items, he grabbed a torch and went on his way out into the dark autumn night for one more round, searching for his laird.

***

The small gap between the curtains cast an oblong shape of morning light on the four-poster bed. David was lying on his side, leaning on one elbow, supporting his head on his hand, staring at Cathy. Her constant fidgeting and mumbling during the night combined with his inner turmoil, had hardly giving him space to rest. Last night was more difficult than he had imagined when Cathy appeared from the shower room wrapped in a bath towel. It felt so natural to be together. By the time he showered, Cathy had been in bed. When he joined her, she had snuggled up close and immediately fallen asleep. He enjoyed feeling her warm body against his, but the situation was surreal.

On the flight to the UK he had wondered how their lives would pan out if they got back together. Before, Cathy was always the one to discourage his genealogy research and had stubbornly been opposed to accompanying him to Scotland. It was ironic she was now under some kind of ancestral spell. What had stayed the same though, was she was still completely locking him out.

Back in the US, David had hooked up with his distant cousin Wayne Stewart. Wayne had told David of the copies of the letters he had given to Cathy and yet she had never shared any of this with him, not on their rare Skype calls, not by email, nothing. Typical Cathy; always attempting to solve a case by herself to such an extent it felt personal. Could they just return to life in Wake Forest as if nothing had happened? Still gazing at his wife, David contemplated on what he wanted. She was an attractive woman. He had never seen her cry the way she did in the Garth Hotel. *In three short months Cat! You are obsessed by your make believe inner demons. How things have changed. Do I still love you? Do you love me?* He smiled. Her nightshirt had crawled its way above her waist, exposing a black string. He ran a finger gently down her back and stopped short at her exposed buttocks, feeling a familiar stirring. *Something* hadn't changed!

Cathy found herself in a room with several doors, feeling an urgent need to choose which one to open. Within an instant the scenery changed. Two cows stood grazing near a river with a hunter ready to aim. A crowd of people surrounded her, a tour of some sort, looking at artefacts. Was it a museum or a church? She tried to focus on the walls but found them to be transparent; only a few stones were visible, some standing up, some fallen over. Next she looked straight into the face of Angus.

David heard Cathy mumble something inaudible. He leaned over to look at her face and found her eyes wide open staring into space.

"Jesus H Christ Cat!" David shouted.

Startled, Cathy turned on her back, looked around her, hardly noticing David's worried look.

"You scared the shit out of me. Your eyes so …"

"I was dreaming, dreaming of stones. We need to get to Lagmore! David, call Duckett."

CHAPTER 85
Monday 31 January 1916, Boston, USA

A loud knock on the door forced Sarah to open her eyes and take in the bedroom surroundings of her Back Bay apartment. Even though it was a clear day, Sarah had been sleeping, finally slipping into relative peace, after what seemed like hours of crying.

She had been dreaming of Alex and found it hard to orientate. The dream had been confusing. Alex had been explaining something to her, but she had been unable to hear his words. Whatever it was he was trying to convey, was disturbing. She had been left with a feeling of loss as if she had forgotten something and should try and find it.

She almost felt incapable of lifting herself from the bed. With a lot of effort she pulled herself up and dropped her legs at the side of the bed.

Another loud rap on the door reminded her why she woke up.

"Just a moment, please," she called out, not feeling any inclination to go to the door. It couldn't be Robert, he would have used his key and she wasn't expecting visitors. When she finally opened the door, daylight flooded in, making her blink, hardly able to distinguish the face of the man standing outside. She only recognised a postman's uniform.

"Mrs Stewart?"

"Yes," was all she could say.

"I have a special delivery; it needs to be signed for." He held out a parcel wrapped in brown paper, tied with flax rope.

A shiver ran down her spine. She knew it was the result of a telephone conversation Sean Devane had with the authorities. It was from Turkey, as promised by the British Military administration.

After having her sign, the postman tipped his cap and took a step backward. With a soft thank you Sarah pushed the door shut with her foot and stood alone in the hallway, her heart pounding, gripping the package she knew contained the belongings of her husband. Tears started flowing again, big drops, leaving wet stains on her blouse. It all became so real. With a cry Sarah sank her body against the wall and felt her knees buckle. There was little else she could do but slump to the floor.

This is how her son found her later, her head resting against the wall, her knees drawn up to her chest, eyes closed and her arms tightly wrapped around the unopened parcel. Gently, Robert unfolded her arms, placed the parcel on the floor, lifted the small woman and carried her to the bedroom, covering her with a quilt. When he made sure she was settled, he walked to the hallway and sat by the table. In front of him were a candlestick telephone, notepaper and pencil. Even though his parents had raised their family in the modest apartment, they did acquire many of the modern appliances of the new era. Given his father's profession, it included a subscription with the American Telephone and Telegraph Company.

"Operator, I would like to place a call please, to Mr Sean Devane in Beaumont, Texas."

In her bedroom, Sarah opened her eyes. She could hear her son's voice and listened intently, wondering what the package had revealed.

The Honda CRV twisted and turned on the narrow road as David and Cathy made their way to Lagmore. David was driving. They sat in silence, but for screeching windshield wipers removing early morning drizzle.

Cathy thought of the first time she had seen the stones. It had been with John. Like this morning it had been raining. Her mind returned to Angus. She shivered, knowing. The hill was to their left.

"Over there," she said, directing David to the exact same layby parking space from her last visit. David pulled over and switched off the ignition. "Are you okay Cat?" His wife's strained features worried him.

"Oh, David, poor Angus, what have I done?" Tears came. David looked puzzled. *What is she blaming herself for?* He leaned over to put an arm around her, but she pulled away.

"I knew I shouldn't have come," Cathy blurted. "I should never have let you convince me to join you in Scotland."

David felt awkward. "Look, we don't know anything yet." The inside windows of the car quickly covered in condensation. Cathy stepped out of the car. She looked up at the grassy hill dreading what was to follow.

She sniffed, glanced at her watch. "Where is Duckett?"

David opened a golf umbrella and held it over them. "Cat, he has to come from Grantown."

Cathy put one foot on the stone wall bordering the hill from the road. "It's quite a climb David. Thought I'd better warn you, and you're not exactly wearing the right shoes." Cathy was wearing wellingtons.

David glanced at his brogues.

Cathy started making her way over the small wall. "I can't wait any longer, come on let's go,"

David gripped her arm. "No, come on. You should know better. How would you like to…" The sound of a car approaching could be heard in the distance. "Here he is now," David muttered.

Peter Duckett stepped out of his black Volvo, accompanied by a police officer. Both men simultaneously said 'Good morning.'

"This is Sergeant Baxter," Duckett introduced. "So Cathy, what's the story?"

"You may find me strange, but I think we should look up there," she said, pointing to the hill. Cathy's face was flushed.

Baxter looked perplexed, "Why Lagmore, Mrs Stewart?"

David was ready to defend his wife, when Duckett commanded, "Never mind the how, who and why, let's go." He joined Cathy on the other side of the wall.

"David, will you please stay with the vehicles," ordered the inspector. Although disappointed, as he wanted to support Cathy, David understood.

It was a difficult trek up the small hill. The grass was long and wet and in some places muddy underfoot. It took them almost ten minutes to reach the brow. The land flattened out and the stones came into view. This was familiar territory for Cathy. She heard the sound of the nearby River Avon and peered at the distant stones. She recognised the five standing grey stones with pointed heads, forming an obvious circle. The furthest stone had fallen. As they got closer, Cathy spotted on the fallen stone an outline of what looked like a bundle of clothes. *Oh Angus.*

Cathy ran towards the circle and immediately Baxter gave chase. She reached the fallen stone. Angus Macpherson was lying on his back, dulled eyes staring blankly at the sky, his face the colour of an old newspaper. His hands were clasped on his chest. The slight breeze was stirring his hair and the flaps of his jacket. Cathy went down on both knees, sobbing holding the edge of the stone, "Angus, I'm so sorry, I'm so sorry."

An out of breath Baxter joined her and said, "Don't touch the body Mrs Stewart."

Cathy glared at the policeman and stood as Duckett caught up.

Peter looked at the dead laird, and said, "It looks like he has been here for a while." He glanced at his mobile and put it back in his pocket. "Bax, you go and arrange a doctor and transport. We'll wait here." He looked at the darkening clouds. "Make it quick."

"He hated this place you know. He told me once, couldn't stand it," Cathy said through her tears.

"Why did he hate the stones Cathy?"

She wanted to tell him the truth. Instead, lips trembling looking at the inspector and back at Angus, Cathy replied softly, "He never got round to finishing the story."

Peter Duckett glanced at the sky. The clouds seemed lower. He then looked at Cathy and shook his head. His curiosity regarding the Macphersons had reached a new level.

CHAPTER 87
Tuesday 8 February 1916, Boston, USA

"It's those darn English. That's who it is," Michael Devane muttered, pounding his walking stick against the leg of a chair on each syllable. "You would think they would listen to reason. They left their soldiers bereft, no food, no water, no supplies and no ammunition."

Sean frowned. His father's sources tended to be biased. He had little time to keep abreast of details of world events. All he wanted was to get his friend's remains back from Gallipoli. They had offered to pay big, but the British authorities refused to co-operate, claiming shortage of men and a war going on as an excuse.

"Look at the state Sarah's in," Michael Devane continued. "No grave to visit and nothing as to what happened." Sean's father tried to hide his anguish.

The package delivered to the Stewart's home had contained only a penknife, his wedding ring, a wallet containing a few dollars, a picture of Sarah and many notes written on scrap paper. Alex's war diary had not been included.

The cable reporting Alex's death had stated, 'Killed in Action.' Despite the efforts of Michael, Sean and the Globe management, nobody managed to get any further details.

"There are letters from a Mr Bartlett and another from a Mr Murdoch," Sean said. "They worked with Alex in Gallipoli. Apparently this Mr Bartlett and Alex spent a lot of time together. Mr Bartlett said he's still investigating the circumstances under which Alex died. Shall I write and offer compensation for any information?"

"Not sure," Devane Senior responded. "Let's wait and see if he comes up with anything. Send a reply thanking him for his efforts. Flaunting cash doesn't always secure the truth. He might come up with some spectacular news just because we pay him."

Sean sighed. His father had become distrusting after his partners let him down over a deal which nearly pushed his business into bankruptcy. He had only recently stopped working, months before his seventy-fourth birthday. His failing construction company was up for sale, but there was little interest from potential buyers. If it hadn't been for Sean's support, his father would have been back where he started forty years ago, when the poverty in Ireland forced him to seek his luck in the States. Devane did well, starting as a worker with the Boston Gas Company working his way to foreman, before starting his own business. He'd always helped others in time of need. Alex Stewart was a good example of Michael's compassion.

"This Bartlett is a journalist as well," Sean announced. "Englishman, I'll try and find out some more on his background."

"Good, let me know what you find. Meanwhile I'll set to work and get a headstone or a plaque organised to commemorate Alex. Sarah and the boys deserve something."

His father's remark reminded Sean of *his* promise to Alex. Subconsciously his hand moved to the letter he was carrying in his jacket pocket. *Alex, why in God's name did you give me this wretched task?*

CHAPTER 88
Monday 14 February, 1916, Boston, USA

Michael Devane sat in the dark in front of the ebbing fire of his living room. The house was quiet. Supper had been served and Breen had gone home. Devane's thoughts were gloomy and he rubbed his ever painful leg.

I'm getting old. Why didn't the Lord take me?

Losing Alexander and seeing Sarah age before his eyes, had taken more out of him than he ever imagined. He looked at the upright clock and shrugged. Almost ten o'clock. He tried to count the number of hours Ireland was ahead of the East Coast. He still found it difficult to comprehend time zones. While he was getting ready for bed, in Dublin it was the middle of the night.

His thoughts drifted back to his native country. He would have stayed in Ireland had it not been for Tricia perishing under the harsh circumstances labouring in Moore Street pottery factory. After the death of their mother Michael Devane wanted a better life for his children. He wiped his eyes with a handkerchief as he recalled how he was left with two daughters, Breda and Mary and two boys, Donal and Sean. His younger brother Charlie and his wife Ealga had taken the girls and Sean into their household so he could seek his fortune in the States. Donal, who had a mental disadvantage, had been admitted to a church institution in Dublin.

I have a lot to be thankful for.

For the first time in years Michael started to feel homesick. He wondered how his life would have turned out had he stayed.

I probably would have joined the Republicans to help kick out the bloody English. Never mind one day soon it will happen!

Michael took a deep breath as if to expel the thoughts from his mind. He reminded himself how successful he'd been in Boston. His wealth had for many years provided security for all the family, including his brother and his daughters who now had families of their own. He'd gone back to visit every few years, but their lives had developed in different directions. In many ways Alexander had been more of a son to Michael than Donal. Michael was embarrassed having such thoughts.

He gripped the armrests of his chair and took another deep breath before pulling himself up. Skilfully, he let his good leg take the weight. He grabbed his walking stick from the side of the fireplace and limped with surprising ease towards the study, pushed on the switch and blinked at the burst of electric light. It had been Sean's initiative to install electric lighting throughout the house. 'Take all advantages of progress,' he had said. It had certainly pleased Breen; no more cleaning oil lamps.

The study was cold and Michael could see a thin layer of ice on the inside of the window. On the desk lay Alexander's scattered belongings, the contents of the parcel, given by Sarah at Michael's request. He picked up the wallet. A small piece of notepaper slipped onto the desk. Michael sat down and put on his spectacles. On the notepaper, written in pencil was what Devane thought to be a telephone number. He then retrieved from the wallet a well-folded sheet of paper. Michael peered at a handwritten list of towns and times. He was sure it was train schedules.

'Glasgow QS Perth, Perth Glasgow QS, Perth GRA, GRA Perth'

He then relooked at the smaller note. 'Ball 321' His lips silently formed the words.

Devane had an eerie feeling. It had been obvious Gallipoli had changed Alexander. Sarah had mentioned how she and Alexander had quarrelled about his plans to return, arguing he wanted to go to Scotland to visit their son at Glasgow University after his work in Turkey was done. But Glasgow was hours away from Perth and Ball 321, Michael suspected, could well be the number of the castle where Alexander was raised. He wondered if Sarah knew.

***

Wednesday 16 February 1916, Boston, USA
"Sarah my dear, you shouldn't have gone to all this trouble."

Sarah Stewart smiled at Devane over her home baked cookies. The incentive to prepare for the visit of their treasured friend had been good for her. For the first time since Alex's passing, she'd paid attention to her appearance and dressed with care. She had also spent a lot of time making sure the house was prim and proper.

"It's good to have you here Michael. It was high time I got back on my feet."

Devane smiled at her fondly. He had returned with Alex's belongings and had placed the small carton on the sideboard.

"Sarah, I would like to ask you something if I may." Stirring his tea he thought of what to say next.

Sarah waited patiently.

"I've returned Alex's belongings," Devane said, giving a slight nod towards the box.

"Thank you. Did you find anything of specific interest?" Sarah asked.

"Well … did you look inside his wallet Sarah?"

"No, I couldn't summon up the courage, not yet anyway."

"Mm, there was something I couldn't quite place, a list of train times, you know like a timetable."

"He was planning on going to London and then visit Michael in Glasgow."

Rubbing his bad leg Devane continued. "The note listed times for Glasgow to Perth and Perth to GRA Sarah. I just thought I would mention it in case … you know …"

Sarah fell silent, deep in thought. "Grantown," she said softly.

"What are you saying Sarah?"

She sat up with a start, "I said Grantown, close to Ballindalloch Michael."

***

The same day after dinner Michael Devane booked a call to Texas.

"Operator! Put me through to Beaumont, 55532, Mr Sean Devane."

Seated behind his desk Michael impatiently tapped his good foot as he waited for the connection with his son. A crackle on the line was followed by the voice of the operator instructing him to go ahead.

"Hello son. Sean, are you there?" Devane shouted into the mouthpiece.

"Dad what brings you to call me at this late hour?"

Miles away in his ranch, Sean Devane had been ready to retire when his home servant answered the phone.

"I'm troubled Sean. I tried to call you earlier today. I may have made a terrible mistake."

"What do you mean by a mistake?"

"I've upset Sarah by stirring up unanswered questions. I was so intrigued I just needed to share it but I couldn't reach you."

"I was out in the field these past few days. What's happened?"

"You know Alexander's personal possessions from Turkey?"

"Yes, what of it?"

"Sarah allowed me to go through them. I was hoping to find something, anything that might help us know what happened to Alexander. I went over to Sarah's house this morning to return them."

"Yes…and?"

"I couldn't help myself son. In his wallet, I found a handwritten list of train times. Train times to a place called Grantown."

"Where?"

"Grantown, Sarah confirmed it's a town close to Balldalloch, you know, where Alexander came from."

295

"Ballindalloch," corrected Sean. He took his time formulating his next remark. "I know why he was making plans to go there."

Michael Devane fell silent.

"Something Alex asked me to keep in confidence. I have a letter from Alex to Sarah. He asked me to give it to her should anything happen to him in Turkey."

"What on earth are you saying son?" Devane shouted, his tone a combination of reproach and fear of what he was going to hear.

"I thought it best to wait a while and not give Sarah too much grief all at once."

"Don't tell me the rogue kept in contact with this Katherine woman." Michael Devane knew all about Alex's time in Scotland, including the circumstances of the friendship with the laird's daughter and his forced departure.

"No, he did not," said Sean firmly.

"Holy Mary Mother of God, what is going on? Are you going to make me come to Texas before you tell me?"

"All right, but remember you must keep schtum. Alex will have to tell Sarah himself."

For a moment Michael misunderstood Sean's words. "What!"

"Alex's letter for Sarah," Sean took a deep breath and told his father everything he knew.

At the other end of the line Michael Devane turned pale and placed the phone back on the receiver failing to hear Sean cry out, "But Alexander didn't know father, he didn't know."

CHAPTER 89
Thursday 3 November 2011, 09:30 am Ballindalloch Castle, Banffshire

Cathy glanced through the window at the stream of cars arriving. From a black limo, she saw the elderly twins Maggie and Euphemia step out into a rainy and blustery morning. Both women were dressed in long black skirts with matching black and white tartan jackets. Cathy watched Christie rush towards them to accompany the women to the entrance. The sisters had been extremely warm to Cathy ever when she had first arrived at Ballindalloch, but now she had her fears and doubts.

I wonder if they blame me for Angus's death. Cathy could sense it; the silence and awkward glances. She had taken it too far. Her actions had brought Diane Cox to Ballindalloch, upsetting Angus more than she realised.

Only close family and friends had been invited to Inveravon Church for the burial ceremony. The tiny church had a maximum capacity of fifty adults and Angus's sons had faced a difficult task to select who should be present. An afternoon reception at the Grant Hotel in Grantown-on-Spey was planned, to facilitate a much larger number to pay their respects to the family.

Without making his presence known to Cathy, Billy came into the room, followed by two men carrying chairs. Since Angus's death, Billy Brocklebank had totally ignored Cathy and avoided any conversation. He needed someone to attack and maybe he was right. Cathy knew she had triggered a sequence of events at Ballindalloch that had sorely impacted the Macpherson family. Even Uncle T was very subdued and pensive towards her. Where does one start pointing the finger and what had it all been for?

Cathy tried to make eye contact with Billy, but failed. It made her feel awkward. She was genuinely concerned for Brocklebank. His appearance was haggard, face grey and his frame even thinner. In search of some moral support, Cathy made her way to her room, where she knew David would be, probably busy working.

As she approached the staircase, Angus Junior walked towards her.

"Catherine, I wish we were meeting under different circumstances. How are you bearing up?" Angus was a tall gangly man with chiseled, pale facial features and a shock of bright red hair.

Cathy felt lost for words and mentally cringed when she heard herself say, "I am so sorry Angus. Your father was a wonderful man."

He glared at her for a moment. "He was indeed. I couldn't believe it when John called me. Please excuse me," he said, and went to join Maggie and Euphemia who were now loitering in the hallway.

***

Cathy threw open her bedroom door to find David busy rifling through a folder. Pictures and papers were scattered on the table in front of him, together with an open hard-back book.

"Working on your travel guide?" she asked.

He looked up. "No, not yet Cat. You okay? You look upset. Has anyone said anything to you?" he asked.

His remark annoyed Cathy, he knew her too well. She sighed and sat on the edge of the bed, "It's more what they didn't say. What are you doing David? We need to leave for church soon."

David took his time. Given the circumstances they hadn't been able to talk at length, which left major issues unaddressed. But what was there to discuss? They both knew where they stood. The exchange and support mechanisms within their relationship hadn't functioned for a long time.

"Just tidying some stuff," he mumbled, waiting for a lecture that this was not the time or place.

Glancing at the untidy bundle of what looked like his genealogy papers, Cathy asked, "Has Wayne given you copies of Alexander's letters to read?"

"Yes, he sent me a lot of material a while back."

"Did you get a copy of the James Macpherson letter to Alexander suggesting a meeting at the Globe?"

David just nodded.

"At first, I thought James would make a good candidate to be my great-great-grandfather," Cathy said. "But it turns out his son Eddie, who I now know for sure is my *great-grandfather*, was only *raised* by James. According to his birth certificate, Edward's mother was Alexandra Macpherson."

Eddie was of no interest to David, but when Cathy mentioned Alexandra, his heart skipped a beat.

"Have *you* made any progress on the Stewarts?" Cathy probed.

"Yes, I have discovered some more about Alexander."

Cathy sat next to him on the couch. "Katherine and Alexander were lovers David."

"You might be right."

Cathy looked closely at him. He was holding something back. Cautiously she continued, "Alexandra, according to the Macpherson family tree was the only child of John and Victoria, but denounced her inheritance at the death of her father." Cathy could see David's interest rise. She decided to not yet mention Diane Cox. She wanted to know if

298

David was willing to follow her trail of thought. "Instead the estate passed on to a Donald, Gordon's fourth son."

Tossing in some more bait she continued, "Alexandra moved to America, where she settled in Hollywood and was contracted by MGM. The birth certificate of her son Edward has no mention of a father." Cathy paused to wait for David's reaction.

"Go on," was all he said.

"I realise it is purely circumstantial David, but I strongly suspect, Alexandra was the daughter of Katherine, and that Alexander was the father."

David picked up the old hardback Cathy had noticed earlier. "You know I nearly missed this page when I was browsing. The book is titled: 'Memoirs of the Dardanelles', 1915-1916, by Ashmead Ellis-Bartlett. Let me read chapter twenty-four, page 303."

Cathy opened her mouth to say something, but David raised a hand in defence. "Listen to this please."

She sighed and slumped back on the couch.

David recited: "I recall many soldiers and sailors during my time in the Dardanelles, some brave, some not, some sad, some depressed, some men wounded, some men dead. One encounter embedded in my brain was of a fellow journalist. We corresponded during the early part of 1915. We first met in August, in a dugout just off 'V' Beach at Helles. He was a charming fellow from the north of Scotland. I recall he offered me some Fry's chocolate. This chap, together with Keith Murdoch was helping me communicate dispatches avoiding censorship. I have written in chapter 17, details of the Asquith letter, but I often wonder what befell the Scotsman. His name was Alexander Stewart from the Boston Globe. Although Alex and I had a few adventures together in Gallipoli, I clearly recall our first meeting. I never had come across such a fellow, and still haven't, with three children so diverse; one black boy, studying in Glasgow, (Alex and his wife adopted the lad), and one boy in Boston. I don't remember their names. His third child however, is easier to recall. I was forbidden to return to Gallipoli after the "Asquith Letter Scandal" but I kept in touch with Alexander Stewart and Keith Murdoch. He was preparing to go back to the Gulf to report on the final evacuation of the British troops from Helles in January 1916 and promised me a copy of his dispatches. During one of our conversations, he asked me to try and find out if a Katherine and Alexandra Macpherson were living at Ballindalloch Castle. He confided in me he had just found out Alexandra was his daughter, born and living in Scotland."

David looked at Cathy and found her looking tense.

"Let me hear the rest David. Go on …"

David continued; "He was planning to meet her after his assignment. Poor bugger never did. Alexander died in Helles and no dispatches were ever received. I did have contact with the Boston Globe and they confirmed he was killed before the actual evacuation. I often wonder what Fate bestowed the Scot."

David stared at his wife. "This means Cathy, like me, you're a descendent of Alexander Stewart … Mrs Stewart."

Cathy paled visibly. She slowly got to her feet, "We need to go. We have a funeral to attend."

Inveravon Church and Burial Grounds, 11:45am

On leaving the church grounds after what had been a simple yet moving service and burial at the mausoleum, Cathy held David's hand. They tried to make their way through a jostling crowd. The scene was chaotic. Although there were two police vehicles present, their lights flashing, there seemed little control to stop the media pushing forward.

A journalist thrust a BBC mike directly in front of Cathy's face, the cameraman behind his shoulder.

"Mrs Stewart why are you still here? You have a habit of attending funerals don't you? What is your involvement Mrs Stewart? What's the connection to Lagmore?"

David pushed the microphone away and put his arm around Cathy's waist. "No comment, leave her alone." The crowd stood back, allowing the couple to make their way to the car.

Sitting in the back seat of the Land Rover, Cathy looked at the many peering faces, all trying to get a glimpse.

Christie turned from the drivers' seat and asked, "Are you okay Mrs?"

Cathy hadn't even noticed Kenny Christie was in the car. "Yes thanks," was all she could say. Christie didn't bother to introduce the elderly gentleman in the front passenger seat.

The man turned to face them. "I know who you are, Mrs Stewart. Nice to meet you both," he said unconvincingly. I am the family lawyer, William Waddell."

Christie carefully maneuvered his way out, avoiding the crowd walking up the small hill towards the road leading to Grantown-on-Spey.

***

Grant Arms Hotel, Grantown-on-Spey, 2:00pm

The family had arranged a sit down lunch for over two hundred guests at The Grant Arms Hotel, by far the largest in Grantown, positioned close to the square in the north of town.

In the white walled spacious dining area, seated at the top table were; John in the centre, to his right Thomas, Maggie and Euphemia. To John's left were; Angus Junior, George and James Grant Senior.

With the local press snapping pictures, John Macpherson made a moving speech before the meal. He paid tribute to his father and focused primarily on childhood memories of his parents, Angus's contribution to the local community, his dedication to his employees and his broader responsibilities as Laird and Chief of the Macpherson Clan. John also read out some selected messages from family and friends around the world.

Cathy and David were seated with four other guests close to the top table. They were just finishing their coffee when a photographer from the Press & Journal newspaper caught Cathy. Cathy winced at the surprise flash from the camera. David turned towards the pressman and gave him an angry glare.

She whispered, "Leave it alone David. Let's call a cab. I need to get out of here."

The dining room was noisy with people either preparing to leave or visit the Macphersons at the top table to pay their respects.

The American couple made their way to the foyer, when from the opposite direction Angus's son George approached, a small, stocky man his head almost completely bald.

He glared at Cathy. "You have some nerve. I don't know why my father tolerated you. You bloody well sent him to an early grave with all your fucking interference."

People within hearing distance stopped and looked on. David defended his wife, "Loosen up my friend ..."

"I'm no friend of yours and certainly not her," George said pointing to Cathy.

John arrived at the scene, and put an arm around his brother, ushering him away. George kept turning towards Cathy. Shaken, Cathy sat down in the lobby.

"I'll go get our coats," David said.

John reappeared and sat down next to her. "I'm sorry, I think George had one too many."

"Oh John, maybe your brother is right. Don't be angry with him."

"Cathy this might not be the time and place ..."

"Taxi ordered and I have our coats," David said. Turning to John he added, "Good speech John. Your father would have been proud of you."

David felt a sudden pang of loneliness. He had genuinely liked Angus. In fact, he had been first to make contact with the laird, long before Cathy arrived in Scotland. Nobody considered how this was not easy for him either, most of all Cathy.

"Thank you David. Cathy, can we meet later tonight at home?"

"Sure."

"Say around eight tonight." Without any farewell, John made his way back to the dining room.

***

"Cat, we need to discuss the Stewart connection in our family line," shouted David, stepping out of the shower. The door of the ensuite bathroom was open and steam escaped into the bedroom.

"Not now David." Cathy was busy changing into casual clothes. Her feet were hurting from the dress shoes she hardly ever wore. "Anyway, I have to go downstairs and look for John. I shouldn't be long." Cathy was still unable to talk about Alexandra. Suspecting was one thing, getting confirmation was another ... She did wonder if David had the same disturbing thoughts.

Cathy went downstairs and walked outside. She welcomed the fresh air. It was dark, the air crisp, not a breath of wind. The castle and grounds now reverted back to the peaceful tranquillity to which she had become so accustomed.

"Hi Cathy," John said. "Give me a few minutes please." John was walking with Mr Waddell and Peter Grant to their cars. Cathy sat on a bench by the flowerbed. Soon John joined her. He was still dressed in his formal clothes.

"You must be tired John. It has been a long day for you."

John nodded. "Yep and I still have many things to do here."

"Will you stay on for a time?" asked Cathy.

"At least for the coming week, I will resign from ... What am I saying?" John looked at Cathy with sadness in his eyes. "You know I once told my father we should all help you in your family research. But I never thought for one moment it would be at such a cost. I am not blaming you Cathy for what happened to Dad. According to the coroner he must have had a weakness in his heart, never properly diagnosed which could have been there for years. With everything which has unfolded here these past few months as well as Doug Stein's death, it must have been all too much for him." John tried to push aside

302

his memory of the last conversation with his father, the issue of Broadside Holdings.

"I never thought I'd hear myself say this Cathy." His face was taut. "I want you to leave. Leave the castle, I don't care if you stay in Grantown, Elgin or go back to the States, it's your business, but not here. Too much has happened. We need a break to settle back into normal life. I hope you understand."

"I do John, I feel much the same. Part of me wished I'd never come at all and yet in some weird way it seemed unavoidable. I have a lot to digest too."

John looked at her pensively and said: "If you'll excuse me I need to return to the family."

Cathy watched John make his way towards the house.

He turned one more time and said, "Let me have your contact details when you've made all the arrangements."

With a deep sigh Cathy walked to a nearby garden bench, her shoes crunching over the gravel. The night was cool, but pleasant enough, no wind and the sky clear with a bright half-moon giving a remarkable amount of light. Cathy looked up at the stars, wondering about the irony of how ancestors never cease to influence life.

CHAPTER 90
Sunday 11 June 1916, Back Bay, Boston, U.S.A.

After church on what was an unusually warm Sunday, Michael Devane and his son Sean, announced themselves at the doorstep of the modest but well equipped apartment of Sarah Stewart.

"It is good to see you both." Sarah welcomed the men who had grown increasingly dear to her over the months. Their support had been huge, nothing too much trouble. When Michael had telephoned to ask if they could visit, Sarah had felt a twinge of anticipation. Somehow, she had known all along that Alex had kept something from her and suspected the Devane's held the key.

"I knew there was more to him missing Christmas," she said, when Sean handed her the letter.

"Alex told me to choose my own good time Sarah. I felt it would have been too much for you, had I given you the letter earlier, but I apologise if you feel I have done you wrong."

Sarah hugged the stocky red haired Irishman. "You did what you thought right Sean. Your best intention is what matters."

Sean felt tears stinging at the back of his eyes. He had never envisaged it would be this difficult. It had caused him many a sleepless night.

"Do you know the content of the letter?" Sarah asked.

"No, of course not, but we did discuss a few things in the Plaza Hotel two days before Alex left."

Sarah wanted to know details of their encounter, cherishing any new moments of Alex when he was still alive. Sean informed her as much as he could without disclosing what Alex confided in him.

"I'm sorry Sarah, but you should hear this from Alex and not from me," Sean finished, nodding at the envelope she still held in her hand.

***

It wasn't till late at night in the solitude of the surroundings where she and Alex had spent so many good years. Her hands trembling she found herself almost incapable of opening the envelope simply addressed 'Sarah,' but the yearning to read her husband's last message to her prevailed.

Boston, December 1915

My Dearest Sarah,

This has been the most difficult writing I have ever incurred. If you are now reading this letter, it means I can no longer be with you in body. As I write this, I can only convey to you how much I love you and the rewards you have provided me. Not only our two wonderful sons, but how you have always shown your affection and understanding to me in our years together. You have been my rock. You are the most wonderful mother and I know you will continue to guide our boys through this difficult and sometimes treacherous world. Keep a special eye on Robert. I think he will always need more support and direction.

I have something to relay my love, and there is no easy way to tell you. I have a daughter, Alexandra, born in Scotland. She is now 19-years old and I planned to visit Alexandra and her mother Katherine in January after meeting with Michael in Glasgow. You have every right to be angry but please never have it stain what we have enjoyed and nurtured. I have only known of Alexandra a few days since the visit of James Macpherson. With all my heart Sarah, I would have told you on my return from Scotland. Don't be upset with Sean, as I abused our friendship to convince him to keep this letter for me. I am so sorry Sarah I could not stay. Please do not assume it is only because of Alexandra. I had to return to Turkey and witness the withdrawal of the troops. The situation in Scotland merely compounded the need to go.

You are the most wonderful woman and human being. You and the boys are well taken care of financially, I am sure in your own time, Sean will provide you with all the details you need. Please tell the boys I love them dearly. I will always be by your side.

Your loving husband,

Alex

EPILOGUE
Saturday 18 February 2012, Wake Forest, Raleigh, North Carolina

Cathy arrived at her parents' house early afternoon. She gave her coat a vigorous shake in the hallway before hanging it on the stand.

"Anyone home," she called out, kicking off her shoes.

"I'm in the den," her father yelled.

She made her way to the small lounge at the back of the house to find Jim kneeling on the carpet, surrounded by papers of every size, shape and colour. He removed his glasses and peered at his daughter, who directed a questioning look. "It's the golf club. The treasurer, Bill Morrison is sick and I volunteered to help out. How did you get on?"

Cathy carefully moved some papers from the sofa, sat down and sighed. "To rent an apartment in Raleigh is so expensive Pop. The realtor is going to arrange a schedule for next week. Mom said she would join me. By the way where is she?"

Jim stood up and carefully stretched, wincing because of an old injury he sustained years ago. "She's gone to the library. Some author is giving a talk on how to write a novel. Is it still raining Cat?"

"Drizzle and humid, you going out?"

"Chuck and I were planning to play nine holes. Listen, you know you can stay here as long as you want."

"I know, but it has been three months and I do need my own space."

"Then kick *him* out. Why should he have the house and …"

"Pop, don't go there, I promise we'll get the house on the market soon."

Jim answered impatiently. "Glad to hear it. Your Mom will be delighted. She hates how he lives there with all his home comforts while you …"

"His name is *David*, Dad, and I just wish you'd stop blaming him for everything. She glanced at her watch. "I'm going for a shower, I'm running late, doing a double shift with Hicks."

It had already been three months since Cathy had landed at Raleigh-Durham, a few days after her showdown with John Macpherson. To some extent arriving home had been an anti-climax. Cathy had not been able to shake the feeling of running away, having left Scotland without closure. The warm reception of her parents in the arrival hall had only given brief respite. The drive home had been dominated by her mother updating Cathy on *all* she had missed. It had made Cathy feel as if she came from another world, which in a way was true.

Gradually, in bits and pieces, Cathy had told her story to her parents; from the day she arrived in Ballindalloch to the day of Angus's funeral, trying to fill in the blanks when her parent's struggled to understand. Explaining her fondness of Uncle T and how he looked like her father had made her emotional.

"You know Pop," Cathy had said, when they had a moment together. "I feel for Duckett. Having Doug Stein's homicide on your patch and then having to hand over the lead to the big wigs is tough."

Jim had reacted with understanding. "I know Cat, but as you rightfully pointed out, this case has international, political or even mafia connections. Maybe you have a soft spot for this Peter Duckett?"

"No Pop, at least not in the way I think you're thinking. Even if he was a pain in the ass at times, I *can* relate to how he must feel."

"It's the same with Diane Cox. John Macpherson told me about his meeting with her in Edinburgh. Quoting John, she added, 'He didn't see the point of Diane coming all the way from New York.' But she is not a bad person Pop. All she ever wanted was some recognition, not for herself, but for Alexandra, her… *our*… ancestor. It was more of a personal thing, a form of justice. Perhaps we should invite her here some day and get to know her better."

The first Saturday after arriving home, Cathy, still jet lagged and all, had met up with Jacki and Sherry at Backfins Crabhouse. Her friends were fascinated with her Scottish adventures, especially the incident with the JCB digger. Their eagerness to hear more even made Cathy exaggerate certain aspects of her experiences, to feed their thirst for thrills. It also helped her cope with the pang of loneliness she felt, being unable to express what it had really been like for her.

Her close encounter with John, she kept secret, even though her thoughts often drifted back to him. Cathy managed to bounce all attempts to get her talking about David.

The Wake Weekly newspaper had pestered Cathy for an interview. She flatly declined, but they published an account of her time in Scotland anyway. To steer away from all the unwanted attention Cathy focused on work where Steve Hicks, her professional partner, saved her life again by not mentioning Scotland once. Knowing Cathy like the back of his hand, Hicks knew well enough when to leave her alone.

Three weeks after her return home she'd had a brief meeting with David, who had stayed on in the Highlands to finish his travel guide on the Whisky Trail. There had been no malice, no arguments, no emotion, merely business, all very amicable, even if they both had the eerie feeling a lot was left unsaid. Both of them however had shied away from the confrontation.

"Before you go for your shower," Jim said, "here's some mail that came for you this morning." Jim reached for an envelope on the coffee table. "I noticed it's from Illinois Public Records. Did you do more research?"

Accepting the envelope Cathy smiled apologetically. "Well, a few weeks ago I was on the web trying to find more on William Macpherson, the ancestor from Chicago."

"The guy that traded booze, don't tell me …" Jim closed his eyes for a moment, "the younger brother of 'Gordon the Bones,' who had a pencil with the inscription right?" He looked on when Cathy retrieved a photocopy of an old-fashioned document.

"This is a copy of his Will. I ordered it online."

Curious, Jim joined his daughter on the couch, in a short careless gesture brushing a bundle of receipts to the floor so he could sit beside her. "Come on then, let's have a look," Jim said, fumbling for his glasses.

Father and daughter leaned over the document in unison.

I, William Macpherson, of Maxwell Street, Chicago, Illinois, make this my last will. First, I direct that all of my debts, the expenses of settling my Estate &c. shall be paid out of my personal estate. Second: I direct that the sum of fifty thousand dollars ($50000) shall be paid to my friend and confidant Clementina Dorrington, formerly Nerlinger of no fixed abode, five thousand dollars ($5000) to Alfred Danaher of Pershing Road (39th Street), Chicago, for his dedication and patience over many years and ten thousand dollars ($10000) to the Charity School (Orphanage) of Grantown-on-Spey, Scotland. Third: All of the remainder of my estate I give to the Executor hereinafter named to be held by him for the following purposes.

The whole estate shall become the absolute equal property of Katherine Macpherson of 63rd Street, Chicago and her daughter Alexandra Macpherson (my granddaughter) their heirs and assigns. I appoint my friend, J.M. Blair, executor of this and I authorize him as executor or trustee to dispose of my personal estate at either private or public sale, and upon any terms that

308

he may think to the best interest of my estate. I also request him to consult my friend E.S. McMurtine in matters pertaining to the estate. Witness my hand and seal this

December 18, 1919

William Macpherson (seal)Witness: Stephen Haig, Clara McMurtrie

Still holding the document, Cathy leaned back and stared at the ceiling, "Well I'll be damned, his granddaughter." Startled, she turned to her father. "Pop, Alexandra was William's granddaughter. That means Katherine was *his* daughter! Never saw that one coming. I dug up the bones of someone who had absolutely nothing to do with it all!" Cathy chewed on her bottom lip, her mind racing. *I wonder if the family knew, even Gordon. Or was it yet another Macpherson cover-up? It certainly gave a whole different perspective to all that happened 7 generations ago.*

Clumsily and as yet unaware of the significance of his daughter's find, Jim placed an arm around her shoulders.

Cathy looked at her father with a lop-sided smile and said, "I guess this now leaves us with choices Pop."

"Meaning?" Jim asked, raising one eyebrow.

The silence that followed Cathy's words was disturbed by the sound of a key opening the front door.

"That'll be your mother," Jim said. "Let's all have a coffee before you decide anything rash…"

READER'S NOTES

CHAPTER 1
The Pullman strike of May 1894 is factual. George Pullman died in 1897 and in 1971 the former 'company town' of Pullman was designated as a national landmark district.

CHAPTER 5
Allan Pinkerton, born in Glasgow, in 1819, founded **the Pinkerton National Detective Agency** in 1850. By the 1890's the agency employed more agents than there were members of the United States Army.

Andrew Carnegie (1835-1919) was a Scottish American industrialist building an enormous steel industry. He went on to become a leading philanthropist for the USA and the British Empire.
See also CHAPTER 63.

Distillers Company Limited (DCL) was a leading Scottish drinks company. It was formed in 1877 by a combination of six Scottish whisky distilleries; Macfarlane & Co., John Bald & Co., John Haig & Co., MacNab Bros & Co., Robert Mowbray and Stewart & Co.

CHAPTER 10
Mary Slessor Mary Mitchell Slessor was a Scottish missionary to Nigeria. Her work and strong personality allowed her to be trusted and accepted by the locals while spreading Christianity. protecting native children and promoting women's rights.

CHAPTER 21
The tragedy of the 'SS Furnessia' is based on the actual sinking of the **RMS Atlantic** on 1st April, 1873.

CHAPTER 23
The Royal Scotsman is owned by the **Orient Express Company**. It is a factual excursion that has Aviemore on the schedule where passengers are coached to Ballindalloch Castle.

CHAPTER 24
Sophia Louisa Jex-Blake (21 January 1840 – 7 January 1912) was an English physician, teacher and feminist. She was one of the first female doctors in the United Kingdom of Great Britain and Ireland, a leading campaigner for medical education for women and was involved in founding two medical schools for women, in London (at a time when

no other medical schools were training women) and in Edinburgh, where she also started a women's hospital.

Edith Pechey (7 October 1845 – 14 April 1908) was one of the first women doctors in the United Kingdom and a campaigner for women's rights. She spent
more than 20 years in India as a senior doctor at a women's hospital and was involved in a range of social causes.

After Sophia Jex-Blake's sole application to study medicine at the University of Edinburgh was turned down, she advertised in The Scotsman for more women to join her. The second letter she received was from Edith Pechey, who wrote:'Do you think anything more is requisite to ensure success than moderate abilities and a good share of perseverance? I believe I may lay claim to these, together with a real love of the subjects of study, but as regards any thorough knowledge of these subjects at present, I fear I am deficient in most.'

Despite her concerns, Edith Pechey became one of the Edinburgh Seven, the first seven undergraduate students at any British University, and proved her academic ability by achieving the top grade in the Chemistry exam in her first year of study. This made her eligible to receive a Hope Scholarship.

CHAPTER 32

Georgi Markov was a Bulgarian dissident writer, was poisoned by a tip of an umbrella on 7th September 1978 in central London. He died four days later. It remains one of the great unsolved crimes of the Cold War.

CHAPTER 41

Alec Boswell Timms was an Australian-born Scotland international rugby union forward. He was sent to Edinburgh University to study as a medical doctor. After finishing his degree he progressed to the College of Surgeons and took the Scottish triple qualifications in 1903.

CHAPTER 48

The 1st Marquis of Dufferin and Ava, was Rector from 1899 to 1902. Born, Frederick Hamilton-Temple-Blackwood.

The 6th Lord Balfour of Burleigh, was Rector from 1896 – 1899. Born, Alexander Hugh Bruce.

CHAPTER 51

Bertie was King Edward VII (Albert Edward) who was king from the 22nd January 1901 till his death on 6th May 1910. His coronation was planned for 6th June 1902, but two days before he was diagnosed with appendicitis which carried a high mortality rate. Sir Frederick Treves supported by Lord Lister carried out a then-radical operation of draining the infected abscess though a small incision. The next day, Edward was sitting up in bed, smoking a cigar.

CHAPTER 63
St. George's School for Girls in Edinburgh; founded in 1888, by women who campaigned for gender equality in education.

GALLIPOLI CHAPTERS 71, 72, 73, 75, 77, 82
Ellis Ashmead-Bartlett and **Keith Murdoch** were the actual correspondents responsible for the 'Asquith Letter'. The beachhead assault in Chapter 73 was based on extracts from the War Diary of Bartlett. The Murdoch dispute (Chapter 82) with the Guardian newspaper involving **Henry Nevinson** is based on fact.

Acknowledgements

The making of *Bloodlines-Touch Not the Cat & Bloodlines-Traces*, as described on www.touchnothecat.com; originated following a dream of Ingrid, combined with Tom's genealogy quest on his McKerley roots.

To set the scene, Tom searched the web for a castle to be the prime location his only criteria being it should be family-owned and preferably still lived in. Thus, 'The Pearl of the North', Ballindalloch, literally popped up and was introduced in the storyline.

While all of the above is true, the content of the Bloodlines series is entirely fictional. It should be especially noted, that the Chief of the Macpherson Clan does not reside at Ballindalloch. We also emphasise that none of our Macpherson characters resemble the members, past or present, of the Macpherson-Grants, to whom Ballindalloch has been the family home since 1546.

Next to bringing both joy and challenge, the writing of the Bloodlines series also brought great company. Editor Hans Offringa, (www.hansoffringa.com), who also wrote a review on 'Bloodlines-Touch Not the Cat', for *Whisky Passion,* , has been very thorough and helpful in regulating the roller coaster ride of writing a sequel. The version now published is much different from the one initially submitted to Hans.

A big thank you also goes to the very constructive feedback from proof readers, David Herron, Cees van de Kroef, Dawn Lemmer, Maggie Myklebust (author of Fly Away Home), George Watson, and Vanessa Sparrow; ranging from forgotten commas, to cultural and structural ideas.

A special thank you goes to Art and Travel writer Vivien Devlin, who, sparked by fate, attended the June 2012 *Bloodlines-Touch Not the Cat* book signing at the tearoom of Ballindalloch Castle. It was Vivien who suggested to insert a murder on the Orient Express' in the sequel. The blog titled: 'A Murder on the Royal Scotsman', posted 13th March 2016 on www.touchnotthecat.com, reveals more on this topic. Vivien also proofread *Bloodlines-Traces* and generously shared her professional writing skills and insights.

Graham Booth, gave shape to the ideas for the cover of *Bloodlines-Traces* and a last thank you goes to Dan Colucci of antiquecamera's.net, who 'supplied' the camera used by Alex Ledingham.

Lightning Source UK Ltd.
Milton Keynes UK
UKOW02f0821220616

276825UK00002B/31/P